*What readers are saying about*
the R E D E M P T I O N *series*

"If I could only put into words what these books have done for my life. Between you and Gary Smalley, I believe I have renewed a dying spirit within myself and my marriage. I feel so much a part of the Baxter family; both books have moved me to tears. I, when I am reading, feel as if I am in their presence as an onlooker. It is hard to describe." —B.S.; Rochelle Park, NJ

"It takes a special talent and great insight from God to write and get into people's hearts as you do." —J.K.; Upper Peninsula, MI

"I have laughed and cried with your characters and have felt drawn to pray for those in the same circumstances. I figure any book that gets a person to pray for another must be great." —A.M.; reader

"You have reached into our family's hearts with precious characters that only the Lord could have placed into your mind to write about. You are, and always will be, a part of my heart—and bookshelf!" —L.; Tampa, FL

"Until this year . . . I never could get into reading. . . . Well, girl, I love your book with Gary Smalley, so down to earth and one that I cannot put down! . . . I am recommending your books to all of my friends and family. All I can say is WOW. Keep up the good work!"                                      —C.P.; reader

"I just completed the first two books in the Redemption series with Gary Smalley. Awesome, just awesome. Again, you've touched my heart. I laughed and cried. I felt their pains and their joys. . . . Thank you for daring to write about the tough issues that even believers face."                                      —S.A.; reader

"God has truly given you a gift to write and not just write, but minister as well. I can feel His Holy Spirit moving in your books. . . . Thank you and please stay open to His leading and continue writing stories that not only touch the heart but help bring healing as well."                                      —N.L.; reader

"My friends and I are hooked on the Redemption series and make it our goal to purchase those books the day they get on the shelf! We literally devour them! The characters are so real, I've got the Baxter house in my mind's eye. I know John and Elizabeth, felt the pain with Luke's wandering, then the joy of his return, and on and on."                                      —L.L.; reader

# REJOICE

## Karen KINGSBURY
## with Gary SMALLEY

TYNDALE HOUSE PUBLISHERS, INC., Carol Stream, Illinois

Visit Tyndale's exciting Web site at www.tyndale.com

*TYNDALE* and Tyndale's quill logo are registered trademarks of Tyndale House Publishers, Inc.

*Rejoice*

Designed by Zandrah Maguigad

Edited by Kathryn S. Olson

Published in association with the literary agency of Alive Communications, Inc., 7680 Goddard Street, Suite 200, Colorado Springs, CO 80920.

**Library of Congress Cataloging-in-Publication Data**

Kingsbury, Karen.
　　Rejoice / Karen Kingsbury with Gary Smalley.
　　　　p. cm. (Redemption series bk #4)
　　ISBN-13: 978-0-8423-8687-6 (sc)
　　ISBN-10: 0-8423-8687-4 (sc)
　　　　1. Married women—Fiction. 2. Mother and child—Fiction. I. Smalley, Gary.
　　II. Title.
　　PS3561.I4873R45 2004
　　813'.54—dc22　　　　　　　　　　　　　　　　　　　　　　　　　　2003024807

Printed in the United States of America

12　11　10　09　08　07　06
12　11　10　9　8　7

TO OUR LOVING FAMILIES,

who continue to give us countless

reasons to rejoice.

AND TO GOD ALMIGHTY,

the author of life,

who has—for now—

blessed us with these.

## AUTHORS' NOTE

The Redemption series is set mostly in Bloomington, Indiana. Some of the landmarks—Indiana University, for example—are accurately placed in their true settings. Other buildings, parks, and establishments will be nothing more than figments of our imaginations. We hope those of you familiar with Bloomington and the surrounding area will have fun distinguishing between the two.

The New York City settings combine real observation with imaginative re-creation.

CHAPTER ONE

THE SWIM PARTY seemed like a great idea, the perfect ending to a perfect summer.

Brooke Baxter West's partner at the pediatric office had a daughter Maddie's age, and to celebrate her birthday, the family had invited ten kids and their parents for an afternoon in their backyard pool.

For two weeks the girls had talked about it nonstop, seeking out Brooke each morning and tugging on her arm. "Mommy, when's the swim party?"

But two days before the big event, another doctor at the office had received word from California that his aging grandmother had only days to live. Before he caught an emergency flight, he'd asked Brooke if she'd take his on-call duty for the weekend.

"You're my last hope," he told her. "My family needs me."

Brooke hated being on call when she had plans to spend an afternoon with her girls. But other than the swim party, the weekend was open, and she could take the pager with her. The chances of getting a Saturday afternoon call were fairly slim. Saturday evening, yes. But not Saturday afternoon.

Now the big day was here, and Brooke was having doubts. She should've called around, found someone else to take the doctor's on-call duty. Her kids wanted her at the party, and if a call came in, she'd miss the summer's last hurrah.

Brooke slipped a pair of shorts on over her swimsuit. She was raising the zipper when she heard Peter's voice downstairs.

"Hurry up, let's go." Frustration rang in his voice. "The party starts in ten minutes."

Brooke rolled her eyes and grabbed her bag—the one with the life jackets and sunscreen. What was wrong with him? He was constantly grouchy; the two of them hadn't had a normal conversation in weeks. Their home was so tense even little Hayley had noticed it.

"Is Daddy mad at you, Mommy?" she'd asked earlier that week.

Brooke had mumbled something about Daddy being tired, and that yes, they should pray for him. But after days of sidestepping him, she was sick of Peter's attitude. He made her feel incompetent and irritating. The same way he'd made her feel ever since Maddie's diagnosis. Didn't he get it? Maddie was better now; no fevers for more than two months.

Brooke headed into the hallway and ran into Hayley and Maddie. "Guess what, girls?" A glance at the grins on her daughters' faces and her smile came easily. "I'm wearing my swimsuit!"

"Goodie, Mommy." Maddie jumped up and down and reached for Hayley's hand. "We can play tea party on the steps."

They joined Peter downstairs and but for the girls' excited chatter, they rode in silence to the house across town where Brooke's partner, Aletha, and her husband, DeWayne, lived.

At three years old, Hayley was still small enough to carry, so Brooke swept her into her arms as they headed up the walk toward the front door. On the way up the steps, Hayley took hold of Brooke's hand and squeezed it three times. The sign Brooke used with the girls to say, "I love you." The love from her younger daughter was the perfect remedy for Peter's coolness.

"You're a sweet girl, Hayley; do you know that?" She shifted her pool bag to her shoulder.

"You, too, Mommy." Hayley rubbed her tiny nose against Brooke's. "You're a sweetie girl, too. Know why?"

"Why?" Brooke and Hayley trailed behind, and Brooke took her time. She loved moments like this with her girls.

"Because—" Hayley tilted her head, her pale blonde hair falling like silk around her wide-eyed face—"I love you, that's why."

The door opened and Aletha smiled at them from the front step. "Hi. The party's out back."

Peter pulled out a smile, the one he wielded whenever they were in public. Brooke studied him, confused and hurt. Why couldn't he smile that way at her? She'd been meaning to ask him, but she hadn't found the chance. She was a few feet from the front door when her pager went off. She exhaled hard as she unclipped the pager from her waistband and stared at the small message window. *Urgent,* it read. The word was followed by the hospital's main number. *Great,* she thought. *I won't get even an hour with them in the pool.*

Peter came up behind her and looked over her shoulder. "What is it?"

"A hospital call." She didn't hide the disappointment in her voice. "Maybe it's nothing."

Several children, breathless and excited, ran into the foyer and surrounded Hayley and Maddie. Brooke ducked into the nearest bedroom and pulled her cell phone from her purse. "Dr. Brooke Baxter West here. Someone paged me."

The nurse on the other end rattled off the information. One of the patients from their office had been admitted with a staph infection. It looked serious. They wanted a pediatrician to consult. Immediately.

3

"I'm on my way." Brooke hung up the phone and returned to the foyer.

Peter caught her look and raised his eyebrows. "Well?"

"I have to go." She pursed her lips. Doctoring was the most exhilarating career she could imagine having. But not when it interfered with her family. "I'll be back as quick as I can."

"It's your own fault."

A ribbon of anger wrapped itself around her heart. "What's that supposed to mean?"

Peter shrugged, his eyes distant. "You took the on-call."

Maddie ran up to her. "Natasha wants us to swim, Mommy. Can we, please? Can we right now?"

"Um, baby—" she looked at Hayley standing a foot away, waiting for her answer—"why don't you wait till Mommy comes back?"

"We can swim then, too. Please, Mommy? Can we?"

Natasha did a little dance nearby and hugged Brooke. Their families had been friends for years, and Maddie and Natasha were best buddies. "Please, can we swim?" Natasha linked arms with Maddie and the two smiled their best smiles.

Brooke could feel the fight leaving her. So she'd miss out on some of the fun. If she hurried, she'd be back in time to join them in the pool. "Okay." She allowed a slight smile. "But let me talk to Daddy first."

Peter had moved into the living room, and Brooke found him and DeWayne seated side by side, their eyes glued to the television. A baseball playoff game was on, and Aletha had joked that having the party at that time could mean the men might never leave the TV.

Brooke crossed the room and positioned herself between her husband and the big screen. "The girls want to swim." The bag in her hands was bulky, and she set it on the floor between them. "Here's the sunscreen and life jackets. The girls need both before they can go out back."

"Right." Peter leaned sideways so he could see the game. "I got it, honey."

The term of endearment was for DeWayne's benefit, Brooke was sure. She didn't appreciate the way he looked past her to the game. "Peter, I'm serious. Don't let them outside without sunscreen and a life jacket. They're not pool safe."

He shot her a look, one that said she was embarrassing him. Then he yelled out, "Hayley . . . Maddie, come here."

The girls scampered into the room and came up close to Peter. "Yes, Daddy." Hayley spoke first. "Can we swim?"

"Not yet." Peter looked hard at Brooke and unzipped the bag. Quickly and with little finesse, he lathered sunscreen into his hand and then tossed the bottle to Brooke. "Do Hayley."

She needed to leave, but this was more important. Moving as fast as she could, she squeezed the lotion into her hand and positioned herself in front of their little blonde daughter. "Here, sweetie. We don't want a sunburn, right?"

"Right, Mommy."

Brooke rubbed the sunscreen over Hayley's arms and legs, her back and neck, and finally her face. She and Peter finished with the girls at the same time, and Peter tossed her the smaller life jacket. He said nothing as they worked, and that was fine with Brooke.

These days, the less he said the better.

She took the blue-and-aqua life jacket and slipped first one of Hayley's arms, then the other, through the holes. Next she latched the buckles down the front and attached a strap that ran from the back of the vest, between her legs, to the front.

Brooke had researched life jackets, and this style was the safest of all.

When Maddie's vest was on, Peter gave Brooke one last glare. Again because of DeWayne seated beside him, he kept his tone light, almost friendly. "There you go. See you later."

Brooke said nothing. Instead she turned and bid the girls a quick good-bye. She found Aletha and promised to be back as soon as possible. A minute later she was in the car, doing a U-turn toward the hospital. With every mile she felt the distance between herself and her daughters. They were playing in the pool by now, getting used to the water, their little-girl laughter ringing across Aletha's backyard.

She stepped on the gas. She'd make this the quickest call ever and be back before the underwater tea party even began. Then— other than her relationship with Peter—everything about the day would play out just like it was supposed to.

Peter was grateful for the National League Championship Series on TV.

Because as much as he liked DeWayne and Aletha, the last thing he wanted was to spend that Saturday with a bunch of doctors. Swimming wasn't his thing, and the current series was easily one of the most exciting ever. Besides, most of the guests were Brooke's friends, people he barely knew. The prospect of catching a game with DeWayne had swayed him to come.

Especially after Brooke took the on-call assignment.

What had she been thinking? Of course she'd get called Saturday afternoon; kids needed doctors then most of all. Soccer injuries, illnesses that had brewed all week at school. Insect bites. Weekends were notoriously busy for pediatricians.

The fact that she'd let the other doctor talk her into taking his on-call was further proof that she wasn't capable. Not nearly as capable as he'd originally thought her to be. Back when they'd met in med school, her confidence and competence had been part of what attracted him to her. But after the situation with Maddie—when she'd insisted that their daughter didn't need a specialist—Peter had seen his wife in a new light.

One that was far from flattering.

An hour passed, and the sound of children came from the other room.

"Okay," he heard Aletha tell them. "Dry off, and we'll have cake."

It was the seventh inning, and his team was down by one. Peter hoped they could keep the cake thing quiet—at least until the commercial. Not that he didn't like birthdays, but he'd had one of the longest weeks in his life. His patients had needed him more than usual, he'd gone without sleep for two days, and now—on his day off—he was spending his Saturday at a kid's birthday party.

At that instant—with the tying run on third and a power hitter at the plate—Maddie and Hayley ran into the room. They were shivering, and their life jackets made a trail of dripping water. "Daddy, can you take off our jackets?"

He glanced at them and then back at the TV. "Just a minute, girls. Daddy wants to see this."

The count was 3–0, but this time the pitch was good. The batter cut and connected, but the ball flew over the catcher and into the stands. Foul tip. Strike one.

"Okay." Peter looked at his daughters again. "Now what?"

"We're dripping, Daddy." Maddie took a step forward. "Can you take off our jackets? Please?"

"Sure, pumpkin." He unsnapped the buckles on both vests and helped take them off. "Give them to Natasha's mommy and ask her to hang them near the bathtub."

The next pitch was a perfect strike, one that caught the hitter looking. Full count.

"Daddy . . ." Hayley stepped up. "When's Mommy coming back? We're a'posed to have a tea party with her in the pool."

"Soon, baby." He leaned around her and watched the man at bat belt one out of the park. The moment it was gone, he and DeWayne stood up and slapped their hands in a high five. "That's my boys."

"Bigger than life." DeWayne gave a few nods and sat back down. "On their way, baby. On their way."

"Daddy . . ." Hayley angled her head. "I love you."

"Right." Peter eased himself back to his seat. His eyes returned to the game. "Love you, too."

"Bye." Maddie turned and dashed from the room, her life jacket slung over her arm.

"Bye, Daddy." Hayley was close on her sister's heels.

"Bye." Peter studied the screen and then remembered something. "Don't go outside without those life jackets."

But the girls were already out of the room.

He stared after his girls, and even with the noise from the game he could almost hear Brooke telling him to find them, make sure they understood about the life jackets. But the game was almost over, and anyway, the kids were about to eat cake. He could remind them about the pool in a few minutes.

His mind cleared, and all his attention centered once more on the game. A single and a stolen base, another single and a sacrifice fly. Two-run lead. If they won this game they'd take a three-two lead and the series would be as good as over.

Instead, the pitcher struck out the next two batters, and in the following inning the other team scored two runs to tie it up. Not until the bottom of the ninth inning did his team score the winning run. The game ended, the win forever in the books, and Peter was thirty minutes into a discussion on the merits of switch-hitting and relief pitching when he heard Maddie call him from the other room.

"Daddy! Daddy, quick! Help!"

He held up his hand to DeWayne. "Just a minute." He raised his voice. "In here, baby."

Maddie tore around the corner. Her hair was dry, her eyes round with fear. "Daddy, I can't find Hayley."

Peter was on his feet, his heart suddenly in his throat. "What do you mean?" Fear dug its talons into his back, his neck. It was all he could do to keep from sprinting toward the backyard. "I thought you were eating cake."

"We did. Then we 'cided to go swimming, Daddy." Maddie's

mouth hung open. "But Hayley said she wanted to be first to get the tea party ready for Mommy. Now I can't find her—"

Peter didn't wait for Maddie to finish. He took off for the patio door, not so much because of what Maddie had said but because of the thing she was holding in her hands. The thing Peter had only that instant recognized.

Hayley's life jacket.

# CHAPTER TWO

PETER COULDN'T BREATHE, couldn't think.

"Hayley!" The word was a shout, a desperate plea that somehow she would answer him. As he ran into the backyard toward the pool, he could feel his body slipping into some sort of robotic mode, where his arms and legs continued to move without cognitive connection whatsoever. *"Hayley . . ."* He screamed her name this time, breathless, frantic. "Where are you, baby?"

He had the attention of the other guests and a number of adults began running alongside or behind him, all of them headed for the pool. Peter rounded a garden section and a cluster of high bushes, and suddenly he saw the water spread out before him. At first glance Hayley wasn't there. . . . *Let her be in a bedroom somewhere, in the play area downstairs, anywhere but here, God. Please . . . not here, God . . .*

Peter was panting now, forcing his feet toward the edge of the pool. Only then did he see the small form at the bottom . . . still, unmoving.

"Hayley!"

"Daddy!" Maddie's scream was high and shrill. "She's in the water, Daddy . . . get her out!"

One of the parents took Maddie's hand and led her back into the house as her words grew hysterical, "Daddy, get her out! Daddy . . ."

Time and understanding and all of existence clashed together in a single moment, a moment when a hundred realizations and actions and memories converged within him.

Hayley was lying at the bottom of the pool, drowning, maybe already dead, and she didn't have her life jacket, and it was his fault because he was watching baseball when he should've been watching her. And Brooke hadn't gotten to say good-bye, and now neither of them would see her baby blue eyes sparkle again, never hear her singsong voice, never know her little-girl arms around their necks after a long day at work.

But she was crying for him, even now, wasn't she? "Daddy, help me! Get me out, Daddy . . . save me!" That was her, wasn't it? Speaking to his heart from the watery grave where she lay?

"I'm coming, Hayley . . ."

And he was in the water, feeling the weight of his clothes and shoes, and diving down deep, deeper, to the place where her body lay, scooping her up and ordering himself to move faster, thinking how small she felt, how still, how it was taking forever to get her out of the water. And he was racing her toward the surface, rolling her up onto the patio while parents ushered their children back into the house. And Aletha was picking up the outdoor telephone, her eyes wide, expression frozen, and he was out of the pool, dripping wet, one shoe still in the water floating to the bottom. And he was standing over Hayley, staring at her blue face, turning her onto her side so the water would drain from her mouth, and he was screaming, "Call 9-1-1!"

"They're on their way!" Aletha was standing next to DeWayne. "God, help us!" And she was grabbing handfuls of her own hair, her arms and legs shaking.

And Peter was leaning over his younger daughter, remembering how it felt to hold her for the first time, how she'd looked at Kari and Ryan's wedding two weeks ago, how she'd wanted to save the rose petals because they were too pretty to drop on the ground, how she'd looked an hour earlier, decked in her life jacket, an angel smile lighting up her face.

And he was feeling for her pulse and finding nothing. Not a single thready beat. And he was pinching her nose, covering her small mouth with his and blowing a single burst of air into her lungs. Chest compressions. One—two—three—four—five. Another short breath. More compressions. And he was forcing himself to keep moving. *Make her breathe . . . now, God . . . please, God. . . .* And he was calculating the time, reminding himself of the details he'd learned in med school. Lack of oxygen for ten minutes, brain damage. Fifteen minutes, irreversible brain damage. Eighteen minutes . . .

And he was staring at his daughter's closed eyes. *Cough, Hayley . . . cough or cry or make a sound. God . . . wake her up!* More compressions . . . more breaths . . . and he was willing her to move, willing her to do anything but lie there, unmoving on the wet patio while Aletha wept somewhere behind them.

And all of it, the entire scene, came together in that one moment, in the time it took him to draw a single breath.

Sirens wailed in the distance, and Peter sat up, pressing his fingers against the artery on the side of her neck, and this time he felt something. The faintest movement, like breath against his skin. A chance. She had a chance. He passed his hand beneath her nose, but the spot was stone still.

She wasn't breathing.

Panic knocked the wind from him, and it took all his effort to suck in enough oxygen to give her one more short burst of air. *God . . . what's happening? Make her move, God, make her breathe. . . .*

Paramedics were racing across the patio, asking him to step aside, none of them recognizing him as one of the doctors at the hospital. And they were covering her face with an oxygen mask, lifting her onto a stretcher and explaining that she needed immediate emergency care.

Peter wasn't sure he could stand, wasn't sure he could speak. But one raspy question came from a tormented place in his soul. "Will she . . . will she make it?"

"We're doing our best . . ."

And with that, Peter knew. He knew because it was the same thing he would've said to the parents of one of his patients. Not when recovery was imminent, because that was the sort of news a doctor didn't hold back. Rather it was the type of thing he'd say when the opposite was true.

When his gut feeling told him the patient didn't have a chance.

Brooke was beyond frustrated.

The call hadn't been urgent at all, and by the time Brooke arrived at the hospital, the child's diagnosis had been adjusted from staph infection to pneumonia. Basic, bacterial pneumonia. Lung X rays showed the infection was bad enough to warrant hospital admission, so the on-site doctor had advised intravenous antibiotics. Brooke verified that treatment, checked that the child was stable, and signed off on the hospital chart.

She was on her way to her car when another call came, this one from the emergency room. A ten-year-old boy had broken his arm at a soccer game; a piece of the bone had punctured the skin. Brooke gritted her teeth and hurried back, confirmed initial treatment, checked the pain-medication doses, and the boy's vital signs. She was finished in twenty minutes.

"Finally . . . ," she muttered as she headed for her car one more time. The party would be halfway over by the time she got there. The birthday song would be sung, cake cut and eaten. The underwater tea party, long over. The girls would be tired of swimming, ready to warm up inside.

Brooke blew a strand of hair off her forehead as she started her car. Peter was right; it was her own fault. She could've turned down the request. Someone else would've taken the on-call duty if she'd held her ground. Her family had to come first.

She glanced at her watch. Ninety minutes had passed since she'd left the party. Peter's game would be over by now, so he'd be away from the television, maybe chatting with the other parents sitting around the pool. At least she hoped so. But then, he hadn't shown interest in any of their friends lately. Since Maddie's diagnosis and treatment for her bladder condition, Peter had been distant to everyone.

Mostly to her.

As she drove back to the party his voice filled her mind.

*"Don't rely on your training, Brooke. . . . Whether it's our kids or one of your patients, talk to the specialists. Don't get too relaxed, Brooke. . . . You're still learning how to do this medical thing, Brooke. . . . Maybe you should practice medicine part-time, Brooke. What if I'm the family doctor, and you stay home with the girls, Brooke? You're a better mother than a doctor, Brooke."*

His comments were a constant series of put-downs.

Brooke clenched her jaw. How dare he think his abilities superior to hers? Besides, the girls were fine, flourishing under the care of their nanny when they weren't in preschool. She had three full days off, didn't she? How many working mothers could say that?

Her irritation with Peter was still churning in her gut when half a mile from the party, a speeding ambulance came from behind and passed her. Brooke shuddered. No matter that she was a doctor, ambulance sirens always made her heart skip a beat. The screaming noise meant one thing: Someone, somewhere was in the midst of an emergency, a heart attack or a car accident or some other life-threatening incident. For the briefest moment, in less time than it took to blink, Brooke wondered if the ambulance was headed for the pool party. But just as quickly the thought was gone. Of course it wasn't. The place was full of doctors; the children would be fine. Watched over, protected, and safe. No one would've let anything happen to them. Unless the ambulance was for one of the adults.

Then, like that, the crazy thought was gone.

Of all the homes in Bloomington, Indiana, the ambulance was certainly not headed for DeWayne and Aletha's place. That was irrational mother-speak happening in her head, the voice that came up and caused a moment of worry whenever the possibility of danger existed. No matter how remote.

As she turned onto Aletha's street, Brooke was thinking about Peter again, but then something caught her eye and her foot froze on the gas pedal. Instantly she felt the blood drain from her face. The ambulance was up ahead, its lights still flashing.

Parked in front of her friend's house.

*Dear God, not one of the children, please. . . .*

Her heart slammed against her chest as she snapped into action. Her car flew past the five houses that separated her from the ambulance. Ten feet away, she hit the brakes and tore out of the car just as a cluster of paramedics came through the front door carrying a stretcher between them, and on the stretcher a figure.

The small figure of a child.

One of the medics held an oxygen mask to the child's face, and in the group of people behind the stretcher was . . .

Brooke grabbed her throat. "Peter!" She ran across the yard, her feet moving only half as fast as she wanted them to go.

His eyes met hers and she knew, knew before she reached the stretcher, before anyone said a word to her that the child being taken to the ambulance was hers.

He jogged around the paramedics and came to her, grabbed hold of her shoulder. "It's Hayley . . . " He was pasty white and trembling, beads of sweat lined across his forehead.

*Shock,* Brooke thought. *He's in shock.* But what had he said about Hayley? She knit her brow and gave a quick shake of her head. "What . . . what happened?"

The medics were moving past her and one of them stopped and put his hand on Brooke's arm. "Are you the mother?"

*The mother?* Brooke wanted to blink and be back in the car, back on the road on the way to the party when the idea that the ambulance might be headed for Aletha and DeWayne's house was nothing more than a random irrational thought.

*The mother . . . the mother . . .*

"Yes . . ." She jerked away from Peter and fell in alongside the moving stretcher. There, for the first time, she got a clear look at her daughter, motionless on the stretcher. She was blue. With frantic movements the paramedic continued working the oxygen bag. Terror flooded Brooke's veins as she kept walking. "What happened?"

"She fell . . . in the pool." Peter was back at her side, breathless and keeping up with them step for step. "She . . . didn't have her life jacket."

Brooke's mouth fell open, and for half a second she stopped and stared at Peter. "What?"

Peter moved his jaw, but no words came out.

The paramedics were moving on without her, so Brooke spun away from him and caught up with the stretcher.

They reached the ambulance, and the first medic flung open the back doors. "Okay." His tone was urgent, his eyes darting from Peter to Brooke. "One parent can come."

"Me." Brooke's response was out almost before the paramedic finished his sentence. She shot a look at Peter. "Stay with Maddie."

Peter took a step back and swayed some. "We'll be right behind you."

"Call my parents."

He nodded, but she barely noticed. She was already climbing into the back of the ambulance, positioning herself next to Hayley, opposite the place where the paramedic was working at a feverish pace.

Another medic shut the doors and the ambulance sped off, sirens blaring.

"Hayley, baby, it's Mommy." Brooke took her daughter's limp hand. "Wake up, baby . . . please."

She gave Hayley's fingers a squeeze, but the child lay unmoving on the stretcher.

Brooke blinked and looked about the inside of the ambulance. This couldn't be happening. It was a dream, a nightmare, right? She wasn't really in the back of a speeding ambulance, watching a uniformed man hold a bag over Hayley's face, was she?

Spots filled Brooke's vision, moving in slow, lazy circles, and a tingling began in her fingertips and forearms. Her breathing grew shallow. Shock, just like Peter. She was going into shock. "No!" She shouted the word. Then twice she blinked, hard and deliberate.

No, she was a doctor, not a victim. Shock wasn't an option—not now.

Her training kicked in and she stared at Hayley, studying her, going over the facts the way she would if Hayley were someone else's daughter. Hayley was here beside her, and they were on their way to the hospital because Hayley had drowned; wasn't that it? Yes. Yes, those were the facts.

But Brooke had no information, and suddenly she was desperate to know. She shifted her gaze hard and fast to the paramedic. "How long—" Brooke fought to form the words—"how long was she under?"

"No one knows for sure. Ten minutes, maybe more."

Ten minutes! Ten minutes while everyone at the party did what? Sat inside and never missed her? And what about Peter? Where was he, watching baseball? While Hayley wandered around the patio deck by herself? While she fell into the pool?

A flash of images tore across Brooke's consciousness. Hayley making desperate little strokes for the side of the pool, panicking, trying to remember what she'd been taught about kicking her feet and blowing bubbles. Brooke could see her, paddling faster, harder as she began to sink.

She would've screamed for her daddy, for Maddie, for anyone who would help her out of the pool. But then she would've needed air, and that first giant gulp would've filled her lungs with water until finally she couldn't remember how to scream or paddle or kick at all, until her mind gave in to the numbing darkness and her body began to drift to the bottom of the pool.

Brooke tightened her grip on Hayley's hand and the images stopped. *Save her, God . . . don't let her die. . . .* Nausea gripped her, and Brooke looked around for a bag in case she had to throw up. When she didn't see one, she closed her eyes again, just for a moment. No, she wouldn't be sick, not now. Hayley needed her; she could throw up later. She released her daughter's fingers and stroked her feathery blonde hair. "Hayley, baby, it's Mommy."

The paramedic continued his efforts. Checking her pulse every few minutes, maintaining the rhythmic squeezing of the oxygen bag.

Only then did Brooke notice the swelling in Hayley's hands and fingers, the way even her face looked bloated. The worse off a drowning victim was, the more swelling she would have. This time panic slapped her in the face, and she had to know, had to ask the question burning inside her.

"Is she going to . . ." Brooke ran her fingers along Hayley's tanned arm and found the medic's eyes. This was the question patients asked *her,* but now she was asking it. She pressed her free hand against her stomach and ordered herself to finish speaking. "Will she live?"

"We have a pulse." The paramedic was breathless, sweat dripping down the sides of his face. "But she's not breathing on her own."

A lump formed in Brooke's throat. The medic's information was obvious. If Hayley were breathing on her own, he wouldn't be giving her artificial respiration. But hearing it, listening to the man's words as he gave the grim report, made everything about the moment more real.

How damaged was her brain, and how soon before they could determine the extent of her injuries and the first step back to normal health and . . . ?

She had a hundred other questions, but no need to ask even one of them. She was a doctor; she knew the answers. Depending on the length of time Hayley was underwater, her brain could already be dead. If it wasn't, if a flicker of life remained, she could spend the rest of her life in a hospital bed hooked to tubing. Beyond that lay several dozen other possibilities.

Hayley could be brain damaged, unable to eat or walk or talk, or she might retain all of those actions, but in a slow, partial sort of way. Just one option was acceptable. And that would only happen if somehow her brain had escaped any damage at all. If Hayley hadn't been under as long as they thought and if she could get past the initial trauma, then maybe—just maybe—she would come back to them, back to the same way she'd been that morning.

But Brooke knew the odds of that as well. She'd studied pediatrics after all. Once a victim could no longer breathe on his own, tests weren't needed to determine whether brain damage had occurred.

It had; it was that simple.

The sirens grew louder, shrieking at her in a sort of pattern that mocked her and made her crazy. It was all her fault, wasn't it? She shouldn't have taken the on-call assignment. If she'd been there, Hayley never would've had a moment alone by the pool. She wouldn't have had a moment alone anywhere. Brooke wouldn't have allowed it.

But Peter . . .

Her own guilt dimmed as she pictured her husband, stuck to the living-room chair, watching the baseball game. As much as it was her fault, it was more Peter's. She'd asked him to watch the girls, to keep an eye on them and make sure they stayed in their life jackets.

She slid her hand around Hayley's again. "Baby . . . wake up, please, honey." Her voice was quieter, less certain. If Hayley couldn't breathe, she definitely couldn't hear sounds. Hayley wasn't there at all, not really. She was trapped in another world, locked in a distant cell where her release depended on one thing only.

Her brain's ability to function.

"We're almost there." The paramedic glanced out the side window and kept his hand on the bag.

He didn't need to tell her that every second counted. She nodded, her eyes locked on Hayley's face. *Move, baby. Show me you're still there. . . .*

But her daughter remained motionless, and Brooke thought of the life jackets again. Neither girl could take them off without help, and a mountain of rage began to form in Brooke's soul. She had asked Peter to leave the jackets on, so that meant someone else must've removed them.

But who? Not Aletha or any of the other mothers. None of them would've taken that risk. And Hayley and Maddie never would've asked one of the other fathers. The mountain grew larger, and a picture began to take shape in her mind, one that imagined Hayley and Maddie running up to Peter and asking him to take off the life jackets. Maybe so they could play upstairs with the other girls or so they could sit more easily on the kitchen chairs while they ate cake.

If Peter had taken off the life jackets, he would've stayed with the girls, stayed with them until they were ready to go back outside or at least stayed in the kitchen with the other adults. That way he would've seen the girls heading back outside.

And if he hadn't . . .

If he'd done nothing more than sit in front of the baseball game talking to DeWayne . . .

The ambulance jerked into the hospital driveway and tore up

to the emergency-room entrance. Someone from the outside yanked the doors open, and the medic joined two others in a flurry of activity as they removed the stretcher and headed inside the building.

Brooke stayed with them, praying with every step, her rubber-soled tennis shoes padding out a muted beat on the hospital linoleum that sounded like *Please, God . . . please, God . . . please, God . . . please, God. . . .*

No other words came to mind, nothing she could force herself to say. The spots were back, and Brooke stared at the stretcher being pushed along in front of her. What were they doing here? And why was Hayley at the hospital, sound asleep? And how come no one was trying to wake her up?

Terror seized her, stopping her, doubling her over for a few intense seconds. She stared at the scuffed hospital floor and then lifted her head. Hayley was getting away from her, hurrying off on the stretcher without her.

"Wait!" Brooke straightened, urged her legs to keep moving.

"You okay?" One of the medics fell behind the group and held his hand out to her.

Brooke took it and felt herself moving forward, felt her feet pick up speed as she dropped the medic's hand and caught up with the stretcher again. *Please, God . . . please, God . . . please, God. . . .* "Hayley!" She had no air, but she found a way to shout the words building within her. "I'm here, baby."

The spots faded again and she remembered where she was, what was happening. They were trying to save Hayley's life. She forced her feet to keep moving, keep taking steps until they took her to one of the private emergency rooms. *Don't let her die, God . . . don't let her die.*

"Get a tube in her." The doctor's voice was familiar, but Brooke didn't look at him, didn't look anywhere but at her daughter.

"Hayley . . ." Brooke's whisper was lost in the chaos of emergency personnel working to get her little girl breathing.

"Hayley." She touched Hayley's matted blonde hair, and her thoughts ran together.

What if Hayley died? What if she wasn't okay? What if she was never the same again? Brooke ran her tongue over her lower lip and tried to swallow. What about herself? What if she couldn't take another minute watching Hayley lying motionless on the stretcher? And where was Peter? Where had he been when this happened?

Wherever he'd been, he'd taken his eyes off her, let her drown. This whole thing was his fault; it had to be.

He probably took off the girls' life jackets and forgot to put them back on. That had to be it. And if they lost Hayley because of his carelessness, then yes, it was his fault. Even if she had taken the on-call shift. As the medical team raced about the room, the realization became an understanding, and Brooke became certain about one more thing.

If she lost Hayley because of Peter's carelessness, their marriage wouldn't stand a chance. Because never, not as along as she lived, would she forgive him.

# CHAPTER THREE

ASHLEY WAS PAINTING AGAIN.

In the first month after her diagnosis, she'd put away her easel and brushes, convinced she would have no time to paint as long as she was seeing doctors and working on a plan to stay alive. But she still hadn't seen a doctor, and all her determinations to let go of painting had changed with Landon's visit. His time with her the week after Kari and Ryan's wedding convinced her that a difference existed between breathing and living.

"None of us know how long we have," Landon had told her the night before he returned to New York. "Don't stop living because of a diagnosis, Ashley."

She'd thought about that often since then, and he was right. At least about part of it. Cole, for instance, and her painting. Even her twenty hours a week at Sunset Hills Adult Care home. She'd told the owner about her HIV blood test, and the woman had checked and found out Ashley could still work there. As long as she handled administrative and social details and left physical care of the patients to the other workers.

Her relationship with Landon would die because that was the

right thing. But otherwise, she would stay engaged in life. Until her strength was gone, she would play with Cole, toss a ball with him or push him on the backyard swings, run with him along the shore of Lake Monroe, and read Dr. Seuss to him each night. She would stay connected with the people at Sunset Hills: Irvel and Edith and Helen and Bert.

And she would paint, pouring her heart across the canvas with every stroke.

All of it as long as she drew breath.

She sat outside her parents' house now, watching Cole as he tried to lasso the horns of a plastic bull's head. The head was a present from Landon. It had two metal stakes that dug into the ground, so that the bull, minus a body, appeared to be gazing ahead in a stiff sort of way, while the horns stood straight up, ready for capture. Landon had also bought him a cowboy hat and a child-size rope, one that was stiff enough to hold a loop and light enough for Cole to toss.

"It's all in the wrist," he'd explained to Cole when they set it up in Ashley's front yard that day.

Now she moved her paintbrush in delicate strokes across the canvas and smiled at the memory. Cole's eyes had been so wide she could see the whites almost all the way around them. His small mouth had hung open. "Are you a cowboy, Landon?"

"Well . . ." Landon had chuckled, casting her a glance across the yard. "Not really. But my uncle was. He taught me how to rope when I was a little older than you."

Cole had been obsessed with capturing the horns of the plastic bull's head ever since.

A breeze brushed against Ashley's face, and she watched Cole from her place in front of her easel. The painting was of Cole this time—Cole with a cowboy hat and lasso, determination etched into his expression.

"Watch, Mommy . . . I got both horns last time." Cole's voice sang out across her parents' front yard.

"I'm watching." Ashley studied him, the easy way he held his arm up and behind him, moving his wrist just the way Landon had taught him. Cole was a natural athlete, a boy who would've thrived under the daily love of a man like Landon.

Ashley dipped her brush into a color that was too light to be brown and painted the fine outline of a rope above the image of her son.

Where was he now, Landon Blake?

Slowly, like the setting sun, sadness clouded her heart. He'd surprised her by showing up at Kari and Ryan's wedding, and for the first twenty-four hours she almost let him change her mind about breaking things off with him. It was his presence that did it, of course. The nearness of him, the smell of his skin, and the way his fingers felt on her face.

His voice was as real now as it had been that evening. "I'm not leaving, Ashley . . . you can't make me go."

And for the first day Ashley could only hold on to him and believe he was right, that somehow they would find a way to be together despite her health. But by the second day, her sanity returned. She couldn't live with herself if she dragged Landon down with her.

Two days before he left, she told him so.

"I need time," she'd told him while they walked along the river behind her parents' house. "I have to see my doctor, make a plan. And you . . . you need to get on with your life, Landon." They stopped walking and she faced him. "You have three months left in New York."

"No, Ash." Something that wasn't quite anger or sorrow filtered across Landon's expression. "Don't do this—not again."

"I'm not doing anything. I'm telling you how I feel. I can't be with you right now; my health has to come first."

Landon fought her on it until the day she took him to the airport. But he agreed on certain points. Yes, he needed to finish up with the FDNY. His position at the Bloomington station wouldn't open up until spring, anyway. In the meantime, she could figure out a plan for her health.

"But after that, I'm coming back for you." They were lost in an embrace at the airport's curbside check-in.

"I'm not sure, Landon." She drew back and searched his eyes.

"Not sure about what?" His tone was more fearful than frustrated. "Ashley, stop fighting me."

With everything in her she wanted to agree with him, to tell him to get back in her car and never leave her side again. But she loved him too much for that. She would never agree to a relationship with Landon Blake, not while she was battling HIV, not when she was facing the possibility of AIDS. But this wasn't the moment to fight him about the facts. Instead of saying anything else, she had leaned in and kissed him on the cheek. "I love you, Landon. I always will."

"That's better." His lips brushed against hers, and the tiny lines around his eyes relaxed some. "I'll call you when I get home."

When he left, she felt physically sick for days, as if he'd ripped her lungs out and taken them with her. But even if it killed her, she needed to let him go. Landon deserved a normal life, a life where she was nothing more than a fond memory. Of course he never would have agreed to that, so she stalled. If she could send him on his way and keep her distance, then eventually he'd move on with his life and everything would work out for the best.

At least that was the plan.

But in the ten days since Landon left, he had called four times. Ashley had done everything to avoid talking to him. Three times when she saw the call was from him, she let the answering machine pick up, and the one time she forgot to check her caller ID, she pretended to be too rushed to speak.

"Where've you been?" He sounded confused, hurt. "I left you messages."

"Landon, I have to run." She sighed loud enough for him to hear it. "I told you. I have a lot to figure out. Give me time, okay?"

The conversation had ended abruptly, and afterwards Ashley had wandered around her backyard for half an hour, until Cole came outside and found her near their old oak tree.

"What's wrong, Mommy? You miss Landon?"

Ashley had managed the slightest smile. "Yes, honey." She took Cole in her arms and nodded, struggling to find her voice. "I miss him a lot."

Cole had wriggled free from her embrace and brushed his fingertips along her brow. "He's coming back, Mommy. You don't need to be sad anymore. Landon's coming back forever. In a few shakes of a rope, remember?"

"I know, sweetie." Ashley hadn't had the strength to tell him the truth. That as long as her blood was contaminated, she couldn't let Landon back into her life or Cole's. "I know."

She still needed to tell the rest of her family. Her parents knew, and Luke, of course. But now that Kari and Ryan were home from their honeymoon, she needed to tell them as well. That way they could form a plan for Cole in case she developed a full-blown case of AIDS.

She set down the smaller brush and picked up one with a broader tip. It was time to paint the sky, time to frame the frozen moment in a hundred shades of blue. She dipped the bristles into a powdery color and was just about to accent the area over the rope when the phone rang.

The cordless receiver sat on a chair a few feet away. Ashley set the brush down, hopped off her stool, and grabbed the phone on the third ring. "Hello?"

"Ashley . . ." The voice at the other end was tight, strangled with fear.

"Yes?" She couldn't make out who it was, but his tone made her heart skip a beat.

"It's Peter." He hesitated, and she heard him release a shaky breath. "Listen, I need your help."

"Of course." Ashley moved closer to Cole. "What is it? What's wrong?"

"Hayley . . . she's at the hospital. I need to be there, but I have Maddie."

*Hayley? At the hospital?* The child was perfectly healthy a few days ago when Kari and Ryan returned from their honeymoon. Ashley brought her hand to her throat and massaged her neck. "What's wrong with her?"

Silence shouted on the other end.

A few feet away, Cole circled the rope three times over his cowboy hat and released it in a perfect loop around the bull's plastic horns. "I did it!" He turned to her. "Did you see that, Mommy? I did it!"

She nodded and put her finger to her lips. "Peter . . . tell me what happened."

"We were at a party. Hayley. . . she fell in the pool. When we found her she was at the bottom."

Ashley gasped. "No . . . Peter, no!" The trees and bushes and grassy carpet around her began to shift, waxing and waning and making it hard for Ashley to focus. She dropped to the ground and crossed her legs, her voice no longer familiar. "Is she . . . how long was she under?"

"We don't know." Peter's tone was more controlled now, but the urgency remained. "I'll bring Maddie over in a few minutes. And please, Ashley . . . could you tell the others?"

She agreed, and the call ended.

But still Ashley remained on the ground, her chin on her chest as she stared at her knees and tried to accept what Peter had said. Hayley had drowned? She'd fallen into a pool without either Brooke or Peter seeing her? It seemed impossible. She glanced up, beyond the tree branches toward heaven.

*Please, God . . . please, let her live. She's just a little girl . . . full of life and hope and laughter.*

As she prayed she included Brooke and Peter, because things between them were already strained. Brooke spent much of her time at their parents' house, even when Peter was home. If something happened to Hayley, all of them would feel it. But for

Brooke and Peter, things would never be the same again. Every day of their lives together would forever be changed.

If their marriage survived long enough to find out.

🌿

Dr. John Baxter couldn't concentrate on anything but Hayley's vital signs.

By seven o'clock that night they were all at the hospital except Erin and Sam, who had already returned to Texas. But other than Peter and Brooke, only John understood the gravity of the situation. He sat in the waiting room glancing every now and then at the others. Elizabeth beside him, Ashley next to her, and Luke at the far end of the sofa. Luke was set to leave Monday for New York, and already he'd called Reagan and explained the situation, that he might wait and travel after they knew more about Hayley's condition.

Across the room sat Kari and Ryan, the glow from their honeymoon dimmed in light of this tragedy. Brooke and Peter were in with Hayley. The children, Cole and Maddie and Jessie, were across town with Pastor Mark and his wife.

None of them talked about what had happened or how long Hayley had been under or who was at fault. In fact they'd said very little, each of them too deep in prayer and fear to think of anything to say.

John had called the pastor a few minutes earlier and given his friend an update. "It doesn't look good." He pinched the bridge of his nose and squeezed his eyes shut. "She could've been under fifteen minutes or more."

"Oh, John . . ." The man didn't say anything else. What could he say? He didn't need a medical degree to understand how serious her condition must be if she had been underwater that long.

"She still isn't breathing on her own." John's throat was thick, and he waited until he had more control. His mind kept screaming the obvious. Hayley might survive. But depending on the damage in her brain, she would almost certainly not live any kind of normal life. "Pray for her, Mark . . . for God's will."

"I'm praying for a miracle."

"Right." A knifepoint of guilt nicked John in the gut. "That's what I mean. Pray for a miracle."

But now, ten minutes later, John wasn't sure.

If she lived . . . if her brain didn't swell in the coming days, and if somehow her mind figured out how to breathe again, exactly how much of Hayley would remain? He shuddered and remembered a boy who had come into the hospital a few years earlier. The child—a two-year-old—had fallen into a muddy part of the river, where he was under twelve minutes before his desperate parents bumped into him and ran him to their car.

Friends and relatives gathered around the hospital in the days afterwards, praying for the boy to survive, and sure enough he did. But he left the hospital two months later an entirely different child. Unable to see or speak or move his limbs, the child was doomed to spend the rest of his life being tube fed, strapped to a bed or a wheelchair.

And John had wondered.

Wouldn't the child have been better off in heaven? Why would God allow him to live, only to confine him to a paralyzed mind and body? to deny him the chance to run and play and live a normal life? The incident was so troubling, John had never actually resolved it. Instead he'd put it out of his thinking until now, until he and his family were the ones praying desperately for life, begging God for Hayley's next breath.

He hung his head and laced his fingers along the back of his neck. *Don't do that to her, God. . . . If you bring her back, bring her back all the way.* Anger welled within him, and he wanted to grab the nearest magazine and throw it across the room. He was a doctor, after all. A doctor! And here he was completely helpless to do anything for his little granddaughter.

*God . . . I want her to live. . . .* He worked his fingers into his neck muscles. *But if she won't be the same . . . if Hayley isn't Hayley*

anymore, if she can't play with Maddie or recognize Brooke—then
God, maybe it would be better if you—

"John?"

"Yes . . ." He looked up and saw one of his colleagues at the
door. Dr. Zach Martinez specialized in brain injuries; the two of
them had finished med school together and started practicing in
Bloomington the same year.

The man's face was grim. "Could I speak to you?"

John gave Elizabeth a look as he stood and followed the doctor out of the room. When they were a ways down the hallway,
Zach turned to him and pursed his lips. "The situation isn't
good, John. You know that."

"Yes." John's knees shook. His arms hung weak at his sides.
"Can you tell anything about her brain yet?"

"It's damaged." The doctor breathed hard through his nose.
"We can see that much."

"Meaning?" John was playing two roles today, doctor and
grandfather. But here and now he wanted Zach to see him as a
doctor, someone who could be trusted with the news, no matter
how bad.

"She has severe brain damage, John."

John took the news like a bullet, the sensation so strong he
staggered back a step. "Severe?"

"Yes." He clenched his jaw. "But that's not the worst of it.
Honestly, the team wanted me to ask you about . . ."

John searched the man's face. The hallway was spinning, and
he took hold of the railing that lined the wall. "About what?"

"Whether the family would consider organ donation." Zach
held up a hand. "I know it's too soon, but if she dies, John, we
need to know what to do."

The floor fell away, and John tightened his grip on the safety
railing. "They . . . they don't think she's going to make it?"

"Her brain's swelling, and it's only been hours." His voice fell.
"Swelling can last for three days after a drowning."

"I know . . ." John leaned against the wall. "Have you talked to Brooke and Peter?"

"Yes." The man bit his lip. "They wanted me to tell you so . . . so you can help them make a decision."

A decision? About whether their three-year-old granddaughter should be cut apart and doled out to a handful of sick kids? The idea seemed ludicrous, as if it were happening to someone else, one of his patients, maybe, or someone on a movie set. But not to him, not to John Baxter.

He closed his eyes and saw Hayley the way she'd looked at his house a few nights ago. She'd been playing with baby Jessie, standing behind her, helping her walk toward Kari.

"That's it, Hayley. What a good little cousin." Hayley had bent down and planted a kiss on the top of Jessie's head. "Okay, honey. Keep walking to mama."

The image broke apart. He opened his eyes and Zach was still standing there, still waiting for an answer. John planted his feet a ways apart and let go of the railing. "Okay—" he gritted his teeth—"I'll talk to them."

By the time he returned to the waiting room, Brooke and Peter were there. Peter sat next to Ryan, his head back against the hospital wall, eyes vacant. Brooke was pale, her lips tight, face drawn, caught between Ashley's and Kari's embrace. As John entered the room, Peter caught his eye.

"We . . ." John coughed and searched for a strength he couldn't muster on his own. "We need to talk."

The others had no idea what was happening, but not one of them asked. The news was bad enough without something getting worse. Brooke pulled away from the others, wiped her sleeve across her face and followed John. Peter came a few steps behind. Out in the hallway, John looked from Brooke to Peter, and back again. "I talked to Dr. Martinez."

Brooke was shaking, her face pale and clammy. She held his gaze and lifted her hands toward him. "Help me, Dad."

Then, as if Peter weren't there at all, she fell into John's arms and wept against his chest. For several minutes she stayed that way, while nearby, Peter shifted his weight from one foot to the other. When Brooke had more control, she stepped back and stood a few inches from Peter, as close to her husband as she'd been all day.

"We can't . . ." Peter cleared his throat and looked at his shoes. After a while he shook his head and shrugged his shoulders. His chin was trembling badly.

"You could wait." John put one hand on Peter's shoulder and the other on Brooke's. "You don't have to make this decision now."

"Of course we want to . . . to help someone else." Brooke's words were high-pitched and jumbled together. "But if we say yes . . ."

Peter gave a hard shake of his head and lifted his eyes to the ceiling for a moment. When he had more control he locked eyes with John. "If we say yes, we're giving up on her."

A knot the size of a bowling ball shifted in John's heart. He thought of Hayley's worsening condition, and suddenly he wondered. Had God heard his prayer, the one he had been forming even as Dr. Martinez came to find him? Was God taking her now because John hadn't wanted her to live, hadn't wanted Hayley back unless she was whole and complete, the way she'd been before the accident?

Was this God's way of honoring his request, his lack of faith that somehow she would be well again if she would live? The idea lay like a cement blanket on his conscience. He leveled his gaze at Peter and worked the muscles in his jaw. "You know the routine, Peter. Telling them yes is only part of the process. It doesn't mean you've given up."

"Dad." Brooke lifted her fingers and covered her mouth for a moment. Fresh tears slipped from her eyes. "How can we?"

"Honey, listen." John looked at her, his hand still on her shoulder. "God is in control; we have to believe that. I know how you feel about organ donations. We've talked about it a number of times."

"The shortage . . ." Brooke hung her head and grabbed three quick breaths.

"Yes." John squeezed her shoulder. How was he standing here, talking to her about Hayley's organs, when he himself wanted only to run or scream or find a way to undo the damage in his granddaughter's brain? He urged himself to concentrate. "It's your decision, but don't make it with your heart. Make it with your head. Then move past it. She's in bad shape, Brooke. You know that. This is only protocol."

Peter slipped his hands into his pockets and looked at his shoes again. He added nothing to the conversation.

"Okay." Brooke sniffed and searched John's eyes. "We'll sign the papers."

John waited a beat and looked at his son-in-law. "Peter?"

"Fine." He said the word fast, as though it hurt too much to let it linger on his lips.

"All right. I'll get Dr. Martinez." John turned and saw the doctor talking with another specialist at the end of the hallway. He motioned at the man, and he came toward them, a clipboard tucked beneath his arm.

John nodded at Brooke and Peter. "They're ready."

The other doctor stepped closer, his voice soft, filled with compassion, as he held the clipboard out and explained the document. His words weren't necessary, of course. Peter and Brooke knew the document well; it was part of their medical training. Brooke reached for the pen first. John watched as she signed her name, her tears leaving a black smudge beneath her signature. Peter signed it next. Then Dr. Martinez tucked the board beneath his arm once again.

He was telling them something in hushed tones, something about hoping for the best and wanting to believe that Hayley would be okay, and how their signatures on the document didn't mean they'd given up on her or her chance for survival. But suddenly, in the middle of his brief talk, a different doctor came hurrying toward them, one John recognized but didn't know by name.

"You're Hayley's family?"

"Yes." Peter lifted his head for the first time in five minutes. His eyes screamed for a reason to hope, a reason to hang on.

Something about the scene made John want to cry, because the news couldn't possibly be good. Peter and Brooke knew that more than anyone else in the family, but now, when it was their daughter's life at stake, they wanted to believe as badly as the distraught parents they often dealt with.

The doctor uttered a frustrated huff. "We're losing her." He glanced at John, and then back to Brooke and Peter. "We thought you'd want to be there."

# CHAPTER FOUR

PETER HAD NO IDEA how to survive what was happening.

He and Brooke had raced to Hayley's room after the doctor's warning, but now they'd been on either side of her bed for thirty minutes without any change in her condition. She wasn't breathing on her own, and her heartbeat was irregular. But her face was more swollen than before, the skin around her eyes thick and bunched so that her eyelids were grotesque slits.

And the whole time, Peter hadn't said more than a handful of sentences to anyone. He replayed the scene from earlier that day, the first few moments when he and Brooke were alone together in Hayley's hospital room. She was already at their daughter's side by the time Peter arrived, and when they locked eyes, Peter wasn't sure what he saw there. Fear and anger, yes. But a strange sort of guilt as well.

He wanted to go to her, hold her and tell her it wasn't her fault, explain how it wasn't his fault either. That from what he'd been able to piece together, after eating cake, the girls had gone upstairs. She'd chattered on about wanting to swim again, but Aletha and the other mothers had told the children no, they could swim later.

All of them headed upstairs, every single girl. Aletha was certain Hayley had been with them. But sometime after they'd pulled out the Barbie dolls, after assignments had been made as to who would have which one and what drama they were going to act out, Hayley turned to Maddie and told her good-bye, told her she wanted to be the first to go swimming.

"No, Hayley. Mommy says we have to stay together in the pool. Plus you need your life jacket."

Maddie remembered every detail, and Peter could only be grateful for one small aspect. She was too young to own any of the guilt, at least for now.

After Maddie told Hayley she couldn't swim yet, Hayley sat near the stairs and pouted. A few minutes passed, and Hayley said she had to go potty. Maybe she never intended to go and instead wanted a reason to head down to the pool. Or maybe she used the bathroom and then got distracted by the view to the outside.

Whatever happened, she managed to get through the patio door without any parents noticing her. After a long time—fifteen minutes, maybe more—Maddie realized that Hayley had been gone too long. That's when she raced downstairs, grabbed Hayley's life jacket from the bathroom, and ran to find him.

Peter had replayed the scene in his head a hundred times since this afternoon.

How could he have possibly known Hayley would slip into the backyard without telling anyone? And even though he was in charge, even though Brooke had asked him to keep the girls' life jackets on, wouldn't she have done the same thing? Wouldn't she have taken them off so the girls could eat cake without dripping water on Aletha's kitchen floor?

He'd gone to Brooke when he first entered Hayley's hospital room. "Listen . . . I can explain what ha—"

"Stop!" She held up her hand and hissed the word. "I should've been there."

Peter's heart sank to his shoes. He'd been right; it had been guilt he'd seen in her eyes. He lowered his voice and made his way to her side. "Brooke, it isn't your fault. Neither of us could've done anything to—"

"You were there, Peter." She pointed one angry finger at him. "You were there and you—" She stopped short and glared at him, her eyes narrow and angry.

That's when he knew she wasn't only blaming herself. She was blaming him. And suddenly he had no excuses for her, no desire to explain what had happened while she was on her call. In the hours since, she still hadn't asked him about the details, the moments that led up to Hayley's drowning.

Other than a few functional statements, he hadn't spoken to her.

He glanced at her now, the woman he'd fallen in love with back in med school. She hovered over Hayley, whispering to her, terror etched in the lines around her eyes.

With everything in him, he wanted to pray for a miracle, beg God to let Hayley live, and not only that, but let her be well again. But he knew the statistics, knew the realities of drowning victims. The doctor was right; any minute now her brain would swell to the point that existence would be impossible. It was only a matter of time.

Because of that, Peter had nothing to say to anyone, really. Not to the doctors, not to Brooke.

And especially not to God.

Rather than pray, he remembered something Ryan had told him once. In the past few months, the two of them had gotten together several times to study the Bible, something that helped make Peter's faith feel real, despite the growing tension in his marriage.

"People think prayers have to be memorized and perfectly spoken." The two of them had been fishing off the pier at Lake Monroe. Ryan chuckled and stared out at the water. "Nothing could be further from the truth." He looked at Peter. "God already knows what we're thinking. Our best, most intimate prayers happen when we're simply honest with him. Feeling happy, thank him. Feeling lonely, cry out to him. Feeling afraid or angry or unsure, tell him. That's the only way you'll ever have a relationship with Jesus."

Peter had taken the words to heart. In the months since then, he had talked to God whenever he felt anything out of the ordinary. Sometimes the conversation felt forced and one-sided. But other times . . . other times he was certain God was there, listening to his thoughts, helping him believe. Sometimes he even felt a thought, an impression on his heart, as if God was actually answering him.

Here, though, with his sweet Hayley girl dying a few feet away, it wasn't that Peter couldn't believe. Rather he didn't want to. Because if God allowed Hayley to die or to live life hooked to machines, then Peter didn't want anything to do with him.

And now, in light of Ryan's suggestion, Peter decided to tell God just that. He gripped the railing on his daughter's hospital bed and closed his eyes. *God . . . what are you doing? Why did this happen?* His breathing grew faster, and he opened his mouth so the sound wouldn't attract Brooke's attention. *You have to make her live; you have to. I can't believe in a God who would let my daughter die, not when she's only started living.*

Peter opened his eyes and studied Hayley again.

*Make her well, God. Otherwise I'll know you don't exist. Because no good God would take the life of an innocent three-year-old. If she dies, then either you don't exist or you're not good. And if that happens, this will be my last conversation with you.*

Peter let his final silent statement swing from the rafters of his mind. But before he could switch gears and try to imagine how much longer his daughter had, how quickly they might lose her, Hayley moved. Not a big movement, but one of her hands definitely moved.

"Hayley?" Brooke lifted her head and studied their little girl. "Did you see that?"

"Yes." Peter was about to reach out for his daughter's hand

when she moved it again. At the same time, a soft moan came from her throat.

Peter didn't wait. He spun around and ran into the hall. "Dr. Martinez, quick . . ."

The doctor was talking with the rest of the team near the nurses' station. He looked stricken, as though the news had to be bad. "Is she—"

"She moved!" Peter heard the hope in his voice. "Come look."

The doctor and three others followed Peter back into the room and surrounded Hayley, checking the monitors and breathing apparatus. Peter and Brooke stepped back against the far wall of the room.

Brooke hung her head, her fists clenched. "Please, God . . . please."

Peter gulped back the lump in his throat and thought about the words he'd been saying to God when Hayley moved. A sense of awe and wonder filled him. Had God heard him, responded to him even though his words had been unkind? He reminded himself to breathe as he waited for the doctors to say something.

After five minutes, Dr. Martinez turned to them and grinned. "She's breathing on her own."

Brooke let out a cry and crossed her arms tight around her waist. "Does that . . . does that mean her brain might be okay?"

Shadows fell across the doctor's face. "We're a long way from knowing. It only means she's clinging to life, clinging by a thread. Her brain could continue to swell, but if she survives the next three days, we'll assess the extent of her damage." The team of doctors moved toward the door, and Dr. Martinez stopped short. "We have a long road ahead; I have to be honest with you."

Peter's awe and wonder dissipated like April snow.

So it hadn't been a miracle after all. Peter clenched his jaw and watched Brooke hurry back to Hayley's side, watched her take hold of their daughter's hand and whisper to her. "Hayley, come back to us, baby. We're here for you. Mommy and Daddy are here, sweetie. We're here, Hayley. . . ."

So she was breathing on her own. So what?

They didn't have hurdles left on the road to their daughter's recovery; they had mountains. Mountains the size of Everest. If she made it through the next three days, she would almost certainly be severely brain damaged, one of those children whose hands and legs were in a constant state of seizure, a child whose mouth would hang open, drooling, making slow attempts at movement.

And if that happened, his threat to God was still intact. He would have no reason to talk to him again, no reason to believe. Once more he looked at Brooke, and though his heart hurt for her, he felt nothing beyond pity. No love or desire, not even a deep friendship. She would resent him forever for not watching Hayley more closely, and what would that leave them? He swallowed and the truth tasted bitter in his mouth. If Hayley didn't recover, it would not only mean the end of his relationship with God.

It would also mean the end of his relationship with Brooke.

# CHAPTER FIVE

ASHLEY WAS BACK AT WORK at Sunset Hills. The residents weren't yet at the breakfast table, so she was going over the work schedule and praying for Hayley.

Always praying for Hayley.

Five days had passed since the child's accident, and her doctors had declared her stable. But in this case, stable wasn't entirely a good thing. She was breathing on her own, and she'd survived the dangerous period of potential brain swelling. But she was still in a coma, still hooked to feeding tubes and monitors. Ashley hadn't wanted to ask, but her father had told the family anyway.

Hayley could stay in a coma forever. She could grow up in a nursing facility, breathing but never so much as opening her eyes.

Her father had kept the family informed. Ashley understood. It was his way of being strong, playing the role he'd always played, even at a time when he was as helpless as any of them to make a difference. With the situation stable and improvement hardly guaranteed, Luke had gone home the day before. He couldn't do anything by staying in Bloomington, and Reagan and their baby son were waiting for him in New York.

Before he left, he pulled Ashley aside and hugged her for a long time. "After thinking about your situation, I decided to get tested." He searched her face. "Lori was very, well . . . very active. I couldn't marry Reagan without knowing." He paused. "I'm fine, Ash, but if I weren't, this wouldn't be the time to tell the family." He took her hand. "Don't do it. Don't tell anyone about your blood test. Wait until this is over."

Ashley clung to him and shook her head against his chest. "I won't. Go be with your baby, little brother."

Since Saturday, she had spent most of her time either watching the children or visiting with Brooke and Kari and their mother at the hospital. So far the children hadn't been allowed into the room. The situation was still too awful, too frightening for the little ones.

Besides, the tension between Peter and Brooke was unbearable. Brooke had told her how desperate things between them had become. "We only talk when we have to, when the doctor asks a question or when we have to decide what to do with Maddie." Brooke's eyes were more dead than alive. "We take turns with Hayley and pass each other in the hallway without saying a word."

The picture Brooke painted was almost as sad as Hayley's small figure beneath the hospital sheets.

"Brooke . . . you need each other." Ashley had pulled her aside the day before. "Go to him . . . say something. Hug him so he knows you still love him."

"I would—" Brooke had turned to the closest window— "but I'm not sure I do."

Ashley had talked about the situation with Kari and Ryan, and the two of them were determined to help. Twice Pastor Mark had stopped by to pray. Both times he took Peter and Brooke aside and spoke to them, but not even that broke the silence between them.

Her father had returned to work by then, but Mom had set up camp in the waiting room, her job clear-cut. She would stay there, taking turns with whoever was in the waiting room, and praying constantly for Hayley to be healed. The stress was getting to her; Ashley could see it. Her eyes had dark circles beneath them; her shoulders hunched more often than not. Her clothes looked looser, too. As though she'd lost weight in places where she had no weight to lose.

This weekend, though Sam had to work, Erin was coming, the first chance she could get away from her classroom in Texas. The entire family was rallying behind Hayley, but still the situation felt as if it was falling apart.

Ashley tapped out a few more lines on the computer and studied the screen. The work schedule for Sunset Hills was finished, and she shifted her gaze to the phone on the desk. She should call Landon, give him an update and let him know how everyone was doing. Reagan had told him about the accident, but so far Ashley hadn't spoken to him.

She was too afraid she'd break down and beg him to catch the next flight.

The phone practically screamed at her to make the call, but she turned away. Later. She'd call him later.

Breakfast had been served in the next room, and she needed time with the residents, time to connect again with Irvel and Edith and Helen and Bert. The new woman was failing quickly, but the others, her special friends, were still about the same. None of them seemed worse for their year or so of living with the Past-Present theory.

Helen still had times when she recognized Sue as her daughter, and Bert still spent hours each day shining the saddle in his room. Edith didn't say much, but she hadn't had a nightmare or screaming episode since they'd taken away her mirrors.

And Irvel . . . Irvel was still Ashley's favorite. She was slower these days, less quick to come up with a social plan for the afternoon. But she was still sure Hank was out fishing, still convinced that come the end of the day he'd join her at the house and hold her close while she slept.

The pictures of Hank, the ones Ashley had hung on Irvel's wall nearly a year ago, were still in place. Ashley dusted them now and then, so Irvel could see the sparkle in Hank's eyes as clearly as she'd seen it all those years ago when they had been together. She talked about him more now, and once in a while she seemed to be talking *to* him. As if he were standing in the room with her.

"Why, Hank," she'd say, "hello to you!" She'd pause, squinting at the empty space in front of her. "What's that? A sixteen-inch trout?" A ripple of laughter would ring across the room. "Hank, you don't need to impress me; I couldn't love you more if I tried!"

The doctor had told them it wouldn't be long for Irvel. Her heart was slowing down, her mind giving way to the incessant ravages of Alzheimer's. But for now, she remained the brightest light at Sunset Hills. Ashley thanked God for her, certain that but for Irvel's love for Hank, Ashley never would've connected with Landon.

And even though she'd chosen to let go of him, his love for her and the memory of their time together would last a lifetime. Enough so that one day, if she lived long enough to be Irvel's age, she would no doubt have conversations with a tall, handsome firefighter who hadn't been a part of her life for decades.

And she just might live that long.

She'd been researching HIV online, and the news was hopeful. Though she would always represent a risk to anyone who was intimate with her, research showed that the right treatment plan could keep AIDS at bay for decades.

*Ah, Landon . . . if only I didn't love you so much.*

The thought lifted and danced in the breeze from the nearby window. Ashley looked out through the old, wood-framed window and stared at the blue sky. It was an Indian-summer morning, a day when fall still felt weeks away. She closed her eyes and let the sun shine against her face.

*Keep him close to you, God. . . . Don't let anything happen to him.*

It was a prayer she lifted on Landon's behalf every day. The easy part. She drew a slow breath and finished. The last part was so difficult it made her stomach ache. *And help him let go of me, of us. He needs to find someone in New York, someone who can give him a future without fear, someone healthy and whole. Please, God. And help me live without him.*

For a moment her mind went still, and though this time she didn't hear an answer from the Lord, she felt his presence. Felt his Spirit in the core of her being, his comfort as close as her heartbeat.

She opened her eyes and realized the familiar pain in her heart. Yes, God was with her, and yes, her prayer came from the most sincere part of her soul. But that didn't make the praying any less painful.

In the distance she could hear the residents at the breakfast table. A smile lifted the corners of her mouth, and she willed herself to get on with the day despite the ache in her heart. She made her way down the hall to the dining-room table. Bert wasn't there, probably eating in his room again. He didn't get up as early as he used to, and his chart said that in the past few weeks he'd been joining the others only for dinner.

The moment Irvel saw her, she sat back in her chair and smiled. Her skin was more translucent now, almost clear. "Hello, dear . . . I don't believe we've met."

Ashley walked around the table and reached for Irvel's fingers. The bones in the old woman's hand were more defined than before. "Hello, Irvel. I'm Ashley. I'll be with you this morning, okay?"

"Ashley." Irvel studied her, and a flicker of recognition flashed in her eyes. "Yes, I remember you, dear. You have the most beautiful hair. Has anyone told you that?"

"Not today, Irvel." She leaned close and gave the woman a careful hug. "Thank you for saying so."

Every now and then Irvel remembered Ashley, and those days

were the happiest of all. Days when Irvel was the best friend Ashley had.

"Hey, you!" Next to Irvel, Helen pointed at Ashley. Her voice was loud, and it knocked the moment on its side. "Tell me something, will you?"

"Hello, Helen." Ashley worked her way around the table and patted Helen's shoulder.

"Back up!" The woman jumped as if she'd been slapped. "That's my sore arm!"

Ashley glanced at the daytime care worker, a kind young woman named Maria, who was still working in the kitchen. Ashley mouthed the words, "Sore arm?"

Maria grinned and shook her head. Her answer was too quiet for anyone but Ashley to hear. "She's fine."

Still, Ashley took a step back. "I'm sorry about your arm, Helen."

"Yeah, well, no one checked it this morning. Spies got to it, I tell you. Spies run the place."

Ashley changed the subject. "How's your oatmeal, Helen?"

"Listen, I'm asking you a question." Helen pounded her fist on the breakfast table.

Irvel clucked her tongue in Helen's direction. "Now dear, that isn't a very nice dinner bell." She smoothed her hands over a wrinkle in the tablecloth. "We're all friends here. No need to get violent. Besides—" she cast a quick smile at Edith, who was staring at her half-eaten oatmeal—"it's not every day we can be together like this."

"I said . . ." Helen spat the words in Irvel's direction. "I have a question." She pointed at Ashley again. "Are you gonna answer me or not?"

"Definitely." Ashley bit the inside of her lip. "What's your question, Helen?"

"Okay, then." She banged her fist on the table once more and glared at Irvel. "Who's this old bird beside me? Because I never invited her to the party and now she hasn't been checked."

"Excuse me." Irvel made a polite tap of one finger on the table between her and Helen. "The old bird flew away an hour ago, and for the record it was a crow. And yes, dear, of course I've been checked." She smiled at Ashley. "We all have, right?"

"Yes." Ashley faced Irvel, but gave Helen a sideways glance. "We've all been checked."

Helen jabbed her finger in Edith's direction. "What about her? Why isn't she cooking something?"

Edith brought her hands up onto the table and began fidgeting with her fingers. "Cooking? Cooking . . . cooking . . . cooking?"

Ashley moved around the table to Edith. "It's okay, dear; you don't have to cook today."

"Not today?" Edith narrowed her eyes and stared at Ashley as though she were desperate for a moment of lucidity. "No cooking?"

"Not today."

"Fine, then." Helen made a loud moaning sound. "If she's not the cook, it must be the old bird beside me."

Irvel looked around as if Helen was perhaps thinking of someone who hadn't yet been introduced to the group. When she realized Helen was talking to her, she made a polite bit of laughter. "No dear, my name isn't Birdie; it's Irvel. But sometimes when Hank brings the boys over, they call me Birdie." Confusion clouded her eyes. "Or maybe it's Irvie." Her face broke into a smile. "Yes, that's it. Irvie."

"Well, Birdie, are you the cook or not?" Helen pointed at Irvel and then shifted her finger to Ashley. "Tell me that, will you?"

"Dear . . ." Irvel tapped again. "I'm not the cook; I'm the eater." She dropped her voice to a whisper. "Maybe you're the cook."

"What?" Helen thought about that for a moment. "Listen . . ." She scowled again. "I don't care if you're the cook, but I have an announcement." She punctuated each word with her fist against the table. "My . . . oatmeal . . . is . . . cold."

"Well!" Irvel raised an eyebrow at Helen. "Excuse me." She looked to Ashley for support. "Maybe this woman should go home. Hank doesn't like me keeping company with violent people."

Ashley was about to offer to warm up Helen's oatmeal when the phone rang. She held up a finger to Helen and reached for the cordless receiver. "Hello?"

"Hi, honey; it's Dad." He sounded better than he had last time they talked. "I've got good news and bad news."

The conversation at the breakfast table grew louder. Ashley moved into the next room and covered her ear. "What is it?" She held her breath. *Please, God, let the good news be about Hayley.* "Good news first, okay?"

"Okay. Hayley woke up about an hour ago." Her father's voice cracked. He cleared his throat and waited. "Sorry." He breathed out. "It's just . . . I wasn't sure if she'd ever . . ."

"She's awake?" Ashley paced toward the television and back to the dining-room entrance. They had all known Hayley might stay in the coma for weeks, months, even. Now, only five days after the accident, this was amazing news. "She's out of her coma?"

"Yes." Her father made a noise that was half laugh, half delirious relief. "Brooke wants us to visit her. The doctor says it's important to surround her with familiar voices."

"Why . . ." Ashley heard something change in her father's tone. "Why familiar *voices*? What about familiar faces?"

For several seconds her father said nothing, and Ashley realized what was happening. He was too choked up to speak.

Ashley dropped to the nearest chair and anchored her elbows on her knees. "Dad?"

"Because of the bad news." His voice was tight, racked with emotion. "They've worried about this from the beginning, but now they know for sure."

"What?" Her heart beat harder than before.

"Honey, . . . Hayley's blind."

# CHAPTER SIX

FOR FIVE STRAIGHT DAYS Brooke had begged God to let Hayley live, let her wake up. She had no doubt that the nightmare would end the moment her younger daughter opened those pale blue eyes.

But now that Hayley had been awake for ten hours, Brooke was beginning to understand. The nightmare wasn't over; it had only begun. The child in the bed who looked like Hayley was nothing like the little girl Brooke had bid good-bye that sunny Saturday afternoon. The differences were terrifying, and sometimes Brooke could barely stand to be in the room with her.

It wasn't the fact that her daughter had so much ground to make up before she'd be well again. Rather it was this: The child in the bed was no longer Hayley. Not her expression, not her personality, nothing even remotely familiar in her face. And definitely not her cry.

From the moment she woke up, Hayley had been crying. She was still crying now, at seven o'clock Thursday evening. Other than a few short naps, she had cried all day.

"It's okay, Hayley." Brooke stroked her daughter's bare leg.

Discouragement rang in her voice, but Brooke could do nothing to change it. "Mommy's here, baby. Shhh . . . it's okay."

The crying grew louder. Not the familiar cry that had been Hayley's before the accident. But a strange, sickly sort of cry, slow and constant like a bleating lamb.

The cry of a brain-damaged child.

"Baby, I'm here; it's okay." Brooke reached for her daughter's hand and braced herself. Hayley's hands didn't feel the same either. They were stiff and turned slightly out, the same as her feet. Brooke wanted to think Hayley was suffering from cramps or a lack of movement. But she knew better. The stiffness meant she was seizing, another symptom of a seriously injured brain.

More crying, and this time Hayley turned her head from one side of the pillow to the other. Over and over and over again.

Brooke watched and felt her insides being ripped to shreds. An hour after Hayley woke up, Dr. Martinez had explained the reason for her crying, for the strange way she looked from side to side a hundred times without stopping.

"She's looking for you." He held Hayley's file, his eyes full of quiet compassion. "We consider it a good sign when a drowning victim shows a desire to connect. It means some part of her memory is working."

"But I'm here." Brooke wrapped her arms around her middle and tried to keep her head from spinning. "All I want to do is hold her and take away her fear, Doctor. If she's looking for me, why doesn't she know it's me beside her?"

"First of all, she's blind. She can't see you, and the darkness is scaring her. It's something new, something she has no frame of reference for." He bit his lip and leveled his eyes at Brooke. "Second, her brain is too injured at this point to recognize your voice. She knows you're there, but she doesn't know you're her mother."

The news had hit like a machete to what was left of Brooke's fragile heart. Of course Hayley didn't recognize her. Brooke remembered lessons she'd done in med school about brain-damaged children. Hayley's symptoms were classic in their presentation. Brooke simply hadn't wanted to believe it was true.

And that wasn't all. Every time one of her family members came to visit, Brooke had to explain the situation again. Now, after a full day of hearing her daughter's unfamiliar cry, a full day of failing to connect with her, of watching her hands and feet grow stiffer with each passing hour, a day of breaking the awful news to her family, Brooke was at the end of her abilities.

The hands on the wall clock moved slower than usual, reminding Brooke that the hours here with Hayley, the months of recovery, were bound to be as tedious as they were painful. Her eyes fell on a framed picture of Peter and her and the girls on the bedside table beside Hayley. Her mother had brought it earlier today.

"When her sight returns, she'll have something familiar to look at." Her mother had cleared a spot on the table and set it up during her morning visit. Then she looked at Brooke. "Maybe it'll help you, too."

Brooke let her eyes move from Maddie to Peter and herself. The picture had been taken at Lake Monroe little more than a year ago, during the Baxters' Labor Day picnic. Brooke remembered playing Frisbee with Peter on the beach, grateful for a chance to drop the professional role and be less serious.

Once, in the middle of their game, Peter threw a floater and ran after it at the same time Brooke did. They collided in shallow water and fell, knees bruised, laughing at their soaked shorts and T-shirts. The collision became a tickling match, the two of them going after each other, wrestling on the shore and chasing each other into the water. By the time they stumbled up the beach and grabbed their towels that day, Brooke felt young and alive and more in love with her husband than ever before.

She gazed out the hospital window. Things had certainly changed since then, and she wondered if the difference was entirely centered around Maddie's illness.

Maybe it was something more; maybe they'd become too busy

for each other, too caught up in building their separate prac-
tices, too given to their daughters when they came home at
night. Or maybe they'd developed some kind of professional
competition. Whose practice would be more successful, more
quickly established?

Brooke studied Hayley again and realized she was tuning out
her daughter's crying, finding a way to survive the situation even
when she knew she couldn't take another minute.

Or maybe the trouble with her and Peter hadn't truly started
until Maddie's illness. The specialist had been just the answer, of
course. The man had known what tests to run, where to look to
find the reason for Maddie's constant fevers. Though she'd never
admitted it to Peter, he'd been right to call the man. He'd been
right and she'd been wrong.

And he'd reminded her of the fact as often as he could. A quiet
comment about her inexperience, or a reminder that he at least
had realized they needed to call in a specialist. So maybe it was a
competition thing between them after all. He saw himself as the
competent doctor; her, the incompetent one. In the past year
she'd gone out of her way to change his mind. She looked the
part—simple, shoulder-length dark hair, little makeup, and a
closet full of rayon skirts and blouses.

And she was active in two organizations that sought to give
women equal pay and respect in the medical field. More than
once Peter had commented that women should spend less time
trying to convince people they were equal and more time acting
it out.

So yes, professional competition had to be part of it. She
soothed her fingers over Hayley's brow.

The only time they didn't seem to be in competition was on
Sundays at church. Since September 11, 2001, they'd attended
her parents' church together, but after Maddie's last illness, their
attendance had been only occasional. It wasn't something they
talked about or agreed on. Rather their conversation was too dis-

tant to make weekend plans, even the simple plan of attending church.

Once in a while Brooke took the girls when they complained about missing Sunday school. But for the most part Brooke spent Sundays grocery shopping, taking the girls to the park, visiting her parents. And Peter spent Sundays in his home office, studying his more difficult cases. In recent months, whole weeks had passed without the two of them sharing a kiss or even a smile.

Whatever the reason, their love had grown cool long before Hayley's accident.

That was the other thing her mother talked about on her visit earlier today. Her relationship with Peter. "You're a pediatrician, Brooke. You know the statistics."

"Statistics?" Brooke wasn't in the mood for counseling. She wanted to spend every moment praying for Hayley, that the fog in her brain would clear at least enough for her to recognize their voices.

"Marriage statistics. In the aftermath of a child's tragedy."

Yes, Brooke knew the statistics. More than 90 percent of marriages ended in divorce after a child's tragic accident or death. But Brooke didn't want to talk statistics. "Mom, this isn't the time, not when . . ." It was one of the few hours when Hayley was asleep. Brooke looked at her daughter and felt a thickness in her throat. When she spoke again, her voice was a strained whisper. "Please, Mom."

"Brooke, I won't lecture you." She took hold of Brooke's hand. "But Hayley and Maddie need *both* of you. God's given you each other as a means of support for times like this."

"Mom . . ." Brooke held up one hand, her heart ice-cold.

"Okay . . . no more. I'm sorry."

And that had been all. After that her mother didn't say a word about Peter or the troubles between them. Peter had returned to work the day before, and he'd been in twice that day to see Hayley. Since Brooke was staying at the hospital, Maddie was staying with her grandparents. Peter didn't feel up to watching their older daughter, not when he was gone until after dinner most nights, anyway.

Both times he'd been by the hospital that day, Brooke had gone to the waiting room with her parents or Ashley, all of whom had been in at one time or another since morning. On his last visit, he left straight from Hayley's room, without even stopping in to say good-bye.

Hayley's crying grew softer now, and she fell still, the way she did before taking a nap

"*That's* right, baby . . . shhh."

Brooke folded her hands on her lap and dug her fingertips into the backs of her hands. She would've given anything to blink her eyes and be at home with Hayley, anything to turn back the hands of time and have her little daughter back once more. She no longer had the energy to think about her husband's behavior. She was completely consumed with watching Hayley, praying for her, trying to see even the smallest bit of hope during her waking hours.

Hayley's crying grew even quieter, the pattern slower than before. Brooke stood and leaned over her, searching her daughter's face, her eyes. She could picture her last moments with Hayley as clearly as if they'd happened only a moment ago. The two of them leaving the car and heading up the walkway to DeWayne and Aletha's house. Hayley jumping into her arms, and Brooke carrying her to the front door.

With Hayley close against her chest, Brooke had felt loved and needed, the way she hadn't felt in weeks. She'd snuggled the child close and felt Hayley take hold of her hand and squeeze it three times. Their secret code for *I love you*. Then she'd whispered in her daughter's ear, "You're a sweet girl, Hayley; do you know that?"

And Hayley had responded in a similar way. "You, too, Mommy." Hayley had rubbed her tiny nose against Brooke's. "You're a sweetie girl, too. Know why?"

"Why?" Brooke and Hayley had trailed behind Peter and Maddie.

"Because—" Hayley had tilted her head, her pale blonde hair shining in the afternoon sun—"I love you; that's why."

Now Brooke took hold of her daughter's stiff fingers and tears filled her eyes. *Hayley . . . where are you, Hayley?*

She swallowed hard and the memory broke apart. Was Hayley, the old Hayley, gone forever? Would she never again have the Hayley she'd held as they headed up the walkway hours before the drowning? Watching her lie there in the hospital bed, drifting to sleep, her brain so damaged she was beyond comfort, Brooke pictured something from her own childhood.

Her mother had loved to sew back then. Until Brooke was ten years old, Mom had sewn matching outfits for the five Baxter kids, including once when she made the girls floral pantsuits in lightweight cotton with matching headbands. Luke had shorts in the same material, and a white shirt, and together the group looked like some sort of kid band from the seventies.

The five of them laughed about the outfits now, but they still appreciated the hours their mother put into the effort. Brooke remembered sitting beside her while she sewed, watching her struggle to thread the needle. Once in a while the thread would dance about just below the needle's eye, until her mother would drop her hands to her lap.

"It's right there. I can see it and feel it. I just can't bring it to the surface."

That was how Brooke felt now.

Hayley was there, just below the surface. But no matter how hard she tried to grab what was there and pull Hayley back, it was no use.

"God . . ." Brooke whispered the words, ignoring the wetness on her cheeks. "I know you're there. I know you saved her for a reason. But give her back her sight, please. Breathe life into her brain, because she's in trouble, God. Please . . ."

Hayley's crying grew loud again, and she began turning her

head from side to side. She still had tubes in her nose where she was being fed and hydrated, so maybe Dr. Martinez was wrong. Maybe she wasn't looking for Brooke; maybe she was sick of the nose tubes. It was possible, wasn't it?

With each minute her daughter's crying grew louder, and a panic began to come over Brooke. Panic and adrenaline. The same feeling she had once when she was in the house and heard a loud crash in the backyard, followed by Hayley's desperate cries. In that moment, she'd had a frantic determination to reach Hayley, cradle the little girl in her arms, and rock away the fear and pain.

It was a mother's instinct really, and now . . . now even though Hayley desperately needed comfort, Brooke could do nothing to help her. The mother's instinct was there, stronger all the time. But there was no way to act on it, no way to do the one thing that would bring peace to both her and Hayley.

The bridge between them was broken in too many places, and now nothing could repair it. Not even an ocean of love for her younger daughter.

She gripped the rails on Hayley's bed and raised her voice. "Baby, Mommy's here . . . it's okay."

More crying, more head turning.

"Sweetheart, I love you." She stood and moved her face closer to Hayley's. "Everything's okay. Jesus is with you . . . he's going to make you better."

The pattern of her daughter's wailing stayed the same. Over and over and over again. Deep sorrowful monotone wails, and finally something inside Brooke snapped. As long as Hayley didn't recognize her voice, she couldn't do anything to help. Couldn't be a mother to her own daughter.

And in that moment Brooke's adrenaline and panic turned to nausea.

She gritted her teeth. Enough. She couldn't stand there while Hayley was suffering, couldn't take another moment of it. A way had to exist for her to mother her daughter, and somehow, someway, Brooke would find it. Without considering protocol or Dr. Martinez's assurance that nothing would help her daughter, Brooke released the lock on the bed rail. She eased it down and then climbed carefully into bed beside Hayley and propped herself up against the headboard.

Then she worked her hands beneath her small daughter and lifted her into her arms. Brooke fought the urge to recoil, because the moment her daughter was completely and fully in her arms, Brooke realized something. The stiffness wasn't only in Hayley's hands and feet.

It was throughout her entire body.

Hayley had always been more clingy, more willing than Maddie to cuddle with Brooke. Maddie was the independent one, the daughter who would give Brooke a quick hug, then be on her way. But now Hayley fought Brooke's embrace, pushed against it and stiffened in a way that left Brooke unsure about whether she'd survive the pain.

"Hayley, it's me, Mommy." Brooke lowered her mouth to Hayley's temple, inches from her daughter's ear. "Hayley, I'm here, honey . . . I'm here."

Brooke hadn't cried much since the accident.

She was a professional, after all. Someone trained to think with her head, not her heart. But with Hayley unwilling, unable to respond to Brooke's arms around her, the tears came like streams. Quietly and without the sobbing some parents showed in emergency rooms, Brooke wept over Hayley, wept for all the missing parts and for the uncertainty of whether she'd ever be whole again.

"Baby . . . shhh. Hayley, it's Mommy." She hugged her daughter to her chest and whispered the words as often as she could, as often as her strength would allow.

If only Peter had watched her, if he'd stayed with the girls until she got back . . .

Hayley's blonde hair was matted to her head. Brooke brought her knees up so Hayley wouldn't roll out of her arms back onto the bed. Clutching her tighter than before, Brooke worked her fingers through her daughter's hair, the way she'd done a hundred times before. "Hayley . . . I'm here. Mommy's here."

And that's when it happened.

Suddenly Hayley stopped crying. For the first time since she'd woken up earlier that day, she was neither sleeping nor crying. Brooke's breath caught in her throat, and in the shock of what was happening she stopped running her fingers through Hayley's hair. Almost at the same time, Hayley began crying again, wailing that constant, sickly slow cry that sounded not even remotely familiar.

Brooke drew short, shallow breaths, desperate to find her way back to that place where for the fraction of a moment, Hayley recognized her voice.

*She knew. I know she did, God. Let her remember again, please. . . .*

No audible response came, but the moment she finished praying, she knew the answer. It was Hayley's hair. The touch of Brooke's fingers in her hair had pierced the darkness and caused her to remember. Even for just a few seconds.

Trembling with the possibility, Brooke gathered herself into a straighter sitting position and cradled Hayley closer than before. Once more using her legs to brace Hayley's body, Brooke worked her fingers slowly and carefully through her daughter's knotted blonde hair.

And once again her crying stopped.

Hayley's mouth hung open, and her eyes held the vacant stare of someone who couldn't see. She still turned her head from side to side, but she was connecting. Somewhere deep inside her brain, she was feeling a bond with Brooke.

A dryness filled Brooke's throat. Why hadn't she thought of this before? Brooke had always run her fingers through Hayley's hair. Whenever the child couldn't sleep or if she'd had a bad dream, Brooke would sit at the side of her bed and play with her hair until she was sleeping once more.

She sniffed and found her voice. "That's right, baby. You always loved this." Brooke felt a smile lift the corners of her mouth, because for the first time since Hayley's accident, the panic and fear and nausea were gone. As awkward as it felt sitting on the hospital bed, holding her stiffened daughter, Brooke was doing the only thing that in this new season of life held any meaning whatsoever.

She was being a mother to Hayley.

Peter was in bed early that night, but it made no difference. Since Hayley's accident, sleep wouldn't come except in useless fits and starts. The rest of his family had settled into a routine by now. Brooke stayed at the hospital night and day, coming home during the day, when he was at work, to change clothes or take a shower. And Maddie stayed with John and Elizabeth.

The idea seemed odd, and no matter how he tried, Peter couldn't make peace with it. While Hayley lay in that hospital bed—forever changed, forever damaged—the people who loved her the most had found a way to go on, a way to exist day to day.

Everyone but him.

Peter rolled onto his side. The room was dark, and shadows shifted near the window. Peter wasn't sure, but he couldn't remember the shadows doing that before Hayley . . .

The thought hung in the air and Peter swallowed. His heart thudded hard against his chest in a pattern that hadn't been regular since the moment he'd seen Hayley at the bottom of DeWayne and Aletha's pool.

A deep pounding ache tore at his head, permeating his brain, his consciousness. He tried with both thumbs to rub away some of the pain, but after a minute it only felt worse. His hands fell back to the bed and he lay motionless for a moment.

Everything hurt. His fingers, hands, both arms for that matter. The muscles in his thighs and calves. All of him hurt the way he had once when he contracted a strain of the Asian flu.

But this time he wasn't sick—not in a viral sort of way.

He'd first noticed the strange sensations in his body the day after Hayley got hurt, the way his feet seemed suddenly heavy and unwilling to move, the way he struggled to open his car door and keep his hands on the steering wheel as he made his way home from the hospital.

Now, though, he had a few ideas about what was happening to his body. He was sleep deprived, for one thing. Anxious, tense, unable to help his little girl. No wonder he was falling apart. The pain in his heart had spilled into his bloodstream, his limbs, his organs, until every part of him hurt.

Finally, today he'd done something about it. He closed his eyes and pictured the scene, the way it had played out this afternoon after his second visit with Hayley.

On his way out of the hospital, he'd gone to the pharmacist and approached the man with a smile. The two had started practicing medicine in Bloomington about the same time; they knew each other on a first-name basis.

"Peter." The man's face was somber. Word traveled fast through the hospital personnel; by then everyone knew about Peter's little girl. "How is she?"

"Hanging in there." Peter managed a grim look, one that hid the trembling in his hands. "It's too soon to tell."

The man shook his head. "I'm sorry, Peter. Really. All of us are."

Peter nodded and kept his eyes down, trained on a spot just in front of his shoes. After an appropriate amount of time, he looked up and angled his head just slightly. "Listen, I've neglected some of my patients lately. Could you look up Joe Benson's chart and give me a refill of his pain meds? I promised I'd phone it in, but I forgot." A quick shake of his head, as if to say Peter couldn't believe he could do such a thing, even with what happened to his daughter. "He called, and I told him I'd run them by his house on the way home."

The pharmacist squinted, troubled. "Peter, you don't have to do that. If he can't come out, I can have someone else run it over to him."

"No." Peter hoped his answer wasn't too quick. "I'll take care of it. Joe's a special patient. His back pain's been an issue for years now." Peter allowed a slight, sad smile. "It'll make me feel useful."

"Okay, then." The man tapped the counter. "You got it."

Peter's heart had been racing within him, but with those words it calmed down for the first time that day. *Amazing*, he thought. *The lie was brilliant.* If Joe ever found out about the prescription, Peter would only have to say there must have been a mistake, that the pharmacist must have gotten his information mixed up.

After a few minutes, the pharmacist returned with the bottle of pills. "Here you go." He handed a small white bag to Peter. "Hope old Joe Benson feels better."

Peter studied the man's face and saw not a shred of doubt. "I'm sure he will."

The memory of that conversation lifted, and Peter turned onto his other side. He hadn't planned to use the pills, not really. Only if he couldn't sleep again. The aches and pains, the dull thudding in his brain—all of it would go away if only he could get some sleep. He'd thought about sleeping pills, but he remembered something one of his patients had told him a few months back.

"Pain pills do it all, Doc." The man had been an addict; Peter was fairly sure. "Everything that hurts feels good again, and you sleep like a baby."

Peter tried to imagine feeling like that, and he could hardly do it. The only thing besides a pill that could make Peter feel that way would be hearing the news that Hayley was well again, that the drowning had been a bad nightmare and her doctors were releasing her to Brooke even now.

But that wasn't about to happen.

A storm was brewing outside and a gust of wind shook the

bedroom window. Again his patient's words ran through his mind. *"Everything that hurts feels good again and you sleep like a baby . . . like a baby . . . like a baby. Everything that hurts feels good again. . . ."*

Peter lay there for only a minute more, and then in a burst he was on his feet. Again his legs hurt, and his feet felt as if he were dragging through cement. But that didn't matter. At this point, he would've walked across the ceiling to find relief. As he made his way to the kitchen, to the vitamin cupboard, where he'd stored the bottle of pills, he thought of the patients he'd seen grow addicted to painkillers over the years.

*I'll be smarter than that,* he told himself. *This is only temporary, until my body learns how to sleep again.*

He was in the kitchen now, his steps coming faster despite the way his feet ached. He poured himself a glass of water, opened the cupboard, and reached for the bottle. One pill, that's all he needed. His body would be highly sensitive to the medication— especially at first. One pill and he'd get his first night's sleep since Hayley's accident.

The bottle shook some in his hands, and he wasn't sure why. Anxiety again? Or lack of sleep? Something. He tightened his grip, twisted off the lid, and took one pill. Popping it in his mouth, he returned the bottle to the cupboard and washed the pill down with a single swig of water.

There. That would take care of the pain and the sleep.

He made his way back to bed. By the time he slipped beneath the covers, he could already feel his body relaxing, feel the pain leaving his limbs and mind. But even as sleep began to overtake him he pictured Hayley. Damaged and changed, lost forever . . . and all because he hadn't watched her, hadn't taken better care of her. And he knew no matter how many pills he might take, there was one terrible, all-consuming pain the medicine could never touch.

The pain in his heart.

# CHAPTER SEVEN

KARI SAT IN THE FRONT SEAT with Ryan for the drive to the hospital.

It was Friday evening, almost a week after the accident, and Brooke had asked if they'd pick Maddie up at her grandparents' house and bring her in to see her sister. At less than two years old, Jessie was still too young for hospital visits, so they'd left her at the Baxter house.

Now Maddie was belted into the backseat, a backpack on her lap. "Aunt Kari?"

"Yes, sweetie?" Kari looked over her shoulder at Maddie.

"Is Hayley in the hos'apul because she went in the swimming pool too long?"

Kari exchanged a glance with Ryan. "Yes, honey, that's why."

"But water doesn't hurt people, does it, Aunt Kari?" Worry pushed her eyebrows into a *V*.

"Well, water can hurt people, yes. If they stay under and don't get enough air."

Next to Kari, Ryan reached out and took her hand. He kept his other hand on the wheel, his eyes on the road straight ahead of him.

Maddie seemed to think about that for a moment. They passed through three stoplights before she spoke again. "You mean Hayley's in the hos'apul because she didn't get enough air?"

Ryan worked his thumb along the side of her hand. Kari looked out the front window again and nodded. "Yes, Maddie, that's the reason. Because she didn't get enough air."

"But she has air now, right? So why can't we bring her home?"

A series of knots gripped Kari's stomach. She wasn't convinced it was time to bring Maddie in to see Hayley. Kari had been there earlier today, and Hayley looked nothing like herself. She was unable to move her limbs, and everything from her strange cry to her vacant eyes made her seem like a different child entirely.

"Aunt Kari, did you hear me? She has air now so why can't we bring her home?"

It was a good question.

Brooke had already explained that every other part of the body could regenerate itself after an injury. But not the brain and not the spinal cord. Yes, they would see possible improvements, but after a year or two whatever damage remained would be permanent. Now Kari looked over her shoulder and found Maddie watching her. "Hayley's brain still needs more air, Maddie. Can you understand that?"

Maddie blinked but said nothing.

She was five years old this fall, old enough to understand that Hayley was sick, if nothing else. But Maddie was having nightmares about her sister, dreams that Hayley was still in the pool or that she had disappeared through the drain at the bottom. Her thoughts were understandable. After all, before she'd been rushed into the house that awful Saturday, she'd seen Hayley lying at the bottom.

Kari shuddered and tried again. "Maddie, do you understand? Your sister's brain needs more air, okay?"

"Okay." She angled her head and lifted the corners of her mouth just a bit.

She was quiet the rest of the way to the hospital. Ryan slipped a CD into the player, and none of them spoke until they were up in the waiting room. Kari and Ryan sat with Maddie on one of the sofas and waited until Kari's mother appeared at the doorway.

"Okay, Hayley's asleep."

Kari studied her mother and wondered when the cloud of sadness that hung over all of them would lift. Her mother's eyes were red and swollen, thick the way they'd often been this past week. She'd admitted to all of them at one time or another that she wasn't feeling well, wasn't up to the task at hand. For the flash of a moment, Kari remembered how they'd gathered in the waiting room the night before and held hands.

They'd prayed for Hayley, of course. For her brain to recover, for her limbs to relax, and her sight to return. But they also prayed for each other, for the strain Hayley's accident had placed on all of them.

Kari took hold of Maddie's hand, and Ryan took the other one. Peter was working late tonight, so they were the only Baxter family here, and that was a good thing. Brooke wanted a calmer setting for Maddie's first visit with her sister.

Brooke had asked them to wait until Hayley was asleep. That way Maddie wouldn't be so surprised at the changes in her sister. Otherwise the child's strange sound and appearance were bound to frighten Maddie.

Kari looked at the small child. "Ready?"

"Mmm-hmm." Maddie's eyes were big and round, and she kept licking her lips. "Will Hayley look sick?"

For a moment Kari said nothing. Then she opened her mouth to speak, but a rush of emotion stopped her. She looked to Ryan for help, and he lowered himself to Maddie's level. "No, sweetheart. She'll look like she's sleeping, okay?"

"Can we wake her up and play with her?"

"No, Maddie." Ryan's voice was calm, soothing. "Not to-night."

Kari bit the inside of her lip. Brooke wanted Maddie's visit to be a positive experience for both girls. Seeing Hayley would relieve Maddie's fears, help her know that her little sister hadn't slipped through the drain at the bottom of the pool. At the same time, Maddie's voice could help restore another fragment of Hayley's memory.

At least those were Brooke's hopes.

But this—these questions from Maddie, the girl's desire to play with her sister—was more difficult than Kari had imagined. She and Ryan surrounded the child, and together they headed down the hall with Kari's mother leading the way.

"Hos'apuls have lots of rooms." Maddie wore her backpack now, and she stared at each door as they passed.

"Yep." Ryan smiled at her. "Lots of people need to get better."

"And Grandpa works at this place, right?"

"Right. And your mommy and daddy sometimes, too."

"That's good."

They reached Hayley's room and went inside. Before even looking at her sister, Maddie went to Brooke, who was sitting in the recliner chair beside Hayley's bed. "Mommy, I missed you."

"I missed you, too, baby." Brooke swept Maddie up onto her lap and hugged her.

After a few seconds, Maddie squirmed herself free and spun around to face the hospital bed. "Hi, Hayley!" Maddie's voice was loud and upbeat. "It's me, Maddie."

Kari stood nestled between Ryan and her mother as they watched the scene.

"Shhh, honey. Use your indoor voice, okay?" Brooke put a gentle hand on Maddie's shoulder. "We want Hayley to keep sleeping."

"Oh." Maddie's tone dropped to a whisper. "Sorry, Mommy." Then she turned back to Hayley. "Hi, Hayley . . . I brought you something." She worked her backpack off her shoulders, put it on the floor, and unzipped the top flap. Then she pulled out Hayley's baby doll, the one with the pink crayon smudge on the cheek and the bald head, the hair having long since been loved off.

Kari felt her heart breaking within her. She worked her fingers between Ryan's and watched Maddie place the doll next to Hayley. As great as the problems between Peter and Brooke seemed to be, the two of them had done a great job teaching their daughters how to love.

Maddie moved the baby doll closer to Hayley's sleeping face. "I'm glad you got out of the pool, Hayley." She patted her sister's arm. "You're not 'apposed to go in there without Mommy or Daddy, remember?"

Hayley took a deep breath and let out a soft moan.

Maddie leaned closer, and Kari could no longer make out what she was saying. Ryan used the moment to motion Brooke to join them by the door. She struggled to her feet and stretched. Her clothes were rumpled, her hair pulled into a stubby ponytail.

At the door, Ryan led them into the hallway and the others followed. Kari stood beside him, her arm around his waist. Today when he came home from his job teaching and coaching at the high school they'd discussed a few things he wanted to bring up to Brooke, so Kari knew what was coming.

*Give Ryan the words, God.*

In some ways, Brooke's future depended on the way she reacted to the things Ryan wanted to say.

"Hayley seems pretty stable." Ryan spoke so only Brooke and Kari and Mom could hear him.

"She is." The pain in Brooke's eyes was deep, but she managed a partial smile. "Every day another piece of her seems to connect with me."

When Ryan looked at Kari, she gave him a barely detectable nod, one that would encourage him to continue with what he wanted to say. "Brooke, I'm worried about you and Peter."

Kari watched the walls go up around her older sister's heart, watched the way her eyes grew hard, her expression stiff. "I'm not worried about me and Peter. Hayley's more important right now."

"I know." Ryan's voice was gentle. "But maybe keeping your marriage alive is the most important thing you can do for Hayley." He hesitated. "Have you thought about that?"

Kari gave her husband's waist a soft squeeze. She was glad he was willing to push Brooke.

Kari studied her sister and saw for the thousandth time that they had little in common. Yes, they both loved their children, and they were both Baxters. But Brooke was a thinker, Kari a feeler. If love didn't make sense to Brooke for intellectual reasons, she could disconnect very quickly.

Now she stood straighter than before and met Ryan's eyes. "Look, I know my marriage is in trouble, but what can I do? Peter is avoiding me, and when we see each other he won't talk." She planted her fists at her angular waist and looked from Kari and their mother back to Ryan. "Besides, he took off Hayley's life jacket." She huffed, and the anger in her tone sent a chill down Kari's arms. "Excuse me for not feeling 'in love' with him right now."

Ryan gave her a few seconds to catch her breath. Then he touched her shoulder so she would look at him again. "That's just it, Brooke. Love isn't a feeling; it's a decision. It's something you choose to do because deep down you know it's the right thing; it's what's best for everyone."

"Okay." Brooke's voice dropped some, the fight gone for now. "I hear you. So why come to *me*, Ryan? Why aren't you giving him this speech?" She gestured toward the hospital room. "He's the one missing."

Kari took a half step closer to Brooke. "That's what we wanted to talk to you about. Both of you."

"Pastor Mark trained Kari in counseling. It was something she did before we got married."

"She helped Erin; I know that." Brooke sniffed and crossed her arms. She kept her eyes on the far wall, looking at nothing in particular.

"Right." Ryan waited until he had Brooke's attention again. "Maybe we could get together, meet a few times a week so you can get through this without hating each other."

"Together or apart?"

Kari looked at Ryan and then at Brooke. "Apart at first, if that would help."

"I don't know." Brooke sighed through clenched teeth and stared at the ceiling for several seconds. When she looked back at Ryan, her expression was softer than before. "Peter won't agree to it. We haven't been to church in weeks. He doesn't like the idea of someone telling him what to do."

They ended the conversation with Brooke's agreeing to spend an hour Sunday talking to Kari in the waiting room, or wherever they could find privacy. Ryan promised to call Peter at their house later that night and see if he'd join them.

"You have to believe your marriage is worth saving." Ryan met Brooke's eyes one last time. "Otherwise no amount of talking things through will make a difference."

"I know." Brooke released a sad burst of air. "That's the problem; I'm not sure it is." She looked at Kari. "But I'll talk. If it would help Hayley, I'd walk across broken glass."

Ryan hugged Brooke and Kari.

Their mother joined them, and she placed her hand along the side of Brooke's face. "Don't give up, honey. God shines a flashlight on even the darkest path. There's nowhere we can go where he hasn't already been."

They went back in the hospital room to check on Maddie and Hayley, and what they saw stopped them in the doorway. Maddie was standing on the bedside chair. She was leaning over Hayley, blowing short puffs of air onto her face.

Brooke didn't run at Maddie, but she moved as fast as she could without startling the girl. "Honey, what are you doing?"

"I'm helping Hayley." Maddie looked up and brushed her dirty blonde hair out of her eyes. "Hayley's brain is hurt, Mommy."

"Yes . . . of course, baby." Brooke was at Maddie's side now, taking her into her arms and hugging her, stroking her hair. "But why are you blowing on her?"

"Because, Mommy." Maddie glanced over her shoulder once more at her little sister. "Hayley needs air."

# CHAPTER EIGHT

LANDON WAS DEEP IN SLEEP when the phone rang.

He smashed the pillow with his elbow and squinted at the alarm clock. Eight-fifteen. For a few seconds he struggled to clear his head. It was Monday morning, his day off, right? So who would be calling him so early? More than a week had passed since Hayley's accident, and still Ashley hadn't phoned. Was this her now then? Missing him, knowing how crazy she'd been to keep her distance . . . ?

On the fourth ring, he grabbed the receiver and hit the Talk button. "Hello?"

"Blake, it's Captain Dillon at the station."

"Yes, sir." He sat up and rubbed his eyes with his free hand. Why would the captain call him this early, unless . . . images from September 11 flashed in his mind. "Is there an emergency, sir? Do you need me?"

"Take it easy, Blake." The captain chuckled on the other end. "There's no emergency. Guess I forgot how early it was."

"Oh." Landon exhaled. "That's okay." He held the pillow against his bare chest and leaned into it. "How can I help you, sir?"

"I know it's your day off, Blake, but a few of the brass are holding a meeting here at one o'clock today, and we'd like you to attend."

"Yes, sir. Of course." *The brass?* Meaning the captains and the battalion chief? Why would they want him at a meeting like that? He leaned back and stared out his bedroom window at the buildings across the street. The questions would have to wait until later. "One o'clock then?"

"Yes." The captain uttered another laugh. "Now get some sleep, will you? It's your day off."

"Yes, sir. I'll do that." Landon hung up and stared at the receiver. His year with the New York City fire department wasn't up until the first of January. It was only October now, too early for his annual review. So what was it?

Landon slid back beneath the covers and tucked the pillow beneath his head. Had he messed up on some procedure, overlooked a detail in one of his recent reports? He didn't think so, but then it happened. And when it did, meetings sometimes took place to discuss the offense.

His empty stomach rumbled in a sickish sort of way. He'd put his entire heart and soul into his job with the FDNY; how could he have messed up a report? Landon stared at the ceiling and thought back over the past few weeks. He'd been distracted, of course. Ashley was always on his mind. And for the past week, ever since Reagan had told him about Hayley, he'd thought constantly about the Baxters.

But he'd gone on with his routine.

Men's Bible study Thursday nights, church on Sundays, volunteer work Monday and Wednesday afternoons—two of his four days off. Nothing out of the ordinary had happened at work in that time, no major fires, no fatalities, nothing that would warrant the scrutiny of the captains, let alone the brass.

For seven minutes Landon allowed himself to consider the possibilities. Seven minutes of worry before he remembered he wasn't alone. *Why the meeting, God? What did I do?*

*My son, do not be anxious. . . . I know the plans I have for you.*

"God?" Landon whispered the word and felt his eyes grow wide. Often he sensed the Spirit's presence when he prayed, heard the quiet echo of a response that had to have come from God alone. But this . . . the words he'd just heard had been almost audible. If it wasn't for the phone call from the captain, he would've known he was dreaming. What was it he'd heard?

*Do not be anxious. . . . I know the plans I have for you.*

The words were a mixture of verses, Scriptures he'd studied last week at the men's meeting. They'd been talking about the uncertainty of life since September 11, the uneasiness of living in Manhattan, the constant news reports that terrorists were planning still more attacks on the city.

And the leader had brought up two Scripture verses.

One from Philippians. *Rejoice always, I will say it again rejoice . . . do not be anxious about anything, but in everything with prayer and thanksgiving make your requests to God, and the peace of God which transcends all understanding will guard your hearts and minds in Christ Jesus.* The leader had underlined the obvious points. Take your concerns to Jesus and he will give you unbelievable peace in exchange.

The second Scripture was from Jeremiah, and it was one Landon was very familiar with. One he'd shared with Ashley a number of times. God knew the plans he had for his people, plans to give them a hope and a future and not to harm them.

Again the leader had connected the dots. With the promise of peace and a future filled with hope, they could live a joyful life.

"Rejoice," the man had told the group. "God wants us to rejoice no matter what our circumstances. With the guarantee of peace and a hopeful future, why should we worry?"

*Rejoice . . .*

Landon thought about that for a moment, imagined himself feeling happy inside despite the pending meeting, despite the fact that Ashley hadn't called him since Hayley's accident, despite her HIV-positive blood, and the fact that she was drawing further away from him throughout the weeks.

At the time, last Thursday night, he couldn't relate to the idea. Yes, the people in the Bible might've been able to rejoice in the face of awful circumstances. But he wasn't living in Bible times. He was living in a city still reeling from the effects of the nation's greatest tragedy ever, a nation stumbling along beneath the threat of future terrorist attacks and an uncertain economy.

"I'm not sure I see it," he'd told the group that night. "I can understand feeling God's peace, believing in his plans . . . but rejoicing? Always? I don't know."

No one had tried to convince him. Instead, the conversation merely shifted to examples from several of the men, ways they'd been able to rejoice in the middle of some pretty awful stuff.

But here . . . with the voice of God still echoing in his room . . . Landon understood for the first time. The only way he could live in a constant state of rejoicing was if he kept his perspective.

It wasn't so different from fighting fires in New York City.

Every now and then a call would come that looked impossible from the first response. But they'd been trained to take the call in stages. Assess the situation . . . strategize . . . and work the plan. Step-by-step, moment by moment. And in that way no call ever felt overwhelming.

The same was true with living a life of joy.

No matter what the situation, Landon could be certain of the bigger picture. God would be with him, giving him strength and peace. And in the end, God's plans were good ones, plans that God himself was pulling together. All that and the promise of eternity.

Landon uttered a single quiet laugh. "I get it, God. I really get it."

What wasn't to be joyful about? Why not rejoice when God already had all the strange and sad details figured out?

He was still marveling over the revelation when he arrived at the fire station that afternoon a few minutes before one. By then he wasn't even a little worried about whatever the meeting held. God already knew the details. Landon would merely go along and give the best, most honest answers to whatever they wanted to know.

"Hey, Blake, we're in the meeting room." Captain Dillon spotted him in the kitchen. The man poured himself a cup of coffee and stuck it in the microwave. He shot Landon a look over his shoulder. "Pretty big meeting, Blake. Maybe you better heat yourself a cup."

Landon hesitated. . . . *"Rejoice always. I will say it again: Rejoice!"*

"I'm good." Landon smiled.

Captain Dillon was right about the brass. Landon entered the meeting room and recognized only half of the six men in the room. Their names weren't necessary; he could see from their uniforms that they were farther up the chain of command than anyone he'd ever met.

"Sirs . . ." Landon nodded and stood at attention.

Captain Dillon entered the room behind him, steaming coffee in his hand. "Have a seat, Blake. This isn't a disciplinary action."

Joyful or not, relief spilled into Landon's veins. His knees trembled as he removed his hat and took a seat at the table with the other men.

Battalion chief Michael Parsons sat straight across from him. He cleared his throat and began the meeting. "We're very happy with your work, Lieutenant Blake. You've been meticulous in following department protocol, and your attention to detail has saved both buildings and lives in New York City."

"Yes, sir. Thank you, sir." Landon sat up straighter and glanced down at the front of his uniform. He expected to see his heart pulsing out past the buttons.

"The purpose of this meeting is twofold." The man glanced at a file on the table in front of him. When he looked up, his eyes shone and a smile tugged at the corners of his mouth. "First, we've chosen to promote you to captain in January."

Landon could feel his heartbeat in his temples. His mouth was dry and his hearing dimmed. What had the battalion chief said? They wanted to promote him to captain? In January? That kind of a move was unheard of. A dozen men at his station alone would've been in line for the position ahead of him.

The chief was explaining the details, how the position was at the smallest station in the department, how the brass had taken into consideration Landon's years of service in Bloomington. "You'll have the worst shifts at first, all nights and weekends. The most dangerous time to fight fires."

"Yes, sir." Landon's heart rate still hadn't returned to normal, and he felt buoyant, as if he were floating, four—maybe five— feet off the ground. "The shifts won't be a problem."

The man broke into a full smile. "I didn't think so."

"You should know, Blake." Captain Dillon grinned at him. "At first I told them they couldn't have you." He shifted his gaze to the battalion chief. "But then I heard the rest of their plans."

*The rest of their plans?* Landon couldn't swallow, couldn't think of anything to say. They had plans for him that went beyond making him captain? The offer was amazing, the kind of promotion a firefighter only dreamed about. But just when he was about to get the rest of the information from the battalion chief, a thought flashed across the core of his soul.

Was that really what he wanted? A promotion? A higher rank in the FDNY? Didn't he want to be in Bloomington with Ashley and Cole?

"That brings us to the other reason we're meeting today." The battalion chief tapped the file in front of him. "We have plans for you, Blake. You're the type of man this department needs, the type we want to build our future around."

Their future? The future of the FDNY?

Landon felt as if he had a mouth full of cotton balls. He ran his tongue along the inside of his lips. "Yes, sir." He hesitated. "You're serious, sir?"

"Yes, Blake." Captain Dillon spread his hands out in front of him. "This is the first phase of a plan to groom you, my boy."

One of the other men leaned back in his chair. "For the top position, Blake. That's what we're talking about. A plan to make you chief of the department."

Landon gripped his knees and tried to keep from swaying. The words were coming at him from everyone around the table now, but he couldn't make sense of any of them. They had a plan to make him chief? fire chief of the entire FDNY?

Captain Dillon was explaining that Landon wasn't the only one chosen for advancement. "Every five years or so, the brass get together and identify the firefighters who most demonstrate what we're looking for in department leaders." He lifted his coffee mug and took a swig. "Not everyone will make it, obviously. But everyone at this table thinks you have an incredible chance."

The battalion chief pushed himself back a few inches and crossed one leg over the other. He tried to contain a smile. "We're fairly sure of your answer; otherwise we wouldn't have asked. But before we begin training you, grooming you for something bigger down the road, you need to be sure it's what you want."

The question was only a technicality. Landon had given his superiors no reason to believe he wasn't enamored with his position in the FDNY. He wouldn't be working here if he didn't love it, right? He managed a tinny laugh. "Of course. Yes, sir."

"What we mean is, take your time and think it over." The battalion chief gave a firm nod in Landon's direction. "It's a lot to take in at once, Blake. The promotion to captain, the plans for your future in the department." He raised his eyebrows. "You'd be committing your future to this city, to the people of Manhattan."

"Right, sir." Landon's mouth was operating separately from his heart and soul. Committing his future to the city of New

York? He gulped and kept his eyes on the battalion chief. "When
. . . when do you need to know?"

"By Friday." Captain Dillon looked at the faces around the table. "That should be enough time, wouldn't you say, gentlemen?"

Agreement came from each of them. Yes, no doubt, five days
should be enough for a young firefighter to commit to a lifetime
in Manhattan. No doubt.

"Very well, then." The battalion chief stood and held his hand
out to Landon. "I happen to think you already know what you
want, Lieutenant. And I'm convinced beyond a doubt that we
made the right choice in calling you here today."

Landon stood and took firm hold of the man's hand. "Thank
you, sir. You won't be sorry."

"I'm sure of it."

The handshakes continued around the table, with several
men nodding their approval and reminding him to make the call
sooner if he was certain about his decision. When he finally left
the room, Captain Dillon followed him.

"I knew what you were thinking in there, Blake." He stood
inches from Landon's face, his expression serious.

Did he know? Could he have read Landon's thoughts about
Ashley and Cole and the life that awaited him back in
Bloomington. He searched the man's eyes. "You . . . you did?"

"Yes." The captain took a step back and crossed his arms.
"You're thinking it isn't fair; you're not next in line for a promotion like this one, right? Isn't that what you were thinking?"

The man was partially right. "Yes, sir. Other men should have
the chance before me."

"You're right, Blake." His voice fell to an insistent hush. "But
other men aren't brass material. The decision to promote you
was unanimous, and in all my years one thing has always been
true when we agree on the man we'll promote."

"What's that, sir?"

"We're right." He brought his tone back to a normal level. "Go enjoy the rest of your day off, Blake."

Landon had taken the subway to the station, but now he wanted to walk, to suck in big gulps of city air and sort through everything he'd just been told. His station was only a block from Central Park. As he left, he took long fast strides toward his favorite path, the one that wound east and then north past several play areas and the skating rink.

The streets were crowded, full of the tourists who came for the fall leaves and milder autumn temperatures. Vendors shouted about T-shirts for sale and off-Broadway theater productions, but Landon hurried past, not paying attention to any of them.

They wanted to make him captain? in January?

Instead of the hundreds of people he passed, his mind saw only one face. His friend Jalen's. Hadn't that been Jalen's dream? To make captain and one day find himself among the FDNY brass? Was he up in heaven right now, nudging God and asking that the plans for Landon's life include his very own long-ago dreams?

Landon walked harder, pushing himself.

For two years he'd been too busy to think about the possibility of promotion. Busy finding Jalen's body in the heap of rubble after the World Trade Center collapsed, busy getting established in the department last January. And most of all busy trying to figure out Ashley Baxter.

He'd done everything he knew to win her heart, but where was she? The answer caused a bitter burst of air to slip through his teeth. She was back in Bloomington avoiding his calls the same way she'd avoided them back when they were in high school.

He was in the park now, shaded by the trees that lined the path. A dark-skinned man in a white coat caught his eye and waved an ice-cream sandwich at him. "Ice cream . . . get your ice cream . . ."

Landon kept walking.

A hundred scenarios could have played out in that meeting room. He could've been under scrutiny for failing to file a report, or he could've messed up on protocol at one job or another. They might have wanted his opinion about a certain call or asked questions about the way a rescue had gone down.

They could've even hinted at a promotion.

But captain? And a shot at one day becoming chief of the department?

All when hours earlier he'd practically heard God tell him to relax, rejoice, because the Lord's plans for his life were set for him? It didn't feel even a little possible that the timing of today's events was a coincidence. Landon let his eyes fall to his feet, the way he was attacking the path despite his cramped uniform dress shoes.

"Hey, fireman!" The voice belonged to a young woman a ways behind him. "Wait up. . . . I wanna get your autograph. Hey, fireman!"

Landon didn't look back. Since September 11, firefighters in New York City had maintained a hero status. Usually he did his best to accommodate requests from the public, but not today. He made a right turn and kept walking, his mind focused again on the matter at hand: God's plans for his life, the way he'd heard God speak to him about plans hours before the meeting with the department brass.

The conclusion was easy.

God wanted him to stay in New York City. Take the promotion to captain, serve to the best of his ability, and work his way to the top of the ladder in a way that would bring the Lord glory. That had to be it, right?

The thought rattled around his heart like a crushed pop can.

If he stayed in New York, he could never have a life with Ashley and Cole. She would never move to Manhattan, not in light of her health. He knew her too well for that. She wouldn't even work with the Midtown Art Gallery after all. Too stressful, too fast-paced. She needed to concentrate on staying well.

The problem was, all his life he'd known the Bible verse about God's plans, the fact that the Lord had a road map for his life, good plans, plans to give him hope and a future. But always—from his teenage days—he'd believed those plans would include Ashley Baxter.

Now, though, God had allowed an opportunity to present itself that had nothing to do with Ashley. One that could easily take him headlong into a life where he would have no choice but to find his way without her.

Was that what God wanted? For him to move on and forget the hold she'd always had on his heart?

He thought about his last conversation with her. She'd done everything but tell him not to call again, going on about how he deserved someone better, someone healthy, and insisting that she didn't want him thinking about her.

A park bench stood a few feet ahead, separated from the path by a thick hedge. Landon slowed his pace, sat down, and laced his fingers behind his head. *Ah, Ashley, where are you now? After all we've been through, we really haven't come that far, have we?*

He would always care about her, of course. And no matter whom God brought into his life in the years to come, he would never love any woman the same way he'd loved Ashley. Even now he would've traded everything about his future with the FDNY for a chance to marry her. But the facts were easy to sort through.

If she were part of God's plan for his life, something would've gone right for the two of them in the past few years. Something. Instead she'd sent him away more times than he could remember, and even though her health problems didn't worry him, they caused her to refuse everything about him.

Even his ring.

Landon sucked in a slow breath through his nose and stared through the brilliant red and orange leaves to the blue sky beyond. As long as Ashley was pushing him away, he'd been determined to keep trying. But this . . . this offer of advancement and promise of a future in the department, this seemed straight from God's office desk.

And if God wanted him to let go of Ashley Baxter, what choice did he have?

He realized then that his mind was already made up. He would tell Captain Dillon in the morning. The offer had come for a reason, even if it wasn't the plan he would've chosen for his life. He should be excited, of course. Any of a thousand firefighters given his opportunity would've been well into planning a celebration by now.

But for Landon, the celebration could come later.

First he had to grieve the idea that for the first time since he was a fresh-faced high school sophomore, his future plans no longer seemed to include the only girl he'd ever loved. And more than that, they didn't include her son.

A boy he would carry in his heart until his dying day.

CHAPTER NINE

L UKE WAS GRATEFUL to be in New York City with Reagan and their baby son, but a piece of his soul was back in Bloomington. Back in the hospital room standing guard over his blue-eyed little niece. He'd stayed as long as he could, and by the time he left for Manhattan, Hayley was stable.

Now they knew more, of course. The child who had been the brightest sunbeam in the Baxter family was blind. Blind and brain-damaged.

Luke found relief the same way he had in Bloomington, back when he'd chosen to be distant from his family. He spent hours staring out the window thinking. He wouldn't start school until January, so the next ten weeks were a gift, really. A chance to bond with Reagan in a controlled setting and help her with little Tommy.

But he still needed his window time.

He was there now, sitting adjacent to a glassy picture window, his legs pulled up on the bench seat beneath the sill. It was his favorite spot in Reagan's mother's apartment, and the view was breathtaking. The distant skyline of Lower Manhattan and enough of the park to make Luke want to sit there for hours.

Sometimes when he looked out that window, he imagined the place where the twin towers stood, the place where Reagan's father had taken the two of them that summer day more than a year earlier. The man would've been disappointed about Reagan's pregnancy, but he would've gotten past it. Tom Decker had been a godly man, a forgiving father who would've loved the boy named for him.

Luke understood better now about the tragedy of September 11. God had helped him with that a month earlier when he'd finally taken the steps to make things right with his dad. He'd been wrong before, thinking God allowed what happened that day or that he condoned it somehow. The truth was much simpler standing where he was on this side of it. Life was tragic, and God . . . God wasn't the problem.

He was the answer.

All of that made sense, but there was still something that didn't: Why was Hayley lying in a hospital bed with a damaged brain? If it was her time to die, fine. God could take her, and yes, they'd miss her like crazy. But at least she'd be free to run and laugh and play in heaven.

Instead, she was trapped in a body that could do none of those things, with a brain that couldn't function well enough for her to recognize her own mother. At least that was the last update he'd heard.

"God, I'm back again . . . I still don't understand. . . ."

"Don't understand what?" Reagan's voice was feathery soft, whispered against the side of his head in a way that had an instant soothing effect on him.

He leaned backward, nuzzling his face against hers. "I didn't hear you come up."

"Tommy's awake." She moved in front of him and lowered her chin, studying him. Her long blonde hair fell like satin sheets down her shoulders and back. The sparkle in her eyes was one Luke was familiar with. She wanted something, no question about it. "Let's take him to the park." She lifted her brow and looked out the window. "Winter will be here soon, but today's too beautiful to stay inside."

She was right. Besides, the fresh air would do him good, maybe help clear the cobwebs from his heart. "Okay." He worked his arm around her waist and pulled her close. "C'mere."

For a long moment, his lips met hers and he felt the familiar desire, the anticipation that in a few short months he could love her completely, the way he was dying to love her.

"You taste good." She gave him a slow smile and caught her breath.

"You look good."

Another smile. "Thank you."

"I'm glad your mother's in the next room." He brought his fingers up to her face and worked them over her cheekbones and into her hairline.

"You know . . ." Reagan let out a quiet giggle. "She's pretty much always in the next room."

"Yes." Luke held his breath for a moment. "And that's a good thing, believe me."

Reagan straightened and studied him, her face angled in a way that made her look irresistible. "Can we?"

Luke reached for her again. "Can we what?"

"The park, silly." She gave his chest a playful push. "Let's take Tommy, okay?"

A low moan sounded from Luke, and he worked his hands down his thighs to his knees. "Okay." He lifted his eyes to the ceiling. "Switch gears, Baxter . . . switch gears."

She was still giggling as she left the room.

❧

At least once a week they took Tommy to Central Park.

Luke liked that it gave them time alone, time to talk about the wedding and the crazy twists their lives had taken in recent months. It also allowed them the chance to talk about the counseling. The pastor at Reagan's church had arranged premarital counseling for them, something Luke hadn't been sure they needed.

But now, two weeks into it, he was grateful.

He wanted the type of marriage his parents had, one where he and Reagan would become so close it was impossible to see one without seeing the other. A marriage that would survive illness and tragedy, wayward children, and a lifetime of change. In counseling they would talk about expectations for intimacy and philosophies on child rearing, finances and faith and frustrations that were bound to come. Dozens of scenarios that could play out in their lives and how they would handle them together with God.

Always with God.

The cab pulled up at the east side of the park. Luke hopped out and went straight for the trunk. A quick flick of the wrist and he had the stroller out on the sidewalk and locked into the open position. At the same time, Reagan unfastened Tommy's car seat and eased him from the backseat. They had a routine now, and to people passing by they probably looked like any other young married couple. It was impossible to tell what they'd been through that past year.

Reagan enjoyed the exercise, and Tommy would take his bottle, mesmerized by the changing colors in the trees. Now that Reagan was recovered from having the baby, she'd started jogging again on her mother's treadmill. A jogging stroller was on her Christmas list.

The mid-October sun was still warm enough that Tommy didn't need a blanket. He was four months old, and he enjoyed being propped up for his walks.

Reagan bunched up two blankets and eased them behind his back and neck. "There you go, little guy. Enjoy the view."

Luke watched, taken by her gentle way with their son. "You're good at this." He grinned at her as he set the stroller in motion.

She covered one of his hands with her own and returned the smile. "Thanks. You, too."

He was quiet then, still caught up in the thoughts that had troubled him before she found him at the window.

"You're distant today." She kept her eyes straight ahead, their pace slow and easy.

"Hmmm. Yes."

She waited a few minutes. "Want to talk about it?"

"Not sure, really."

Another minute. Reagan gazed up at the changing leaves and narrowed her eyes. "Remember what the counselor says?"

"About silence?" He gave her a side-glance and stifled a grin.

"Yes. Troubled silence." Her eyes shone. "Remember? There are two ways to handle silence from your spouse." She looked straight ahead again. "Allow it, and hope it doesn't become a pattern. Or push a little and find a way to talk about it." She deepened her tone to sound more like their counselor. " 'And only by talking will your relationship grow.' "

"Okay." Luke chuckled and slipped his free hand into his jeans pocket. "I'm sorry."

"So . . ." They walked another ten yards. Her tone wasn't as easygoing as before. "What is it, Luke? I hate when you get like this."

"Like what?"

"Like . . . like quiet and distant." Her smile was gone, but she kept moving, keeping in step with him. "It makes me think you're mad at me."

"Mad at . . ." An understanding dawned in his heart. He slowed to a stop and faced her. "You think I'm having doubts about the wedding?"

For the first time that morning, a shadow fell across her face. He looked straight into her soul and saw the fear she kept hidden there. "Sometimes." She shifted her eyes to the path beneath their feet. "I'm sorry." Reagan angled her face so she could see him again. "It's just that . . . I don't know. It all happened so quick, and . . ."

"Reagan." He placed his hands alongside her cheeks and searched her eyes. "I'm more sure about marrying you than I've been about anything in my life." He pulled her into his arms and held her while the occasional businessperson or jogger passed by. After a while he drew back and kissed first her right eyebrow, then her left. "We've been through this." He paused and flexed the muscles in his jaw. *Please, God . . . let her see how much I love her.*

Reagan's eyes glistened and she gave a few quick nods. "I know. I'm just being stupid."

"Not stupid." He kissed the tip of her nose this time. "Forgetful, maybe. But not stupid."

She sniffed and uttered a frustrated laugh. "Okay, so I have a bad memory." Her eyes danced and she looked all the way to his heart. "Tell me again, Luke . . . so I'll know for sure."

"Reagan . . ." He wanted to pull her into his arms again and never let go, never leave her worrying for a single moment that he wasn't sure about the commitment they were about to make. "I don't feel guilty or obligated or pushed into marrying you." His words were softer than the breeze, meant for her alone. In the stroller, Tommy cooed and then went back to his bottle.

"You don't? Really?"

"Really." Times like this Luke understood better how hard the past year must have been on her. Reagan Decker had always been the picture of confidence, the only girl who hadn't fallen over herself when he asked her out. But now . . . now she needed his reassurance, and he was glad to give it. "I don't feel rushed into marriage; I feel grateful. Because you, Miss Decker—" his lips met hers and lingered for several seconds—"are the love of my life. And I can't wait to be married to you."

"Me, too." Her expression eased, and she gave a sheepish shrug of her shoulders. "Just checking."

They began walking again, and Luke narrowed his eyes at a

play structure far in the distance. "I guess I'm thinking about Hayley."

"Oh." A breeze picked up and swirled a handful of leaves onto the path before them. Reagan adjusted Tommy's bottle and exhaled in a tired sort of way. "What's the latest?"

"My mom calls every few days, but so far she's about the same. Awake but struggling. Stiff . . . hard to console . . . they're certain she's blind."

Reagan had heard the news before, but she winced all the same. A minute passed before she said, "It doesn't seem fair."

"Yeah. I guess that's what I was thinking." He kicked at a loose bit of gravel and let his eyes fall to Tommy's face, his perfect hands. "It doesn't make me doubt God, the way I doubted him after the terrorist attacks." He looked at her. "But it makes me wonder."

She looped her arm through his as they kept walking. "It makes us all wonder."

"I mean, God could take her, right? Take her to heaven where she could be the Hayley we all knew and loved." Something caught his attention, and he looked to the right, where a little girl was doing cartwheels for an older woman sitting on a bench. As Luke studied her, he could almost see Hayley's face on the child, doing something Hayley would never be able to do. He looked at Reagan again. "But now . . . now she might never get out of bed. It's hard."

"The timing is interesting."

"Yep. If it had happened six months ago, I might never have found my way back to God. Too many reasons to be angry at him."

"You don't feel that way now, do you?"

"Not at all." He tightened his grip on the stroller. "Now I can see the truth for what it is. God has a plan for her, even if we don't understand it."

"Right."

"But still . . ."

"Still we have to pray for a miracle." Reagan gave him a sad smile. "Nothing is impossible with God, remember?"

"Definitely."

He was quiet again. "Watching Brooke with Hayley, the patience she shows, the way she massages Hayley's stiff arms and legs for hours at a time." Luke shook his head. "It was a picture of love, you know?"

Reagan stopped this time. "You, Luke Baxter—" she locked eyes with him and tapped his collarbone with her fingertip— "are also a picture of love."

"Aw, shucks . . ." He grinned. "Only when my hair's combed."

"No, silly." She poked at his ribs. "Even if you didn't have a stitch of hair at all."

"Really?" He was teasing her. The mood between them had lightened, and he felt his heart lift ten feet because of it.

"Yes." She poked at his other side. "Even when you're a hundred and one I'll still go to bed every night amazed that we found each other again."

"Thanks to Ashley." He raised his eyebrows at her.

She grinned. "Thanks to Ashley."

"And God."

"Mostly God."

Luke hugged her close again, keeping his face back far enough so he never lost sight of her eyes. "Makes me think of something my dad told me last year, back when I didn't want to hear anything he said."

Reagan tossed her hair over her shoulder. "What's that?"

"He told me love meant honoring the other person." He reached up and brushed his thumb across her cheek. "That's what you did, Reagan. You thought by staying away from me you were honoring me, giving me my space." He raised his eyebrows in a teasing sort of way. "You were wrong, but . . ."

"But I meant well; is that it?" Her eyes held that familiar shine. "Is that what you mean by *honor*?"

"Mmm-hmm." He started to kiss her, just as Tommy spit his

bottle out and began to fuss. Luke leaned closer to the stroller and made a funny face for their baby's benefit. Tommy giggled and waved his hands in the air. "Is that right?" Luke pretended to give him a few serious shakes of the head. "So that's what you think about all this stopping and starting, huh?"

He shot a quick look at Reagan and raised a single finger in her direction. "Hold that thought." Then he bent down and repositioned the bottle until Tommy had it in his mouth again.

"As we were saying . . ." His lips found hers again. "Did I mention I like this part of talking?"

Reagan laughed and pulled back. "Finish, Luke . . . you were saying something about honor."

"Right." He relaxed his hold on her. "An honoring kind of love puts the other person first. And that's what I want to do for you, Reagan."

"Right now?" She was playing with him, savoring the moment the way he wanted her to. "Because I think Tommy needs a new diaper."

"No." He kissed her one more time, long enough to leave her breathless. Then he looked past the moment into a future he couldn't wait to start with her. "Not for right now, silly." His tone was soft, serious. "For the rest of our lives."

## CHAPTER TEN

THE FIREFIGHTER BY ASHLEY'S SIDE was more handsome than ever.

And growing taller all the time.

Cole adjusted his Halloween costume and slipped the plastic face mask over his eyes. "Think they'll recognize me, Mom?"

"Nope." Ashley pictured Irvel and Edith and Helen, already gathered around the breakfast table. "Definitely not, Cole." She patted the top of his helmet. "They'll think you're a real fireman, for sure."

He puffed his small chest out as the two of them walked up to Sunset Hills's front door. Ashley had an hour of paperwork, and Cole wanted someone to admire his look. Ashley's mother had picked up the costume when she was shopping in Indianapolis this past weekend. It was nicer than most firefighter costumes. Real canvas coat and pants, and stencil marks that made it a close replica of the uniforms worn by the FDNY.

"Just like Landon!" Cole had danced around when his grandmother gave him the package. "Now me and him can be twins!"

Ashley had ignored the way Landon's name made her heart

hurt. Instead, she admired the costume and agreed that yes, in the little uniform he was the mirror image of Landon Blake.

The novelty hadn't worn off in the days since. Cole had worn the costume everywhere except to bed, and now that Ashley had errands to run this morning, he insisted on coming with her, dressed as Firefighter Cole.

Ashley turned the door handle and let Cole go in front of her. "Not too loud."

He peered at her through the helmet's protective shield. "Okay!"

The pants bunched up around his knees and ankles, but he moved as fast as his legs would carry him. "Hello, everybody." He tore into the dining room before Ashley could stop him. "Don't be afraid. I'll save you!"

"Cole . . ." Ashley was only a few feet behind him, but it was too late.

Edith covered the top of her head as if the ceiling were falling on her. "Help . . . help . . . help . . ."

"Now!" Helen slammed the palms of both hands onto the tabletop. "Stop that man! Stop him right now."

"Excuse me." Irvel tapped Helen on the arm. "I believe your gentleman caller is shorter than before."

"Hi, everybody!" Cole's voice was muffled beneath the play helmet.

"Good morning." Ashley put her hand on his shoulder and smiled at the ladies. It was time to bring order back to the breakfast hour. "Cole wanted you to see his Halloween costume."

"He's a spaceman!" Helen looked at the others around the table. "Spacemen are dangerous, I tell you. Dangerous! We can't have spacemen in the house. Who's going to check him?"

Edith's eyes were wide, and she leaned hard in the opposite direction of Cole. Her voice was a quiet whimper. "Save me . . . save me, someone. Save me."

"I'll save you, Edith!" Cole took a step closer, but Ashley jerked him back beside her.

"Cole, honey, they don't understand." She whispered near the ear of his helmet. "They have a hard time making sense of things, remember?"

"Help." Edith's eyes were completely round now, the single word a pathetic squeak.

"Shhh." Ashley stepped in front of Cole. "It's okay, Edith. You're safe now."

"Spacemen are never safe." Helen crossed her arms and huffed. "Someone check that little man." She stomped her foot. "He needs to be checked!"

Irvel looked at Ashley and smiled. "What planet did you say you were from, dear?"

"Planet?" Usually Ashley had an answer for her friends at Sunset Hills, but this conversation was still far from under control. "I'm from down the street, Irvel. I've already been checked."

"Oh." Irvel studied Ashley as though she were seeing her for the first time. "Well you do have lovely hair; I'll give you that." She pointed at Helen. "But Gertrude here said you were from outer space." She made a polite lift of her napkin and dabbed around her mouth. "Of course, Hank doesn't like me cavorting with space people. Not while he's fishing."

"Who's Gertrude?" Helen snapped the comment at Irvel and then sneered in Ashley's direction. "The old bird's lost her marbles; that's what I think."

Irvel smiled at Cole and gave him a quick wink. "I like marbles; how 'bout you?"

"Yeah." Cole's eyes lit up. "Marbles are great! Especially the clear ones with the sparklies inside."

"Yes, dear boy. Exactly." Irvel gave Cole an emphatic nod. Then she leaned close as if this part was for Cole alone. "That Gertrude next to me, she doesn't like marbles."

"Oh." Cole raised his eyebrows.

Ashley was about to intervene, when Irvel frowned at Helen. "You know . . . Hank doesn't care much for Gertrude. Too violent." Then she tapped Helen's hand again. "Listen dear, you better hurry."

"Hurry for what?" Helen slammed her fist onto the table. Her fork spun around on the edge of her plate, teetered for a moment, and fell onto the floor. "I'm not going anywhere until someone gives me a mask. If he gets a mask, we should all have a mask, and if we all have a mask then she should—"

"Excuse me." Irvel made a dainty cough so Helen would stop shouting. "Your gentleman caller is shrinking."

"Cole . . ." Ashley brought her face close to his. "Take off the helmet. Maybe that'll help."

"Okay."

She could make out Cole's grin from behind the plastic shield. He whisked off the helmet and tucked it beneath his arm. The move was fluid and natural, the same way she'd seen Landon remove his helmet on the times they'd visited him at his fire station.

"See . . ." Cole's voice was bright and cheerful. "I'm a fire-fighter, not a spaceman!"

At that moment, Bert came shuffling into the room. He looked from Cole to Ashley and back again. "Fire?"

"No, Bert." Ashley went to him and helped him the last few steps to the table. "No fire."

"Fire!" Helen raised her voice. "The kitchen's on fire!" She pointed at the place where Maria was working on the dishes. "See . . . flames everywhere! Taking over the place. Big flames!" Her tone changed and her eyes filled with fear. "Help! Someone put out the flames!"

The others looked toward the kitchen, and Irvel leaned close to Ashley. "Maybe she needs her medicine."

"Yes, Irvel." Ashley bit her lip to keep control. "Maybe she does." She winked at Cole. "Okay, partner. Time to try out the costume."

Helen was still shouting about the flames and how come no

one was putting them out. Cole had to struggle to hear her. "What should I do, Mommy?"

"Pretend you have a hose and you're putting out the fire in the kitchen."

Cole shot a quick look at the kitchen. "But there's no fire."

"I know." She nudged his arm. "Pretend."

A grin spread across Cole's face, and he mustered up as serious an expression as he could. "Don't worry! I'll put out the fire!" He held up a pretend hose and sprayed pretend water toward Maria and the kitchen. "*Shhhhh . . .*" He continued the sound effects until everyone around the table was quiet, mesmerized by the drama at hand.

Finally Cole let his hands fall to his side. Out of breath from the effort, he turned and smiled at Helen. "The fire's out."

For once, Helen was speechless. She sat back in her chair and looked at her half-eaten scrambled eggs.

"Well." Irvel brushed the crumbs off her hands and took hold of her teacup. "That was exciting."

"Help. Help . . . help . . . help." Edith studied the palms of her hands, turned them over and studied the backs, and then started with the palms again. "Help."

"I think she has a splinter, Mom." Worry spilled into Cole's voice.

"No, honey, she's just tired."

Maria folded the dish towel, set it near the sink, and joined them, taking the nod from Ashley. "Come on, Edith; let's get you cleaned up."

The two women left, and Irvel tapped Helen's arm again. "Gertrude, dear, I think you've offended your gentleman caller." She dropped her voice to a whisper and pointed nervously in Cole's direction. "His head . . . he's lost his head!"

Helen glared at Irvel and flapped her arms like a bird. "Crazy old goose!" The fire danger forgotten, Helen pounded her fist— this time against her knee. "Ouch!"

"Excuse me." Irvel looked at Ashley this time. She made a

subtle attempt at pointing to Cole without being noticed. "I think Gertrude scared that little man. Could you help him, dear? His head fell off."

The moment Maria was back in the room, Ashley directed Cole down the hallway. "Okay, so maybe letting you in here with your costume wasn't the brightest idea." She ushered him into the office. "You can watch cartoons in here."

"But, Mom, they liked me."

"Yeah, I could tell." She blew at her wispy bangs and cleared a stack of paperwork so Cole could sit on the oversized office chair. "They always act like that when they're having fun."

Cole giggled. "I liked putting out the fire."

"I thought you would."

Ashley flicked the channels until she found an old Mighty Mouse cartoon. "Okay, buddy. Sit tight. I'll be done in a minute."

"Can I watch it with my helmet on?"

"Hmmm." Ashley put her hands on her hips. "You won't be able to see as good."

"That's okay; please, Mom?" He lifted the helmet up, waiting for her permission. "Firefighters can't always see good."

"True." She lowered her chin to her chest, teasing him. "Okay, Firefighter Cole, go ahead."

He slid the helmet over his head and put the plastic shield in place. "Thanks, Mom." His words were garbled.

"Wait a minute." She lifted the shield and planted a kiss on his forehead. "Love you."

"Love you, too."

Back at her desk, she paused a moment and studied him, her little firefighter, lost in the oversized costume, watching cartoons. The moment made her long for an easel and a paintbrush.

Her work that day was fairly mindless. Plan the schedule for the coming week and make a list of supplies they needed. The tasks gave her time to think about Landon. He would've loved

102

Cole's costume, and the thought gave her an idea. Maybe she should take his picture and send it to him.

But wouldn't that give him the exact message she was trying to avoid? That she still thought of him, still wanted him involved in Cole's life? in hers? She stared out the window at the almost-bare trees. A windstorm had passed through a few days earlier, and the leaves that had looked so brilliant a week ago now covered the ground.

*God, why can't I get him out of my heart? I want to let him go; you know that. But everything reminds me of him.* She glanced at Cole again. *Everything . . .*

A memory filled her senses. She and Landon having dinner in New York City the night he had asked her to marry him. She'd told him that it wasn't possible, that she could never subject him to a life of uncertainty, a life of misery and loss. But he'd been determined. Even now, with Mighty Mouse playing in the background, she could hear his voice from that night, see his face.

*"I want to marry you, Ashley. We'll find a way to make it work; we have to . . . no matter what happens."*

She sighed and concentrated on the list in front of her. A gallon of bleach, three rolls of paper towels, a pack of sponges . . . the words on the list blurred.

Did Landon still feel that way, that he'd marry her no matter what? Or was he rethinking the situation because of her cool behavior and her determination to battle her health issues alone?

She still hadn't decided on a doctor or a treatment plan. Instead she spent hours on the Internet, reading about ways to build her immune system. She was taking nearly twenty daily vitamins and herbs, but it wasn't enough. She knew that.

Her father talked to her about it often. "You need to get in, see a doctor, Ashley. The medicine out there can keep you healthy for a long time."

But the medicine had side effects. Swelling and weight gain, and who knew what else. Besides, there was another reason why she hadn't sought treatment. The moment she did, she would have to admit that things were different. For the rest of her life she'd be an HIV patient, fighting for one more year, one more month.

The notion was exhausting.

Ashley turned back to the list in front of her. Liquid soap, laundry detergent . . .

The phone rang, and Ashley jumped. Sunset Hills didn't get many calls. She picked up the phone and clicked the On button.

"Hello?" She doodled an *L* at the top of the supply list.

"Hello, madam. Is this Sunset Hills Adult Care Home?"

"It is." Ashley scribbled a lazy *A* next to the *L.*

"Good. This is Henry Wellington the third, and I'm looking for a quiet place to live."

"I'm sorry . . ." The voice was vaguely familiar, but Ashley didn't recognize the name. "I'm afraid we don't have any openings at this time."

"I see. Well, I won't need a bed for another two months. My memory is fading faster than a fall sunset."

Strange. Usually the initial call came from a doctor or relative. Ashley couldn't remember ever receiving a call from a prospective patient. "Two months?"

"Yes . . . two months. At least I think I'll need it in two months. I have trouble remembering."

Ashley thought about the woman at the far end of the house. Her doctor had said she'd be moved to a nursing facility in six weeks. Ashley flipped the pad of paper to a blank page and positioned her pencil. "Actually, that might work. Tell me a little bit about yourself."

"I don't know much anymore." The man sounded older with every few words. "But I have one memory I'll never lose."

Ashley twisted her face. *What in the world?* "Did you want to tell me about the memory, sir?"

"Yes, I'd like that." He drew a long, slow breath. "In my mind I see a beautiful girl . . . a girl who can paint masterpieces. A girl with the most beautiful hair . . ."

"Is that so . . . ?" It was a trick; Ashley knew it now. But she still couldn't make out the voice. Was it Luke? or her father? "Tell me more."

"It's too tragic, really. She never loved me, poor Henry Wellington."

"No?"

"No . . . because she was always in love with this firefighter in New York City."

A smile filled Ashley's face. "Landon?"

"Yes, I believe that was his name."

"Landon . . . stop!" She laughed and spun the chair so she was facing the window again. "I believed you!"

He chuckled on the other end. "I've been brushing up on my snobby retiree voice."

"It worked."

A comfortable quiet filled the lines between them. "How are you, Ash?"

"Okay." The pretense fell away, and she couldn't keep herself from missing him, wishing he were here beside her instead of a thousand miles away.

"You haven't called."

She twirled a piece of her hair and angled her face closer to the receiver. "I've been busy."

"Yeah . . ." Something in his voice changed just enough to catch her attention. "Me, too."

"Luke says he talked to you." Her heart was pounding, demanding that she not betray her decision to let him go. *Keep it simple, Ashley . . . nothing too emotional.*

"I went by and saw them." Landon uttered a sad chuckle. "He and Reagan can't wait for the big day."

"None of us can." She bit the inside of her lip. "We haven't thought much about it with Hayley still in the hospital."

"I'm praying for her every day. That God will let her see again."

Ashley squeezed her eyes shut and pictured Landon, jeans

and white T-shirt, sitting on the leather sofa in his Manhattan apartment, praying for Hayley's eyes. "Thank you, Landon. That . . . that means a lot."

"Any updates?"

"She's still in the hospital." Ashley opened her eyes and peered out the window at the blue sky beyond the trees. "Her doctors are trying different medications, looking for something that'll stop her seizures. She can't go home until she's more stable."

Landon hesitated. "How does she look?"

"When she's sleeping?" A robin landed on the front lawn and then took to flight again. "Like the same little girl you'd remember. But when she's awake . . ." Ashley's voice cracked. "Oh, Landon . . . she looks . . . she looks so different."

He didn't say anything for a moment. "I'm sorry."

His words were like a caress against her hurting soul. "Her mouth hangs open and she drools." Ashley looked across the room at Cole. He was still caught up in the cartoon, and she was glad. She didn't want him to hear the truth about Hayley. "Her arms are rigid, and her legs get so stiff they sometimes kick straight up." She waited until she had more control. "I'm sorry."

"Don't be. You've probably been strong for Brooke, but all of you have to be feeling this . . . the loss."

"We are." Ashley leaned back in the chair and stared at the peeling paint on the ceiling. "I see it in Mom, especially. She's always been so strong, the family ringleader, ready to find the good in any situation. But now . . . she looks tired. I think this one's put her over the edge."

"How about your dad?"

"He gets quiet when we talk about Hayley. I'm not sure what he's thinking."

"And you? Tell me you're seeing a doctor, right?"

Landon always asked, each time they'd talked since her last visit to New York City; she'd known the question was coming. "I haven't picked one yet."

"Ashley . . ."

"I know. I'll get on it. I've had a lot of distractions."

"Yeah." He was quiet again. "Me, too."

She sat a bit straighter. What wasn't he saying? Ashley was scared to prod, terrified he'd tell her he'd met someone, or that he'd finally decided she was right about the two of them breaking ties.

But he'd left her no choice. "Busy?"

"Sort of. Lots on my mind."

Ashley worked to find her voice. "Fire stuff or . . . or something else?"

"I have to tell you something, Ash." Landon released a breath, and the sound of it rattled what remained of Ashley's nerves.

Here it was, the part where Landon would finally tell her he was ready to move on. She bent forward over her knees. "Okay."

"The department brass talked to me and offered me a promotion." He paused and though his words were quietly serious, a hint of excitement crept between them. "Ash, they want to make me captain. Can you believe it?"

"Captain?" She muttered a sound that was more shock than joyful release. "Wow, Landon. That's amazing. You've . . . you've only worked there a year."

"I know . . . it doesn't seem real."

A hundred questions begged for Ashley's attention. Was he serious? Had he accepted an offer that would keep him in Manhattan for another few years? And why would that be so hard to believe? Of course he'd accepted it. Hadn't she been telling him to get on with his life? Hadn't she avoided his calls every time he phoned for the past two months?

He was talking to her again, saying something about the promotion, about that not being all they had talked to him about. She forced herself to focus.

". . . so then the battalion chief tells me the captain position is only the beginning." He made a disbelieving huff. "Get this, Ash.

He tells me they want to groom me for the top job. Fire chief of New York City."

"Aren't . . . aren't fire chiefs a lot older than you?"

Landon's tone was a strange mixture of pride and sorrow. "They're talking about a long-term plan, Ashley. Fifteen, twenty years. I'm not the only one they're looking at, but they like me. They made that much clear."

"Wow." Ashley was desperate for something to say. The last thing she could do is make Landon doubt his future in Manhattan. Especially now, with the opportunity of a lifetime hanging in the balance. "That's amazing, Landon."

The enthusiasm leaked from Landon's voice. "They gave me some time to decide; it's a big commitment."

"Yes." Ashley's heart was racing beneath her linen blouse. *No, Landon . . . no. Don't tell them yes . . . not when I'm still in love with you. Please, Landon.* She swallowed the desperate cry and kept her tone upbeat. "It's huge."

Landon waited. "I took a walk that afternoon and thought about my life, my commitments and priorities. For a long time I asked myself if there was any reason, any possibility that you would change your mind, that you'd tell me yes, you still wanted me. I even thought about calling you and asking you.

"But then the answer came to me without having to make the call." He made a sound, and she could almost see his sad smile through the phone lines. "I knew what you'd tell me. You'd say, 'Landon, go for it. Make a life for yourself in New York, because I can't promise you anything.'" He exhaled in a tired kind of way. "Right, Ash? Isn't that what you've always said?"

She hated that he was right, that those were exactly the words she would've said.

"I'm right, aren't I?"

"Yes." The word was a dagger to her heart, to everything she'd hoped and dreamed those past two years about sharing her life with Landon Blake. "You're right."

"I thought so." A tinge of bitterness colored his tone. "All my life you've refused me, Ash. My schoolboy attempts back when we were kids, my effort at being your friend when you came home from Paris, and after we found something special, you still refused me. My ring, my time, even my love and—"

"Landon . . ." She couldn't listen to another word. "You don't understand. It's not like that. I didn't want to refuse you. You mean more to me than . . ." She stopped herself. No matter how she felt, it would only be selfish for her to tell him now. He deserved his freedom, even if it meant leaving him with a lifetime of misunderstandings.

"More than what? Tell me, Ashley."

She cleared her throat, desperate for the right words. "What I mean is, I don't want your pity. I need to move on, find a doctor, and you . . . you deserve a life of your own. Can't you understand?"

"Sure." His tone was kind, as if he finally understood. "That's what I thought."

"So you . . . you've made up your mind?" She held her breath, not sure why.

"I accepted the position the next day."

The chair wasn't moving, but Ashley felt herself sway all the same. The ground felt like liquid and the sounds around her came in spurts. She clenched her fists and ordered herself to get a grip. *Help me, God. Isn't this the right thing? Isn't it what I wanted all along?* The question was an easy one. No, she didn't want Landon to tell her he'd made a twenty-year commitment to New York City. She wanted to be well and normal; she wanted to tell him to quick get on the next plane for Indiana before she died from missing him.

He was talking again. ". . . and the captain position starts in January at one of the smaller stations. The hours aren't good at first, but they'll get better."

She leaned back in her chair and stared at her hands. They were trembling, reacting to the news even if she had to pretend everything was okay. Did he want her to congratulate him? Did he really think she wanted all the details, the information about the shift and the station and the hours he'd be keeping?

"Look, Landon . . ." She shifted her gaze to Cole once more. The cartoon was almost over. "I have to go. Cole's with me and . . . well . . . we have errands to run."

"Ash . . ." He sounded frustrated and a little panicked. "Tell me what you're feeling. Please . . ."

"What I'm feeling?" She stood and walked the few steps toward the window. "What am I supposed to feel?" Her throat hurt and she willed herself to sound calm. "Okay, listen. I'm happy for you, Landon. I'm glad you believed me and decided to make a life for yourself in New York. I'm glad you're happy, okay? It's what you've worked hard for."

"Wrong, Ashley." His voice was thick. He waited a long time before finishing his thought. When he did, his words were slow, measured. "I've worked hard for *you*. But I can't have you, so I'll settle for a future with the FDNY. Understand?"

And there it was. No matter what he'd said, no matter that he'd made a decision that would affect the rest of his life, he still wanted her. Still wanted her to change his mind and tell him she'd take him back. "What am I supposed to say, Landon?"

"Nothing. I wanted you to know, that's all. And maybe someday . . ."

"Maybe someday what? You want me to tell you that maybe I'll move to New York and look you up? One day when I have my health under control. Is that what you want me to say?"

"No." He paused, but only for a heartbeat. "I want you to tell me you love me. And that this wasn't how you wanted it to end."

She shut her eyes tight against the wave of sorrow that welled inside her. "Oh, Landon . . ."

"Please, Ashley." His voice was calmer now, as deep and passionate as if he were looking straight into her eyes. "If it's true, please tell me."

She made a fist and pressed it against the glass pane. *I can't do this, God.*

*I am with you, daughter . . . even now.*

The holy assurance breathed a strength into her soul, a strength she hadn't known before. She steadied herself and held the receiver closer to her face. "I love you, Landon." Chills ran down her spine and she opened her eyes, more sure about this than anything she'd ever said in her life. "I'll always love you. This . . . this wasn't how I wanted it to end."

He was quiet, and she could picture him replaying her words, absorbing the reality of them, the truth about how she felt. Finally he said only this: "I love you, Ashley. Call me sometime."

The conversation was over as quickly as it had begun, leaving Ashley with one devastating possibility. In all likelihood, she and Landon might not speak again for weeks, months even. He would be busy, moving on with his life and the climb up the FDNY ladder. In fact, other than Luke's wedding, she might never see him again.

Swiftly, suddenly, Landon Blake was out of her life.

The reality weighed so heavily on her chest, she had trouble filling her lungs. Because Landon was her only love, the way Hank was Irvel's only love. And no matter how she tried to justify her decision to let him go, she was certain Irvel wouldn't have agreed.

And that made Ashley even sadder because maybe she hadn't learned as much as she'd thought from the old woman. Irvel would never have understood any reason for letting go of that kind of love. Even now Irvel's love for Hank was stronger than Alzheimer's or reality or the confines of an adult care home. Stronger than her need for air.

A person who loved like that would never let go, not for health or money or job titles. That person would cling to the other at all costs.

Even after death took one of them home.

# CHAPTER ELEVEN

T HE G O O D N E W S came as a complete surprise, and that Thursday it gave Elizabeth reason to throw a dinner party.

All week she'd felt stronger, more willing to face the mornings. For the first time since Hayley's accident, she had enough energy to get through the day, and that had to be a good sign. She'd started to worry that maybe her lack of energy didn't have anything to do with her granddaughter's accident. Maybe there was something wrong with her, too.

But after getting the call from Erin two days earlier, after getting excited about the dinner party, she dismissed the idea that she might be sick. Her tiredness had nothing to do with her health. She was merely staggering under the reality of Hayley's situation.

"Ashley?" Elizabeth craned her neck toward the stairway and waited for an answer from her middle daughter. Cole was out back playing, and Ashley was working at the easel in the upstairs guest room.

"Yeah, Mom?"

"Could you help me with the salad, please?" Elizabeth didn't need the help so much as she needed the company. She treasured the moments with her family more since Hayley's drowning, if that was possible. Every day was golden, and no one knew when things might change. Life had at least taught her that much.

"Sure." She heard Ashley climb down off her stool. "Be right there."

Elizabeth opened the refrigerator and pulled out a bag of fresh vegetables. A head of lettuce, two green peppers, an onion, and a tomato. She set them on the counter and checked on the chicken covered in the refrigerator and marinating in her special sweet-and-sour sauce. Time to start cooking; her family would arrive in less than an hour. She lifted the casserole dish into the oven, adjusted the dial, and heard the heating element click on.

Then she leaned against the counter and watched Ashley come off the stairs into the kitchen. "Let me wash up first."

Elizabeth studied her. Something wasn't right with her, something in her eyes. "You okay, honey?"

Her answer was quick. "Fine."

"Do you have an appointment yet?"

"No . . ." Ashley smiled and locked eyes with her for a few seconds. "It's okay, Mom. Years could've gone by before I found out about the blood test. There's no need to rush into treatment. Besides, I'm not ready to be a full-time patient yet. I feel too good still."

"But it could help."

"Mom . . ." Ashley lifted her eyes from the running water where she was washing her hands. "Can we talk about something else?"

Elizabeth winced, cut by her daughter's question. She'd always prided herself in not pushing her kids, not nagging them. Setting an example, teaching them the ways of God, and then letting them make their own decisions. But now . . . now nothing seemed certain. She rolled up her sleeves and pulled two knives from the drawer—one for Ashley, one for herself.

After a few minutes of silent chopping, Elizabeth froze over a piece of green pepper and looked at Ashley. "Sorry. I don't mean to push."

Ashley leaned closer and kissed her on the cheek. "I know. We're all feeling it these days."

"I guess." Elizabeth pushed the knife through the pepper again. "It's just . . . I don't think I can handle anything else happening, you know?"

A distant look flashed in Ashley's eyes and she nodded. "I know."

Elizabeth drew a deep breath through her nose. "That's why I'm glad about tonight." She gave Ashley a quick smile. "There's a reason why we called everyone together for dinner."

"A reason?" Ashley stopped and stared at her. "You mean an announcement or something?"

"Yes." Elizabeth gave her a teasing look. "And you'll have to wait like everyone else."

Ashley hesitated, as if she might beg for details. Then she seemed to change her mind as she went back to chopping. "Good. We could all use a little happy news."

After that they worked in silence, and Elizabeth thought about the gathering tonight, the people who were coming. The list was shorter these days, and that was something else that troubled her. Ryan and Kari and Jessie would be there, and Ashley and Cole. Brooke would come with Maddie, as long as things were stable for Hayley. But Peter had declined, and earlier today Elizabeth had shared with John her fears about their daughter's marriage.

"Things are bad between them." They'd been on the patio off their bedroom, sharing coffee and a morning Bible reading. "Peter's worried about Hayley, obviously. But something else."

John had gazed into his coffee cup. "One of the pharmacists told me Peter's been picking up more painkillers than usual. Says they're for his patients, but some of the patients have names the pharmacist hasn't heard of."

The river of fear and worry in Elizabeth's soul was already at flood levels. She stared at John and set her cup down. "You think . . . you think he could be using them? for himself?"

"It's possible. I can't figure why else he hasn't been around."

"He and Brooke weren't doing well before . . . before the accident." Elizabeth folded her hands tight against each other. Her fingers were cold, the way they always were lately. "Maybe that's why."

"Maybe."

The memory of that earlier conversation faded, and Elizabeth scooped the green-pepper pieces into the salad bowl. Either way, Peter wouldn't be here tonight, and Elizabeth was beginning to wonder. If Hayley was ever well enough to go home, would she have a family to go back to?

Poor Hayley . . . lying there in that bed, trapped in a body that no longer remembered how to be a little girl. Sometimes at night Elizabeth could do nothing more than go to bed early and cry herself to sleep, remembering the happy sprite Hayley had been before the accident, the way she'd looked all decked out like an angel at Kari and Ryan's wedding.

No, it would be a long time before Hayley would join them for dinner. Maybe never. And Hayley wasn't the only one missing, of course.

Erin and Sam were gone, making their new life far away from Bloomington. They were doing well in Texas from everything Erin had told her. The teaching job was perfect, and Sam was making strong inroads with his company's management team. They'd stay in Texas indefinitely, no doubt. Or at least until Sam was ready to work for another firm.

Then there was Luke . . .

She'd always known he would leave home one day, but it all happened so fast. His rebellion after September 11, the way he kept his distance while God chased him down, and then as soon as their son was back in their lives, he was gone again. Off to

New York, where he and Reagan and Tommy would maybe find time once a year for a visit back to Indiana.

A single tear slid down Elizabeth's cheek, and she wiped it with the back of her hand.

"Mom?" Ashley set her knife down and looked at her. "You okay?"

"Yes." Elizabeth sniffed and reached for a tissue from the box beside the sink. "I'm sorry. I promised myself I'd be happy today."

"It's okay." She put her arm around Elizabeth's shoulder. "You don't have to be happy all the time, Mom. You've spent a lifetime being happy for us, celebrating with us, making sure we had happy times together. This—" she shrugged and tossed her free hand in the air—"this is one of those sad seasons, that's all."

"Yes." Elizabeth crumpled the tissue in her fist and gritted her teeth for a moment. "But it's against my beliefs to be like this."

"Against your beliefs?" Ashley raised her eyebrows, her face a mask of sorrow and amusement. "Meaning what?"

"Meaning depression, sadness." She waved her hand in the space above her head, as if she was searching for the right words. "I've always believed Scripture when it says 'rejoice always.' No matter what the circumstances."

"Yes." Ashley reached out and wiped at another tear on her mother's cheek. "But it also says that Jesus wept." She cocked her head, her eyes sympathetic. "Oh, Mom, don't you see? The joy we have in Christ is always there. But sometimes it's a season of sorrow, and that's okay, too. Otherwise Jesus wouldn't have cried."

Elizabeth took another tissue and blew her nose. "I guess I never thought of it that way."

"Well, it's true." Ashley picked up her pile of vegetable pieces and tossed them into the bowl with the green peppers. "And if the sadness doesn't go away, talk to your doctor. Sometimes we need medicine to help us feel like ourselves again." She raised her eyebrows. "And that shouldn't be against your beliefs either."

"Listen to you." Elizabeth made a sound that was more laugh than cry. "Miss I-Don't-Want-to-See-a-Doctor giving *me* medical advice."

"Someone has to."

The mood lightened and by the time they set the table, the others began arriving. Kari and Ryan took turns holding Jessie, their moods lighter than they'd been in weeks. Ryan's football team had a winning record and hopes for the postseason were high.

"Ryan's brilliant." Kari hoisted Jessie onto her hip and gave her a sippy cup of juice. "The Giants don't know what they're missing."

"My guys are talented, that's all."

Kari waved her finger at him and smiled at Elizabeth. John and Ashley were listening, too, all of them working in the kitchen. "Don't listen to a word. He's brilliant, I tell you. Perfectly brilliant."

Elizabeth laughed, and the feel of it was wonderful. Like having her first drink of water after a year in the desert. "We've seen the games, Ryan. Kari's right."

"Not that Elizabeth would know." John leaned close and gave her a quick kiss. "Last Friday she asked me why some players ran backward after the ball was snapped."

"Hmmm." Ryan chuckled. "Can't really trust that opinion now, can I?"

"Cole and I are coming to the game tomorrow night." Ashley grinned. "After we do our trick-or-treating. Cole wants to wear his firefighter uniform."

"That's good, because we play the crosstown rivals." He raised one eyebrow as he carried a stack of napkins to the table. "Things could get pretty heated."

"Cole will be ready." Ashley raised her voice so Cole could

hear her in the next room. "You already put out one fire today, right, Cole?"

"Right, Mommy!" Cole jumped up and down and assumed his firefighting position, pretend hose raised high in the air.

Elizabeth looked from Cole back to Ashley. "He did *what?*" She pulled the chicken from the oven and carried it to the hot pads on the counter.

"We were at Sunset Hills." Ashley made a face. "Pretend fires break out all the time over there."

They all laughed and moved to the table.

A few minutes later, Brooke and Maddie arrived with news that Hayley was doing better, responding to the latest seizure medicine. Conversation shifted from football and firefighting to Thanksgiving and Luke's approaching wedding in New York City.

"That reminds me . . ." Elizabeth set her fork down and waited until she had everyone's attention. "I picked up a block of *Lion King* tickets for Sunday before the wedding." She looked at the faces around her and realized how long it had been since they'd had a normal night like this one. "Will everyone be there by then?"

"I'm not coming until Tuesday." Brooke's smile was tinged with sorrow. "If Hayley's well enough to go, that is. If not, I'll stay behind with her."

"Okay." Reality tugged at Elizabeth like a giant deadly tentacle, but she pulled away, refusing to let it drag her down. She looked at the others. "How 'bout the rest of you?"

Cole clapped his hands. "I love *Lion King*, Gramma. Take me . . . take me!"

"Me, too . . ." Maddie stood up at her seat. "Simba's my friend, Gramma."

More laughter. Ashley offered to take Maddie with her to New York on Saturday before the wedding, so the child could sit with Cole at the play. When the discussion was over, everyone but Brooke had agreed to come.

Elizabeth reminded them of the itinerary for the rest of the week of the wedding. Sightseeing and *The Lion King* on Sunday, Niagara Falls on Monday, shopping on Tuesday, and the wedding rehearsal Tuesday night. The wedding on Wednesday, Christmas Eve, and then Christmas Day at Reagan's mother's apartment, complete with stockings and toys for the children. After that they would be on their own until most of them flew home again the following Saturday.

They were just about finished eating, the plans for Luke's wedding and Christmas in Manhattan more clearly defined. Elizabeth began clearing plates, going on about how good it was to be together and how wonderful it felt to look forward to all that lay ahead.

She was about to thank everyone for coming when John nudged her. He leaned close and whispered in her ear, "Aren't you forgetting something?"

For a moment, she only stared at him. Then, with a quick gasp, she remembered. The good news! The reason she and John had invited them for dinner in the first place. She gave John the nod. "You do it."

"Your mother and I have a little secret to share with you." John stood up and took the cordless phone from the kitchen counter. He looked at Elizabeth. "Is this a good time?"

Curiosity filled the faces of the others around the table, and Ryan whispered something to Kari. She shook her head and looked back at John, waiting with the others for whatever John was about to do.

Elizabeth couldn't contain her smile. She checked the clock on the wall near the stove and nodded. It would be six o'clock in Texas; Erin was expecting their call anytime after five. Moments like this were hallmarks in the Baxter family, times when good news was savored and shared in a single, celebratory moment. She nodded at John. "Go ahead and call."

John punched in a series of numbers, then clicked a button on the phone so that the ringing on the other end filled the space above the dinner table.

"Hello?" Speakerphones always made the voices sound tinny, but even so, Elizabeth could see the others recognize Erin's voice.

"Hi, Erin. It's me, Dad. I'm at the table with everyone . . ."

A chorus of greetings came from Kari and Ryan, Brooke and Ashley. Even the children chimed in with high-pitched hellos.

"Hey, everyone . . . wish we were there." As happy as Erin sounded, a faint tinge of homesickness hung in her voice. "Did Mom and Dad tell you our news?"

The others sat up a bit straighter around the table as John answered the question. "No, honey. Why don't you tell them yourself?"

Erin made a light, laughing sound. "Okay." She paused for a moment, "Sam and I are going to adopt. We've found a baby and started the process. The baby is due in six months." She gave a short squeal. "Isn't that awesome?"

The news was met with hoots of joy and the sound of Brooke and Ashley and Kari all talking at the same time.

"I'm so happy for you, Erin." Kari put her arm around Ryan and leaned close to him. "I knew God wanted you to adopt."

"Yeah, little sister." Brooke clapped her hands. The sadness that had darkened her eyes since Hayley's accident remained. But at least she was smiling. "You'll love every minute of being a mom."

"That's for sure." Ashley pulled Cole close and kissed his forehead. "Way to go, Erin! How'd you find the baby?"

"That's the miracle part." Erin's voice was trembling as she told the story. "Sam was meeting with the pastor once a week, just to be connected, and he mentioned we were thinking of adopting.

"The pastor got this strange look on his face and asked Sam how soon." Erin paused long enough to catch her breath. "Sam told him very soon, actually. And then the pastor said that he'd just met with a woman the day before whose daughter was going to have her third child out of wedlock. Each of the kids was being raised by a separate family member, and the woman's daughter had no interest in being a mother. This time the daughter wanted to give the baby up to a Christian family, through a private adoption, if possible."

Elizabeth felt the hair on her arms rise, the same way it had the first time she heard the story.

"A few days later we met the birth mother and signed the initial paperwork. She's absolutely sure about the adoption, and she showed us pictures of her other children." Erin's voice was pinched with emotion. "They're beautiful. I wish you could see them." She grabbed a few quick breaths. "Now all we have to do is wait."

"God is so good, isn't he?" John spoke the words toward the telephone, but he met the eyes of everyone in the room, even the children.

Again, Elizabeth felt a fullness in her heart, a knowing that someday soon the black cloud she'd been living under would lift. She had never understood why God hadn't granted Erin and Sam children. Back before the move, she'd wondered if it was because their marriage wasn't as stable as it should be. But now . . . now the answers seemed as clear as water. God wanted them to parent a child who otherwise might not have had a chance in the world.

Erin's sisters made another round of congratulations, with promises to call her separately and talk about the impending adoption in more detail. Erin asked about Hayley, and Brooke sounded upbeat.

"She's responding to the antiseizure medication, which is a big step. And the more time I spend massaging her muscles, the less stiff she is."

"That's good." Sadness rang in Erin's voice, even though Elizabeth knew she was trying to hide it. "We're praying for her every day, for nothing less than a miracle."

"Thanks, Erin. That means a lot."

"Is Peter there? Tell him Sam's going to call him later this week."

The question was innocent enough, an assumption really. If Brooke was there, of course Peter was there. And Elizabeth realized she hadn't been honest with Erin about the situation between Brooke and her husband.

"Uh . . ." Brooke looked around the table and a hush fell over the room.

"What's the matter, Mommy?" Maddie stood up and wrapped her arms around Brooke's neck. "Why's everyone quiet?"

"It's okay, baby . . ." Brooke took Maddie's fingers and held them against her cheek, as if she was trying to quench the sadness that was suddenly building within her.

"Brooke, are you there?" Erin sounded confused. "What's wrong?"

John clicked the button and took the call off the speakerphone. "Erin, honey, Peter's not here. Things haven't been the same with him for . . ." John walked out of the room, his voice hushed as he went.

Brooke ran her hand over Maddie's back and looked from Ashley and Kari to Elizabeth. "I think we need to get going."

"Brooke . . ." Elizabeth moved around the table toward her oldest daughter.

No words were necessary. Led by Elizabeth, the group formed a circle around Brooke and hugged her, as if the combined love from all of them together might somehow fill the hole in Brooke's heart.

Ryan's voice, strong and steady, lifted from the midst of them. "Father, we have no answers, nowhere to turn but to you. Our hearts ache at the thought of Peter trying to walk through this maze of pain by himself, without Brooke, maybe even without you." He hesitated. "Whatever it takes, Lord, bring him back. Let him see that Hayley needs him; Brooke needs him. And please, Jesus, breathe new life into our little Hayley. You saved her, now please . . . we beg you, make her whole again."

The moment ended, and in quiet, hushed tones Brooke, Ashley, and Kari gathered their children and headed off into the night. John was still on the phone with Erin in the next room, so Elizabeth was alone again, by herself and back at the shores of a sorrow that still swelled in her soul.

It was a moment when she wanted to trudge slowly to her bedroom, peel off her clothes, and slip into her nightgown, despite the fact that it wasn't close to bedtime. A moment when she wanted nothing more than to grieve the tragedy of Hayley's accident, the gravity of the situation between Brooke and Peter.

But instead she remembered what Ashley had said. They were supposed to be joyful. "Rejoice always"; that's what the Bible said. But it also said that Jesus wept. And the thought of that was suddenly more comforting than anything Elizabeth had known since Hayley's accident. Jesus wept. Even amidst perfect joy, he cried tears of pain. Certainly when he looked down from heaven at Hayley, he cried even now.

And that meant that none of them were really alone. Because Christ was with them in every moment, every season of life.

Even in this, their season of sorrow.

John had just hung up the phone from talking to Erin when he heard Ryan begin to pray in the next room. His first instinct was to hurry back into the dining room and join them. But then he heard the prayer move toward Hayley's situation and how badly all of them wanted a miracle for her.

That's when he knew he couldn't be there.

Because though he wanted desperately to believe it was possible, he had been a doctor too long to believe in a miracle this time. Hayley was brain damaged, brain injured. He'd gone over the tests a number of times. When a child went without oxygen as long as Hayley had, the situation was no longer gray. Odds didn't exist for healing in a drowning as serious as this one.

The results were the same 100 percent of the time. Children with Hayley's type of brain damage didn't get better. Not ever.

No happy ending awaited his darling granddaughter somewhere down the road. No, she would be fed by a tube, dressed in a diaper, drooling over herself for the rest of her days. Eight years, ten at best, and then death would come. Hayley's body would atrophy, taking the brain's lead in finally accepting an inability to continue.

Ten years of heartache before Hayley would be free of the prison her mind and body had become, free to run and play in the fields of heaven.

John hung his head and felt his body bend beneath the pressure. The prayer he'd uttered that first night came back to him, and he thought again of the ramifications. While everyone else had prayed for Hayley's next breath, John had prayed for God to take her home.

He had known the score, known the type of life she would face, and so he'd asked God to give her freedom instead. But the guilt from that prayer ate at him still, nibbling at his soul and robbing him of even a moment's peace since then.

The worst part was a fear he hadn't shared with anyone, not even Pastor Mark. Maybe Hayley had lived as a way of punishing him for his lack of faith. He hadn't thought God capable of making good out of her life, and so he'd asked the Lord for her death. Instead, Hayley lay hooked to tubes and monitors, unable to see or speak or connect with any of them.

"Is that what you're doing, God?" His voice was a tormented whisper. "Are you punishing me by letting her lie there that way? by letting her live?"

Even now John wanted nothing more than to believe like the rest of them, believe that somehow a miracle was possible, and Hayley's brain could heal itself, bring her back to a place where she was Hayley again. But it simply wasn't possible. Hayley's kind of brain damage went beyond traumatic injury, beyond anything the medical profession had ever seen healed.

"I want to believe, God . . ." John sat on the edge of the sofa in the den and gripped his knees. He knew the Scriptures, knew the times when Jesus promised that nothing was impossible with God or that the Lord was able to do immeasurably more than all they could ever ask or imagine.

But healing Hayley's brain?

A hundred answered prayers came rushing to John's mind. Elizabeth's recovery from cancer all those years ago . . . Luke's return to the family . . . the renewed faith for Brooke and Ashley . . .

"Yes, God, you're able . . . I know you're able." John clenched his jaw, willing himself to get past the hurdle of unbelief. "Increase my faith, Lord. Please."

Sweat beaded on his forehead. He'd never prayed with such fervor in all his life. Because as much as he was convinced that Hayley had lived as a means of punishing him, he was also convinced that his unbelief could keep her from getting well. No, he had nothing if he didn't have his faith, and that was the biggest problem of all. As hard as he was trying and as awful as he felt about it, John couldn't muster the faith to believe God could heal his Hayley. Not this time.

Not when conventional medicine told him her recovery was completely and totally impossible.

## CHAPTER TWELVE

WINTER HAD COME to Bloomington, and the rain and sleet matched Peter's mood. Especially when the pills wore off.

It was eight o'clock, the same time he'd been getting home to the familiar old house every day for the past month, ever since his family had left him. Since Hayley's drowning and Maddie's move to the Baxters' house, and Brooke's determination to stay at the hospital. Not that he blamed them—not when the whole situation was his fault.

His hands shook as he slipped the key in the door.

*More! Find the pills . . .*

His body screamed at him, and he did his best to obey. The keys fell to the wet cement, and he wiped the rain from his eyes. "Come on; get inside!" He hissed the words, and this time he was grateful to be alone.

He was always alone now; he would be alone for the rest of time. His family didn't need him, didn't want him. He'd done enough; he knew that much by looking at Hayley, at the strange, slow way her sightless eyes drifted about the room, at the painful seizures that attacked her body every moment she was awake.

Yes, he'd done quite enough for his family; they were far better off without him.

What he hadn't counted on was the pain. An aching emptiness that robbed him of his ability to think or feel or sleep. Even his ability to practice medicine. Of course, all that changed a few days after Hayley's accident, when he first discovered the pills.

For years he'd known about them. A number of med-school students lived on them, popping them between class like so many jelly beans. Med students and—once he started practicing medicine—several doctors, too. Doctors who'd started on the meds to lessen the stress, the anxiety that came with the job. A few of them, doctors Peter knew personally, couldn't stop, couldn't get through the day without the magic of Vicodin or Percocet.

"Aren't you worried?" he'd asked one of his colleagues once, half a dozen years ago. "You know the risks . . . you more than the patients."

"Listen, Peter, I have one bit of advice for you." The doctor had lowered his voice, a fine layer of sweat on his brow. "Don't start, okay? Don't ever start."

Another time he'd asked a different doctor what the attraction was. "They're addictive; they'll kill you."

The man's response haunted Peter to this day. He'd squared his shoulders, leveled his gaze at Peter, and said, "Without them, life will kill me first."

Five days after Hayley's drowning, Peter knew exactly what the man meant. By then he couldn't sleep, couldn't eat, couldn't think. Couldn't live a minute of life without replaying the scene in his mind and changing the ending:

He's watching baseball with DeWayne when Hayley and Maddie rush into the living room and ask him to take off their life jackets.

"Girls." He would grin at them, raising a single finger in their direction. "Now what did Mommy say?"

The girls would give up, aware of their mother's rule, and Maddie would do the talking. "Keep the life jackets on."

"That's right." And Peter would walk the girls into the bathroom, find a towel, and dry them off so the jackets wouldn't drip water in Aletha's kitchen. When he'd rubbed the water off, he'd kiss their foreheads—first Maddie's, then Hayley's—and tell them to go have cake. "But whatever you do, keep the life jackets on."

Or a different scenario:

Maddie and Hayley come into the living room and ask to have the life jackets off, and Peter agrees. "But only while you're eating cake. If you want to swim again, you need the jackets. Otherwise you can't go in the backyard at all."

Twenty minutes later, Hayley would scamper into the room carrying her life jacket. "Here, Daddy. I wanna swim again."

Or still another possibility: fifteen minutes would pass. Not twenty or thirty, but fifteen. And he'd realize it had been too long since he'd seen the girls. "Just a minute," he'd tell DeWayne. "I'm going to check on the girls."

He'd trot up the stairs and find them playing with Barbies, Hayley pouting against the far wall. He would drop to his knees and hold his hands out to her. "What's the matter, Hayley . . . why so sad?"

And she would come to him and wrap her arms around his neck, peering at him with those big blue eyes of hers. "I wanna swim, and Maddie won't go with me."

"Maddie wants to play with the girls, but I have an idea."

"What?"

"How 'bout we get your life jacket on and I take you out in the pool. I'll sit at the edge and watch you swim, okay?"

The story lines were endless. Playing over and over in his mind until he thought he might go crazy. Why hadn't he listened to Brooke in the first place, kept their life jackets on just in case they went back outside? Couldn't he have been more clear about the importance of staying inside as long as the jackets were off? Wasn't there something else he could have said, something more specific that would've kept Hayley from going outside? And why had he sat there so long watching television when he had no idea where the girls were? What would it have hurt for him to check on them, offer to take Hayley swimming so she wouldn't have to go alone?

He had no answers for himself, and that only added to the pain. A constant buzzing in his brain, a breathless, pounding ache that knew no end. Once that first week he'd tried drinking. He bought a fifth of vodka and drank half of it while watching *SportsCenter*.

The drink numbed him for sure, but it also knocked him out. When he came to the next morning, vomit covered his bedsheets and the pain was worse than ever. It was the next day at work that he hit on the idea of pain pills. At two o'clock that afternoon he had visited Hayley again and checked her charts. Her brain-scan results were horribly poor, pointing to a vegetative life. It was the first time he'd been forced to realize the truth about the accident.

Hayley was gone forever.

He would never again see her playing with her doll on her bedroom floor, never hear her singing songs with Maddie, never see her run or skip or write her name. She was gone.

As he left the hospital that day, he had turned into the pharmacy and found his old friend behind the counter. The rest had been little more than a blur.

The medicine didn't make him feel loopy or inebriated the way the vodka had. Rather it gobbled up the anxiety. Peter knew it was working because the next day—his first full workday under the influence of painkillers—he noticed something that hadn't happened since Hayley's drowning.

He'd gone fifteen minutes without thinking about it.

Fifteen minutes that felt like a lifetime, and a strange giddy feeling rose up in Peter. If he could take an occasional pill now and then and limit his visits to Hayley, he might get through an hour or two of life the way it used to be.

Even with all his medical training, Peter couldn't believe the slippery slope he'd been on since that first day. How one pill a day had become two, and two had become four, and four had become more than he cared to count.

He blinked and the recent past collided with the present. Why wouldn't the key fit into the front door, and how long had it been since he'd had a pill? Finally—after four attempts—Peter slipped the key into the hole and the door opened. He stumbled in and dropped his things on the chair. These days he carried a bottle in his pocket, but now it was empty. Something he hadn't noticed until he was halfway home from work.

That was okay; he'd planned ahead. Weeks ago he'd made up another patient name, had the pharmacist fill another prescription, one he could keep at home in case of a moment like this. In case he was suddenly out of pills.

"Okay . . . where are you . . . ?"

The kitchen swayed and the floor buckled beneath his feet. Betty had warned him about this. She was his head nurse, his right hand at the office. A week after he started taking the pills she'd walked in on him as he was taking one. Her face had gone pale and she'd politely stepped out of the office.

But later she had come to him and told him how it was. "My son was addicted." She kept her voice low, not willing to betray his secret. "You need more to make it work, Dr. West. More all the time. And before you know it, you're hooked and it's too late. My son said the floor would move beneath his feet if he didn't get his fix." She searched Peter's face. "I know you're going through a hard time, but please . . . don't make it worse."

Her words had come too late.

This past week he'd been taking one pill every hour on the hour. The whole time he convinced himself that he was okay as long as he wasn't taking more than one. But four pills over four hours was a problem, no matter what he told himself.

He tried to hold steady, tried not to sway, but the kitchen floor wouldn't stay still. The vitamin cupboard was at the far end of the room near the stove, and in that moment it felt like a world away. Peter held his hands out and took small shuffling steps until he was close enough to grab the edge of the counter and use it to keep his balance.

"Where are you?" He shouted the words, and the sound of his voice banged against his conscience, amplifying the steady, searing pain in his head. With a quick grab, he opened the cupboard door and swept his hand across the first shelf. A dozen bottles fell onto the counter, and his fingers fast-danced over them, searching the labels, looking for the pain meds.

The room began to spin and he felt himself shaking harder, faster. His heart raced and he wondered, *Is this it?* Would he die right here in the kitchen? He squeezed his eyes shut, and when he opened them the room was no longer spinning.

Reason interrupted the moment.

He was a doctor; he had taken classes on pain management, hadn't he? He could think of something else, outlast the pain at least until he found the pills. His heart rate slowed, but then picked up speed again. He knocked another row of bottles off the second shelf and searched them with quick, frantic movements.

Vitamin A, calcium, vitamin C . . .

His legs were weaker than before, and without any sense of control, he dropped to the floor. Tears filled his eyes. "Help me!" He still wore his dress shirt and tie, still had on his white jacket, but his mind wouldn't tell him what do next. "Help me . . . I need the pills . . ."

It wasn't a prayer really. He hadn't spoken to God since that awful day in Hayley's hospital room. But he needed help from somewhere, whoever or whatever was willing to give it to him. Then, in that instant, he spotted something on the floor, tucked against the floorboard. An amber bottle with a white label, half full of pills. A bottle of—

Could it be? Was it?

He snatched at the bottle and tried to read the label, but his hands were moving too hard for him to get a good look. That and the fact that the floor was still moving. With every ounce of his remaining strength he used both hands and his knees to steady the bottle. Then—and only then—could he read the label and see that . . .

Yes! Yes, he'd found them.

It took another minute to remove the lid and struggle to his feet. He had two pills beneath his tongue minutes before he found the strength to pour a glass of water. At first—weeks ago—the taste had been bitter enough to make him gag. But water wasn't always available when he needed a pill, so he'd learned to take them dry.

By the time he brought the water to his mouth, the pills were long since dissolved, their effects already playing out through his system. "Steady, Peter . . . stay steady." He gripped the edge of the kitchen sink and waited.

Three minutes, five . . . seven . . . ten.

And gradually, moment by moment, everything was right with the world.

The kitchen floor no longer spun, the walls were stable, and he gave a shake of his head. A shudder passed over him as he considered what might have happened if he hadn't found the pills. But no matter; at least he'd found them.

Sweat dripped down his face, so he took off his white coat, his tie, and white button-down shirt. Even his undershirt felt too hot, but he left it on. He didn't like the way his ribs stuck out when the shirt was off.

He looked around and realized the mess he'd made near the vitamin cupboard. *Crazy*, he told himself. *Crazy to get that bad off*. He was picking up everything, putting the bottles back where they belonged when the clock caught his eye. He hadn't eaten since breakfast. He wasn't hungry; the pills took care of that, too. But he needed to eat. Otherwise he wouldn't have the strength to get through another day.

A quick tuna-fish sandwich and an apple—that would take

care of the food problem. He ate without tasting a bite, and then headed into the TV room and flipped on ESPN. It was football season—Peter's favorite. He sat motionless, his mind numb from the meds, content to be consumed with midseason statistics and predictions about who would make the play-offs. Two hours passed and his hand began to twitch. First a little, then enough so that both arms were shaking.

This time he was ready.

He pulled the bottle of pills from his pocket and popped two more. Now that he'd done it once, two pills wasn't a problem, not really. Not when he'd waited two hours between doses. What was the difference? One pill every hour or two pills every two hours. He wasn't addicted, of course not. An addicted person would need more per hour, right?

Once the pills began working, his arms fell still against his body and he grew tired. Too tired to leave the chair or do anything but hit the remote and turn off the television. He could sleep in the recliner; he'd done it often that month.

It wasn't until he was almost asleep that something occurred to him. He hadn't thought about his family once that entire night, not since his last appointment at work. No images of the wife he'd pledged a lifetime to, or the father who had walked out of his life when he was just a boy, or the cheery little Maddie who had always played checkers with him.

And most of all, not a single thought about Hayley and how she should've been upstairs dreaming by now, tucked into her own bed next to her favorite doll. Her blonde hair should've been fanned out across the pillow, that precious smile of hers still on her lips.

It should've been that way. If only it weren't for him.

# CHAPTER THIRTEEN

ASHLEY VISITED THE HOSPITAL as often as she could, and her time there had brought about something neither she nor Brooke had expected.

After a lifetime of being related, the two sisters were finally getting to know each other. But even then, most of the time Ashley tried not to talk about Peter. What advice could she possibly offer about staying with the person you loved? Especially after she'd just ended things forever with Landon Blake?

Forever love wasn't her territory; it was Kari's.

Still, she looked forward to the occasional nights when she'd leave Cole with her parents and Maddie and head for the hospital to spend a quiet evening with Brooke. Ashley would stroke Hayley's hand, and she and Brooke would get into the kind of conversation the two of them had never had before Hayley's accident.

The night after Thanksgiving was one of those nights.

November was almost past, which meant Hayley had been in the hospital two months. Her progress seemed tedious and slow, at least to Ashley. Brooke had become the optimist in the group, believing she was seeing movement in Hayley's fingers, certain that Hayley was tracking her around the room with eyes that were supposed to be blind.

Hayley was asleep when Ashley arrived, so she pulled up a chair next to Brooke and leaned back, searching her sister's expression. The hum of the machines in the background was strangely comforting, and the nurses had dimmed the lights in a way that relaxed Ashley, made her feel even more talkative.

"You okay?" Ashley searched her sister's eyes.

"Yes." She shrugged and looked at Hayley. "I keep thinking tomorrow will be the day she wakes up and tells us she's okay."

Ashley bit her lip. "It could happen."

"I know." Brooke smiled but it fell short of her eyes. "I'm praying for it every day."

Hayley began to stir, and soon she was making the strange and constant moaning sound that accompanied her waking moments. And while that aspect of her recovery hadn't changed, for weeks now she'd been able to stop crying whenever any of the family talked to her.

The crying grew louder. Brooke looked at Ashley and nodded. "Go ahead."

"Are you sure?" Ashley was excited and anxious all at once. Hayley's medication made her sleep much of the day, and Ashley hadn't seen her awake for the past few weeks. Usually Brooke was the one who went to her when she needed comforting.

"Yes. It's good for her to remember more than me." Brooke smiled. "See if you can make her laugh. That's her newest thing."

Ashley stood and leaned against the rails that ran along Hayley's bed. "Hey, little girl, it's me. Aunt Ashley."

The sound of Ashley's voice had an instant impact. Hayley stopped crying and blinked. Ashley watched her, hating the way the child opened and closed her eyes, each movement painstaking and deliberate, in slow motion. Further reason to believe that the brain damage she'd suffered was very serious.

As Hayley woke up, she held her arms out in front of her, both hands stiff and turned outward. Next, her right leg kicked straight up in the air and stayed there, bouncing a few inches in either direction.

Ashley placed her fingers on Hayley's right calf. Her small muscles were hard and stiff. Ashley massaged them, the way she'd seen Brooke do. Almost immediately, Hayley's leg relaxed enough that it returned to its position on the bed. *Oh, Hayley, you're so different.* Ashley kept her thoughts to herself.

Tears blurred her vision, but her voice was happy, upbeat. "Hey, silly girl, where's your smile, huh?"

Again in a way that was painfully slow, Hayley turned her head and looked at Ashley. Not at her face or at the space near her, but right into her eyes. Ashley sucked in a quiet gasp and shot Brooke a look over her shoulder. "Hey, come here. You have to see this."

"I know." Brooke smiled. She joined Ashley at the side of the bed and stared at Hayley. Even before Brooke began to talk, Hayley shifted her gaze to her mother. "That's what I've been saying. Looks like she can see you, doesn't it?"

"She can; I swear she can!" Ashley gripped the bed rails and uttered a giddy sound. "Brooke, I can't believe this; look at her! She can see; I have no doubt."

Brooke took Hayley's stiff fingers and worked her thumb into the child's palm, relaxing her little hand some. "I keep telling her doctors that, but in here they don't see me as a professional. They think I'm a delusional mother, believing what I want to believe about Hayley's condition."

"Hayley . . ." Ashley tried again and waited until her niece looked her way. Then Ashley made a goofy face, one that always made Cole laugh. "That's right, silly head; where's your little smile?"

And right then Hayley opened her mouth and laughed! Not the normal wind-chime laughter that had been her trademark before the accident. But a series of short breathy sounds, the way Edith at Sunset Hills laughed. Still, it was something. It meant

Hayley could hear Ashley and that she knew what was being said. Also, that somehow she understood she was being played with, and that it would be an appropriate time to laugh.

Ashley kept working her fingers into Hayley's calf muscles—first the right leg, then the left—and finding ways to make her respond until ten minutes later a nurse came in with a long needle.

"Time for her meds." The nurse's eyes looked tired, as though a lifetime of seeing children like Hayley had left a permanent mark.

Brooke moved back and motioned for Ashley to do the same. As they did, Hayley began to cry, and her arms and legs, which had been calm while they were being massaged, grew stiff and rigid once more.

"She wants us." Ashley stared at her niece wide-eyed. As often as she'd been by to visit, she'd never seen Hayley so responsive. "Brooke, she knows who we are and she doesn't want to be alone."

"I know." Brooke's eyes were wet, but her smile took up her whole face. "Now you can see why I'm so hopeful. She's coming back to us, Ashley; I really think she is."

As soon as the nurse was finished, Ashley returned to her place by the bed. Hayley was crying again, turning her head from side to side. "It's okay, sweetie; we're still here." Once more she took hold of the child's stiff leg and eased her thumb into the tight muscles. And once more Hayley stopped crying and found Ashley's eyes. "That's right, Hayley; where's your happy smile, silly?"

The corners of Hayley's mouth stretched and filled her face, and she pressed her head back into the pillow. The action reminded Ashley of something—something she couldn't put her finger on until . . . She gasped out loud. "Brooke, she looks like a newborn. That smile . . . it's the same one she had when she was two months old."

"Right." Brooke's tone was sure and confident. "That's what

I've been saying." She moved back in place beside Ashley. "Now if we can just get the doctors to see it."

Ashley was quiet, continuing to massage Hayley's legs and arms and hands. After a while, as they often did when she was with Hayley, tears formed in her eyes and spilled onto the child's hospital sheets. They were strange tears, really. Not like any Ashley had ever cried before. The tears didn't involve her sinuses or even the sound of her voice; they simply came. Falling like rain whenever she spent time with Hayley.

"I want her out of this bed so bad, Brooke." Ashley dabbed at her cheeks, but it did nothing to stop the flow. "I want her to sit up and tell us she's only teasing, that she's really still in there, still the Hayley we know."

"Exactly." Brooke's eyes never left Hayley. "I want her to tell me how she's feeling, if she's alone or afraid or if her legs hurt when they cramp up. I want her to ask about Maddie and talk about going home again." She sniffed. "I want her to eat with a spoon, not through a tube in her nose."

"I picture her on her fourth birthday." Ashley wiped at her tears again. "Riding her tricycle, playing catch with Cole . . . eating birthday cake with the other kids."

Brooke's voice held a quiet resolve that hadn't been there before. "Then we have to pray that way, Ashley. You and me and everyone else who knows her."

"I am, Brooke. Every day I am."

They were quiet then, and after fifteen minutes, Hayley fell asleep. Brooke and Ashley took their chairs again, the tears gone for now. Once they were settled, Ashley leaned forward and rubbed her sister's knee. "Okay . . . what's on your mind?"

Brooke shrugged. "I'm wondering, I guess; why Peter isn't here, why he thinks his being gone will make it easier for us."

A conversation came to mind, one Ashley and Kari had shared earlier today. Ryan had dropped in a few times to see Peter, and each time Peter had acted strangely. Ryan had talked about Peter's behavior with Ashley's dad and they'd reached the same conclusion: Peter might be taking something to get through the ordeal.

Ashley studied her sister, not sure how much she should say. "Have you talked to Dad lately?"

"Yes." Brooke rolled her eyes. "Peter isn't taking drugs. He might be drinking, but he wouldn't abuse his privilege as a doctor; I know him better than that."

"I don't know." Ashley didn't want to argue the point. But maybe if Brooke considered the possibility she might look a little closer at how Peter was spending his time. "Doesn't it seem strange that he isn't here more?"

Brooke shifted so she was facing Ashley. "He's guilty, Ash. That's why he isn't here. He's chosen to cut himself off from me and the girls and the accident, because that's the easiest way he can get through it."

"You think so?"

"I know so." She turned back to Hayley. "The guilt's tearing him up."

These were waters they hadn't crossed. Most of the time Ashley and Brooke spent these hospital hours talking about happier times, the years since the girls were born, the fun moments they'd shared as a family, Brooke's insistence that God was going to work a miracle and give them Hayley back again, whole and well.

Ashley closed her mouth and followed her sister's gaze, allowing her eyes to fall on the blonde girl, still sleeping peacefully a few feet away. *Give me the words, God. I don't want to hurt her.*

A reassurance came over Ashley, and she felt the muscles in her shoulders ease some. "When's the last time the two of you talked?"

"Peter and me?" Brooke glanced at her, but looked immediately back at Hayley. "Days. He was here last Saturday for a few minutes—nothing more."

Ashley rubbed Brooke's arm, willing her tone to sound kind

and gentle. "Then how do you know, Brooke? What if he is using something?"

Brooke's eyes became stony cold. "What if he is?" She shifted her gaze to Ashley's, but just for a few seconds. "He's the one who walked out on this family." Her chin quivered and her voice shook. "I refuse to chase after him, and I absolutely won't beg him to take part in what's happening here. Not when . . ."

Ashley waited until she was sure Brooke wasn't going to finish her sentence. "Not when what?" She leaned a bit closer to her sister. "Not when it's his fault you're here?"

Brooke tilted her face upward and looked at Hayley again. Her expression remained frozen, her body still as if she might break if she moved an inch in either direction. Despite all that, a stream of tears forged its way down the sides of her cheeks.

Ashley wasn't sure why she didn't let the issue go, but for some reason she felt God leading her, directing her to talk about what happened. Maybe then her sister would have a chance to work through the accident.

"Brooke . . . is that what you think? That it's his fault?"

She didn't say a word, but her head moved up and down twice, and the tears came harder, her shoulders shaking with the sobs she was holding back. It was the first time since Hayley's drowning that Ashley had seen Brooke break down this way.

"I . . . I asked him to keep their life jackets on . . . to make sure the girls didn't go near the water without them."

Ashley knew only a few of the details, whatever Peter had shared with Ryan the night of the drowning. The detail about the life jackets was new. "Have you talked about what happened that day? With Peter?"

"No." A momentary guilt colored Brooke's eyes. "I don't want to talk about it. I can't stand the thought of picturing Hayley's last few minutes, the events just before she . . ." Brooke covered her face with her hands and hung her head. "I can't do it, Ashley. I wasn't there to help her."

Ashley felt her eyes grow wider. What had her sister just said?

She hadn't been there to help Hayley? A strange pounding sounded in Ashley's ears, and a rush went through her veins. In all the weeks while they'd sat vigil beside Hayley, Brooke had never said anything indicating her own guilt.

Until now.

Brooke sat unmoving.

Great, heartbreaking sobs shook her back, and she kept her face covered with her fingers. Ashley slid her chair closer to her sister's and eased her arm around her shoulders. "Oh, Brooke. You think it's your fault, too."

Her sister sat up straighter, but kept her hands over her eyes. "I agreed to be on call. I should've put the girls first, and then—"

"No, Brooke." Ashley's voice was firm. "No. A million times no. God wants you to let go of that. Both you and Peter would do a hundred things differently if you had that day to do over again. So you took an on-call job. So Peter watched a baseball game. Those aren't deadly decisions, Brooke; can't you see that?" Ashley leaned her head against Brooke's. "What happened to Hayley just happened, that's all. Blaming Peter, blaming yourself won't take you back in time and let you fix it. All you have is to-day, maybe tomorrow. None of us know even that for sure."

"Yes, but . . ." Brooke let her hands fall to her lap, and her eyes had the frightened look of a lost child. "If it wasn't our fault, then . . . then that leaves only God. Don't you see, Ashley? If I believe this is God's fault, I'm not sure I could ever trust him again. I have to blame someone else." She gave a slow shake of her head. "God sees all things, right?"

"Right." Ashley swallowed her fears. This conversation was way beyond her abilities, but still she felt the peace of God inside her, encouraging her to go on.

"Okay—" Brooke sniffed—"here's the problem. I just found God again, Ashley. All those years when we were kids and Mom and Dad took us to church and talked about Jesus? I never really believed—not until after September eleventh. I don't know; maybe that was the first time I ever needed God." She made a sad ironic huff. "Now I believe every bit of it. God is real . . . Jesus died for my sins . . . I want him as my friend and Savior so I can get through life here and spend forever in heaven, okay? I believe all of it."

She took four quick, jerky breaths and knotted up her features. "I can understand Hayley's drowning because of something we did; because I shouldn't have been on call and Peter shouldn't have been glued to that stupid baseball game." Her eyes narrowed, bright with pain. "But if it wasn't my fault, if it wasn't Peter's fault, then I'd have to believe God allowed my daughter into the backyard by herself. And then instead of causing one of the adults to check on her, I'd have to believe that same God watched her fall into the pool and did nothing to stop her, nothing to save her."

"That isn't true." Ashley removed her arm from Brooke's shoulders and met her stare straight-on. "Hayley's alive, isn't she?"

A handful of emotions flashed across Brooke's face. Surprise and anger, fear and desperation, and finally an understanding that came and grew stronger with every passing minute. The fight inside Brooke was gone now, and once more she peered through the bed rails at Hayley. For a long while neither of them said anything, but Ashley could sense the change in her sister. Something she'd said, something God had given her to say, had touched Brooke and even now it was working its way from her head into her heart.

After several minutes, Brooke stood. When she opened her mouth to speak, her words were barely more than a whisper. "She is alive, isn't she?" She took Hayley's hand in hers. The hint of a smile played at the corners of her lips. "I never thought of that before . . . that maybe what happened to Hayley wasn't anyone's fault. Maybe it just happened, and God in all his mercy saved her life."

"Exactly." Ashley stood next to Brooke and stared at her

niece. "We're all praying for her, Brooke. Even Peter must be praying."

Brooke ignored the part about Peter. She was quiet for a moment, and then she said, "Mom told me Pastor Mark has churches around the country praying for Hayley, thousands of people."

"Right. And you know what, Brooke?" Ashley remembered Hayley's slow, strange laugh and the way she'd used her eyes earlier that evening. "I have a feeling God's not finished with her yet. "

# CHAPTER FOURTEEN

THE BEST NEWS OF ALL came three days later on the first of December.

At Brooke's prodding, the doctors decided to retest Hayley's vision, and that morning three of them entered her hospital room together, their faces a mix of shock and exuberance.

Dr. Martinez took the lead. "Brooke, we have no explanation for the information we're about to give you."

Brooke rose from her chair and faced the men, all of them doctors she'd seen at the hospital over the past few years.

"Hayley can see." A sound that blended awe and joy came from the doctor's throat. "We checked her every way we knew how and there's no question about it. Her vision has returned completely."

An explosion of color and light flashed through Brooke's mind, as if the news had given sight again to her, too. Hayley was sleeping, but Brooke took hold of her hand anyway, her eyes still on the three doctors. "People all around the nation are praying for this little girl, gentlemen. She's getting better; that's the only explanation."

Dr. Martinez raised his clipboard a few inches and let it fall back to his side. "All we can tell you is this: It's working." He flashed a smile at her, one that said he shared her faith. "Tell everyone to keep praying, okay?"

The other two doctors shifted their weight from one foot to the other, their eyes intent on the floor tiles. Med school didn't teach doctors how to handle three-year-old drowning victims who spent fifteen minutes underwater and then regained their sight. Brooke understood the uneasiness of the two men. Medical books taught nothing about God.

One of the two stepped forward, the lines on his forehead more pronounced than before. "We, uh . . . we have no explanation for what's happened with your daughter."

Brooke smiled, willing them to understand. "I know prayer isn't conventional medicine, Doctors." She looked down at her daughter. "But you said it yourself. There's no other explanation."

An hour later Brooke's father knocked on the doorframe and leaned his head inside the hospital room. "Can I come in?"

"Sure." Brooke hadn't stopped smiling all day. "Did you hear the news?"

Her father came to the opposite side of Hayley's bed and held on to the railing. He looked from Brooke to Hayley and back again. "She . . . she can see? They're sure?"

A ripple of gentle laughter spilled from Brooke. "Wait a minute, Dad. You're Mister Prayer Man, remember? 'Never underestimate the power of prayer'; wasn't that you? Every time I bombed a test or struggled in any way?" She grinned at him from the other side of Hayley's bed. "What do you mean 'are they sure?' " Her smile pushed up into her cheeks. "Dad . . . she can see!"

Since the accident, her father had been quiet and tense. Normally the strength of the family, in light of what had happened to Hayley, he seemed distant, almost irritated. Brooke hadn't talked to him about it, because her father hadn't stayed in the hospital room more than ten minutes at a time.

Now, though, relief filled her father's features and his eyes welled up. "Brooke—" his gaze held hers—"I have a confession."

He sounded serious, and Brooke took quiet steps around the bed and faced him, her back to Hayley. Was it something about Peter, something her father knew that she hadn't found out yet? She steadied herself against the bed railings and searched his face. "What?"

Her father reached out and took her hand in his. "Remember that first night, when we got the news about Hayley?"

"Yes?" Brooke reminded herself to exhale. Whatever this was, it hurt him badly. She'd never seen him look so tormented.

He shifted his attention beyond her to Hayley, and he shook his head. "Her doctors gave me the numbers from her initial tests and—" he tossed his hands— "she didn't have a chance, Brooke. I couldn't tell you that then, but I knew the truth. Children don't recover from that kind of brain damage."

"Okay . . ." There had to be more to the story. Brooke waited, her eyes trained on her father's face.

"So I prayed something awful that night, honey." Her father's chin trembled and he clenched his jaw until he had control. "I prayed that God would take her home. Because according to her tests, she would never get out of this hospital bed, never know any of us, never even wake up."

Brooke had experienced more emotions in the past two months than in all of her life until this point. Standing before her, admitting his frailties, was the man she idolized, the one who had praised her abilities since she was a child, the one who had encouraged her to apply to med school. John Baxter, the strongest man she knew. All that and he was only human after all, human like everyone else.

"Dad . . . it's okay . . . really." His admission sent her into his arms, and for a moment their roles seemed reversed—he, the repentant child; she, the forgiving parent. She pulled back and studied him, the sorrow in his face. "We all thought about it, Dad. At one time or another, all of us. It was easy to think she'd be better off in heaven, running and playing the same as she'd done before the accident."

"But now . . ." John nodded his head toward Hayley, and his voice dropped to an agonizing hush. "Now she can see!"

"Yes!" Brooke felt an otherworldly joy fill her heart, spreading out from her veins into her limbs and heart and soul. A joy that went deeper than the ocean and higher than all the mountains in the world combined. "Yes, she can see!"

Her father looked at Hayley again. "I doubted God, Brooke. For the first time in my life I doubted."

"But, Dad . . . look at how much God loves you." Brooke took gentle hold of his shoulders. Her father would never know how close she felt to him in this moment, knowing that her hero could make mistakes and be big enough to admit them. She looked over her shoulder at her younger daughter. "He loves you enough to laugh at the limits you put on him." She met his eyes again. "The limits all of us put on him."

"But not you, Brooke." Her father kissed her forehead. "You believed from the beginning."

"Because if I didn't believe . . ." Brooke choked back the lump in her throat. "If I didn't believe, I would've drowned right there beside her."

Her father twisted up his face and gave a hard shake of his head. Brooke had never seen him look more broken. "I'm sorry." He squeezed his eyes shut for a moment and hugged her close again. "Forgive me, Brooke. I promise . . . I promise I'll believe now."

Brooke's heart hurt within her, because she had known all along. Deep inside she'd been sure that her father wasn't completely with them, and she hadn't known why. Only that she didn't seem to have his support, his confidence the way she'd had it all her life. But now . . . now Hayley wasn't the only one who had her sight back.

Her father did, too.

She framed her father's face with her hands. "God can do anything, remember, Dad?" Her voice was pinched, tight with emotion, but she smiled anyway. "You taught me that."

"I remember." Her father's eyes were bright with unshed tears. "And here's something else." He reached into his coat pocket and pulled out a small folded piece of paper. "Open it." He handed it to Brooke and let his eyes drift to Hayley.

The paper was fragile, cut out of a newspaper or catalogue perhaps. She opened it and there inside was a picture of a small pink bicycle, complete with white streamers and a floral basket. Brooke knit her brow and looked at her father. "I . . . I'm not sure I understand."

"It's for Hayley." He pointed to the picture. "I bought it an hour ago and parked it in the garage. It'll be there waiting for her."

"Dad . . . are you serious?" Brooke clutched the picture to her heart. His renewed faith in Hayley's future was the greatest gift he could've given her.

"Yes." He smiled for the first time that morning. "Because God *can* do anything, Brooke. Anything at all. And on the day when Hayley can ride that bike down the driveway, I want to say I was the first one who believed it could happen."

When her father was gone, Brooke took her place in the familiar chair near Hayley's bed and pulled her Bible from her overnight bag. She wanted to find something about this . . . this indescribable joy, the feeling brimming inside her unlike anything she'd ever felt.

It was strange, really. Because even with the strides Hayley was making, she still had a million miles to go. Even after

Ashley's talk the other night, she was still bothered by feelings of guilt about her role in Hayley's accident, about Peter's role.

In many ways their lives were still in massive disarray, total confusion. Maddie was living with her parents, and the two of them saw each other only an hour a day when Brooke visited the Baxter house. She was still living at the hospital, sleeping in the reclining chair next to Hayley's bed. Things at work had moved on without her, and the other doctors had filled in with her patients since the accident. Peter never came by, never called, or even talked to her at the hospital.

Hayley was making strides, yes, but she still lay confined to a hospital bed, unable to move or speak or eat without the nose tube. Still, somehow, Brooke had never felt happier, never known with more certainty that God was moving and working in her, around her, never been more convinced that he had every aspect of their future figured out.

Somehow Hayley would get better; Brooke had no doubt.

Hayley would go home soon—the doctors had said that—and the four of them would find their way back to being the family they used to be. The joy within her seemed to promise as much.

But still, she hadn't studied the Scriptures about this strange new kind of joy. Hayley was asleep and Brooke wasn't expecting visitors. She opened the Bible and flipped to the concordance at the back, where she found a list of key words and their locations in the Bible.

She stared at the list of words and tried to think of the right one. *Joy* . . . or *joyful*. Or maybe *rejoice*. One of those had to be listed. She was turning to the *J* section when she heard someone enter the room. Her eyes lifted from the Bible to the door, and she felt her heart skip a beat.

"Hello." Peter stopped before moving farther into the room. "I hope I'm not interrupting."

"No." Brooke didn't know what to say. This was the most he'd spoken to her in weeks. Usually he'd spend ten—fifteen—minutes standing at Hayley's bed, and then give her a terse nod on his way out. She closed the Bible and set it back in her bag. "Sit down if you want."

"Okay." He took a chair near Brooke, reached up and cupped the back of his neck, massaging his muscles for a moment. When he lowered his hand to his lap, his fingers shook. He seemed to notice the way they trembled, and he made tight fists of both hands. His eyes lifted to hers, and he looked twenty years older than the last time they'd sat face-to-face this way. "Brooke . . . we need to talk."

In a rush, Brooke realized something. She and Peter hadn't had a joyful discussion in months. Forget joyful. They hadn't even been civilized to each other since long before Hayley's accident. Now, with Peter almost always gone, with the two of them not speaking, she had in some ways written him off, forgotten about him.

But Peter's tired, lackluster tone brought back all Brooke's old feelings. How dare he question her medical abilities? And what kind of nerve did he have, leaving her alone to handle the tragedy with Hayley? He was an unfeeling coward, a man who had carelessly risked the safety of their children so he could watch a baseball game and . . .

The inner diatribe went on. And in a tangible way she felt bitter sarcasm pushing joy out of the way.

"We need to talk?" She leaned back in her chair and lifted her eyebrows in his direction. "You think?" She hardened her eyes. "Our daughter's been in the hospital for two months, and you haven't said five sentences to me. Yes—" a mean-sounding exhale came from deep in her throat—"I'd say we need to talk."

Peter hung his head. He seemed unable to find the strength to lift it again, but he did so anyway, meeting her look head-on. "I didn't come here to fight. This whole thing's been just as hard on me."

"I can tell."

"Brooke . . ." A flicker of anger danced in Peter's eyes and then burned out. "Brooke, I'm moving out this weekend."

She stared at him, not believing what he'd just said. "You're what?"

For all of her anger at him, all the reasons she was frustrated, even disgusted with him, she had never for a moment expected a statement like that one. She felt light-headed and sick to her stomach all at once, and she gripped the arms of her chair. Her voice was there, but barely. "What did you say?"

He breathed out through his nose and shook his head. "It's over, Brooke. You and I both know that."

She needed a glass of water, needed a way to stop the scene taking place between them. "So we go from arguing and tragedy straight to divorce, is that it?"

Peter dropped his jaw and let his mouth hang open for a minute. "I . . . I guess. I don't see any other way." He looked at Hayley's sleeping form. "I talked to her doctor. They think she'll be coming home a week from today." He lifted his shoulders, defeated. "You and the girls deserve the house; I'll be in an apartment by then. I thought you should know."

She stared at him, speechless. Her emotions ran wild and she considered slapping him, screaming at him, throwing something at him. *Fight, Peter,* she wanted to yell. *Fight for what we used to have; fight for the sake of our girls, for Hayley.* But he'd surrendered their marriage before the battle had even begun.

And despite her strong desire to pound her fists on his chest and rail at him for leaving her alone since Hayley's accident, she also wanted to fall to her knees, crawl to him and wrap her arms around his waist. Let her head fall on his lap and weep for how much she'd missed him, how she still longed for the way they used to be.

No words came, but a memory formed in her head, a picture of the two of them the year he graduated from med school. They'd snuck up to the school fountain with a box of detergent and a bottle of dishwashing liquid. Together they sprinkled the soap around the watery perimeter. Then they tossed the empty box and bottle in a trash can, grabbed hands, and ran for the bushes. There they giggled and held each other, laughing about their "clean" getaway and how the professors would react the next day when soapsuds poured from the fountain down into the courtyard.

But laughter had turned to passion that night, and most of the next hour they stayed in the bushes, kissing and whispering about the future.

"Know when I first fell in love with you, Peter?"

He'd kissed her lips, her jaw, the arch in her neck. "When you spotted me in chemistry?"

She giggled and shook her head. "No, when you handed me that dead frog. Remember? We were in biology class and you passed me the frog I was supposed to dissect that day. You told me, 'Don't worry; he didn't feel anything.'" She drew back and grinned at him. "After that I knew you were the most caring, compassionate man. A guy just like my father. And just like him, I knew you'd make the best doctor in our class. I couldn't be more sure."

They'd kissed again, and by the time they snuck out of the bushes that night, soapsuds had formed a knee-high wall of bubbles around the fountain.

They'd grabbed hands, and this time they ran as fast as they could back to the dorms. Peter bid her a breathless good night with a promise. "I'll never love anyone like I love you, Brooke. No matter where life takes us, no matter what happens, we're supposed to be together; I know it more than I know anything else."

Brooke blinked and the memory was gone. Peter had proposed to her the next year, and as she'd stood before her family and friends pledging to love Peter forever, she believed with all her heart that he was right. They belonged together.

Never would she have guessed they would wind up like this.

"You need to say something." Peter spread his fingers across the legs of his work pants, and again his hands were shaking.

This time he crossed his arms. He looked at her, but not with passion or remorse.

And in that instant, what remained of Brooke's feelings for him lifted and took flight. Who was she kidding? The two of them had been finished for a long time. In his absence she'd felt happier than before, more free. That had to mean something. "Okay." Her eyes locked on his. "You're right. We've both seen it coming."

Peter nodded. "Let's make it easy on each other. The divorce-attorney thing." He stood and slipped his hands into his pockets. "I'll give you whatever you want, Brooke. But it'll be better for Maddie and—" he looked at their younger daughter— "Hayley . . . if we handle it in a friendly way."

A friendly way? Breaking a commitment to love and honor for a lifetime? How could that be even somewhat friendly? She dismissed the thoughts and forced herself to look at him. "Will . . . will you file soon?"

"I already have." His shoulders slumped some and he shifted his feet, anxious to leave. "I'm sorry, Brooke. I . . . I didn't see any other way."

"Well, then . . ." She stood also, but instead of going to him, she went to Hayley's bedside and took their daughter's fingers in hers. The shock was wearing off. In its place the sarcasm was back. "I guess it's all neat and tidy."

Peter's knees were trembling now, and Brooke wanted to ask if he was okay. But the answer didn't really matter. They moved in separate worlds now, and whether either of them would ever be okay again didn't seem to matter.

Hayley began to stir and her sad, slow cry filled the room. Peter took a few steps toward her, gave her toes a single light squeeze, and then looked one last time at Brooke. "I guess we'll be in touch."

"I guess."

His feet moved faster than before as he headed for the doorway. If he'd looked, he would've seen fresh tears in Brooke's eyes, tears of futility and failure, tears for an uncertain future. He did stop just before leaving, but he didn't turn around. Instead, in a voice free from undue emotion, he said only two words.

"Good-bye, Brooke."

And with that, the man she'd married, the man she'd given her heart to, walked out of her life forever.

# CHAPTER FIFTEEN

PETER SLIPPED INTO the first rest room he could find. His hands were shaking hard, and he'd been frantic to get out of there. She'd looked at his fingers, his knees. No way she could've missed the way he was losing it, but at least she hadn't asked any questions.

He'd told her the truth. The divorce had been coming long before Hayley's accident. It had nothing to do with his guilt, with the way he still wanted to rewrite the ending to that awful afternoon. And it certainly had nothing to do with his current love affair.

The one he was having with the painkillers.

He didn't use the bottles anymore. Too risky. He kept them in a plastic sandwich bag. That way he could reach them easier, and no one would know what they were or whom they belonged to if somehow he lost track of them at work. Or worse, if someone besides his nurse, Betty, saw him taking one or two.

Usually two, if he was honest with himself.

The thing was, they continued to work, continued to take away the biting, driving pain in his head, the constant wondering about what he could have done differently. A few pills and there it was, like magic. Peace and normalcy. The ability to see patients and function like a human being.

The ability to live as if his marriage weren't falling apart and he weren't moving into an apartment this weekend. As if Hayley weren't fighting back from brain damage because he'd lost track of her at a friend's party.

Yes, the pain pills were a great equalizer, the doorway back to the living.

He pulled the plastic bag from his pants pocket, fumbled with the opening, and whisked two pills straight to his mouth. Again he had no cup, so he turned the sink water on, bent over, and sucked in a quick swig. The pills would be working their wonder on his system in ten minutes.

He'd researched the medication a few times in the past weeks, and what he found told him he wasn't addicted. Not the way some people got addicted. Case studies told him of high-ranking businesspeople taking four and five pills every hour and still functioning.

Some days Peter took two pills an hour to get the same relief he used to get from one. But four or five? Peter laughed at the idea. No way he'd ever need that kind of medication, not when two were doing the job quite nicely. By the time he got to the car, he was feeling like himself again. He even hummed something by Kenny Chesney while he drove by the postal station and purchased a dozen packing boxes.

Not much in the house was exclusively his.

At home that evening he started in his office and packed his old medical books and two years' worth of *Sports Illustrated* magazines. He was halfway through the second bookcase when he had the first thought of Brooke since leaving the hospital. Years ago he'd written her letters and they were in a box somewhere in the office, weren't they? Letters he'd written to her the year they married.

Suddenly, strangely, as if his life depended on it, he stood up and glanced around the office. He had to find the letters, had to know how he'd felt about his wife back before everything changed. His eyes fell on the closet and he remembered. He'd put them in a box on the top shelf when they moved into this house.

What had he said to Brooke that day? "Some rainy Sunday afternoon let's take them down and read them together, okay?"

She'd slipped her arm around his waist and smiled. "I'd like that, Peter."

They'd had many rainy Sunday afternoons in the past years, but the box had stayed on the office-closet shelf, untouched. Was there a reason they hadn't made time for celebrating their love? Or had they gotten too caught up in their careers to care anymore?

Peter froze for a moment and studied his hands. He wasn't shaking—not yet. But the numb feeling around his heart and soul was wearing off. Otherwise he wouldn't have thought of the letters in the first place. He straightened his shoulders and ordered himself to be calm.

Twenty minutes until the next pills. He wouldn't take them sooner, wouldn't fall victim to addiction the way others had.

He wove his way around the half-filled boxes, opened the closet door, and peered at the top shelf. At the back on the right side was a simple gray box. He reached up, pulled it down, and stared at it, mesmerized as he crossed the room again and did a slow drop into his office chair.

The lid came off easily, but Peter hesitated. Why had he stopped writing letters to her? When had the business of life taken precedence over its beauty? And how come it had taken Hayley's accident and the undoing of his marriage to even remember about the letters?

As he peered inside the box, a heaviness settled around his heart. He remembered writing letters, but this? The box held a hundred folded pieces of paper—some, delicate-colored stationery sheets; others, scrawled across legal paper. He saw one near the top of the stack, written on a pale blue sheet, and carefully separated it from the others.

His fingers began to tingle—the first real sign that the medicine was wearing off. He told himself to read the letter first; the pills would be there. He opened the letter and found the beginning.

> Dear Brooke,
>
> It's early in the morning, too early for daylight, and I have just come off the longest hospital night shift in my life. Hour after hour I reminded myself that when my training's done, I don't want to work another night as long as I live. But still, the night wasn't all bad. Because no matter how many people walked through the emergency-room doors in the past hours, I didn't go ten minutes without thinking of you.
>
> I don't believe in God or a higher power, not with all my years of science and medicine. You know that. But here, as I write this, I could swear that something bigger than ourselves brought us together. How else could life have matched me up with someone like you? Maybe it's that whole fate thing or karma or reincarnation. But I could search the world over, interview every woman I might meet along the way, and I'm convinced I would never find one like you.

Peter took a break, looked at the date at the top-right corner, and calculated how old he must have been when he wrote it. Twenty-seven, almost twenty-eight. He would have been doing his internship, serving time in the emergency room at night; and Brooke would have been finishing med school. He moved his eyes down the page and found his place again.

> I love being married to you, Brooke; I love that you make me laugh and look forward to tomorrow. I love that we can play tennis and backgammon and still find time to talk medicine. My cases, your courses, and all our dreams about the future.
>
> Isn't it amazing, really? I've known you for three years, and I can't remember what it was like to live without you. In every way imaginable, life is turning out just like I hoped it would. The way I dreamed about ever since I was thirteen.
>
> You know about my father, how he walked out on us when I was eight years old. But I'm not sure I ever told you this: After he left I went four years believing marriage was a death trap, promising myself I'd

*never get married, never put my children through the pain my dad put us through.*

*But in my eighth-grade year, something changed.*

*My friend Steve had me over to his house a couple times that summer, and I saw something I'd never seen before. His parents sat together and talked together and held hands. They actually liked each other, and the feeling I had at his house was one I remember to this day. That was the year I started dreaming that maybe . . . just maybe . . . marriage could be a good thing if only it could be like it was for Steve's parents.*

*And now, in some unbelievable cosmic event, I'm in a marriage just like that, convinced that no matter what, I will always love you, always like you, and never, ever leave. Not in a million years. Our children—when we have children—will never know what it feels like to wake up day after day wondering whatever happened to their daddy. Because you're stuck with me forever, okay? Of course, I'm not worried about your leaving either, because you couldn't find anyone who makes a meaner cup of coffee.*

*Hey, Brooke, have I told you lately how proud I am of you? You're not only a brilliant med student, but one day you're going to make a wonderful doctor because you care about the little details. That and because you really care about people; I've seen that in your classwork. One day when you have your own practice, I'll be your biggest fan, honey. I can't wait.*

*Well, I'm tired and I want to sleep. But I'll leave this out so you can read it when you wake up. I love you more with every breath.*

*—Peter*

When he was finished reading the letter, his hands trembled more than before. He started at the beginning and read it again, his eyes narrowed, puzzled by the words he'd written. On the third time through, he was shaking too much to make out the writing. He set the blue pages down on the floor, pulled the plastic bag from his pants pocket, and grabbed two pills.

He popped them in his mouth in record time and watched the clock, watched the second hand march slow and steady around the circle. Four minutes . . . five. Sweat beaded across his forehead. His legs began to shake and his heartbeat doubled, pounding harder, faster, harder, faster.

Eight minutes, ten.

Peter felt his breathing quicken. Something was wrong. The pills usually worked in ten minutes, but this time . . . this time he was getting worse. Maybe he was having a heart attack or a stroke. Maybe he'd taken too many pills in too few hours, and now he was having a reaction.

Maybe he was dying.

"Come on . . ." He whispered the words. Relief would come; it had to. The pills guaranteed it.

But instead, sweat popped out along his arms, back, and upper chest, and at the twelve-minute mark it had soaked through his shirt. Did he need more medication? Was that the problem? Had the two-pill dose become too small or had he waited too long to take them? He felt like he was running a race, and again the floor began to move beneath him. But instead of pulling off to the side and catching his breath, he couldn't. Nothing could ease his pounding heart or the fact that he couldn't take a deep breath.

Maybe something was wrong with the pills; maybe they were defective, inactive for some reason. He opened the plastic bag again and fingered another two pills. *Come on, Peter, what could it hurt? Go ahead . . . take them . . . take them and you'll feel better.*

The voice in his head taunted him, the feel of it, angry and defiant. Angry enough that it scared him. He stared at the two additional pills. No, not yet. He released the hold he had on them and closed the plastic bag. He would wait; if he didn't have relief at the twenty-minute mark he'd take them for sure.

Thirteen minutes. His heartbeat stumbled some and shot into an irregular rhythm, one that could be dangerous if it didn't convert back to normal. He started high-chest breathing, never fully exhaling, never fully inhaling, grabbing quick mouthfuls of air and feeling like he was suffocating all at the same time.

The symptoms were familiar to him, but he'd never experienced them himself. He was short of breath, unable to find that sweetly calm pattern of breathing he'd always taken for granted.

And what was his heart doing? He felt his pulse. *Thud.* Silence. *Thud, thud, thud.* Long silence. *Thud, thud, thud.* Silence. *Thud, thud.* Long silence.

Too much silence.

He held his breath and tightened his stomach, pushing against the panic, urging his heart to beat and find a way back to a steady rhythm.

Six seconds . . . seven . . . suddenly his heart gave a loud *thud* and flipped into a normal pattern. Far too fast, but regular at least. Gradually, his legs and then his arms stopped shaking and his breathing slowed.

Fourteen minutes since he'd taken the pills.

Another minute and he could feel his body stop sweating, the wetness no longer running down his arms and ribs. He studied the clock, shocked, frightened.

A little more than seventeen minutes after taking the pills, his body was finally feeling normal again. Six minutes longer than it had ever taken before. And that was a bad thing. He stuffed the plastic bag of pills back into his pants pocket and exhaled. No, it was a terrible thing.

It meant he'd have to start taking them sooner or take more of them. And that would make it hard to lie to himself about whether he did or didn't have a problem. If he needed more than two pills every hour to feel okay, then he couldn't lie about it another day.

He had a problem.

But if he could wait out the seventeen minutes, maybe he wouldn't have to increase the dose. He'd survived, after all. It wasn't as if he couldn't go through that again if he needed to. It would be better than increasing the dose and winding up in some detox center.

The awful anxiety forgotten, Peter picked up the letter again. Key phrases jumped off the page at him, taunting him and telling him how far he'd fallen since those long-ago days.

*I love being married to you, Brooke; I love that you make me laugh
and look forward to tomorrow. . . . I will always love you, always like you,
and never, ever leave. Not in a million years. Our children—when we
have children—will never know what it feels like to wake up day after
day wondering whatever happened to their daddy.*

The words couldn't have been more foreign if they were in
Spanish. He went over each of those statements again and realized something sad. Not one of them was true today. Not one.
He hadn't loved being married to Brooke for a year or more,
hadn't found reasons to laugh or look forward to tomorrow
when the two of them were together. She was too caught up with
the kids and her career to care much for him, so he'd stopped
loving her a long time ago. He was pretty sure he didn't even like
her.

Brooke was different now. When was the last time they played
backgammon or talked medicine together? For that matter,
when was the last time they'd laughed at the same thing? No,
Brooke was too busy building her practice, making a name for
herself as the latest up-and-coming pediatrician in Bloomington.
Too busy giving herself to her patients to have anything left for
him.

And the girls?

He wasn't sure about Hayley, because with any kind of luck
she would probably forget he ever existed, forget she ever had a
father who let her wander out to a backyard pool by herself. But
Maddie would certainly grow up knowing what it felt like to live
without a father.

The fact should've made him sad, as though he'd failed somehow. Instead he felt nothing but inevitability, an understanding
of what his own father had gone through because sometimes
marriages died. And when that happened, kids simply had to
find a way to understand.

He gazed at the letter one more time. His belief system was
much different back then. Fate or karma? Cosmic twists? Rein-
carnation? How immature he'd been to believe in any of that.

Not a stitch of evidence existed for those beliefs. They were nothing but romantic meanderings, wishful thinking.

Long before Hayley was born he'd stopped believing anything of the sort. Life and everything about life could be explained by science. Scientific method or scientific discovery or scientific theory. One of the three.

Then, after September 11, he'd agreed to go to church with Brooke, and the strangest thing happened. The idea of God— one God, the creator of Earth and everything in it—began to make sense. Certain scientific discoveries or unexplainable phenomena were proof that God existed, after all. Creation, a great flood, a crucified Christ brought back to life, an empty tomb. All of it had suddenly seemed real, more real than a lifetime of textbooks and scientific ideas. Pastor Mark's sermons spoke to his heart and for a while, life had meaning and purpose that went beyond careers and relationships.

But at the same time, something began to die in his marriage. Peter huffed. That's what he got for going to church and believing in God. Not that faith caused them to grow apart, but it sure hadn't helped.

Peter returned the letter to the top of the stack and put the lid back on the box. Nothing good could come from reliving the way he'd felt about Brooke all those years ago. In every way he could imagine, she'd been a different person back then. The letters told him that much. But they told him something else, something sad and unavoidable.

He was a different person, too.

# CHAPTER SIXTEEN

By THE MIDDLE OF DECEMBER Ashley still hadn't seen a doctor. Luke's wedding was coming up fast, and then the holidays. Waiting a few more weeks wouldn't hurt. Besides, doctors wouldn't schedule new patients this late in the year. Not when they weren't showing symptoms, and Ashley wasn't.

Other than the way she missed Landon, she felt fine.

It was Monday afternoon, just before three o'clock, and Ashley was at her parents' house finishing a painting. Kari was back to modeling part-time, now that Ryan's football team was out of the play-offs, but today she and their mother had taken Jessie, Cole, and Maddie to lunch and the indoor play park so Ashley could work in the Baxters' upstairs guest room.

The day was cold, a few inches of snow on the ground and more expected that evening. Ashley loved the way winter made her feel; something about the cold weather drew her family together and made the Baxter house practically glow with warmth and love. The atmosphere was perfect for painting.

The picture she was working on was a combination of recent images that had touched her heart. The foreground showed the back of a small boy decked out in a firefighter costume. The child was holding hands with an older woman, who from the back looked a great deal like Irvel. The two were standing on the sidewalk in front of a country fire station, an American flag flying from a pole outside.

The little boy was saluting.

Ashley studied it, the way the sky came to life and made the flag more pronounced. It was good . . . very good. Landon would've loved it. She bit her lip and thought about him. Where was he and what was he doing? Was he busier now, training for the new position?

And did he ever think of her?

She let her eyes move down the painting to the quaint firehouse. Funny how so much of her art reflected Landon and his line of work. As if even the core of her creativity could do nothing but be inspired by him, even now when their lives were finally headed in different directions.

Something about the lawn in front of the firehouse wasn't quite right, and Ashley picked up her smallest paintbrush. She mixed pale yellow with a summery green color and added a few selective wisps to the grass. There. She sat back and studied it.

"Perfect." She whispered the word, and then she did the thing she'd taken to doing now that she was painting again. She hung her head, closed her eyes, and spoke the words out loud. "God, thank you for letting me paint. Use this piece, this work, to soften hearts for you."

When she opened her eyes, she stared at the painting a little longer and knew for sure. This one had to go to the gallery. After getting the results of her blood test earlier in the fall, she had decided not to continue exhibiting her work in New York. Instead, she'd taken a few of her pieces over to the best-known local art shop, the one near the university. The owner had been thrilled.

"I can see why they sold so well in Manhattan." The woman was in her forties, her shop a fixture in Bloomington for the past decade. "I'd love to sell your paintings."

"I won't be working full-time, but if you're willing, I'd like a place to showcase my work. Even if it's only one piece a month."

The woman had agreed, and now Ashley thought the piece she'd just finished would be the first one she'd take in. The shop was small, nothing like the intense, high-stakes, leather-and-mahogany storefront in New York City. Piece of My Art, it was called. And it was comfortable for Ashley's new, slower pace.

She heard a car in the driveway and smiled. They were home, and she could almost feel Cole's arms around her neck. They came through the garage door, and Ashley heard Cole announce that he was going to find his mommy.

"Where's my best mommy? Here I come!"

Ashley smiled. She and Cole were so much closer now; something else for which Landon would always deserve credit. Her son burst into the room and stopped when he saw her easel. Ever since he was a toddler, he'd known not to run up to her if she was painting.

"Still coloring, Mom?" He was bundled in a sweatshirt, turtleneck, and blue jeans.

"Nope. All finished." She set her paintbrush on her tray, wiped her hands on her apron, and climbed down off the high-backed stool. When she was a few feet from the easel she held out her hands and he ran to her, jumping into her arms. "How was the play park?"

"So fun, Mommy. Me and Maddie raced on the slides." His cheeks were ruddy, his dark blond hair matted and sweaty from playing so hard. "That's the bestest place. Even baby Jessie had fun with the other babies."

"Good." Ashley gave him a quick kiss on his forehead. He tasted salty, and she breathed in the smell of him, a mix of faint shampoo and buttered popcorn. "Sounds like me and you have to go soon."

"Maybe tomorrow!" Cole's eyes lit up, and he slid back to the floor.

"Maybe." She took his hand. Her brushes needed cleaning,

but they could wait a few minutes. "Let's go talk to Grandma and Aunt Kari."

They bounded down the stairs together. Ashley found her mother and sister talking in quiet tones in the kitchen. Her mother was dabbing at her eyes. Ashley stopped short of them and looked down at her young son. "Uh . . . Cole, why don't you go upstairs and play in the toy room."

"Okay." He ran past the sofa, where Jessie was lying asleep, still bundled in her jacket. He stopped short and spun around. "Hey, Grandma, can I play with the Lincoln Logs?"

"Yes, Cole."

Ashley made eye contact with her son. "Just clean up whatever you take out."

"All right." Cole flashed her a grin and he was off, bounding back up the stairs, oblivious to the drama playing out in the kitchen.

Ashley looked at her mother and stifled a deep sigh as she approached her. Since Hayley's accident, her mother still hadn't rebounded. Not to the cheerful, upbeat person she'd been before.

"Hey . . ." She smiled, hoping to lighten the mood. "Cole says you had a great time."

Kari turned and leaned against the kitchen counter. She had her hand on their mother's shoulder. "The kids were great."

"Good." Ashley shifted her gaze to her mother. "What's wrong?"

Their mother gave a quick shake of her head and bit her lip. She held up a single hand, as if to say she couldn't explain just yet. "I'm sorry."

Kari took over. "We stopped by Brooke's house on the way home to drop off Maddie."

"Is everything okay with Hayley?" Ashley felt her heart drop a notch. Hayley had gone home a few days ago to be with Brooke and Maddie.

"Yes." Kari looked at their mother's shoulder. "It was just

hard. It's one thing seeing Hayley in a hospital bed. Any progress looks good there. But seeing her strapped to a wheelchair . . ."

Their mother reached for a tissue and used it to dab her eyes. "She's doing so well. But still . . . I can't imagine the day when she'll ride that pink bike in the garage."

"That's why we have to pray." Ashley took another step closer and looked from her mother to her sister and back again. "God's going to heal her, Mom. I know it."

Their mother nodded. "That's not all." She sniffed and her red, swollen eyes met Ashley's. "Peter's moved out. I think I hoped it wasn't really going to happen. Like maybe Peter was only feeling guilty about Hayley, and that when he found out she was coming home, he might change his mind."

"And now Brooke isn't sure if she's going to Luke's wedding." Kari made a sad face in Ashley's direction. "Mom didn't cry until she got in the car. I think it was hard for her, pretending to be strong for Brooke."

"Mom . . ." This time Ashley came up along the other side of their mother and hugged her. "I'm sorry."

"It's my fault." Mom managed a weak smile. "I pray all the time for Brooke, and I know God hears me. One of these days everything will work out, and life will make sense." She hung her head for a moment. "All my life I've taught you kids to look for the joy, look for the reason to be happy despite your circumstances. And now . . ." Her voice cracked as she looked up again.

Ashley finished for her. "Now you need us to tell you, right?"

"I guess."

Ashley met Kari's eyes, and the two exchanged a look that said they were up to the task. If their mother needed them, they'd be there for her. The same way she'd always been strong for them through every twist and turn in their growing-up years.

"I think this calls for a cup of tea." Ashley turned and snatched the kettle from the stove top. She filled it with water, turned on the burner, and pulled three of her mother's delicate china cups from the antique hutch that stood between the kitchen and dining room. "Remember what you used to say?"

Mom couldn't resist a single short laugh. "Nothing in the world that God and a good cup of tea can't fix."

"That's it." Kari walked her to the table, and a few minutes later they were talking about Luke's wedding, doing just what their mother had always taught them.

Look for the good in any situation.

Even one as grim as Brooke's.

## CHAPTER SEVENTEEN

AFTER A WEEK of putting it off, Ashley and Cole went to visit Brooke and the girls. From the moment they pulled up out front, the visit was difficult. How could it be anything else? Everywhere Ashley looked she could picture her blonde niece, skipping across the grass, playing duck-duck-goose with Maddie and Cole, keeping up in footraces.

The memories inside Brooke and Peter's home would be just as painful. Ashley held Cole's hand as they made their way up the walk, but halfway there she stopped and touched her fingertips beneath Cole's chin. "Don't forget what we talked about."

"Okay." Cole lowered his eyebrows and gave her a serious nod. "Hayley's still not better even though she's home."

"Right." Ashley was tired, not quite up to the visit. "And she can't run and play like before. Not until—" she drew a slow breath and found her voice again—"not until she's better."

"Okay, Mommy."

Brooke opened the door then, and Ashley was struck by the look on her face. It was peace, perfect peace. Anguish and sorrow and pain, yes. But overriding all of the devastation she'd suffered that season was a peace that shone from the center of her being. "Hi, guys." She opened the door wider. "Thanks for coming."

Ashley's eyes met Brooke's and held for a moment. They'd talked about this, about how Cole would react since this was the first time he'd seen Hayley since her accident. Now they could only watch it play out.

Cole hugged Brooke and looked past her toward the dining room. "Where's Maddie?"

"Upstairs." Brooke roughed up Cole's bangs and grinned at him. "She's waiting for you."

Cole ran his tongue over his lips and shifted his weight from one small tennis-shoed foot to another. "Can I say hi to Hayley first, Aunt Brooke?"

"Yes, honey. She's at the table. She's just about to have apple-sauce." Brooke stooped down, her hands spread out above her knees. "Come with me, okay?"

Knots formed in Ashley's stomach, and she hugged herself to ward off the horrible feeling. "Sure, Cole. Let's go say hi."

Cole reached back for Ashley's hand. "Together, okay, Mommy?"

Again Ashley and Brooke exchanged a glance. Cole understood something had changed; he must have. Otherwise he would have run ahead to find Hayley, the way he'd done a hundred times before.

The three of them went to the dining room, and Cole stood back for a moment, clinging to Ashley's hand, his chin on his chest as he peered at Hayley. She was strapped to a small wheelchair, her head angled sharply to one side. Ashley followed Cole's gaze as he looked at her hands, hanging small and limp against the wheelchair arms, and as his eyes lifted to her mouth, which hung open.

"I think she's hungry." Cole looked at Brooke.

"It's okay." Brooke's eyes glistened some. "She can eat after you say hi."

One finger at a time, Cole released his hold on Ashley's hand,

and with nervous steps he walked the few feet separating them until he stood in front of Hayley's wheelchair. Ashley studied her niece, the way her eyes followed Cole. She seemed to notice him. Yes, but there wasn't a glimmer of recognition. Ashley tapped Cole's shoulder and nudged him forward, her tone soft so it wouldn't startle Hayley. "Talk to her, honey. She sees you."

Cole looked at Ashley over his shoulder. "What do I say?"

His question tore at her heart, and she could only wonder how it made Brooke feel. Ashley gave a quick look at her older sister and searched for the right words. "Pretend she's healthy, Cole." Again her voice was a quiet whisper. "That's the best way to talk to her."

Cole nodded and pulled himself up a bit taller than before. Then he turned and leaned closer to Hayley. "I'm glad you're back home, Hayley. I missed you when you were gone."

A noise gurgled up from Hayley's throat, and her mouth lifted into a smile.

"Cole! See." Brooke gave him a half hug from behind. "She likes when you talk to her."

Ashley was thinking the same thing. Cole looked back at Brooke. "Is it okay if I touch her?"

"Yes, honey." Brooke brought her fingers to her mouth and hung her head for a moment. "Please, Cole. Go ahead and touch her."

Hayley was moving her head now, turning it in that slow robotic way from one side of the chair to the other. From past experience, Ashley knew she was about to cry. But the moment Cole reached out and set his fingers on top of Hayley's hand, she grew still.

"Hayley, can I tell you something?"

The little girl lifted her eyes to Cole's, and for a moment she looked almost well again.

Cole swallowed big. "I talked to Jesus about you, Hayley." He worked his fingers around hers and held her hand, the way he'd done so often before her accident, she the little cousin, he the big-brother type. "I asked Jesus to make you better so we can run races again, okay?"

The corners of Hayley's mouth lifted again, and she uttered a short sound that could've passed for a laugh.

"'emember, Hayley?" Cole stuck his thumbs in his ears and waved his fingers at her. It was something he'd seen Helen do at Sunset Hills Adult Care Home, the sign the old woman made to show that one or more of the people at the table with her had perhaps lost their mind. Cole thought the gesture was hysterical. When he'd showed it to Hayley and Maddie a few months ago at the Lake Monroe picnic, both girls had fallen to the ground laughing.

Now, Hayley watched Cole with a look that was more intent than before. When her eyes lifted to see his waving fingers and his thumbs stuck in his ears, she began to laugh. Not a normal laugh, by any means. But a laugh that was more genuine, more like Hayley than anything Ashley had heard since the accident. She glanced at Brooke and knew. Her sister had seen it, too. Something about Cole's communication was taking Hayley to a cognitive level she hadn't so far reached.

Encouraged by Hayley's laughter, Cole kept waving his fingers and making a face, and this time he also pumped his legs and made a goofy circle around Hayley. Once more Hayley reacted, the tone of her laughter changing, becoming more natural with every passing second.

Finally Cole stopped, breathless and grinning. He went to Hayley's side, leaned in, and kissed her on the cheek. "I love you, Hayley."

Her eyes found him, and this time Ashley was sure. Hayley knew him, remembered him. Even through the fog of brain damage the bond between the two was intact. Hayley made a throaty sound, almost as if she wanted to answer him.

Cole patted her on the head and gave her a smile as genuine as it was sweet. "I'm glad you're okay, Hayley. I'll come back later and we can play more."

With that, he flashed a grin at Ashley and Brooke, his hesitancy forgotten, his childlike assessment of his cousin all that the moment needed. Never mind that she wasn't the same child she'd once been; never mind the distance she had to cover in order to find her way back to that place. The way Cole saw it, if Hayley could laugh at his jokes, she was just fine.

When they could no longer hear his feet pattering up the stairs toward Maddie's room, Ashley sat across from Hayley, and Brooke, beside her.

Brooke looked at her and lifted her shoulders. Tears filled her eyes, but rather than cry she let loose a laugh that released the tension. "Okay, then." She dabbed at the wetness on her cheeks. "When he kissed her, I thought I was going to lose it."

"Me, too." Ashley sniffed. "I'm glad I brought him."

"That's why she's home." Brooke drew a long breath and shifted her eyes to Hayley. "So things can start feeling normal again."

Snow was falling outside, and a vanilla candle burned on the kitchen counter. Brooke began to spoon-feed applesauce to Hayley. "She isn't stiff anymore; did you notice?" Now that they were sitting across from each other, Ashley could see that Brooke's eyes looked tired, the lines around her eyes more pronounced than before. But there was no denying the hope in her voice.

"Yes." Ashley looked at her niece, the way her mouth hung to one side, how her head rested motionless against the back of the wheelchair. The way to feel comfortable around this new Hayley was to never picture the way she'd looked before the accident. Only then could the situation seem positive. "She doesn't seem like she's in pain."

"It's the medication." Brooke dipped the spoon into the applesauce and held a small amount near Hayley's mouth. "They've found the right mix of muscle relaxants and antiseizure drugs. It's been wonderful, really."

Ashley crossed her legs and managed a smile. *Wonderful?*

Wonderful would be the day Hayley could jump down from the wheelchair and run upstairs *with* Cole. The day she could stick her thumbs in her ears and wave her fingers right back at him. But that wasn't what Brooke needed to hear. "I'm glad, Brooke." Ashley reached across the table and squeezed Brooke's fingers. "She's making strides for sure."

Brooke nodded and moved the spoon closer to Hayley's lips. As Hayley felt it, she bobbled her head ever so slightly toward the spoon and opened her mouth wider than before. Brooke eased the spoon past her lips and used the roof of Hayley's mouth to brush the applesauce off the spoon. Ashley watched the process, aching at how painfully slow it was.

*God, she's in there somewhere. Heal her, Lord . . . please.*

A verse flashed in Ashley's mind, one Pastor Mark had shared with them that past Sunday: *Now to him who is able to do immeasurably more than all we ask or imagine, to him be glory forever and ever, amen.*

*Yes, amen, God. That's exactly what I know you'll do with Hayley. Immeasurably more than all we could ask or imagine.* A sense of peace washed over Ashley's heart. She could do nothing but believe it was true, that God would continue healing Hayley the same way he continued to work on all of those who loved him.

"Look!" Brooke's tone was shrill and upbeat. "She's swallowing, Ash. She's really doing it. Do you know how huge that is?"

"Wow!" Ashley watched her little niece, the way she made slow smacks with her mouth until the applesauce slid off her tongue down her throat. "Can she drink yet?"

"This morning she took the smallest sip from one of her old sippy cups." Brooke looked at Hayley, and Ashley was struck by the love in her sister's eyes. A love stronger than anything she'd shown before the accident. "I'd say she's at the developmental stage of about a four-month-old."

"Mmm-hmm." Ashley was sad again. Glancing up, she could see the kitchen and with it another dozen memories of Hayley jumping up onto the counter to grab a cup for water or running in and snatching two cookies before Brooke could stop her. Hayley had been a sunbeam of light and little-girl laughter, but now . . .

Ashley blinked and the memories disappeared. *God, help me focus . . . help me be positive for all of us.*

Brooke set the spoon back in the applesauce and dabbed a napkin at the corners of Hayley's mouth. She was going on about how great the situation was. " . . . and her doctors say we should keep seeing improvements for the first two years. Some drowning victims make giant strides, and others make very minimal advancement." She looked at Ashley again. "But after Hayley got her vision back . . . anything's possible, Ash. Really. She's relearning a month of behavior every week to ten days."

The conversation fell quiet for the most part, Brooke intent on helping Hayley finish at least half the jar of applesauce. When she was done feeding her, Brooke cleaned the child's nose tube and reinserted it. Ashley could only watch for small moments at a time.

Next, Brooke went to the refrigerator, pulled out a bag of medicine vials, complete with attached clean needles. Expertly, Brooke transferred two vials of medicine into a small tube taped to Hayley's lower arm.

Ashley marveled at her sister's ability. She was as gentle and patient as anyone Ashley had ever seen. All while remarking occasionally about how well Hayley looked or how far she'd come or how she was making more sounds lately, trying to remember how to talk.

"You're trying, aren't you, Hayley girl?" Brooke nuzzled her nose against Hayley's.

In return, Hayley made her slow laughing sound.

"That's right, baby. Mommy knows you want to talk."

Ashley looked on, amazed. How much her older sister had changed in the past two years. Watching Brooke work with Hayley, seeing in person the light in her sister's expression, the hope in her voice, Ashley was struck by a thought. Here, before her eyes, was something good that had come out of the disaster of September 11. If it hadn't been for that awful day, Brooke never would've felt driven to come to church, to learn more about God, and eventually to develop a personal relationship with him.

A silent shudder made its way through Ashley. How awful, how desperate the situation with Hayley would've been without the hope and joy Christ brought to the picture.

When Brooke was finished, she unstrapped Hayley from the chair, cradled her in her arms, and motioned at Ashley. "Let's sit in the living room."

Ashley followed, mesmerized at the way Hayley's eyes stayed locked on her mother's face while the two of them sat in an oversized leather recliner. The moment they were situated, Brooke began working Hayley's right foot, flexing it first up and then out in a series of gentle moves that were obviously a part of some physical-therapy program.

Brooke smiled at Ashley. "What do you hear about Luke and Reagan's wedding?"

Ashley angled her head, her eyes locked on her sister's. "Mostly that you're thinking about staying home."

"I probably should." The light in Brooke's eyes dimmed some. "I won't have Peter to help me with the girls, and with Hayley, well . . . it might be too much."

"Can she . . ." Ashley hesitated. She hated asking too many questions about Hayley, in case she hit on an area that might be hard for Brooke. "Can she travel? Is it okay for her?"

"Definitely." Brooke released Hayley's foot and began working the left one. "She's very stable. I would have to keep her in a car seat on the plane, but she's completely mobile. Anything I do for her here—her meds, her therapy, her feeding tube—all of it can be done somewhere else." Brooke looked down and cooed at Hayley. "Right, sweetie? You could hit the road anytime, huh?"

Ashley didn't understand. "So why not go, Brooke? We want you there."

"Because the rest of you are spending a week in New York City, aren't you?"

"Yes." They would be staying from one Saturday to the next, through Christmas. "Erin and Sam, Kari and Ryan and Jessie, Mom, Dad, me and Cole . . . all of us fly in Saturday afternoon."

"See, that's just it. I don't want Hayley away from her doctors for that long. So if the wedding's on Wednesday, that means I'd be flying in by myself on Tuesday, and back out Friday, the day after Christmas." She lifted her eyes. "I'm not real excited about that, Ashley. It's one thing to care for Hayley. But Maddie *and* Hayley . . . by myself . . . traveling to a place as crazy busy as Manhattan? That might be too much."

"Hey . . ." Ashley leaned closer. "I was serious about taking Maddie to *The Lion King*. She could fly in with me and Cole on Saturday. Then when you arrive, you and Hayley could share a room with us. That way you could focus your attention on Hayley."

"Hmmm." Brooke considered that for a moment, and she lifted her eyebrows. "That's an idea."

"It's a great idea." Ashley rested her chin on her hands. "Even if you only came for a few days, Brooke. It won't be the same without you."

Brooke began massaging the muscles in Hayley's calves. "Did I tell you I'm going back to work?"

"Work?" Ashley lowered her eyebrows.

"Yes. Two days a week." She looked at Ashley. "I have a nurse coming to stay with Hayley those days." She hesitated. "I have no choice, Ashley. With Peter gone I'll have to bring in some money. His child support won't be enough."

"Child support?" Ashley hadn't even thought of the possibility that Brooke would face financial struggles, too. It was one more reason to feel depressed about her sister's situation. "So he's serious about the divorce?"

"He's seen an attorney. He doesn't want a fight; he'll give me half of everything and let me stay in the house, but still . . ." She drew Hayley closer to her chest. "We were used to living on two doctors' salaries. Eventually I'll need to work at least three days a week."

Ashley clenched her teeth and swallowed her anger. Couldn't Peter see what he was doing to Brooke and the girls? Was he so blind? "I'm sorry, Brooke."

"It's okay. I can feel God telling me that somehow he'll get me through. I hang on to that every minute of the day. Even when I'm crying my eyes out. Believe me."

"So two days a week, huh? You've already got it lined up?"

"Yes. But I don't start until after the first of the year." A slow spark filled her eyes. "You know what? About the wedding, why not?" Hayley had fallen asleep in her arms. She stood, struggling to hold the child against her chest. "Can you take that blanket from the back of the couch and lay it on the floor for me?"

"Sure." Ashley did as Brooke asked.

"Thanks." She laid Hayley on her side and bunched up the blanket to keep her propped that way. When Hayley was settled, Brooke flipped a switch and flames in the gas fireplace sprang to life. The effect was wonderful, especially against the backdrop of falling snow through the adjacent windows and with the candle burning in the next room.

Brooke sat on the sofa a few feet from Ashley. "Are you sure you could take Maddie?"

"Of course." The idea was taking root, giving Ashley a reason to smile without having to work at it. "Cole loves Maddie. He'll be less bored on the flight if he has his cousin with him."

"And I truly want to see Luke get married. He and Reagan have been through so much." Brooke leaned against the sofa, her expression wistful. "Makes me think of you and Landon Blake."

Ashley felt her smile fade. "Yeah." No matter how much time passed, his name would always make her heart hurt.

Brooke studied her. "I haven't heard much about him lately. Is he coming home when he's done his year?"

"No." Ashley didn't want to talk about Landon, but Brooke needed to know. She'd been too involved with Hayley to realize what was happening outside the hospital walls. The situation with Landon was one of the things she had missed.

"Really?" Brooke's eyebrows came together, her expression curious. "You were in Manhattan a few months ago, right? Wasn't he planning to come home?"

"He was, but . . ." Ashley folded her arms and pressed them against her middle. "He got a promotion." She tried to smile, but her mouth wouldn't obey. "He'll be a captain after the first of the year."

"So . . ." A grin tugged at Brooke's lips. "Does that mean you'll be spending more time in New York?"

Ashley shook her head, and then leaned back against the arm of the sofa. It was no use hiding the truth from Brooke; she would find out sooner or later. "Things are over between us, Brooke. They have been for a few months now."

Pain filled Brooke's eyes, and she reached out and took hold of Ashley's hands. "Oh, Ash, I'm sorry." She hesitated and for the first time that day she looked defeated. "What is it about love, anyway? How come we can't figure out how to make it last?"

"Life is never that easy."

"No—" Brooke looked at Hayley, sleeping on the floor— "it isn't, is it?" She found Ashley's eyes again. "I really thought you and Landon would find a way."

"Me, too." Ashley's eyes stung.

"So . . ." Brooke released Ashley's hands and searched her face. "What happened? Can I ask?"

"Well . . ." Ashley's eyes were brimming now, making it hard for her to see.

"Hey." Brooke scooted closer, her eyes never leaving Ashley's. "You don't have to tell me; it's okay."

Ashley shook her head. "No, it's not that." She blinked and

the tears subsided. "Nothing happened between Landon and me; that's not the problem."

"It's not?" Brooke sat back a bit.

"No." Ashley dried her cheeks with her fingertips. "I love Landon more than ever."

Brooke narrowed her eyes. "Did he . . . did he find someone else?"

"No." Suddenly Ashley knew it was time. Time to share the bigger truth with Brooke, the one that she'd only shared with her mom and dad and Luke and Landon until now. "It's me, Brooke. Something's wrong with me, and I can't . . . I had to let him go."

The color drained from Brooke's face. "Something's wrong with you?"

Ashley didn't want to keep her waiting. She steeled herself against any more tears and leveled her gaze at her sister. "Remember when I went to Paris? I came back with Cole, but I never talked much about his father."

Brooke's eyes were wide, fearful. "I remember. None of us wanted to ask, unless you wanted to talk about him."

"Right." Ashley pulled her legs up onto the sofa and hugged her knees. "He was an artist, someone famous. He . . . he was married, but he was very active outside his home."

The surprise showed in Brooke's eyes, but she said nothing.

"I was taken by him, I guess, impressed by his talent." Ashley's stomach hurt. The story never got easier to tell. "After a while I started sleeping with him, and before too long, I was pregnant."

Brooke was patient, her expression sympathetic as she waited for the rest of the story.

"I found out later that he had affairs with men and women." Ashley wrinkled her nose. The words tasted bitter on her tongue. "Anyway, a few months back I got a call from someone at the art gallery in Paris." She closed her eyes for a moment and then met Brooke's stare, willing her to think the same of her when she was finished telling the story. "Cole's father died of AIDS, Brooke. I was on a list of people who might be affected."

Brooke's lower jaw fell and her mouth fell open. "No, Ash."

"Yes." Her eyes were dry now. This part of the story was simple, dispassionate, factual; it was the part about losing Landon that broke her heart. "I went to a clinic an hour outside of Bloomington and had my blood tested." She nodded. "I'm HIV-positive, Brooke. And that's why I can't be with Landon." Her eyes grew watery again. "I told him to move on with his life. I can't risk infecting him, Brooke. I won't do it."

No words came for Brooke. Instead she wrapped her arms around Ashley's neck and pulled her close, holding her for a long time before drawing back and searching her eyes. "You're serious?"

"Yes."

"Oh . . ." Brooke gasped and put her fingers to her mouth. "What about Cole?"

"I had him tested at his last checkup. I told the doctor I wanted it for his records, and the man didn't ask any questions." Ashley inhaled. "Cole's fine. His blood is normal."

"And what about you? Are you hooked up with a good doctor?" Brooke barely took time to grab a breath. She sat up straighter and continued. "We have several specialists here because of the university, and any of them would have access to the latest medicine, the latest technology, so you couldn't be in a better place. Is it Dr. Mayer in the west medical building or—"

"Brooke." Ashley held up her hand and gave a short shake of her head. "I'm not seeing a doctor yet." She let her knees fall into a cross-legged position. "I'm taking protein supplements, vitamins to boost my immune system. I want to wait until after the holidays before starting treatment."

"What?" Brooke's eyes flew open twice as wide as before. She stood and paced the length of the sofa and back, her eyes never leaving Ashley's. "What are you saying, Ashley?" She kept her voice quiet, even though her tone was intense. "You mean you've known you're HIV-positive for months now and haven't seen a doctor?"

"Now you sound like Dad."

"Dad knows?" The revelations seemed to be hitting Brooke like a series of bombs. "Dad knows and he hasn't forced you into one of the local offices?"

"He's tried."

Brooke stopped pacing. "So what's the reason? Don't you realize that early treatment can keep AIDS from developing for years, decades, even?"

"I've researched it." Ashley rested her elbows on her knees. "It's okay if I wait." Her voice dropped some. "I guess I'm not ready for the side effects. Not ready to feel different because of some strange chemicals in my blood."

Brooke opened her mouth as if she wanted to argue with Ashley, but then her shoulders fell and her lips came together. "Okay. I understand. But get in as soon as the holidays are over, Ashley. I mean it." The fight was gone from her voice. "Anything could trigger AIDS if you're not in treatment."

"I know."

For a moment neither of them said anything. The only sound was Hayley's quiet snore, the distant laughter of Cole and Maddie, and the soft whir of the fire. Finally Brooke pursed her lips and looked at Ashley. "What does Landon think about it?"

"He wants to marry me." Ashley squinted against the stinging in her eyes. "He took the promotion because I refused his ring." She folded her hands. If only her stomach didn't hurt so much. "I won't put him at risk, Brooke; I won't do it."

"Well, then, there's another reason to see a specialist."

"What?" Ashley moved her feet back to the floor. She sat near the edge of the sofa and looked at her older sister. Her heart beat suddenly faster than before. "Why would that give me another reason to get treatment?"

"Because these days they can work with couples, Ashley. So that Landon wouldn't have to face any significant risk."

Their conversation continued for another hour, but through every part of it, Ashley could only think of what Brooke had said. They had ways to work with couples. It was something she hadn't considered, not once since receiving her diagnosis. HIV was a death sentence for most people; of course Landon would be at risk.

But if he wouldn't be . . .

Ashley tried to tell herself that the revelation didn't mean anything, because every case was different. And of course it would still be risky for her and Landon to marry. And most of all, he'd committed his future to New York City, a place where she couldn't possibly live—healthy or not. A city like that would kill her creativity.

But she couldn't shake the feeling of hope that had come over her. A feeling that had started with Cole's interaction with Hayley and continued on with the idea that maybe—just maybe—her blood wouldn't represent a risk for Landon.

When the visit was over, Brooke and the girls moved to the door to tell Ashley and Cole good-bye. Maddie pushed Hayley's wheelchair, and once more Cole walked in front of her, turning every few seconds to make a silly face or say a silly rhyme. Anything to make Hayley laugh.

In the car, Cole waited until he was buckled in. Then he said, "I thought you said she was hurt, Mommy. But she's the same old funny Hayley."

Ashley did a sad, quiet huff, her heart bursting with gratitude for the simplicity of her son's love.

"Yes, Cole. Just the same."

And as she thought about their visit and Cole's easy acceptance of Hayley's new condition, Ashley could only beg God for one thing.

That however much ground Hayley did or didn't gain over the next few years, everyone who met her would see what Cole had seen. That deep down she wasn't a brain-damaged child or a drowning victim fighting various stages of vegetative behavior.

But rather she was simply Hayley. The same old funny Hayley.

✎

The day had been so good, Brooke couldn't resist. She'd had time to think about the situation with Peter, and these days her anger toward him rarely surfaced. Yes, he'd made a mistake. He'd taken his eyes off Hayley when he should've been watching her. He'd taken her life jacket off instead of keeping it on her like he'd promised he would do. But obviously the pain of what had happened that day was hurting him as much as it was hurting her.

And clearly he wasn't handling the pain.

She wasn't sure if her family's suspicions about the pain meds were founded, but she could see in Peter's face that he was tormented. In the past days more often than not she would be working with Hayley or helping Maddie with her bath and an image would come to mind. Peter, the way he looked that night at the hospital room, holding on to Hayley's feet as she cried. The helpless look in his eyes and the vacant stare as he bid them both good-bye.

He wasn't trying to destroy their family; he himself was already destroyed, devastated by what had happened. Since that awful Saturday he'd done nothing but spin wildly out of control. And even though they'd been at odds before Hayley's accident, Brooke couldn't find it in her heart to hate him now.

Tonight, with their home so warm and inviting, Brooke wanted a second chance, an hour or two to welcome Peter back, to take him in her arms and rock away the pain and horror of all they'd been through. She thought of his awful behavior, the cold way he'd treated her, and she knew she wasn't feeling these things in her own strength. But living in the hospital, watching Hayley regain her sight and find a connection with her family again, had changed something in her heart.

Whatever it was, Brooke simply had no room in her life for hatred.

Maddie was watching a video in the next room, and beside her, Hayley sat strapped to her wheelchair. Maddie had her hand on top of Hayley's, her fingers making soft circles on Hayley's wrist.

Brooke looked in on them and the feeling in her heart swelled. *Peter should be here; if he could see this, feel it, maybe we'd still have a chance.* . . .

She didn't wait another minute. Turning her back on the girls, she headed to the kitchen and picked up the phone. Working from a slip of paper where she'd written his new number, she dialed Peter and waited.

"Hello?" He sounded tired, as though maybe he'd been sleeping.

"Oh." She hesitated. "Did I wake you?"

"Brooke?" Irritation tinged his voice. "What time is it?"

She shot a look at the clock on the microwave. "Not quite eight."

"Okay." He sounded more awake but no less irritated. "What's up?"

"Well," Brooke's courage melted like the vanilla candle. She could no longer remember why she was calling or what had been so pressing that she'd had to call him. "I guess I wondered what you were doing." A tense pause hung between them. "We're all settled and, I don't know, there's a fire in the fireplace and the girls are . . ." Her words ran together and she clenched her fists. "The girls are awake and I thought maybe you could join us for an hour or so and . . ."

Silence.

"Peter?"

"Brooke, I'm half asleep. I don't think . . ." He exhaled hard. "Not tonight."

"Okay, I just thought . . ." Her voice trailed off and anger replaced her goodwill. "Never mind, Peter. Go back to sleep."

"Don't be mad, Brooke. I was tired, okay?" A sound that seemed half moan, half cry came from him. "I want to keep a friendly front. For the girls, anyway."

"A front?" Was that what he thought this was? Her way of keeping up a good front for the girls? or at least for Maddie? All the hurt from the past few months came back threefold. "Good-bye, Peter."

She hung up before he had a chance to say anything else, before his words could do more damage. Her angry mood lasted until she rejoined the girls. If Peter didn't want to be part of the family, so be it. She could do as he asked; she could put up a friendly front. But next time she would know better than to believe they had a chance to ever reconnect again.

"Hi, Mommy." Maddie pointed at the television screen. "It's the best part, where the prince comes back and they live happily ever after."

Brooke slipped in between the girls and put one arm around Maddie, her other arm alongside Hayley's. As the movie played out, the joy from earlier today soothed her soul, and her anger faded once more. Peter wasn't being himself; he was in too much pain to be part of their lives. At least for now.

After she tucked Maddie in and made sure Hayley was safely situated in her bed, she wandered about the house remembering. She remembered the beginning of her days with Peter, the promises they'd made to each other, and the way he'd wanted nothing more than to be a father.

No wonder her heart had grown soft toward Peter. He was the father of her children, the love of her life. Yes, he'd walked out but he couldn't stay gone, couldn't stay away forever. Even now—though it went against all reason—her desire to pray for him was stronger than her desire to hate him.

*That has to be you, God.*

*Yes, daughter, pray . . . pray often.*

The response was a subtle whisper, a reassurance that, indeed, her feelings of hope and grace toward her husband were nothing she had mustered up on her own.

Brooke closed her eyes. *Be with him, God. He's been mean and awful, but I know he has to be hurting. Maybe even hurting himself.* She remembered how his hands had trembled back at the hospital that night, the night he told her he wanted a divorce. Maybe her family's suspicions were right; maybe he was taking something to numb the pain.

A sigh made its way through her clenched teeth. *Help me look for ways, Lord, ways to include him, to bring him back to me and the girls. Sometimes it all feels so hard.*

A faint scent of vanilla brushed her senses and reminded her of the day's warmth, the progress she'd seen with Hayley. Peter would come around eventually, and when he did, he would see how wrong he'd been. She yawned and rolled onto her side. Watching *Cinderella* with the girls had been the closest thing to a normal night they'd shared since Hayley's accident. Maddie had been so sweet, clasping her hands and squealing about how wonderful it was that the prince had returned, how happy that life would have a happy ending after all.

As sleep found her, Brooke allowed herself to remember the days when Peter wouldn't have considered missing such a night, back when he'd been every bit her Prince Charming. Her last thought was a simple one. A wish, really. That somehow God would change Peter's heart—the same way he'd changed hers—and that one day soon they'd stumble onto the best part.

The part where the prince would come back and they would all live happily ever after.

# CHAPTER EIGHTEEN

FROM THE MOMENT THEY ARRIVED in Manhattan, Elizabeth felt better than she had since summer.

The family had four adjoining rooms at the Marriott Marquis in the theater district of Manhattan's Midtown West area—Kari and Ryan and Jessie in one room, Erin and Sam next to them, Ashley and Cole and Maddie in the third room, and Elizabeth and John in the fourth. Brooke and Hayley would stay with Ashley when they arrived on Tuesday.

Once they were all checked in, they had dinner at the hotel and firmed up plans for the week.

"This is gonna be the bestest fun time," Cole announced that night.

And so it was.

On Sunday, Luke and Reagan joined them on a tour of the city, complete with a visit to the Statue of Liberty and a cruise around the harbor. It was the first time Elizabeth had been to the city since the terrorist attacks, and she and the others were quiet as they took in the changed skyline.

"Still makes you want to cry, doesn't it?" She leaned her head on John's shoulder, her voice a whisper.

"It really happened." John narrowed his eyes and gazed at the place where the twin towers had stood. "Until you see it for yourself, I guess it's hard to believe."

The twelve of them had an early dinner together at a place near Central Park, and then walked to the New Amsterdam Theatre on Forty-second Street for a performance of *The Lion King*.

When they were filing in, Ashley leaned over and kissed Elizabeth's cheek. "Thanks, Mom . . . for making this happen." She held Cole's hand as they made their way down to their seats. "Cole's never seen anything like this."

When they were all seated, the lights dimmed, and the theater came to life with a procession of dramatically costumed actors, each playing an animal from the play.

"Hey, Grandma." Cole tugged on Elizabeth's sleeve. "They're real! I can't believe they're real!"

Elizabeth wasn't sure which was more fun to watch, the stunning drama taking place on the stage or the awe and wonder on the faces of her grandchildren. In the end, she split her time watching both, grateful that from the beginning of the play, Maddie and Cole were captured by the story.

Afterwards they walked down Forty-second Street and found an ice-cream parlor where they relived the play's highlights.

"We'll have to come back in a few years when our little girl can enjoy it." Erin took Sam's hand and grinned.

Elizabeth raised an eyebrow. "Little *girl?*"

"Wait a minute." John lowered his ice-cream cone. "Are you making an announcement?"

Sam chuckled and looked at the faces around the table. "We found out the day before we left. The birth mother is having a girl."

"Yay!" Kari held Jessie's hand in the air and made a victory hoot. "A girl cousin for you, Jessie." She high-fived Erin across the table. "That's perfect."

"Hey, boy cousins are good, too." Cole crossed his arms and

194

made a half-serious pout. "I'm the only boy cousin in the family."

"Don't worry, Cole." Ashley grinned at Erin and Sam. "They'll adopt a boy next, right guys?"

Erin laughed and slipped her hand into Sam's. "Sounds fine to me."

Ashley nodded at Kari and Ryan. "And I'm sure Aunt Kari will have a boy one day, too, right?"

"If I have anything to say about it." Ryan chuckled and kissed Kari on the cheek.

"Do we have a name for this newest little granddaughter?" John anchored his elbows on the table.

Elizabeth studied him. In light of the moment, he looked younger, more full of life than he had in years.

Erin and Sam exchanged a look, and Erin grinned at the others. "Amy Elizabeth." She looked at Sam again. "We came up with that on the plane ride here."

"Really?" Elizabeth felt giddy, her heart even lighter than before. Amy Elizabeth? A grandchild with her own name? She smiled at Erin and Sam. "I'm honored."

"That's beautiful." Kari punctuated the statement by raising her ice-cream cone in the air. As she did, her top scoop bobbled off the cone and splattered chocolate on her white shirt. Kari peered down at her blouse and muttered, "Very nice, Kari."

Ryan stifled a laugh, but then couldn't contain it. He patted Kari on the back, "We'll call this one Grace."

"I've called her that since she was four." John laughed. "If only her agent could see what goes on when the cameras are off!"

Kari stood and did a little curtsy for the group, and then held up a finger as she headed for a stack of napkins at the front counter.

Everyone was still laughing, and the conversation splintered into several silly discussions. Elizabeth watched them, the happy way they looked, and she wished with all her heart that the moment would last forever. They were together, whole and healthy, this side of so many uncertain times: Erin and Sam's marriage troubles; Ashley's jaded attitude after Paris; Luke and Reagan's separation, the way they almost missed out on finding each other again; Kari's traumatic times with Tim and his murder and her struggle about when to let go of her husband's memory, when to move on and let herself be with Ryan the way she'd dreamed since she was a schoolgirl.

Watching her family now, Elizabeth was reminded of a Scripture about Mary, the mother of Jesus. The Bible mentions that after Jesus was born, Mary pondered what was happening around her and treasured the moment in her heart. That was Elizabeth now, knowing that her family was together only for a short time before life would take them in different directions again.

But here, now, celebrating Christmas and Luke's wedding in New York City, knowing the joy of being together, Elizabeth pondered every moment and treasured the sum of them in her heart. Where she would treasure them until she drew her last breath.

Monday sped past as the family took a tour bus to Niagara Falls, over the bridge to the Canadian side, where the view was amazing. The trip would take six hours each way and would make for a full day with only two hours at the falls, but Elizabeth watched her family and didn't think any of them minded. The ride was pleasant and gave them all a chance to visit, commenting often on the sights and the excitement ahead with Luke's wedding.

They arrived at the falls at just after one o'clock, and despite the cold weather, the sun was brilliant overhead, glistening off the ice that floated at the basin. The mist from the falls was thick enough that they purchased rain slickers for the group and walked along the pathway overlooking the dramatic flow of water.

Maddie grabbed hold of the handrail and peered over the

stone wall at the mighty force of water. Her eyebrows lifted and in a voice only Elizabeth and John could hear, she said, "I'm glad Hayley didn't fall in there."

Elizabeth's heart slipped to her knees. She lowered herself to Maddie's level and soothed her hand over the child's hair. "Me, too, sweetie."

"Know what?" Maddie took hold of Elizabeth's hand, her eyes wide and earnest.

"What?" Elizabeth kissed Maddie's cheek and silently thanked God for healing her of her fevers. She couldn't imagine life without this precious granddaughter.

"Hayley can't swim anymore." Maddie looked over her shoulder at the roaring water rushing down the falls. "Her arms and legs don't work; that's why."

"No, they don't work yet." Elizabeth bit the inside of her cheek and brushed Maddie's damp bangs off her forehead. "But one day God will make her arms and legs better. Maybe she can swim then, okay?"

"Well . . ." Maddie looked at Elizabeth again, but this time her expression was stern, like a miniature Brooke. "Only if she wears a life jacket."

"Yes." Elizabeth swallowed back the lump in her throat. "Only if she wears a life jacket."

The rest of the group was a few feet ahead, so Elizabeth took Maddie's hand and the two skipped together until they caught up.

Ryan was saying, "Maybe we should take the boat trip, get the other view of all that water."

"Actually—" Elizabeth made a subtle motion to Maddie—"we can see it pretty well from here."

A look of understanding filled Ryan's face. "True. Besides, we'd get too wet down there, right, Maddie?" He made a funny face at the child and patted his own head. "I can't let my fancy hairdo get all messed up, can I?"

Maddie giggled, and the sorrow that had come over her was suddenly gone.

They took an entire roll of film, breaking into small family units, and then asking a passerby to finish the roll with pictures of the entire group.

Before they left, Cole pointed at the falls and looked at the grown-ups around him. "Did God build that thing?"

Ashley smiled at her son. "Yes, only God could've built Niagara Falls."

"God's a good builder." Cole planted his hands on his hips and studied the force of the water. Then he turned to the rest of them and patted his own head. "When he was finished with all that water, he built me and Maddie and Jessie and Hayley." He gave a serious nod of his head. "That means God's a busy guy, I think."

Elizabeth smiled and covered her mouth with her fingertips so Cole wouldn't see her giggle. Of all the grandchildren, Cole would always be special. For three years of his life, he was with her and John more than he was home with Ashley. It wasn't until Landon became a greater part of Ashley's life that she seemed to wake up and realize what she had in that special son of hers.

Ashley hadn't called Landon, hadn't asked him to join the group this week. Things had obviously cooled in their relationship, and Elizabeth could only figure it had something to do with her health. Ashley would never have wanted to put Landon at risk, but still . . .

Landon belonged with Ashley—and he definitely belonged with Cole.

The thought reminded Elizabeth of her daughter's uncertain health. Another reason to hold on to today, to rejoice in the moment. Because tomorrow held no guarantees. If God had taught her one thing over the years, it was that. However good or bad a season was, it would change. Nothing stayed the same.

They were tired when they returned from Niagara Falls, but they made time for carriage rides through Central Park. By the time they reached the skating rink, a light snow had begun to fall. As they strapped on skates and made their way around the ice, Elizabeth took another mental picture, one she knew she would recall forever. She couldn't have scripted the moment any better.

Tuesday they met for breakfast and afterwards, the guys headed for the city golf range, and Elizabeth and the girls took two cabs to Fifth Avenue. The next few hours took them to FAO Schwarz and a dozen other high-ticket stores.

"This is torture!" Kari had two bags full of gifts hooked to Jessie's stroller, and it wasn't lunchtime yet. She kept stopping the group every few feet, marveling over one window display or another. "I'm falling in love with everything I see."

Elizabeth grinned. "You always were a shopper, Kari."

"I know what I'm getting you for Christmas." Ashley gave Kari a teasing elbow to the ribs. She had rented a stroller for Cole and Maddie as well. Otherwise the walking would've been too much for them. "A suitcase so you can carry it all back to Bloomington."

"The question is . . ." Kari cast a quick smile at Ashley. "Will we have enough wrapping paper?"

Reagan had been walking next to Elizabeth. Now she took a few quick steps and squeezed in between the sisters. "Not to worry." She slipped an arm around each of their shoulders. "My mother has an entire carton of wrapping paper. She hits the sales when Christmas is over. All year long we have to navigate a forest of Christmas wrapping paper every time we use the storage closet."

"Mother!" The word came in unison from Kari, Ashley, and Erin. All three of them turned and looked at Elizabeth and surrendered to an instant case of giggles.

"Okay, okay . . ." Elizabeth held her hands up in mock surrender. "Reagan's mother and I have something else in common."

The shopping trip ended and that afternoon, they all met up at the hotel to wait for Brooke's arrival. She called Elizabeth as soon as she and Hayley were in a cab headed for the Marquis.

"We made it!" Brooke sounded tired but happy. "Meet me in front of the hotel."

When the cab pulled up, Elizabeth, John, and Ashley were on the sidewalk ready to help. Brooke stepped out first. "Yeah . . . we're here!"

Her face was lit up, and Elizabeth studied her. She should've looked worn-out, defeated, and devastated over the turns her life had taken in the past three months. Instead, Brooke seemed genuinely joyful. Stronger than before, and more connected to the rest of them. Maybe because for the first time in her life, she couldn't rely on her own intelligence. As a result, she'd had to depend fully on her faith, and that, in turn, had brought life to her heart, life she hadn't really had before.

John stepped forward and helped release Hayley from her car seat. "How was the flight?"

"Good." Brooke lifted the strap of one of her bags onto her shoulder and went around to the trunk for the other one. "Hayley slept the whole way."

At that moment, the child woke up and looked dazed, a vacant stare on her face. Her nose tubes were out, but her mouth still hung open. A wet spot on her pink T-shirt was proof she'd been drooling. Her eyes grew wide, and she looked at the faces in front of her, fear written across her expression.

"Let's get her upstairs where it's quiet." Elizabeth came to Hayley and smoothed her fingertips over Hayley's forehead. Seeing Hayley again, being reminded once more of how she wasn't even close to the way she used to be, made Elizabeth's head and heart ache. If only she could give her granddaughter a nudge or a tap, a gentle shake, anything to wake her up and bring her back to the high-spirited pixie she'd been before the accident.

"Here, I'll do the stroller." Ashley took it from Brooke and popped it open. Then she motioned to John, and the two of them strapped Hayley in, while Brooke found a bellhop to help with her luggage.

Hayley started to cry, the repetitive monotone sound that all of them were now familiar with. But only Elizabeth, who had stayed next to her, could hear it. She stooped down and hugged Hayley close. "It's okay, baby; we're here. Everything's okay."

Then, despite the crowds of people bustling around them, despite the noise from the street, Hayley stopped crying. She looked at Elizabeth and peace replaced the confusion in her eyes.

"That's right, Hayley." Elizabeth smiled at her. "We're here, honey."

And then Hayley did something Elizabeth hadn't seen her do since the accident. With her eyes still focused on Elizabeth's, she smiled the way she used to smile. A smile from days gone by. And despite the miles of recovery that lay ahead, the ache inside Elizabeth was instantly gone. Because the smile on Hayley's face wasn't merely a handicapped child reacting to external stimuli. It was Hayley, her Hayley, knowing Elizabeth's voice and letting her see that she remembered, that somewhere inside, Hayley was still there.

For Elizabeth, it was the highlight of the trip to that point.

After Brooke and Hayley were situated in Ashley's room, the group rested for a few hours and then set off for Luke and Reagan's rehearsal. The wedding was to be in Reagan's family church, a century-old cathedral in the Upper East Side, not far from where Luke and Reagan and her mother lived.

With all the activities from the past few days, the reality of why they had gathered in Manhattan hadn't really hit Elizabeth. But now, situated in the second row of the church, watching the minister go over the details of the ceremony with Luke and Reagan, she was struck by the truth.

Luke was about to get married.

Her only son was going to pledge his life to a woman other

than herself, a woman who was perfect for him in every way. But still . . .

She watched him, tall and handsome, his blond hair cut short, the angles of his face striking as he joked with the minister and cast frequent smiles at Reagan. Suddenly she remembered her own mother, the conversation they'd shared in the days after Luke was born.

"Enjoy him while you can," her mother had said. "A daughter's a daughter for life; a son's a son till he takes a wife."

Every now and then while Luke was growing up, her mother's words had come back: *"A son's a son till he takes a wife."* And she'd known it wasn't true. Maybe for other mothers, but not for her and Luke. Out of five children, he was her only boy, and she'd been convinced that he would marry a local girl, raise a family a few miles from the Baxter home, and spend his life stopping in for weekend dinners and summer barbecues.

She studied Luke.

He would stay in touch. She would receive calls on holidays and her birthday, and once or twice a year he'd bring Reagan and his family home. But for the first time, Elizabeth realized that her mother had been right. Come tomorrow evening, Luke would be gone from her life, gone to a bigger purpose, a grander priority.

"Elizabeth?" She looked up and saw Reagan's mother, Anne. "Can I sit by you?"

"Of course." Her sadness took a backseat as the two women smiled at each other. "Reagan is simply glowing."

They were quiet for a while, listening to the pastor lead Luke and Reagan through the parts of the ceremony, watching Kari and Ashley and Erin and Brooke giggle and whisper as they tried to figure out in what order they would walk down the aisle. Across the church, Ryan and Sam talked football with Reagan's younger brother, Bryan.

"Tomorrow should be beautiful for everyone." Elizabeth smiled at Anne.

"Yes." Anne leaned closer and said, "Can I tell you something?"

"Sure . . ." Elizabeth angled her body toward Anne's so she could hear her better.

"You did a wonderful job with Luke. I love him like he's my own."

"Thank you." Elizabeth clutched her bag to her waist and willed her eyes to stay dry. "I wouldn't want him to marry anyone but Reagan."

"They're good for each other." Anne looked at the young couple again. "I've wondered if it's been hard on you, having Luke so far away from home."

Elizabeth lifted her fingers to just beneath the corners of her eyes and caught two tears before they could fall. "Yes." She forced a single laugh. She wouldn't cry, not now. "I miss him."

"He's a good daddy to Tommy." Anne shifted her gaze back to Elizabeth. "It's hard to believe six months ago they weren't speaking to each other."

"Six months ago Luke was a different person." Elizabeth smiled despite the heaviness in her heart. "But not really. I always knew he'd come back."

"I guess I see the changes more than you, but it's amazing." Anne shook her head. "He and Reagan read their Bibles every morning, and Luke's been adamant about doing things right this time around, keeping away from Reagan until after the wedding."

"He's so much like his father."

Anne bit her lip and her chin quivered some. "If I don't get the chance tomorrow, tell John how much it means to me that he's walking Reagan down the aisle."

"I'll tell him." Elizabeth's heart went out to the woman beside her. Tomorrow's wedding would be bittersweet for both of them.

Anne Decker looked at their children, facing each other in front of the church. "I prayed for this day, Elizabeth. And now here it is." A sad smile tugged at the corners of her mouth. "I only wish Tom could be here."

Elizabeth gave the woman's hand a tender squeeze. "He will be, Anne. God'll give him a front-row seat."

# CHAPTER NINETEEN

IT WAS AFTER TEN when Elizabeth and John closed their hotel-room door behind them. John tossed his jacket on the bed and sank into the adjacent sofa. "That went well, don't you think?"

"Yes." She hung her coat in the closet and took the seat beside him. "I still can't believe he's getting married tomorrow." A pause settled between them, and she met John's gaze. "Weren't we just at the hospital having that boy?"

John smiled and tapped the tip of her nose. "I believe we've seen a few seasons since then."

"Maybe a few, but not twenty years, John." She drew a slow breath. "Where did they go?" She stretched out and let her head rest on the sofa back. "Remember what my mother told me after we had Luke?"

"What a handsome baby?" John shifted so he could see her better. His eyes danced the way they often had since their first date.

"No." Elizabeth searched his eyes. She enjoyed moments like this—quiet, unhurried times when she and John could connect after a busy day. "She told me a daughter's a daughter for life . . . a son's a son till he takes a wife. Remember? It made me mad because Luke was my only son. I didn't want to think of him that way."

"I remember." John raised one eyebrow. "Your mother was surprised it upset you. She thought you were hormonal."

"Anyway—" she gave him a pointed look, then felt her eyes grow distant again—"the thing is, she was right. I realized that tonight."

John crooked his elbow around her neck and rested his hand on her shoulder. "She wasn't right, silly. Luke will always be part of our lives."

"But not as much. His focus will be here, with Reagan and Tommy, where it should be."

They were quiet for a moment, and finally John nodded. "I see what you're saying."

"It made me think of something else."

"What?" His tone was light, and he ran his fingers along her upper arm.

"You know how we always made a special note every time our kids had a first? First smile, first teeth, first steps . . . that kind of thing?"

"First day of school, first choir performance?" John cocked his head, remembering. "We had a lifetime of firsts, didn't we?"

"Yes, and we celebrated every one." She reached up and laced her fingers through his. "But along the way we forgot something."

"We did?" John raised his brow, amused in a relaxed sort of way.

"We did." Elizabeth stared out the window. Snow was falling again, slow dancing in lazy circles toward the floor of Manhattan. She turned to John. "We forgot to mark their lasts."

He gave her a strange, bemused look. "Their lasts?"

"Yes." Elizabeth sighed. "Okay, think of Luke. Just yesterday he would pick me a handful of wildflowers from the field behind our house, run inside, and jump into my arms. I'd catch him and hold him, his legs wrapped around my waist. We'd grin at each other, our noses touching. He'd give me the flowers, slide back down, and be on his way."

"Okay . . ." John seemed to be having trouble following her.

"Don't you see?" Elizabeth searched his face. "One day he did that for the last time. It was the last time he ever ran and jumped in my arms and gave me wildflowers. Only I didn't know it was the last time." She paused, her eyes suddenly watery. "I took no pictures, threw no party, made no note of it in a journal or a baby book. We simply moved on to another stage of life and never looked back."

"Oh." A softness filled John's eyes and he nodded. "I see."

"Our children's growing-up years were full of lasts, and I never knew it." She let her mind drift. "Last time I fed them a bottle. Last time they colored a picture for the refrigerator door. Last time they made angels in the snow."

John smiled. "Last time they played in the pond out back."

"Last time they needed me to drive them somewhere."

"Yes," he chuckled. "Last time they asked for advice about romance."

"Exactly."

They were silent again, until John gave her a light squeeze. "I never thought of that."

"I know. Me neither." She stood and sauntered across the room to the table and chairs in the corner. The top drawer held five pieces of stationery, and Elizabeth removed all of them. She glanced back at John. "Are you staying up?"

"For a while." He gave her a slow smile. "I like the snow." His eyes fell to the stationery in her hand. "You writing something?"

"A letter . . . for Luke."

John nodded. "I'm glad."

Every now and then, Elizabeth had the strongest desire to write. It wasn't something she did often; she kept no regular accounting of the days, the way some people did. But she had a journal full of random thoughts, precious moments that might otherwise have been lost in the slow pull of time. And once in a while, on lonely winter nights or cool summer mornings, the need to write was too strong to ignore.

This, the last night before Luke married Reagan, was one of those times.

She turned the chair so it faced the window and steadied the paper on her lap, a New York tourist magazine beneath it. The lights of the city dimmed through the veil of falling snow, and in a rush of school days and birthday parties and summer vacations, time ran in reverse and she allowed herself to go back, back to the days when Luke was just entering their lives.

Through the lens of yesterday she searched the moments, looking for the lasts, but nothing came to mind, and Elizabeth understood why. It was like she'd told John. The last times went by without fanfare. Certainly if she'd known it was the last time Luke would jump into her arms and give her wildflowers, she would've done something to mark the moment.

At the very least she would've held on longer.

With that thought, she positioned her pen over the hotel stationery and began to write. The words came easily, straight from a quiet corner of her heart to the linen page. Rather than a letter, her thoughts formed a poem, and in thirty minutes she had it written. Exactly the way she felt, there on paper.

She let her eyes read over it one more time. Then she turned and saw that John was reading his Bible.

"Hey . . ."

He looked up, his eyes more tired than before. "I was just about to turn in."

She stood and set the pen and magazine down. "Want to hear what I wrote?"

"Definitely." John closed his Bible and set it on the coffee table. "Do you like it?"

"Yes." She brought the pages to the sofa and sat next to him again. "It's exactly what's in my heart."

"Okay." He folded his arms and smiled at her, true and genuine, his love warm enough to melt the snow outside. "Go ahead."

Elizabeth returned the smile, her heart brimming with a kind of joy and sorrow she'd never known before. The kind reserved for a mother the night before her only son's wedding. "Okay." She cleared her throat and let her eyes fall to the paper.

> *"Long ago you came to me, a miracle of firsts*
> *First smiles and teeth and baby steps, a sunbeam*
> *   on the burst.*
> *But one day you will move away and leave to me your*
> *   past,*
> *And I will be left thinking of a lifetime of your lasts.*
>
> *"The last time that I held a bottle to your baby lips . . .*
> *Last time that I lifted you and held you on my hip . . .*
> *Last time when you had a binky stuck inside your mouth . . .*
> *The last time that you crawled across the floor of this*
> *   old house.*
>
> *"Last time when you ran to me, still small enough to hold,*
> *Last time when you said you'd marry me when you grew old.*
> *Precious, simple moments and bright flashes from the past,*
> *Would I have held you longer if I'd known they were*
> *   the last?"*

Elizabeth looked up. "Good so far?"

"It's amazing." John's eyes were damp. "Keep reading."

"All right." She steadied the paper and found her place.

> *"Your last few hours of kindergarten, last days of first*
> *   grade . . .*
> *Last at bat in Little League, last colored paper made.*
> *Last time that I tucked you in for one last midday nap . . .*
> *Last time when you wore your beat-up Green Bay*
> *   Packers cap.*

"*Last time that you caught a frog in that old backyard
    pond . . .*
*Last time when you ran barefoot across our fresh-cut lawn.*
*Silly scattered images to represent your past.*
*Would I have taken pictures . . . if I'd known they were
    the last?*

"*The last dark night you slipped in bed and slept between
    us two,*
*When last I read to you of God or Horton Hears a Who!*
*Last time that I smelled your hair and prayed after
    your shower . . .*
*Last time that we held devotions in the evening hours.*

"*The last time you were M. J. in our games of give-and-
    go . . .*
*Last time that you made an angel in the melting snow.*
*I never even said good-bye to yesterdays long passed.*
*Would I have marked the moments . . . if I'd known they
    were the last?*

"*Last piano lesson, and last soccer goal you kicked . . .*
*The last few weeks of middle school, last flowers that
    you picked.*
*Last time that you needed me for rides from here to there . . .*
*The last time that you spent the night with that old
    tattered bear.*

"*Last time that I helped you with a math or spelling test,*
*Last time when I shouted that your room was still a mess.*
*Time and life moved quicker, taking pieces of your past.*
*Would I have stretched the moments . . . if I'd known they
    were the last?*

"*The last time that you needed help with details of a
    dance . . .*
*Last time that you asked me for advice about romance.*

*Last time that you talked to me about your hopes
    and dreams.*
*Last time that you wore a jersey for your high school team.*

*"I watched you grow and never noticed seasons as
    they passed.*
*I wish I could've frozen time, to hold on to your lasts.*
*For come tomorrow morning life will never be the same.*
*You'll pledge forever to your girl, and she will take
    your name.*

*"And I will watch you, knowing God has blessed you
    with this day.*
*I never would have wanted, Luke, to somehow make
    you stay.*
*They say a son's a son until he takes for him a wife.*
*You're grown-up now; it's time to go and start your
    brand-new life.*

*"One last hug, one last good-bye, one quick and hurried
    kiss . . .*
*One last time to understand just how much you'll be missed.*
*I'll watch you leave and think how quickly childhood sped
    past.*
*Would I have held on longer . . . if I'd known it was your
    last?"*

Elizabeth lowered the paper to her lap and realized that her
cheeks were wet. She dabbed at her eyes, looked at John, and the
two of them uttered a quick bit of laughter. His eyes were red,
tears trickling down both sides of his face.

"Well . . ." He pulled the back of his hand across his cheeks. "I
think that about says it."

"There's just one more thing I have to do."

He reached for her hand, pulled her to her feet, and eased her
close to him. "What's that, my love?"

"Survive the wedding."

# CHAPTER TWENTY

BROOKE SAT BY THE WINDOW of the room she was sharing with Ashley, mesmerized by the swirling snow.

"Hope they can keep the roads clear for tomorrow." She looked over her shoulder at her younger sister. "Otherwise half the guests won't make it."

Ashley was lying on the far bed next to Cole, stroking his forehead as he fell asleep. She peered out the window and studied the snow for a moment. "It'll be fine. The forecast says no more than an inch between now and tomorrow night."

"That's good." Brooke settled back in her chair. "It definitely works for the wedding theme."

"Yep."

Brooke fell quiet again. She was exhausted, but even so, she would forever be glad she came to New York. Before getting close to God, before realizing for herself how real he was, she had seen her family in a pragmatic light. They were the people she'd been raised with, the ones she shared holidays with. But she hadn't felt a heart connection.

Now, though, watching the way they rushed to help her with

Hayley, seeing the love they had for each other, Brooke felt as if her emotions had undergone laser surgery. Where before she had seen things one way, now she saw them as they really were, and that meant she had to be here in New York, had to see her only brother pledge his life to his sweet Reagan.

On the near bed she heard Maddie stir, and she turned toward her. She and Maddie were sharing the bed, and the hotel staff had brought up a special oversized crib for Hayley. That way Brooke didn't have to worry about her falling off the bed or waking up on a strange floor and not knowing where she was.

In the days before the trip, Hayley had made amazing strides. She was taking small sips from a cup now, and when she was on the floor, she would roll toward the sound of Brooke's voice.

"Impossible," Dr. Martinez had said at their visit last week.

But Brooke had spread out Hayley's blanket and laid her down. "Hayley, come to Mommy. I'm over here."

Then, as if on cue, Hayley had craned her neck in Brooke's direction and begun rolling.

"See?" Brooke grinned at the doctor.

"But . . . her tests. She was underwater more than fifteen minutes."

"You and I know that, but I guess God doesn't." She smiled at Hayley. "And he's the one calling the shots this time."

Cole had fallen asleep, and Ashley climbed out of bed and joined Brooke near the window. "Pretty."

"Yes." Brooke looked out the window again. "Makes Manhattan look quiet and dreamy."

"Mmmm." Ashley sat on the arm of Brooke's stuffed chair. "Makes me think of Landon."

Brooke found Ashley's eyes and saw the hurt there, the loneliness. "Have you talked to him? since you've been here?"

"No." Ashley lifted her chin and looked out at the snowy city again. "I'll see him at the wedding. That'll be hard enough."

"Are you sure he's coming?"

"Oh, yeah." Ashley bit her lip and narrowed her eyes. "He'll come."

"You're going to see him anyway; why not call? He could've joined us this week, Ash. We all miss him."

"For what?" Ashley angled her face, her voice resigned. "For another round of hope and heartache?" She looked at Brooke. "It's over between us. I have to be able to come to Manhattan without running to him the minute I touch ground."

"I see." Brooke gave a slight nod. "And what if that doctor you're seeing in January tells you that I'm right, that there're ways for HIV patients to keep their partners safe?"

"That's crazy, Brooke." Ashley huffed, her words quiet because of the sleeping children. She returned her gaze to the window. "The risk would always be there. And even if he never became infected, he'd spend a lifetime worrying about me, maybe watching me die. I can't do that to him, no matter how badly I miss him. He deserves a normal life."

"He doesn't want a normal life." Brooke's words were slow, measured. Something about the night invited her to be completely honest with her sister. "He wants you, Ash. Only you."

"He'll get over it." She gritted her teeth. "We both will."

Brooke waited, letting Ashley's statement settle in her heart. But no matter how she considered her sister's words, she didn't agree. "You're wrong." She met Ashley's eyes once more. "Landon loves you with a crazy kind of love. The way Ryan loves Kari."

Ashley opened her mouth, but nothing came out. Instead she bit her lip as if she might weep otherwise.

"So what if you die young?" Brooke hugged herself to ward off the chill from the window. "If you only had three years together, so what? That's a thousand tomorrows, a thousand sunrises and sunsets. A thousand nights to know you're loved beyond life, beyond anything this side of heaven."

"Brooke." Ashley dabbed her fingertips beneath her eyes and made a light sniff. "Don't."

"Don't what?"

"Don't tempt me."

"Well . . ." Brooke thought about Peter, wherever he might be this cold night, two days before Christmas. "I can think of something worse than being loved like that."

Ashley's face softened. "You and Peter?"

Brooke nodded. "I . . . I keep asking myself what I did to make him leave."

"Oh, honey . . ." Ashley leaned over and hugged her, holding her close for a long while before pulling back. "You didn't do anything. Peter has a lot to figure out."

Their conversation wound down, and thirty minutes later, after they'd brushed their teeth and washed their faces, they climbed into their separate beds. Again Brooke was glad she'd come, glad for the new bond she'd found with Ashley.

Brooke reached up and turned off the light. "G'night, Ash."

"Good night." Ashley lifted her head. "Thanks for talking to me."

"I meant every word."

An hour later, when everyone else in the room was making soft snoring sounds, Brooke rolled onto her back and stared at the dark ceiling. She couldn't sleep, couldn't get thoughts of Peter out of her mind. It was one o'clock, midnight in Bloomington. Before she'd left for New York, she'd called Peter and told him about the trip.

"They'd love you to be there." She'd tried to keep her tone even, nothing pushy or forceful.

"I appreciate that." Peter sounded distant, his words more formal than before.

Brooke hadn't known what to say. She dug her elbows into her knees and pressed the receiver to the side of her face. *God, give me the words* . . . "So . . . would you think about coming? Just for a few days?"

"Listen, Brooke." He dropped the pretense and sighed. "I couldn't go to the wedding with you. Everyone would think that . . ."

Her heart skipped a beat. "That what?"

"That we were working things out."

"Would that be so bad, Peter? Couldn't we try? Pastor Mark knows a counselor who—"

"No!" He muttered something under his breath. "I'm sorry, Brooke. My mind's made up."

The conversation felt like poison to her system, and no matter how hard she tried she couldn't shake it, couldn't rid herself of the memory. The thing was, something magical happened at weddings. Brooke had noticed it at Kari and Ryan's wedding last fall, and at a handful of other weddings before that.

As the couple were exchanging their vows, married people throughout the church couldn't help but remember how it felt when they were the couple standing before God and man, when they were the ones promising forever to the person they'd fallen in love with.

Brooke liked to look around at weddings and watch the way couples sat a little closer as the ceremony went on, how they held hands and exchanged what they thought were private glances and furtive smiles. A wedding was the ultimate reminder that when the smoke screen of busy schedules and demanding children and bill paying lifted, what still mattered was the bond between a husband and a wife and God himself.

With all her heart, Brooke had hoped Peter would come, because maybe if he watched Luke and Reagan exchanging vows, he might find his way back. But with him a thousand miles away, there was no telling what he was thinking, or whether he would even care that she and the girls were gone.

Still, no matter how bad things with Peter seemed, Brooke remained convinced that somehow God would bring them back together. Yes, her anger toward him flared every now and then, but she couldn't stay hateful for long. Not when she spent most of her free time with Hayley. The child had an angel-like quality about her now, her eyes full of a contagious light and innocence.

After a day with Hayley, Brooke's heart simply was not capable of hating anyone or anything.

Even Peter.

In her old life, Brooke would've thought the situation with Peter through and known intellectually that her marriage was over. On paper, it looked that way. But she had a new way of looking at life now, through the eyes of a believing heart. Because of that, and because of what she'd seen modeled in her family, she knew one thing to be true about love.

It was a decision, a choice.

*I believe that, God. . . . I'm willing to wait, to keep praying, keep begging you that Peter will change his mind. Whatever it takes, Lord. Touch him, reach him, make him want us again. Please . . .*

**Rejoice in the Lord always. I will say it again: Rejoice!**

Despite the uncertainty and despair that sometimes welled within her, Brooke smiled. The verse was the same one that flashed in her head every time she prayed about Peter. "Okay, God," she whispered. "I'm rejoicing."

Moments like this she understood what God was doing. He wanted her to rely on him, on his strength and grace and peace. Not just in a wishful sort of way, but for every moment, every breath. It was how she was surviving with Hayley, how she was able to lift her head off the pillow in light of Peter's decision to divorce her. Her joy was no longer dependent on Hayley's health or Peter's love.

It depended on God alone.

And for that reason the joy she felt was as real as life itself.

If Peter didn't want to be with her right now, so be it. She would bend the ear of the one who knew her husband best, the one who was even now healing her younger daughter from an accident that should've killed her. The one who was not only helping her through the ordeal, but allowing her joy in the process.

If God could heal Hayley's brain, certainly he could heal

Peter's heart. And one day she would tell anyone who would listen that God Almighty hadn't worked just one miracle in her life.
  He had worked two.

# CHAPTER TWENTY-ONE

SOMETHING WAS WRONG.

Peter lay in bed and watched the comforter vibrate. *Stop,* he ordered it. *Stop now!* But the blanket kept moving, propelled by the way his body shook from head to foot. He looked at the clock. Midnight. So why was he shaking? Why was his body crying out for more pills? His routine hadn't changed a bit from yesterday, had it?

Home from work at eight o'clock. Three hours of pills and frozen pizza and *SportsCenter,* then a quick rinse off, another two pills and lights out. That was half an hour ago, but still Peter couldn't fall asleep. The pills weren't working as well as before; that had to be the reason.

He held his breath and exhaled in a long burst. He couldn't lay on his left side. In that position, every heartbeat ripped through his body, pounded through his veins and limbs, and straight into his brain. *Boom . . . boom . . . boom . . . boom.* Peter flipped onto his right side and felt the slightest relief. At least in this position his heartbeat was more subtle, less likely to keep him awake.

But lying on his right side he could see out the window, and that meant watching the strange movement of a mass of gnarled tree branches outside his apartment window. They'd never scared him before, but tonight . . . tonight they seemed haunted, moved by some supernatural force, by a wind that wasn't causing a stir anywhere but outside his window.

"Stop!" He hissed the word in the direction of the branches. "I'm not afraid of you!"

His brain was responsible for the mess he was in. If only he could think about something else, replace his irrational fears with a different set of thoughts, then his nerves were bound to calm down. Yes, the mind was a powerful thing however it was used. As long as he was thinking about the pills, about the bizarre scene outside his window, he couldn't possibly find peace. But what else could he think about?

Peter tapped his forehead and suddenly it hit him. His family! He could think about Brooke and Maddie and Hayley. They were in New York City, weren't they? He closed his eyes and pictured Brooke pushing Hayley down the concourse in her special stroller, Maddie beside them, all three excited about the trip to Manhattan.

His trembling settled some.

The stimuli of taking Hayley on a trip like that could actually speed her healing process. He'd read case studies of that happening. Brooke had been right to make the effort and take her along. And Maddie—at five years old—was bound to get a kick out of New York at Christmastime.

Christmastime?

Peter's eyes flew open. The girls would be gone for Christmas? The shaking grew worse again. Why hadn't he thought about that? He'd told Brooke he didn't want to go to Luke's wedding, and that was still true. No point making people think he and Brooke had a chance.

But he hadn't realized he was going to miss the girls' Christmas.

A buzzing started in Peter's brain, and he cursed himself.

*Stupid. Thinking about Brooke and the girls could never calm you down,* he told himself. He was the bad guy, the one who had ruined everything. He'd done everything but lock the three of them in a car and push them over a cliff. The buzzing grew louder and became a pain. An aching, throbbing pain.

Then it spread.

Down his face and along his throat, through his chest and deep into his heart.

And there, for the first time since he'd moved out, he missed Brooke and the girls so much he could barely breathe, as if by thinking about them he had tapped into the single most obvious source of his pain. All along he'd thought the pain came from guilt. The certainty of knowing that Hayley would be fine today if he'd taken more interest in her safety that afternoon. The awareness that he'd walked out on his family long before moving his things into the apartment. But maybe at the root of all the desperate hurt was a single thorn. The thorn of wanting life the way it had been a year ago, back when he and Brooke still had a marriage to save.

Peter sat straight up in bed and swung his feet onto the floor. His heart was racing now, shaking the same way his arms and legs shook. He flipped on the light and saw the bottle sitting on the table beside his bed. Not the plastic bag with a dozen pills for the day, but the entire bottle.

In case he needed an extra dose.

A thought hit him then. What if he didn't need a pill to take away the pain? It was like a splinter, wasn't it? Festering and irritating the flesh around it, the resulting infection wouldn't go away with a dozen weeks of antibiotics. No, it would only clear up one way.

Remove the splinter.

Okay, so what if his stubbornness was the splinter? What if the solution to his pain was to make things right with Brooke again? to run to her and apologize for everything he'd ever said or done, to get counseling for the two of them, to promise that no matter how hard things got, he would never, ever leave again?

If she were there beside him, maybe the pain would go away all by itself.

He stared at the bottle of pills and suddenly, in the recesses of his mind, he heard a strange voice, angry and hissing.

*You're an idiot, Peter . . . an idiot!* The dark words filled the center of his being, and he jerked his head first one way, then the other.

"Who said that?" He looked out the window; the tree branches were moving again. Beyond them everything else on the street looked still. But not the branches outside his window.

The strange voice laughed at him, a slow, evil laugh. Peter slid back against his headboard, so at least his back would be covered. Then he pulled the covers up to his neck and stared at the bottle of pills.

*Go ahead. Take two. No, take more than two . . . take them all. That would stop the pain for good, wouldn't it?*

"Brooke!" He closed his eyes and whispered her name. Even though he'd avoided her as much as possible since Hayley's accident, when he did see her, he couldn't help noticing that she was filled with some kind of . . . some sort of peace. There was no other way to describe it. A peace that seemed almost phony.

And something else.

She'd been happy. Not the kind of happy she used to get when she'd receive a compliment from a patient or when she figured out a particularly difficult diagnosis. But a happiness that grew from inside her, maybe even as far inside as her soul.

His hands were shaking so hard he could no longer hold the blanket up. Instead he tucked the edges in behind his shoulders and used his chin to keep it in place.

*You look like an idiot, Peter . . .*

The voice was back, and Peter's eyes darted about the room. "Who are you?"

*You know who I am . . . you work for me.* The voice laughed.

*Brooke and the girls would make things worse, not better. Every day, every hour, looking at that little girl and knowing it was your fault. All your fault. It is your fault, Peter. You can't run from the truth. It's all your fault.*

"It wasn't my fault!" Peter raised his voice. "She was supposed to wear a life jacket . . . she knew that!"

The evil laugh grew louder. *Take the pills, Peter. That's the only certain relief, and you know it. Take all of them. Then you can go to sleep and never wake up again.*

"No!" His heart was beating faster than he'd ever felt it. He was panting to catch his breath, but he was determined to have the last word with the voice, whatever it was. "No, I don't want that." He began to cry, but nothing came from his eyes. "I want help!"

The voice was silent.

Peter waited, listening for the laugh, the taunting words. But they were gone. He let the covers fall back to his waist and stared at his hands. They were shaking so badly, his forearms hurt.

His eyes found the pills again. Maybe he'd forgotten to take the eleven-o'clock dose. He took the bottle, steadied his hands enough to twist the lid off, and tried to pour two into his hand. Instead, a pile of pills landed in the center of his palm.

Peter stared at them and wondered how it would feel.

The pain would be gone in less than a minute; he was sure about that. But then a few minutes after that he would fall asleep, and most likely that would be the end. They would find him in his apartment sometime in the next few days, after he didn't show up for work the day after Christmas. By then his body would be rotted; they'd have to have a closed-casket funeral for sure.

His eyes moved to the full bottle of water next to the spot where the pills had been. He could do it, couldn't he? He could end it all and never have to explain to Brooke why their marriage fell apart, never have to figure out a way to make a life for himself between visits with Maddie and Hayley. And never again would he have to see his once bouncy, cheery little daughter strapped to her wheelchair, brain damaged.

He looked at the pills; his resistance was wearing down.

Why not do it? He would die someday anyway, right? How good would life be when he needed painkillers to get through an hour of it? Dying would be blissful relief compared to the constant anxiety of not knowing when the medicine would wear off, not knowing where he'd be—with a patient or in a meeting with the other doctors—when his body began to tingle and shake and scream for relief.

He reached for the water bottle, popped it open with his teeth, and then sifted the pills about in his hand. Fifty pills at least— definitely enough to end his misery. For a moment, he hesitated. If he was really going to do it, shouldn't he leave a note, some sort of final parting words for Maddie and Hayley?

A picture filled his mind.

Hayley strapped to her wicker wheelchair, her head and mouth hanging to one side, a steady drip of drool falling onto her shirt, her hands contorted, turned outward.

No, there would be no letter. Parting words could never excuse his behavior, the way he'd allowed her to fall into the pool that horrible Saturday. If only God had been real . . . if only he'd sent angels to catch Hayley or cause him to sense her danger, the way people in those miracle shows sometimes sensed things.

But no, God wasn't real. And if he wasn't real, heaven wasn't real. Hell, either. So the pills were the perfect answer, weren't they? A chance to stop shaking once and for all, to get sleep that wouldn't last merely a few hours. But sleep that would last forever.

He lifted the handful of pills to his mouth, dumped them past his lips and onto his tongue. Words seemed to match the rhythm of his heart, beat for beat.

*Sorry, girls . . . sorry, girls . . . sorry, girls.*

He brought the water bottle to his mouth and had it to his lips, had it tilted and ready to down the deadly dose of pills, when without warning he gagged and a wave of vomit came spewing up through his throat and out of his mouth, taking every one of the pills with it.

The mess landed on his bedspread. And before he could do anything about it, another wave followed, and another, and another. When finally his stomach stopped convulsing, Peter stared at the dozens of pills in the mess and realized something.

He wasn't shaking.

But he hadn't been sick, hadn't felt ill or nauseous, not even a little. How could his body have vomited right then, at that exact moment?

*God?*

The silent word echoed in his mind, sending reverberations through his heart and soul and veins.

*I AM, son. . . . I AM WHO I AM.*

This voice was different than the previous one. Quiet and gentle and strong all at the same time. If Peter hadn't known better, he'd think himself the victim of some heavenly melodrama. The voice of evil versus the voice of good.

Not so much because he believed, but because he wanted to hear the good voice again, Peter said, "God . . . is that you?"

*I AM WHO I AM, son. Repent and be saved.*

Two colleagues had told him the pills could do this. Take them long enough and you'll hallucinate when you need a fix. Your head could be filled with strange sights and sounds that weren't really happening. But something about this experience was different, real.

Peter wasn't sure, but it almost seemed as if God himself had saved him from certain death, maybe even caused the pills to rush out of his mouth moments before Peter would've swallowed them. Again Peter studied his hands and arms, even his legs, and he slid out from the dirty sheets, amazed.

He wasn't shaking even a little. Not a single pill had made it down his throat, but still he wasn't shaking.

It was a miracle.

But . . . if it was a miracle, then somebody had to work it. And that somebody just might be God, right?

*I AM WHO I AM, son.*

Peter backed up and pressed himself against the wall next to his bed. *I am who I am?* Wasn't that the biblical name for God that had most impressed Peter? *I AM.*

Back before Hayley's drowning, Peter had clung tightly to that name. What more could anyone say after that? A name like I AM meant that God always was, always is, and would always be at the center of life. It meant he was everywhere, working his will in every situation. And it meant his word was perfect and true, with no beginning and no end.

But if that was the name Peter appreciated most, then no wonder it had come to him just now. It must've been a figment of his imagination, a subconscious way of finding peace in the wake of the evil voice.

Peter took hesitant steps toward the bathroom and found a roll of paper towels. The mess on his bed had to be cleaned up before he could try again to sleep. He shuddered as he swept the wet, disintegrating pills into a paper towel and threw them into the trash can. If they'd made it down his throat, he'd be dead by now. And what sort of example would that be for Maddie and Hayley?

His body was still calm, not shaking, so he had no reason to take a normal dose of pills. His next fix could wait until morning. Instead he washed his hands, climbed into bed again, and turned off the light.

When he blinked his eyes open the next morning he stared at the ceiling and tried to make sense of the thoughts in his head. Some kind of nightmare, maybe—that had to be it. Strange voices and tree branches scratching against his window. Whatever had been going on, it had all been a crazy dream. But as sleep wore off, the images grew more vivid, the bottle of pills, the strange evil voice countered by the intense, peaceful whispers. The half-empty bottle of pills on his bedside table and the mess in his bathroom trash can.

It hadn't been a dream after all; it had been real and true, and except for a strange twist of fate he should be dead. He pressed his head back into the pillow. Something else had carried over from the night before. He was still missing Brooke and the girls, wanting them as if his next heartbeat depended on their place in his life, wishing with all his soul that they were in the next room, making breakfast and waiting for him to join them.

And then there was the strangest thing of all.

It was time for a fix, but he wasn't shaking or anxious or in any kind of pain except one.

The hurt of missing his girls.

# CHAPTER TWENTY-TWO

CHRISTMAS EVE DAY in Manhattan dawned like something from a dream, and Ashley wanted to set up an easel and start painting it. Snow had stopped falling just after midnight, and by morning, sunshine shone across Manhattan, streaking down between the buildings and casting splashes of white and silver on the snowy ground.

Ashley stood at the window and studied the scene while she waited for Brooke to finish dressing Maddie. They should be leaving now, heading out for their meeting with Reagan and her mother, but Ashley couldn't bear to walk away from the window.

Then she had an idea. She zipped across the room to her bag and pulled out her camera. Before a minute passed, she'd captured the scene a dozen times, all from slightly different angles.

"To help jog my memory," she told Brooke, "when I sit down next week and try to re-create it on canvas."

"Now you'll have enough pictures for three paintings." Brooke grinned and brushed the wrinkles out of her silk blouse. "Let's go."

That morning's meeting had been planned for weeks.

Reagan had asked if Ashley and Kari and Brooke and their mother would meet with her and her mother at their home the morning of the wedding.

"You can each share your favorite Scripture with me, and the reason why it's helped you in marriage or in life. Maybe share a story, something that will help me be a better wife to Luke or a better mother to Tommy." Excitement had filled Reagan's voice when she told the others about her idea. "Then I'd like you to pray for me and Luke, that we'll always put God first and that we'll find a way to grow stronger, more in love, as time goes on."

At the same time, Luke planned to come to the Marriott and meet with their father and Sam and Ryan. The kids would stay with the women, and they'd all meet up again for a late lunch and to get ready for the six-o'clock wedding.

Ashley loved everything about the morning plan. Prayers and special Bible verses seemed so much more meaningful than anything else they could have done hours before the wedding. It was something she would've wanted to do if she and Landon had been able to move on with their plans, if her blood test had been negative.

Because it took more effort to transport Hayley, Ashley and Brooke and the children started out earlier than the others and were the first to arrive at Mrs. Decker's apartment. Reagan answered the door, and Ashley could almost feel the warmth from her glow.

They talked for a few minutes about the snow and the wedding, and then Brooke excused herself to get Hayley set up at the far side of the room in her special stroller, where she could eat and watch the happenings around her. Unless she got fussy, at which point Brooke would have to prepare a dose of medicine for her and lay her in one of the back bedrooms.

Cole and Maddie stood nearby, watching Brooke work with Hayley, moving her limp arms and fastening the belt around her waist. Ashley was about to go to the children, offer them some other activity, when Reagan's mother appeared from the kitchen. She smiled at Cole and Maddie. "Okay, you two, follow me! I have coloring books, crayons, and a movie all ready!"

Their eyes lit up and they started after her, but then Cole stopped and looked at Hayley. "You can come, too, Hayley." His eyes lifted to Brooke. "Can Hayley come with us? She loves to color."

Ashley looked at Brooke and winced. Very few times did her sister allow the pain of Hayley's situation to show in her eyes. But in light of Cole's innocent question, this was one of them. She walked up to Cole, tousled his hair, and gave him a sad smile. "Not today, honey. But one of these days I'm sure she'd love to join you."

"Yeah," Maddie looked at Cole. "Hayley's different now."

"Oh." Cole looked from Maddie and Brooke back to his cousin strapped in the chair. "I think she's the same old funny Hayley." He took a few running steps toward her and patted her head. "I'll color you a picture, Hayley, okay?"

Hayley opened her mouth and made a sound that seemed part moan, part laugh.

"Okay." Cole nodded his head and looked at the others. "Hayley said she wants me to color her a Christmas tree."

"Thank you, Cole." Brooke kissed him on the top of his head. "She'd like that very much."

Cole nodded, grabbed Maddie's hand, and skipped to catch up to Reagan's mother. Ashley caught Brooke's eye and understood the momentary pain there. No matter how well Hayley was doing, it was still heartbreaking to hear her big sister call her "different."

Ashley sat on the living-room sofa next to Reagan and shifted her thoughts to the reason they were gathered this morning. No question her future sister-in-law was glowing. Whatever her dress looked like, however she styled her hair and did her makeup, nothing about her would rival her eyes today. Because in them, without a doubt, was the look of love and certainty and commitment.

The glow of a woman about to promise her life to the man of her dreams.

"You look beautiful." Ashley took Reagan's hand and gave it a tender squeeze. "Are you nervous?"

"No." A blush came over Reagan's cheeks. "I've been in love with your brother for a long time, Ashley. You know that." She paused, searching Ashley's face. "But before the day gets busier, I want to thank you."

Ashley gave a slight shake of her head. "For what?"

"For telling Luke about Tommy." She lowered her chin, her eyes dancing in the glow of Christmas lights from the nearby tree. "I sometimes wonder if we'd be together now if you hadn't said anything."

"You would've told him someday."

"That's just it; I kept finding reasons to wait because I was sure he wouldn't want anything to do with either of us—not based on his life at the time and the fact that he was living with that other girl." Reagan shrugged. "I might've waited years."

"I guess." Ashley thought of Luke, the way they'd been when they were children. "Luke is special to me."

"Yes."

Ashley felt warm at the thought. "I guess it was only right that I played a small part in all of this."

The doorbell rang and Reagan excused herself. She greeted Kari and Erin and their mother. The group stayed by the door, chatting about the events of the day.

Ashley looked at the Christmas tree, at the star nestled on top, and closed her eyes. *God, I went out on a limb that day, telling Luke about Reagan and Tommy, but you led the way. And now . . . I'm awed at your faithfulness. Bringing Luke back . . . using me to bring the two of them together. It's amazing, and it's all you, God . . . but thanks for using me in the process.*

Everyone had arrived, and Reagan's mother pulled several

chairs into a circle in the living room. When everyone was seated, Anne Decker explained again what they were doing, and then she offered to go first. She had her Bible on her lap, and she took a piece of paper from inside it.

"The verse I want to share with Reagan is one I've shared with her since she was a little girl." Anne gave Reagan a smile that spoke of days gone by. She shifted her gaze to the others. "We raised Reagan with an understanding of Scripture, and from her baby days, her father and I prayed over her."

Ashley watched the woman, mesmerized. How difficult the events of the past year must have been on her, yet clearly she'd come out stronger. A woman of faith had no other choice.

Anne Decker's eyes shone and she looked at Reagan again. "The verse is your favorite, honey. Jeremiah 29:11. 'I know the plans I have for you,' declares the Lord, 'plans to prosper you and not to harm you, plans to give you hope and a future.' " Reagan's mother took a tissue from a box beside her chair and pressed it to the corners of her eyes. She gave a single laugh and shook her head. "I'm sorry. I told myself I'd at least get through the *morning* without crying."

When she was more composed, she looked at Reagan again. "Your father and I prayed that verse over you several times a week from the day you were born, Reagan. And always we believed it was true, especially after you brought home a certain nice young man a year ago this past summer.

"Your father took the two of you to his office in the twin towers, and later that night, after the four of us went out, he told me he had a feeling about Luke." She looked at Ashley's mother. "That Luke was a kind young man, one who must've come from a good family."

Reagan angled her head, clearly touched by her mother's story. "I never knew that."

"He didn't want you to know." Anne smiled. "You were his only daughter; he didn't want to rush you."

A bit of soft laughter came from around the circle, and Reagan gave her mother a half smile. "I can see Dad saying that."

"Anyway, the reason I wanted to give you this verse is because there were times in the past year when I thought God had forgotten his plans for both of us. Your—" she held the tissue to her nose and hesitated—"your father's death . . . your pregnancy . . . and then it didn't seem like we'd ever see Luke again."

Reagan had tears on her cheeks now. "I know."

"But today, honey, today here we are." A sound that was more laugh than sob worked its way up from Anne's throat. "Here we are, and Luke has turned out to be exactly the kind of young man your father thought he'd be. The two of you have Tommy and each other, and a love for God that I've watched grow stronger every day these past months." She gave a dainty lift of her shoulders. "God was right all along. In his time, the prayers we prayed for you really did come true. God knew the plans he had for you after all. And so . . . I give you this verse because no matter what happens between you and Luke, no matter where the circumstances of life take you, I want you to know it's true. God knows the plans he has for you, Reagan, plans to give you a hope and a future and not to harm you."

Ashley's own cheeks were wet, and she looked around the room. Not an eye was dry. Reagan's mother stood and handed Reagan the verse. Then Anne looked at Ashley. "Would you like to go next?"

"Sure." Ashley made a quiet sniff. She had written the verse she'd chosen on a card, and she pulled it out now. It had taken several days before she'd settled on the right Scripture. In the end, it wasn't a conventional verse, one people quoted often or tacked at the bottom of artwork.

But it was the verse she and Reagan had most in common.

Ashley looked at the bride-to-be and prayed that the girl could see her heart, hear it in what she was about to say. "Reagan, you and I have something very precious in common, something the rest of our family might not understand." She hesitated, her hands trembling. "Their names are Cole and Tommy." Ashley allowed a sad smile. She and Reagan had never talked about this before. "You and I know what it feels like to do something outside the will of God, something that grieves his heart. We know how it feels to be the black mark on our family's name, and we know what it's like to wind up with the gift of a miracle child on the other end."

Reagan nodded, her expression tender.

"But maybe the thing we know most of all is the grace of God, his forgiveness. Because after the choices we made, his forgiveness was sometimes all that kept us going." Ashley accepted a tissue from her mother. "The verse I'm giving you is from Colossians 1:13-14: 'He has rescued us from the dominion of darkness and brought us into the kingdom of the Son he loves, in whom we have redemption, the forgiveness of sins.'"

In the corner of her eyes, Ashley caught her mother taking a tissue for herself.

"Redemption." Reagan smiled. "That's perfect, Ashley."

"And the thing is, you'll need it all your lives. I really believe that. Through the mountains and valleys of life you'll always come out okay if you and Luke can remember how God rescued you from darkness, rescued all of us from darkness, really. And how he's given you redemption through his Son. God's redemption is why Cole is such a blessing, why he loves the Lord and wants to live for him. And redemption is why you and Luke found your way back together again, and why I'm convinced your lives will be a beautiful thing forever."

Ashley's mother went next. She started by smiling at Reagan and waiting, massaging her throat the way she often did when she was too choked up to speak. Finally she said, "I'm giving you a verse I've given my children often through the years." She looked briefly at Erin, Brooke, Kari, and Ashley. "It's sort of the Baxter family mantra, I guess. And all my life I've never offered it to anyone but my children. But today you'll be taking my son for your own, and . . ." She bit the inside of her lip and closed her eyes for a brief moment.

"And I want you to know that I refuse to see today as losing my only boy. Instead . . . instead in my heart I'm taking you on as a daughter, Reagan. One of my own. And because of that I want to give you our family's special Scripture." She made two short sniffs and unfolded a piece of floral paper. "It's kept us together when times were tough, and it's reminded us that we are called to be one, called to love. It's from Colossians 3:12-14:

" 'Therefore, as God's chosen people, holy and dearly loved, clothe yourselves with compassion, kindness, humility, gentleness and patience. Bear with each other and forgive whatever grievances you may have against one another. Forgive as the Lord forgave you. And over all these virtues put on love, which binds them all together in perfect unity.' "

The words to the verses pushed Reagan over the edge. She hung her head for a minute and pinched the bridge of her nose. Then she stood and crossed the circle to Ashley's mother. "Thank you for loving me, Mrs. Baxter. After today—" her words were muffled, lost in the embrace—"after today I'll have two mothers. And the words of those verses will be a part of our family forever, too."

Kari was next. While Reagan returned to her seat, Kari slid her fingers beneath her eyes and drew a slow breath. "Well . . . no one told me not to wear mascara this morning."

Her comment gave the group a chance to laugh, to release some of the emotion in a way that lifted the mood. When the group quieted down again, Kari took out a note card and met Reagan's gaze. "You don't know me that well." She smiled. "Something I'm sure will change as we share our families in the years ahead."

"Yes." Reagan crossed her legs and leaned forward, connecting with Kari across the circle.

Kari's smile faded some. "You have something in common with Ashley, but Reagan, you also have something in common with me. The reality of a loss few people can grasp." Kari sniffed. "At the most difficult times of my life, this Scripture kept coming to light. In sermons, in conversations, in sympathy letters I received. And truthfully, I didn't want to hear it. Something about it sounded too predictable, too plastic."

Kari exchanged a quick look with their mother. "But the truth is, God wanted me to own this Bible verse, take it to heart and look for ways it was playing out in my life. Because it was." She opened the card and let her eyes fall to the words inside. "It comes from Romans 8:28: 'And we know that in all things God works for the good of those who love him, who have been called according to his purpose.'

"See . . ." Kari looked up, her eyes a reflection of her heart. "It's that last part people forget about when they use that verse. Things don't simply work for the good. They work for the good of those who have been called according to his purpose. In other words, things work to the good for those who don't fight life's ups and downs, but roll with them, allowing God's purpose to be bigger than all their hopes and expectations combined." She knit her brow. "When God's purpose is the main thing in your life, all things will work to the good. Every time. Does that make sense?"

Reagan gave Kari a sad smile, her eyes locked with Kari's. "Definitely."

Kari stood, hugged Reagan, and gave her the card. "Welcome to our family, Reagan."

Erin took a piece of paper from her purse and held it up. "I'll go next."

Reagan shifted her gaze in Erin's direction. "Okay."

"I brought you three short verses because for me, when it comes to marriage, they can't be separated. My sister Kari taught me that." Erin looked at Kari and then back at Reagan. "You may not know this, Reagan, but Sam and I nearly walked away from each other last year." She hesitated, holding the piece of paper against her heart. "Somehow after we married, we forgot about a simple miracle formula that every married person must remember."

Erin looked at the piece of paper. "The first verse is from 1 Corinthians 13:13: 'And now these three remain: faith, hope, and love. But the greatest of these is love.'" She set the paper down again. "I used to read that and think the same thing the world thinks. The answer to a happy marriage is love—pure and simple." Erin smiled and shook her head. "But God showed me it was deeper than that. The second verse is from Ecclesiastes 4:12: 'A cord of three strands is not quickly broken.'

"I knew that verse, too, and I thought I understood what it meant. With God in our marriage, we wouldn't fall apart. And that was true, but I wasn't sure how that worked exactly. Did it mean twice-a-day Bible studies? or constant prayer? Did it mean regular church attendance?"

A few soft giggles sounded from Kari and Anne Decker.

"No." Erin shook her head. "You need each of those things, but they're not the best way to have God always a part of your marriage. I didn't really know what the cord of three strands meant until I nearly let my marriage fall apart. Then Kari put the first two verses together with this one from 1 John 4:16, which says, 'God is love.'"

Erin held up three fingers. "The only way to have God in your marriage is to have love. And the only way to have love is to have God. They cannot be separated from each other because God is love. Every time you love Luke when you don't feel like it, every time you let love come from your words and your actions, you are letting God be part of your marriage. And believe me . . . nothing in the world can tear apart that kind of bond."

"Thanks, Erin." Reagan nodded, thoughtful.

A hush fell over the room, and Ashley looked at her lap. Landon had loved her that way, hadn't he? With a God-kind of love? But still here she was, alone, afraid even to call him, afraid of how she'd react when she saw him tonight at the wedding.

It was Brooke's turn. She crossed her arms and sat straighter in her chair. "Reagan, I'm so glad you asked us here today, asked us to share verses that mean so much to each of us. Mine is short and to the point."

Brooke looked at Hayley, sitting a foot away. "In the past few months God has taught me the secret of being content in every situation, whether life brings tragedies—like what happened to my younger daughter, or triumphs—like you and Luke marrying today. Spending time with Hayley, I can't help but be touched by her sweet spirit. I'm so . . . so glad she's alive." Brooke's voice cracked and she paused a moment.

"I believe with all my heart the secret is in our attitude. Life's circumstances don't improve by being anxious or angry or upset. But God calls us to rise above our circumstances, and that starts first in our attitudes."

Brooke pulled out a pale blue index card with dark writing. "From Philippians 4:4: 'Rejoice in the Lord always. I will say it again: Rejoice!'" She handed it to Reagan, who was seated beside her. "If you and Luke can figure out that point, you'll survive whatever journey God takes you on."

"Thank you." Reagan looked at Hayley. "I think we've all wondered how you've held up these past few months, and now—" she looked at the Bible verse in her hand—"maybe now we know."

"Yes." Brooke patted Reagan's knee. "It wouldn't have happened any other way."

They were finished, and Reagan held the cards and letters in her hand. "These verses will be precious to me forever, not just in my marriage to Luke but in every area of my life."

Anne Decker stood and motioned for them to gather around Reagan. "Let's pray for her, and then I have breakfast ready in the next room."

They prayed for twenty minutes, asking God that Reagan and Luke would live out not only the verses shared this morning but every part of Scripture, so that their marriage would be filled with life and love and laughter. Prayers were said for Tommy and for whatever other children the couple might have. Finally Ashley's mother prayed that after today they wouldn't be just two families with something in common.

They would be one family, connected and joined together by God himself.

# CHAPTER TWENTY-THREE

T HEY WERE THE LONGEST three minutes of his life.

Luke stood at the front of the church and counted the seconds until Reagan would appear at the back door. In the meantime, he surveyed the fifty people gathered at the church and tried to take in the miracle happening around him.

Soft organ music played in the background, something traditional from Bach, but Luke barely noticed. His eyes moved to the front row, where his mother smiled at him. She looked beautiful, as young as Luke remembered her looking when he was a small boy.

Before the service she'd pulled him aside and kissed his cheek. "If I cry during the service, remember one thing." Her whispered words had been upbeat. "I couldn't be happier for you, son. Really."

His eyes met hers and she gave him a slight nod, something none of the others would've noticed, but something that told him she meant what she'd said. No matter that his marrying Reagan would take him from Bloomington; it was the right decision, and his mother was nothing but glad for him.

Other faces jumped out at him from the church pews. Erin

and Sam. Ryan and Kari with Jessie; Brooke and Hayley. His eyes held the image of his blonde niece a few beats longer. She was awake, looking at the lit candles that marked each aisle. It was a miracle she was here at all, but Luke wanted more.

*God, heal her, please. Bring her back to us.*

Luke was still praying, still begging God about his niece, when the music changed and a hush fell over the church.

The wedding party was fairly simple. Reagan had asked Ashley to be her maid of honor, and Luke's father was his best man. Cole was the ring bearer; Maddie, the flower girl; and Reagan's brother, Bryan, was an usher. Now the teenage boy had taken his place a few feet from Luke.

The first one down the aisle was Ashley, and from the moment she entered the church, Luke saw her eyes find his and stay there, connected.

He didn't need words to hear what she wanted to tell him.

She had been his big sister, the one he'd played with and laughed with and loved the most while he was growing up. Now, minutes before his big moment, it was only right that she have this chance to let him know what she felt about his decision. That it was good and right and wonderful. Even if she could only tell him through eye contact.

He felt a smile tug at the corners of his mouth. *I hear you, Ashley . . . I hear you.*

Her eyes told him one more thing then. No matter how quickly the years went by after this or how infrequent their visits might become, she would never forget the endless yesterdays of the idyllic childhood they'd shared. He winked at her and knew that she understood.

He wouldn't forget either.

Cole and Maddie were next—Cole decked out in a blue suit, his grin wide and mischievous; and Maddie in a fluffy white dress, her blonde hair hanging in ringlets around her face. Cole was a bit older, but no question Maddie, her chin held high, was the responsible one. Four times Cole spotted someone he knew, and each time he veered toward the edge of the aisle, waving and pointing, and each time Maddie pulled him close so they kept moving, walking together at an even pace.

The antics earned the children muffled bits of laughter from the crowd, but Luke cocked his head, touched. Wasn't that just like family? One walking the straight and narrow, the other veering off the path? And just like family, one kept the other in line so that somehow they'd finish the walk together.

That had certainly been the case for him in the year after the terrorist attacks.

Cole and Maddie found their places beside Ashley, and again the music changed. This time the traditional wedding march sounded throughout the church and everyone rose and faced the back door. Luke's heart beat hard against his chest.

The door opened and Reagan appeared, her arm looped through his father's. The picture they made was enough to drop Luke to his knees, but he remained tall and strong, waiting for his bride. For the first few steps, Reagan whispered something to his father and the two of them chuckled. Then they looked straight ahead.

Luke studied the man he admired most. How was it possible that only a year ago he'd been ready to walk away from his father forever? And how close had he come to throwing away the faith and future God had planned for him? The answers caused him a slight shudder, but it was gone almost as soon as it hit him. Those days were in the past; God had returned him home and restored everything about their relationship.

And now his father was walking Reagan down the aisle.

Luke's eyes shifted to her. She was stunning, every detail of her dress and bouquet. But it wasn't until they stopped a few feet from him and his father lifted the lacy veil from around her face, that Luke could see her eyes, see the way she was looking past his father, to him alone.

He had expected to see a twinge of sadness in her face, the reminder that her father wasn't here to see this day, to walk her down the aisle. She felt those things, because she'd told him so the night before at the rehearsal. But now that their wedding had finally arrived, her expression held no sadness whatsoever.

It held a look he'd never seen before. A sheer, unabashed devotion, a trust that from now until the end of time she would stay by him, honor him, believe in him. Defining love with every passing day, every hour.

Every single breath.

Landon crept into the church just after Ashley headed down the aisle. He hadn't wanted her to see him until after the ceremony, hadn't wanted anything to take away from the fact that her baby brother was getting married. No question Ashley didn't want him interfering with the moment. In fact, he'd almost chosen not to come.

He'd talked to Luke a few weeks earlier and found out the family's itinerary. The Baxters had been in New York City since Saturday, and Ashley hadn't called once.

He slipped into a pew near the back and peeled off his black wool jacket. Beneath it he wore a dress shirt and tie, not that he expected to stay long. He'd simply watch the ceremony and spend a few minutes at the reception. That way he could congratulate Luke and Reagan, and be on his way.

By the time he got situated in the pew, the wedding march was playing, and with every note Landon felt the air being sucked from his chest. He was supposed to look at the bride, the way everyone else in the church was doing. But he would never hear that song without thinking of Ashley, without remembering the excitement he'd felt in the days before giving her the ring, before asking her to marry him.

And now, helpless to stop himself, he shifted his gaze from the bride to the maid of honor at the front of the church. What he saw made his heart skip a beat. Ashley wasn't watching the bride either.

She was watching him.

Their eyes found each other and held, Ashley's glistening as she studied him, searching his heart. No question it was a look of love, the kind that long ago he'd only dreamed of seeing in Ashley Baxter's eyes. But here, in light of all they'd decided about their future, her expression ripped at his understanding.

*What is it about her, God? And why can it never work?*

His question filled his senses and blocked out even the music, everything but the pair of eyes staring at him from the church front. The connection between them was so strong it was almost physical. Regardless of the wedding procession or the guests gathered to witness the ceremony, Landon had to summon all his strength to keep from striding to the front of the church and taking Ashley in his arms.

After Luke and Reagan stepped before the altar, even after the minister greeted the audience, Landon held Ashley's eyes. But then the cold slap of reality hit him in the face. She hadn't called, hadn't wanted to see him; all that they'd shared was over. Torturing each other now would do nothing but make tomorrow more painful. He shifted his eyes toward the wedding couple, but his heart refused to follow.

What was it about her? Ashley had her mind made up; he would not be a part of her future or Cole's. Landon had known that long before coming here today. It was why he was training for the captain position, why he was willing to marry his future to the FDNY rather than wait a lifetime for Ashley to get past the fear of her HIV diagnosis.

He could feel her eyes on him still, but Landon kept his attention on the young couple. The minister was wrapping up, explaining that Reagan and Luke's special Scripture was from Jeremiah, that God knew the plans he had for each of them, and how this wedding was part of God's plan.

It was time for the vows, and Luke went first. He spoke of the simplicity of love, how it was the most basic and necessary element in a marriage and how, when it was right, it was more beautiful and rare than any diamond. Then he promised Reagan a lifetime of simple love, shared moments walking through the park or laughing over a game of tennis, the journey of parenting and growing old and believing that through every phase in life, the best was yet to be.

Reagan went next. She talked about the love each of their parents had shared, and how they were fortunate to be surrounded by the best mentors of all. Then she promised to be Luke's best friend and lover, the one besides God whom Luke could turn to for everything, the one who would hold his hand through the journey of life.

Tears shone in Reagan's eyes as she finished. "Life is uncertain." She sniffed and looked at her mother for a moment. "We know that better now. But if our life together lasts one day or twenty thousand, it will all have been worth it because all we have for sure is today, this minute. And I'll cherish every minute with you, Luke. As long as God gives us today."

Landon leaned forward in the pew and looked to the floor. He had heard everything Reagan said, but one part was running over in his mind again and again: *"If our life together lasts one day or twenty thousand, it will all have been worth it."*

Reagan and Luke were exchanging rings, but Landon wasn't listening. The simple profound truth spoken in Reagan's vows caused him to look once more at Ashley, to see that yes, she was still watching him.

Had she heard it? Had it clicked, what Reagan had said?

From the back of the church, he couldn't read her expression completely, but fear seemed to be one of the emotions calling out to him.

"Come on, Ashley," he whispered. No one was sitting near him, so the sound of his words faded before anyone else heard them. "We could have today, couldn't we?"

She knit her brow and gave a slight shake of her head, as if to

say she couldn't understand him, couldn't try to understand him
while the ceremony was still going on. She shifted her attention
back to Reagan and Luke.

Landon willed her to understand.

They could be together, couldn't they? Okay, so she thought
it was unfair to sentence him to an uncertain future with her, but
so what? All of life was uncertain, right? Wasn't that what Reagan had said a minute ago? If he could marry Ashley and live a
day with her, a week, the minutes would be the best of his life,
something he wouldn't trade for a lifetime of mediocrity.

Wasn't that what he'd been trying to tell Ashley since she'd
found out about her blood test? Life was too short to borrow tomorrow's pain for today. If Reagan's mother had known that her
husband would die a young, tragic death, she still would've married him. Because love doesn't care when it dies.

Only that it had a chance to live.

# CHAPTER TWENTY-FOUR

THE RECEPTION WAS IN FULL SWING, but so far—other than a quick wave—Ashley had avoided Landon.

She'd seen him, of course. Seen him the moment he walked into the church. And despite her determination to make their time together at this wedding nothing more than a passing hello, her eyes had betrayed her.

No one needed to hand her a mirror for her to know that much.

The love that passed from her eyes to his in those first moments was something she had no control over. He looked amazing, dressed in the same blue shirt and black slacks he'd worn the day he'd proposed to her. And as their eyes held during the ceremony, she wondered a hundred questions. Whether he'd worn the suit on purpose, and whether he'd known that by coming in at the last minute she would have no choice but to see him, feel his presence like a tangible force in the room.

But then, midway through Reagan's and Luke's vows, Landon had mouthed something, spoken something meant for her eyes alone, and in an instant she realized what was happening. By letting herself get lost in his eyes, she had given him too much of the truth, too clear a picture of how much she still loved him.

And though she couldn't read his words, she didn't have to. No matter that he'd made a commitment to the fire department, the things he would've said to her in that moment were no different than what he'd said to her the last time they were together.

They could work it out; they could find a way; they could be together.

Everything she wanted him to say, everything she wanted to believe.

But it wasn't going to happen, because Ashley wasn't going to let it. Rehashing the reasons would do nothing but make her sad and frustrated, and that wasn't how she wanted to spend her time tonight. It was Christmas Eve, after all. Her brother was married to Reagan, and before time pulled them from the moment and propelled them into the new year and all its uncertainty, Ashley wanted to celebrate.

From the moment she entered the decorated reception hall, she made herself busy. Reagan's mother had hired a caterer to serve dinner, and each table was bedecked in Christmas red and white, with a pinecone centerpiece. At one end of the room was a dance floor and a deejay, who was, at the moment, playing something soft and instrumental.

Ashley found Anne Decker talking to one of the caterers. She came up beside her and tapped her shoulder. "Can I help?"

"Everything's done." Reagan's mother smiled. "But I'd like you to meet my friends." She led Ashley to a table of women, most of whom attended her church. Ashley went gladly. Anything to delay coming face-to-face with Landon.

"We've heard a lot about you." One of the women smiled at her. "You helped Reagan and Luke find their way back together."

The conversation continued and when it slowed, Ashley caught a glimpse of Landon off her right shoulder. She turned left and practically bumped into Brooke and Kari and Erin. The sisters talked about highlights from the wedding, how their father had walked Reagan down the aisle with the same kind of pride Reagan's father would have if he'd been alive.

After half an hour, Reagan's mother took the microphone from a podium at the front of the room and asked people to find a table. "Dinner will be served in a few minutes, and then we'll dance."

People made their way to the round tables, and Ashley scanned the room. She hadn't seen Cole in several minutes, but suddenly she heard his voice, high and animated. Her eyes followed the sound, and sure enough, he was kneeling in the chair next to Landon, his arms wrapped around Landon's neck.

Ashley drew a long breath and headed toward them.

"Mom!" Cole called out to her long before she reached the table. "Look who's here!"

She hadn't told him Landon might attend the wedding. With the distance between them lately, Ashley hadn't been sure he would come. "Yes, buddy." She met Landon's eyes and tried to hide her feelings with a smile. "Isn't that great?"

"It's the best news ever!" He slid onto his bottom and reached for Landon's hand. "Come on, Mom. Sit down."

Ashley wanted to sit next to Landon, but instead she took the chair on the other side of Cole. Every few seconds she reminded herself of the truth. Nothing could come from letting her heart loose on a night like this. She turned her attention to Landon. Her tone was light as she smiled at him. "We keep meeting up at weddings."

"Yes." Landon's grin was slow and easy. Not the desperate look he'd had earlier during the ceremony. "Makes you wonder, doesn't it?"

Cole was watching them, listening, his head turning from Landon to Ashley and back again. He tugged on Landon's sleeve. "Hayley's here."

Something softened in Landon's eyes. "I know, pal. She looks good."

"That's what I think." Cole lowered his voice as if he wanted to add something private. "But Maddie says she's different." His tone grew loud again. "She can't swim anymore."

"Maybe one day." Landon gave Cole a sideways hug and kissed the top of his head.

"Yeah, maybe."

Dinner arrived then, and they ate amidst small talk and reflections of the wedding. Through every minute of it, Ashley had to remind herself to stay seated, to not get up and move closer to Landon, where she would finally be close enough to smell him, to breathe in the reality of his presence.

When the meal was over, Reagan's mother used the microphone again and invited them to gather around the cake table.

Cole was on his feet instantly. "Can I go, Mom? Please? Maddie's up there."

Landon brought his face down alongside Cole's and batted his eyelashes at Ashley. "Yeah, Mom, Maddie's up there."

"Fine." She was laughing before she could stop herself, before she could remind her heart not to reengage, at least not beyond a surface level. "Go get a good spot."

Cole was gone before she finished her sentence, and Ashley raised a single eyebrow at Landon. "Aren't you going to join him?"

Until then Landon had been trying to match the easy banter she'd established when she sat down. But now he met her eyes and held them. "I don't want cake, Ash."

"Oh." Her heart rate doubled. "Okay."

He pointed to the empty chair between them. "Think Cole would mind if I took his chair?"

"Actually . . ." She glanced at Cole, lost in the crowd of people ready to watch Luke and Reagan cut their cake. "I think he'll be a while."

Landon smiled and in one fluid motion he slid into the chair beside her. The attention of the wedding guests was completely focused on the cake table, so both of them turned their attention toward the newlyweds. As they did, Landon's arm brushed against hers and stayed that way. She was wearing a sleeveless black dress, one with long, elegant lines and a skirt that fell just above her ankles. Even through his suit jacket she could feel his warmth against her bare arm.

"You look amazing, Ash." He kept his gaze straight ahead, but his voice was different, the pretense stripped away.

For a moment she held her breath, searching for a way to keep things simple. But the idea was as unrealistic as asking herself not to breathe. "You, too."

The big moment had arrived, and together Luke and Reagan eased a white-handled knife into a cake covered with baby roses.

Landon eased a bit closer. "You've been avoiding me."

"No." They both still faced forward, pretending to be caught up in the wedding-cake drama. "I had people to visit."

"Oh." A slow chuckle sounded from deep in his chest. "Okay."

This time she turned her head and met his eyes. "What?"

"Come on, Ash. I know what you're doing, and can I tell you something?"

Her heart pounded in her throat, but she said nothing, waiting for him to continue.

"You don't have to worry, Ashley. We've already made our choices about the future. But tonight . . ."

His eyes held hers and she felt every bit of her resistance falling away.

"Tonight let's not pretend we don't care, okay? That's too much work." The corners of his mouth lifted and a sparkle lit his eyes. "Especially on Christmas Eve."

In the background, the cake-cutting moment had passed. The deejay switched the music to something slower and called Luke and Reagan to the dance floor. Ashley and Landon watched the wedding couple dance, but Ashley could think only of Landon's last words: *"Let's not pretend we don't care, okay?"*

When the song ended, the deejay played another slow song

and invited the guests to join Luke and Reagan on the dance floor. Landon stood and held his hand out to her. "Come on, Ash. Dance with me . . . please."

Ashley looked at him and felt herself getting lost. And in that moment, she knew it was too late. It was Christmas Eve, her brother's wedding reception. No matter how hard she worked at it, she couldn't pretend she didn't love Landon. She didn't want to pretend. Not for one minute more.

"On one condition."

Landon eased his fingers around hers, working his thumb along the back of her hand. "Anything."

"We can't talk about tomorrow."

In all the years they'd known each other, Ashley had only slow-danced with Landon one other time—at Kari and Ryan's wedding. And then only for one song, since they'd been too busy talking to spend time on the dance floor. But now he led her to a spot several feet from the deejay and turned to face her. For a moment they froze and she would've given anything to undo the facts so she could enjoy the dance.

He put one hand around her waist and took her fingers with his other hand. He swayed slowly, more intent on her than the music. For a minute they did nothing more than move subtly across the floor and stare at each other, searching for scraps of yesterday.

Toward the end of the song, Landon slowed to a near stop. "Okay . . . you know it's coming."

"What?" She had her other hand around his waist, and she drew an inch closer so she could hear him above the music. Her emotions were as varied as the Manhattan skyline.

"The question." He gave her a lazy grin, the one she'd seen a hundred times in her dreams.

"What question?" She was playing with him, feeding off his teasing tone, praying they could keep it light until the clock struck midnight and her glass slippers disappeared.

He blinked and the silliness faded from his eyes. "Do you miss me, Ash?"

She clenched her teeth to keep from pulling him close, from drawing him near and kissing him right here in front of the other wedding guests. *Resist him,* she told herself. *It can't go anywhere.* But in light of his question, she had to answer, had to let him know the obvious. "With every breath, Landon."

His feet kept moving to the slow beat, but he squinted at her hair. Then with careful hands, he ran his fingers down the side of her head. "You have the most beautiful hair." He raised his brow. "Has anyone ever told you that?"

She held her breath to keep from giggling, but it didn't work. The laughter built within her and escaped in a burst that left them both chuckling as they sauntered off the floor. "You sound more like Irvel than Irvel does." She bopped him on the head and took the seat beside him at their table.

Cole was dancing with Maddie, staying close to Reagan and Luke. Every now and then he'd look at Ashley and Landon and wave at them from across the room. In turn, they'd wave back and keep talking.

"So tell me, how *are* Irvel and the gang?"

"Good." Ashley was grateful for the laughter between them. It meant they were making the best of the situation without working themselves back to a place that would hurt too much to leave. "I'm worried about Irvel. She's slower these days. Talking to Hank as though he's standing beside her half the time."

Landon shrugged. "I can relate."

"What?" Ashley grinned, refusing to let the conversation grow deep again. "You talk to Hank, too?"

"Okay." He chuckled, and his head dropped a bit. "You got me. I talk to Hank all the time."

They laughed again, and when the music changed to a faster beat, he took her hand and the two of them spent the next half hour dancing with Ashley's sisters and the bride and groom.

When the reception ended, everyone made their way to the

street and a line of cabs. Ashley hung back with Landon, together but apart, not sure how to say good-bye with everyone clustered around.

"When do you leave?" Landon leaned close, obviously aware that this might be it, their last night together for a very long time.

"Saturday." Ashley wore her long wool coat, but still she was cold. The snow was falling again, and she allowed herself the luxury of standing closer to him, their bodies touching as they talked. Her mother and Erin and Sam, even Luke and Reagan had already returned to the hotel. Only her father and Brooke remained, working to buckle Hayley and Maddie into the cab while Cole hopped about on the sidewalk.

"Ash . . ." He waited. His breath hung in the air like a wisp of smoke.

She looked up at him, unaware of anything but his nearness. "I have to go."

"Not yet." His eyes held hers, and he angled in so he was partially facing her. "I'll take you home."

"I . . . Landon . . . what about Cole?"

At almost the same instant, Brooke called out from the cab. "Ashley, I've got Cole." She motioned to him. "Come on, buddy. You can go back with Aunt Brooke."

"Are you sure?" Ashley's heart was beating so hard she expected it to affect her voice. If she were smart she'd go now, take Cole by the hand and join Brooke, her father, and the girls in the cab. But she couldn't do it, couldn't leave Landon standing there no matter what her common sense tried to say. "Okay, Brooke. I won't be late."

She smiled at Ashley. "I'm not worried. You have a key, right?"

"Right." Ashley took a few steps closer to the cab. "Cole, be good for Aunt Brooke, okay?"

"Okay, Mommy." He skipped over and hugged Landon. "Are you coming to the hotel, Landon? Maybe we can watch a movie."

Ashley watched Landon's struggle, how the muscles in his jaw flinched. "Hey, Cole, jump up here for a minute."

Cole backed up a few feet and took a running leap into Landon's arms. "Can you, Landon? Can you come back with us?"

"Not today, tiger." He let his forehead rest against Cole's. "But maybe I'll see you again before you go, okay?"

"Okay." Cole's expression fell. "When are you coming back home where we live?"

Ashley watched Landon's gaze fall to the ground. When he lifted his eyes, Ashley wasn't sure if it was the freezing air or Cole's question, but his lashes were damp. "I'm not sure, buddy. One of these days, okay?"

"Come on, Cole." Brooke poked her head out of the cab. "We're waiting, honey."

Cole wrapped his little-boy arms around Landon's neck and held on for several seconds. "I love you, Landon."

"Oh, Cole." Landon buried his head against Cole's. "Love you, too." He eased the child to the ground, and the two waved at each other once more before Cole ran to the cab.

Landon took a step back, closer to Ashley. Together they watched the cab pull away. Landon turned to her. "I hate this part."

"Me, too." Ashley pushed her hands deep into her coat pockets and shivered. "Where's your truck?"

"This way." Landon held out his hand.

Ashley hesitated only a moment. Then she eased her fingers between his and didn't resist when he slipped both their hands into his coat pocket. His truck was in the back parking lot. They climbed in and Landon started the engine. It was just after ten o'clock, and at that hour—especially on Christmas Eve—they'd be back at her hotel in twenty minutes.

Landon leaned against the driver's door and studied her. "Want to talk somewhere?"

For a few seconds Ashley thought about saying the right answer, the one she had rehearsed for this moment: *No, Landon, take me back to the hotel. Nothing good can come from this.* But her heart spoke before her head remembered the words. "Okay."

They agreed to go back to the Marriott for coffee, but halfway there, Landon pulled into a parking lot near the south end of Central Park and grinned at her. "I have a better idea."

Again her head demanded that she refuse him, beg him to take her back to the hotel before she fell any more in love with him. But instead she smiled at him, and when he opened her door, this time she easily slipped her hand in his. "We're walking through Central Park?"

"Not quite." He led her across the street and down half a block to the place where half a dozen horse-drawn carriages waited.

"Landon!" Ashley's voice fell to a whisper. "What are you . . . ?"

He lifted one shoulder. "It's Christmas Eve, Ash." His eyes met hers and lingered. "Maybe our last."

The carriages were all different, and Landon picked one where the back curved up over their heads, protecting them from the light snow. He climbed in, then helped her up. Once she was inside, the driver spread a fur blanket over their legs.

"It'll take a minute to warm up." Landon put his arm around her and pulled her close.

Again she couldn't find the strength to fight the moment. Everything light and easy about the night was gone now, and Ashley leaned her head on his shoulder, snuggling closer. Tomorrow didn't matter. "Thanks, Landon."

They were four blocks into the park before either of them spoke.

"I liked what Reagan said." He tightened his hold on her and looked at the bare trees that lined the pathway.

"Reagan?" Ashley sat straighter and found his eyes.

"Her vows. The part about life being uncertain, and love being worthwhile . . ."

"If you had one day or twenty thousand." Ashley sighed and looked straight ahead again. "I heard it."

His voice was soft, a caress against her soul. "And . . ."

She rested her head against the back of the carriage. "And it doesn't apply to us, Landon. If Reagan and Luke only live a handful of days as husband and wife, at least those days will be healthy and safe." Space had crept between them during the conversation, and a chill made its way down her spine. "I can't even give you that."

"Hey." He touched the side of her face, and she looked at him once more. "You're giving it to me now."

Her breath caught in her throat. "Landon . . . you know what I mean."

"But you haven't given me a chance. I want to work with you on this, Ashley."

"No!" She raised her voice a notch. "It isn't fair to you; I won't do it. You're here; your job is here. And this—" she waved her hand around in the air—"this is some kind of Christmas fantasy. Some moment not connected to yesterday or tomorrow, okay?"

He studied her, waiting a handful of heartbeats before the fight left his eyes. "Okay." He closed in and kissed the tip of her nose. "I'm sorry."

What else could either of them say? Ashley lifted her chin a notch. "Me, too." *Keep your distance; come on.* A cool breeze swirled several snowflakes into the carriage.

The ride was half over, and while the horse's hooves clopped in the background, Landon faced the path ahead and again they were quiet. Ashley ached for a way to break the silence, to tell him that yes, of course Reagan's words had applied to them as well. To hold him and kiss him and pray that he might come back to Bloomington with her. She hadn't expected him to kiss her, not even on the tip of her nose. But then she hadn't expected to be alone with him in a horse-drawn carriage on a snowy Christmas Eve in Central Park.

"I want to ask you something." Landon shifted his body so he could see her. "Now, before the ride's over."

"Okay." Her lips were suddenly dry, her heart once more skittering about inside her chest. He had a right to tell her he never wanted to talk to her again, and if that was the case, she had to accept it. Dragging out the ending of their relationship was proving hard on both of them.

He opened his mouth to speak, but instead, in a pull too strong for either of them to resist, he eased his fingers along the side of her face and drew closer.

Ashley knew what was going to happen, but she couldn't stop herself, didn't want to stop. Their lips touched and he kissed her, melted her in a way that dissolved every reason why she should pull back and have him take her home.

The kiss continued, changing from quiet desperation to urgent. Ashley pulled away first, her lips burning from his warmth, the magic of being with him this way. She closed her eyes and tried to ignore the way her breathing was quick and jagged. *Why, God . . . why does it always come to this when I know we're not supposed to be together?*

Landon was still close, his mouth inches from hers. He whispered the words, slow and thoughtful. "Do you still love me, Ashley?"

She opened her eyes and felt herself falling into his stare, lost in his feelings for her. "Yes, Landon. I always will."

"Okay, then." He exhaled and allowed a bit of space between them. "Stay with me, here in New York, until New Year's Day; would you do that, Ash? I have the week off, and Brooke could take Cole back on Saturday. Then you could get a hotel closer to my apartment. We'll spend Christmas with your family tomorrow, walk along Fifth Avenue, and go to Times Square on New Year's Eve."

"Landon . . ." Ashley tried to contain her smile. She was about to tell him his idea was crazy when he started in again.

"We won't talk about the future, Ash. But you won't be seeing a doctor until you get back and then . . . well, by then everything will be different. You'll be in and out of appointments, and I'll be—"

"You'll be a fire captain." Her heart danced around inside her chest like a small child begging for one more carnival ticket.

"Yes." He lifted her hand to his lips and kissed it. "Please. I'll go crazy knowing you're here and not seeing you."

She felt the corners of her lips inch up into her cheeks. She would have to change her return date, but her ticket allowed for that. "Did you say art museums?"

"And Coney Island dogs." Landon kissed her again, but not as long as before.

Ashley looked at him and bit her lip. The thrill from a moment earlier faded some. "What happens when the week's over?"

"We ask God to help us find a way to say good-bye."

"Again."

"Yes." He eased his arm around her shoulders once more. "Again."

It was after eleven when the carriage came to a stop. Before taking her back to the hotel, Landon took her to a midnight Christmas Eve service at a church in downtown Manhattan.

They held hands as the preacher talked about making every minute of the new year count, about turning it into a gift for God, the way he'd turned the Christ child into a gift for all of mankind.

By the time Ashley got in that night, Brooke and the children were asleep. She tiptoed to the bathroom, brushed her teeth, and climbed into bed. She was glad no one else was awake, glad to keep her feelings about the night to herself. She'd set out that night intent on having only a friendly conversation with Landon. Instead she'd made plans to spend the coming week with him.

She didn't want Brooke's approval or Cole's excitement. Her relationship with Landon was over, so she didn't want to spend one minute talking about the decision she'd just made. It was crazy, impulsive, and in the end it would hurt both of them when the week was over. But it was Christmas, and come January, everything about Ashley's life would become more complicated. Yes, the reality of her situation would not change because of a week in Manhattan. In fact, there were a hundred ways she could've convinced herself to stay clear of Landon Blake next week, but all of them combined didn't carry the weight of one single truth.

They might never have a chance like this again.

# CHAPTER TWENTY-FIVE

CHRISTMAS, in all its bittersweet array of emotions, was over, and Brooke had a full heart as she packed her suitcase. She and Hayley were catching a plane in the morning. Her parents would keep Maddie, and on Saturday Cole would fly home with them so Ashley could stay through New Year's.

Brooke folded a pair of slacks and nodded to Ashley. "Could you hand me the sweater in the closet? I almost forgot it."

Ashley grabbed it and tossed it to her. Then she flopped onto the bed, careful not to disturb Cole, who was sleeping on the other side. "Great day, huh?"

"Wonderful." Joy and the hint of sorrow filled Brooke's eyes. "Too bad Peter missed it."

"Yes."

They were quiet for a spell.

"It was fun, watching all the kids together, knowing that Reagan and Luke are finally married."

Brooke raised an eyebrow at her. "Come on, Ashley. It was fun because Landon was there."

"Well . . ." Ashley sat up and pulled her knees to her chest. "Maybe."

"Please." Brooke's hands fell to her sides, the pair of pants forgotten. She stared at her younger sister. "You two look like parts of the same whole. And when Cole's with him . . ."

"I know. I'm glad we'll have this week."

Brooke released a slow sigh. "You could have more than that if you were willing."

Ashley's smile dimmed. "We've been through that."

"I know." Brooke picked up the sweater, folded it, and set it into the suitcase. "I just think you're being crazy, Ash. The man's perfect for you and Cole; he'll never love anyone like he loves you. It's written all over everything he says and does when you're together."

Ashley bit her lip and looked at Cole. "I know. I see it, too."

"But today was good for more than that reason. It was seeing Mom and Dad with all the kids, watching Mom's face glow the way it hasn't in months. And Hayley, sitting nearby as she responded to her cousins and aunts and uncles. All of it was wonderful."

"Except for Peter." Ashley angled her face, her eyes narrowed.

"Except for Peter." Brooke stopped folding again and stared out the window. "I think I know what happened, Ash."

"What?"

"I stopped needing him." She dropped to the edge of the bed and let her eyes fall on Hayley's sleeping form. "When we met, I needed him because he was a doctor and I was a lowly med student. A dozen times a week I asked him for advice or help with a study sheet. He was tall, intelligent, everything to me. Boyfriend, confidant, study partner, and a raving success on top of it. In a professional sense, he was everything I wanted to be."

An understanding look filled Ashley's eyes. "And then you became him."

"Exactly. Bit by bit I accomplished everything he'd done, and maybe . . . maybe I didn't need him anymore."

"He started seeing you as competition instead of a wife."

"Exactly."

The idea was so new it hadn't taken complete root in Brooke's heart, but for the first time she could connect the dots of her past. Maddie's health, Hayley's accident—those things had added to their problems, but they hadn't caused them.

And neither had Peter, really.

Brooke turned to Ashley, her head reeling. "It was my fault, Ash. I became his equal, and I didn't see him in the same light anymore, didn't adore him." She lifted one shoulder. "He didn't know how to handle it, or even how to love me." She could hear the anger in her tone, anger because maybe it wasn't her fault after all. She was allowed to be successful, too, wasn't she?

Ashley was on the same track. "Now wait. You're allowed to be his equal. It wasn't your success that put distance between you." Her eyes softened. "It was something you said a minute ago." She paused. "You stopped needing him."

Brooke felt the truth drop like a rock to the basement of her heart. "I did, didn't I?"

"Yes. Sometimes it looked like you were single, and Peter was along for the ride. Lately, I can't remember seeing you ask for his advice or look at him the way a man needs to be looked at."

Brooke let loose a sad laugh and studied her younger sister. "How'd you get so smart?"

"Mom." Ashley smiled. She traced a series of invisible hearts on the hotel bedspread. "The two of us talk more these days. She and Dad believe love is about honoring the other person, making them feel special, needed." Ashley slid to the edge of the bed and let her feet hang over. "So maybe that's what's wrong with you and Peter."

Brooke thought about the past year, how she'd reacted when Peter wanted to phone a specialist, and later, when he'd made an appointment with the doctor without checking with her. She'd taken it as an affront to her medical training. Instead, maybe

Peter was merely being the leader of their family, taking the man's role of looking out for Maddie the best way he knew how.

Then, after Hayley's accident . . .

"Peter must've felt worthless after Hayley got hurt."

"I'm sure."

"And I didn't help much." Brooke squinted across the room. "I've always tried to be smarter than everyone else." She was calm, the reality sinking in. "I thought I could earn Dad's love if I was like him."

Ashley smiled. "We all thought that, but you know . . . we were all wrong." She looped her arm through Brooke's. "Dad loved all of us, whether we were coming home from Paris pregnant or earning a medical degree."

"You're right."

"Maybe you tried to earn Peter's love the same way." Ashley blew at a wisp of hair and cast Brooke a sideways glance.

"The whole time proving I was as capable of medicine as he was."

"Right."

Brooke felt nauseous, thinking of the times when she'd worked to make a medical point or hold her ground on a method of treatment. She'd all but lost their relationship in her struggle to be a good doctor. Air leaked from her lungs in a tired, defeated way. "All he wanted was for me to honor him, allow him to lead me."

Their conversation played out, and the more Brooke talked about it the more certain she felt. However badly torn apart her marriage was, she had played a part in its destruction. She would have to find a way to tell Peter her thoughts, but not until she was back home.

Talk turned again to Ashley and Landon. "So . . . you and Landon for a whole week, huh?"

"Yep." Ashley was on her feet, slowly making her way toward the window. She showed no interest in talking about details. "We both need to be back at work on the third."

"Well, little sister—" Brooke gave a light laugh—"I want to

tell you to stop fighting yourself and love the man, go ahead and make plans for the future. But I know that's not what you want, so . . ."

"You're wrong, Brooke." Ashley looked over her shoulder. "I want it more than I want life. But I won't do that to him." She turned back to the window. "There's a difference."

"Okay." Brooke's tone softened. "But you're not beginning something with Landon; you're ending it." She stood and joined Ashley near the window. The view outside was wetter than before, most of the snow having melted. "All I'm saying is be careful."

"I won't be alone with him, if that's what you're thinking."

"It's not." Brooke held her breath for a moment and then exhaled hard. "You've been that route. No one needs to lecture you on making smart choices physically." She turned to Ashley. "I'm talking about being smart emotionally."

"Too late for that." Ashley let her head fall softly against the window. "Leaving him will kill me, Brooke. I already know that."

"Okay, but I'm thinking about him. Be careful, Ashley. Don't break his heart."

Ashley said nothing, but after a while Brooke heard her make a few sniffing sounds.

"Hey, it's okay, Ash. You'll be okay." Brooke hugged her from the side and they stayed that way for a while.

Then Brooke resumed her packing, thinking about their earlier conversation and the truth it held. Indeed, she had stopped needing Peter, stopped admiring him for the work he did each day, stopped acknowledging his accomplishments. Stopped recognizing the place he had as leader in their family.

In that light, small wonder that he'd grown distant from her and the girls.

Ashley was still at the window, lost in her own thoughts, so Brooke moved about the room with as little noise as possible. She placed a final few belongings in the suitcase and zipped it.

Already she had outfits laid out for the trip tomorrow. One last check of the closet and she was ready to turn in for the night.

She was headed for the bathroom when she stopped and looked at her sister, still motionless across the room, staring out at the city. "You okay, Ash?"

"Yeah."

Brooke stared at Ashley's back for a moment longer and anchored her hands on her hips. Ashley wasn't okay; neither of them was.

However and why ever Brooke had stopped needing Peter, she was sure of one thing. She needed him now, needed him to help her with Hayley, to believe that one day they'd all be whole again. And most of all, she needed him to hold her and care for her and make her feel like a girl in love again.

There was only one problem.

Peter thought it was too late.

# CHAPTER TWENTY-SIX

THE WEEK WAS A BLUR of gold and silver moments, the type Ashley would remember as long as she lived. And that was a good thing, because this time after she said good-bye to Landon, memories would be all she had left. They'd have to last not just a month or a year.

But a lifetime.

They'd spent Christmas Day with her family, enjoying the re-action of the children as they opened their presents and taking part in a raucous game of Pictionary that evening. Landon gave her a book of famous Americana paintings, and she gave him a sweater from Saks.

After dinner, they'd been clearing dishes when they bumped into each other in the kitchen doorway. Landon had grinned and pointed above Ashley's head. A sprig of mistletoe hung there. Ashley felt her cheeks grow hot. Her family had rarely seen signs of her relationship with Landon, and now . . . with permanent good-byes just around the corner, she hesitated about the wisdom of kissing him.

But only for a moment.

"It's okay, Ash." Something sad played in Landon's eyes. "I know we're not alone, but no one's looking."

"Landon, it's not that. Just that—"

"Shhh." He held a finger to her lips and leaned in.

Then with tender lips he kissed her, and the sensation left her breathless. The closeness of him, the way he'd lingered near her face, his breath against her cheek. All of it.

Ashley had swallowed hard as she moved back to the living room. When he sat next to her, she spoke close to his ear, so only he could hear what she was saying. "That kind of kiss makes me glad we're not alone."

He only smiled at her and said, "Me, too."

On Friday they hit Chelsea Piers, Manhattan's famous amusement park. Ashley rode the roller coaster with Landon and Cole six times before calling it quits. That evening the group caught a movie, and the next morning the others flew back to Bloomington.

The next three days passed in a blur of walks through Central Park, happy conversations about Cole and the people at Sunset Hills, and dinners at a handful of well-known cafes. They window-shopped on Fifth Avenue, skated under the lights in the park, and drank coffee in her hotel restaurant.

Before Ashley had time to calculate how quickly time was passing, it was Wednesday, New Year's Eve. Until then, they'd avoided Landon's apartment, and the plan had stayed the same since he'd talked to her at Luke and Reagan's wedding. New Year's Eve would be spent at Times Square, watching the sparkly ball drop slowly into the crowd at the stroke of midnight. Outside, where temptations would be minimal.

But without saying anything to Landon, Ashley could feel her resolve falling away a little more each hour. When it started raining sleet late Wednesday, they both knew it was time to talk about the backup plan. Ashley had been dying to go to his apartment, to be where he lived and slept and ate his meals, to relax on his sofa and feel—for even a day—that she still had a chance at forever with him.

With the change in weather, the decision was made. They would order in pizza, watch the ball drop on his TV, and spend their last night together without the distraction of crowds or parties or any other thing.

They ate dinner at his small kitchen table, and Ashley told him about Cole's Halloween costume, the way he'd made such a stir at Sunset Hills.

"So there's Helen, shouting that Cole's a spaceman, and what does Irvel say?"

"What nice hair he has?" He bit into a piece of cheese pizza and grinned.

"No." Ashley laughed. "That's what she told me."

"Okay, then . . ." Landon swallowed the bite and chuckled again. "What?"

"She says she thinks Helen's gentleman caller is shrinking. You know, because Cole's only four feet tall."

Landon almost lost his food. "No."

"Yes." Ashley set her piece of pizza back on the plate. She hadn't laughed this hard since before Hayley's accident. "And Helen's having a fit, shouting at people, flapping her arms like a bird."

"She wants to visit the moon with Cole, right?"

"No." The laughter came harder now. She could still picture the look on Helen's face as the situation that morning went from bad to worse. "She says everyone needs a space helmet. If Cole gets one, everyone gets one."

"Of course." Landon wiped a napkin over his lips. "And what about Bert?"

"That's the best part." Ashley waited, catching her breath. "Bert shuffles in, sees Cole in his firefighter costume, and wants to know where the fire is."

"I bet that was a hit."

"Definitely. Next thing Helen's pointing at the kitchen, convinced the sink's on fire."

"Poor Cole . . . probably wanted to run back to the car." Landon ran the backs of his hands beneath his eyes, struggling to grab a mouthful of air between bouts of laughter.

"Not at all." Ashley exhaled hard and again waited until she had more control. "He used his imaginary hose and put out the fire."

"Of course." Landon pretended to have a hose in his hand while he put out invisible flames in his own kitchen. "Why didn't I think of that?"

They laughed a while longer, and one story blended into another. He told her about a few friends he'd met at work—Barry and John-John—both men in their early thirties, married with two children apiece.

"They find something funny at every call." Landon was settling down, leaning back as his voice returned to normal. "I guess a little humor on the job helps."

Ashley wasn't sure. September 11 aside, fighting fires in New York City had always been a deadly venture. "Even when it's dangerous?"

"Yes." Landon's lips came together in a straight line, his eyes deeper than they'd been in a while. "Especially when it's dangerous."

Conversation drifted to things at church, and Ashley shared that she was reading the Bible more with Irvel and Edith. "They don't remember their names half the time, but still, hearing God's Word brings them peace. A peace that doesn't wipe them out the way drugs do but makes them feel almost normal again."

The evening wore on. They finished the pizza and took seats next to each other on his leather sofa. Landon flipped on the television and hit the mute button. "No point hearing a bunch of commercials. When it's closer to midnight I'll turn it up."

*Closer to midnight.*

The thought hit Ashley like a poison arrow and lodged somewhere above her heart. Midnight would come soon, and with it, the new year and the changes that would take them apart, probably forever. Midnight and an hour to tell Landon good-bye. She crossed her arms and stared at her lap.

He slid closer to her on the sofa, as though he'd noticed the change in her. He reached out and ran his fingers along her wrist and the tops of her hands. "Tell me."

"Hmmm?" Her eyes lifted to his and she managed a smile.

"What're you thinking?"

She shrugged. "About us—how my flight leaves in the morning. How different things'll be next year."

"It's been a nice week." He wrapped his fingers around hers and found her eyes. "Like something from a dream."

"Yes." She didn't blink, didn't want to lose a single second of the connection she felt to him. In some ways she had expected them to spend more time alone, kissing or holding each other. Instead they'd kept busy—sightseeing, shopping, skating. Drinking coffee and talking late into the night. For all the days they'd had together, this was the first time they'd really been alone.

His lips opened then, and his eyes pleaded with her. She understood. He wanted to ask her one more time, plead with her to see it his way, to give him the chance to love her, whatever it cost him. But she closed her eyes and gave the slightest shake of her head. *No, God, don't let him talk about it now. I can't take it. . . .*

When she blinked open, the moment had passed. "A lot's happened this year, Ash. Have you thought about it?"

"Not all at once, I guess."

"Really?" He stretched and his leg brushed up against hers. Ashley wondered if he noticed, if the sensation of his straightened leg beside hers was causing him as much conflict as it was causing her. If it was, he didn't let on. He looked straight ahead out the window at the dark sky and lit-up city. "I try to do that every year, think about the highs and lows, the changes, and how all of it's helped me grow." He looked at her again. "You know, taking stock, a chance to see how far I've come in the past twelve months."

Ashley listened to him, and already the pain was taking root in her soul. How had she missed the beauty of this man all those years ago? She should never have gone to Paris, with Landon waiting in Bloomington. That way, the two of them would've married. Cole would be his, and she would be healthy.

"I thought about it last night." He placed his hands behind his head and laced his fingers together. His leg was still alongside hers. "Getting settled at the department, finding out about Reagan, seeing your paintings in the local art gallery." He leaned over and kissed the side of her head. "By now I thought we'd be finishing wedding plans of our own, but that was before your blood test."

"My entire year can be summed up with that one phone call, the one telling me . . ." She couldn't finish the sentence. Instead she stared out the front window and allowed herself to imagine how different things would be if she'd gotten a negative result instead.

"Can I tell you something, Ash?" He angled his head so he could see her better. "The test didn't change anything for me." His eyes shone with a kind of love only he was capable of giving her. "You changed it."

"Me?" She ran her tongue along the inside of her lip. "Not me, Landon. The test. Otherwise, I'd be wearing your ring now."

"No, Ashley. It wasn't the test. It was you—you not believing that sick or not, you're all I want. All I've ever wanted."

The conversation was creeping dangerously close to areas that still needed to be off-limits. She crossed her arms and let her gaze fall to her lap again. "I'm sorry, Landon." Her tone was little more than a whisper. "I pray that one day you'll understand."

"Ah, Ashley. I'm sorry." He pulled one hand out from behind his head and looped it around her shoulders. His tone was kindness and resignation. "I understand *now*. I just never want you to walk away thinking I was afraid of a blood test. This . . . what we have . . . it's stronger than that."

Their eyes locked, and slowly, deliberately, like a dance step that had been building since Reagan and Luke's wedding, the two of them came together in an embrace that needed no words.

It was fifteen minutes before midnight, the time when they'd agreed to turn up the volume and watch the ball drop over a wet and icy Times Square. But in all the world, Ashley could think of nothing but the way she felt in Landon Blake's arms, the way she would ache for his hug all the days of her life.

The way whatever time they shared now would have to last them a lifetime.

In movements too small to measure, his lips found hers. They hadn't kissed since Christmas Day under the mistletoe, but here, on New Year's Eve, neither of them had doubted for a minute that they would find their way back to this place, to the passion of coming together and kissing the way they'd wanted to all week.

Landon's hands found her face, and his fingers wove their way into her hairline. "Ashley . . ."

Her name was all she needed to hear. She knew him well enough, heard in his tone the things he wasn't saying. That he had been honest a moment earlier, that he loved her and wanted her and couldn't bear the thought of what the morning would bring.

"I know, Landon." Tears stung at her eyes as she tilted her head back, savoring his trail of kisses along her jaw, her cheekbone, the soft area near her ear. "I know."

In the time since she'd told him the truth about Paris, the two of them had crossed the sea of desire into dangerous waters only a handful of times. Always at this point—at the place where kissing was simply not enough, where their bodies shared a craving that could be satisfied only one way—common sense would prevail and someone would pull back.

But tonight, more was at stake than ever before. Because tonight was the ending of a year, more than that, the ending of an era. Tonight a page would turn and a new chapter would begin, one that would send them so far in separate directions, a night like this one wasn't only unlikely.

It was impossible.

And because of that, Ashley couldn't bring herself to stop.

She slid closer to Landon, kissing him on his lips and his face, moving her mouth lightly down his neck even after she heard him moan from somewhere deep within. "Landon . . . I love you." For a moment she drew back and found his eyes, saw the passion there, and in the distance she saw the two-minute countdown clock in the corner of the television screen.

1:05 . . . 1:04 . . . 1:03 . . .

He moved his lips over hers, kissing her even as he followed her gaze. "Hey . . . one minute." Landon eased himself from her, stretched, and spread a feather blanket on the floor. He tossed a pillow toward the top, just in front of the TV. "Come on." He took her hand and pulled her down beside him. "Let's watch it."

Ashley looked at the screen, the sound still muted. Fifty seconds. All that was left of the old year, the old Ashley Baxter, was less than a minute. Landon reached for the remote control, the desire of a moment earlier on hold but hardly forgotten. He clicked the Sound button and suddenly the room filled with the sounds Ashley expected to hear on New Year's Eve.

Hooting, hollering, shouting people, arms raised, faces lit with smiles and laughter; Dick Clark explaining in that unique voice of his that, yes indeed, another year had passed them by; and in the background a band playing "Auld Lang Syne"—all as the ball lowered the rest of the way over Times Square.

Ashley sang the words quietly to herself: *"Should auld acquaintance be forgot and never brought to mind? . . ."*

Landon stretched out on his stomach, his eyes on the screen, hand still tucked in hers. And she sat cross-legged on the floor beside him, her knee up against his ribs. The counter on the screen slipped to :10 . . . :09 . . . :08 . . .

"Ashley . . ." Landon rolled onto his back and held his arms out to her. "Happy New Year."

She came to him, allowing herself to lay partially across his chest as they hugged and the countdown finished itself.

:03 . . . :02 . . .

And Ashley's lips found his again, her chest over his as they kissed the slow, happy kiss of celebration, but more quickly this time, the kiss turned hot and dangerous. Landon groped for the remote control and dimmed the volume to almost nothing.

"Where were we?" He worked his hand through her hair and drew her to himself.

Ashley was breathless from the feelings assaulting her senses. An unquenchable desire, a terrifying understanding that this was the most dangerous place they'd ever put themselves into, and an inability to stop regardless of the consequences. All those feelings at the same time.

"Baby . . ." Landon eased himself onto his side so the entire length of his upper body pressed against hers.

They were close here, too close. The nearness of him, his kisses and gentle fiery touch were more than Ashley could handle. But as weak as she felt, she managed the simplest prayer. *God . . . help.*

And though her desire didn't diminish a bit, Ashley suddenly pictured where the moment was headed—and the image it gave her made her stomach turn. Not the idea of Landon's body against hers, or the way it would feel if they could give in to their passions, but the bigger truth.

She was contaminated.

And if she couldn't control herself here, on the brink of goodbye, she could hardly expect to be in a relationship with him and go a lifetime without physical intimacy. Landon could say what he wanted about finding a way to make their relationship work.

The truth was, given the opportunity, she would willingly love him in a way that could do more than harm him.

It could kill him.

He was drawing closer to her now, and though she still savored every moment of his touch, his nearness, she suddenly pulled herself from the moment and sat up on her knees, breathless from her warring emotions. "Landon . . . see? This is why."

His eyes were still clouded with a desire that made him look irresistible. He took her hand and gave a slight shake of his head. "Ashley . . ." The whispered word hung in the air between them. "Come here, baby. Don't worry . . . I only want to kiss you."

Then, in what felt like some strange sort of vision, instead of seeing Landon strong and well, she saw him sick. Sick with HIV because she couldn't control her passions. "No, Landon. This—" she lifted her hands, palms up, and searched for the right words— "this could kill you, Landon. Don't you see?"

"No, baby." He ran his fingers along the length of her arm and searched her eyes. "We could kiss like this forever, and it would never hurt me."

"Landon." Her voice was louder, frustrated. "You and I both know where this goes. We're minutes away from you having the same diagnosis as me!" Her legs shook, but she forced herself to stand up. "I have to go. Please . . ." She held her hand out to him. "Come say good-bye to me."

At first he stayed on the floor, his hand stretched out to her, waiting for her to change her mind and fall back on the floor with him. But after nearly a minute, his expression changed. He took her hand and pulled himself to his feet. Gently, the desire faded from his expression, his voice. He framed her face with his fingers. "I'm sorry, Ashley. I didn't mean for it to get . . . well. I didn't mean it."

"I know." She pressed her fingers against her legs and tried to still her shaking arms. "This is why, Landon. I can't . . ." She let her head fall forward and stared at the floor. Her heart was still beating hard, her breathing not quite back to normal. "I just can't."

His arms came around her waist and he held her, not the way he'd held her minutes ago but in a sad, desperate way indicating that once he let go, he might never be the same again. She eased her arms up and toward his neck. As long as they held on this way, she wouldn't have to leave, wouldn't have to tell him good-bye. Because whenever they let go, there would be only one thing left to do.

He whispered against her face the words she longed to hear. "I love you, Ashley. If this is the last time, then I'll say it again. I'll never love anyone like I love you."

Ashley pulled back a few inches, just enough to find his eyes. "I love you, too. Never wonder about that." The tears came quickly, slipping onto her cheeks and falling to the floor. "I need to go."

She searched his eyes, looking for some crazy way of escape, some possibility that the past five months had been nothing but a nightmare, and that really she was healthy and well, her blood tests normal, and that her time with Landon this week could go on forever.

"This isn't the end, Ashley." Landon moved his thumb across the trail of tears on her face. "I'll never believe that."

They kissed one last time, but Ashley was already straining toward the door. Holding on longer at this point would only make leaving that much harder. When she pulled away, she could barely make him out through her tears. "Good-bye, Landon."

He wouldn't say it. Instead he held his palm up and kept his eyes locked on hers until she slipped through his front door and closed it behind her. She made it to the elevator before she broke down, and as she left his building and looked for a cab, she ignored the curious looks from the occasional passerby.

She could've lost her way or had too much to drink or been the victim of a mugger. This was New Year's Eve in New York City, after all, and no one cared about one young woman crying as she waited for a cab.

That was fine with Ashley.

She didn't want anyone but Landon caring for her, anyway. The air was cold and damp, and she shivered as a cab pulled up to the curb and sprayed gutter water on her ankles. Ashley dragged her coat sleeve beneath her eyes and stifled a series of deep sobs.

Just before she slipped into the backseat, she felt it. The feeling she'd had as a little girl when her mother would stand at the door watching her, checking to see that she was doing her chores. That was how Ashley felt now, as though she was being watched from behind. And not just watched, but studied. Stared at.

She had one leg in the cab when she looked over her shoulder up at a bank of windows in Landon's apartment building, and that's when she saw him. Standing there watching her, his hand still raised. She mouthed another good-bye and held her hand up as she eased herself into the cab and shut the door. The last thing she saw was the haunting image of his face, and something she couldn't quite make out until the very last second—something that would make her doubt forever the wisdom of leaving him.

Landon Blake was crying.

# CHAPTER TWENTY-SEVEN

PETER STARED AT THE TELEVISION SET, at the revelers in New York City, and he was struck by a thought more profound than any he'd had that week.

He couldn't take it. Couldn't take another year of drifting further from his family, of rewriting the ending to that fateful Saturday when Hayley fell in the pool. Couldn't take another year of looking for a reason to live between pills.

A year felt like eternity, a death sentence. A torture worse than hell.

Peter flicked the Power button on the TV remote and the screen went black. Never mind a year; he couldn't take another month, another day. Not even another hour.

He squinted in the darkness and tried to remember when the problem had gotten worse again. Just a week ago he'd tried to kill himself with the pills and something had stopped him, caused him to vomit. At the time he'd been so relieved he'd wondered if maybe God himself had intervened. But the next day around noon the shaking returned with a vengeance.

Two pills an hour had become three now, and even that didn't seem to ease his racing heart, the way the floor swayed, the pounding in his head.

Peter caught a bit of moon reflecting on the pill bottle beside him. He couldn't kill himself, wouldn't try again. That would be no sort of legacy for Brooke and the girls. Besides, he was stronger than that. He needed pain meds, yes, but he didn't have to take an entire handful.

Four.

Maybe that was the answer. Four an hour, the level he'd seen some patients and doctors reach. Never mind that most of them wound up in treatment. Peter wouldn't go that route, not ever. Not unless taking his own life was the only other option.

He reached for the pills and the water bottle beside them. Forty-five minutes since his last pills and already his heart trembled, head and mind twisted with the beginnings of an unbearable ache. He eased the lid off and spilled four pills into his hand. Four pills. Peter stared at them, shocked and anxious at the same time. This would be the answer; it had to be.

*Call for help, Peter. Don't take the pills.*

The water bottle slipped from Peter's hands to the floor. He looked about the room, eyes wide. Who had said that? And where were they? The voice sounded like it was coming from the television set, but he'd turned it off minutes ago.

"Who are you?" He hissed the question, pressing his body into the recliner and tightening his grip on the pills. "Get out of my house!"

*Don't take the pills, son. . . . Come to me, you who are weary and carry heavy burdens, and I will give you rest.*

"Stop!" Peter held the pills to his palm with two fingers and pressed his hands over his ears. "Get out of my house now!"

The voice was silent.

Peter relaxed and eased his hands back to his lap. The four pills were still intact, still pressed against the palm of his right hand. "Good!" Peter grumbled. His headache was getting worse, and the fine muscles in his arms were twitching. "Stay gone!"

He blinked and considered his actions. What was he doing? Talking to someone who wasn't there? Holding a conversation with a disembodied voice? He gritted his teeth and groped around the floor for his water bottle. His fingers felt the smooth plastic and he took hold of it, hating the way it shook in his hands. *Four pills, man. Take the pills and go to sleep.*

Then without giving another moment's consideration to strange voices or warnings or the dangers of taking four pain-killers at once, he peeled back his fingers, popped the pills into his mouth, and washed them down with half the water. The minute they were down, a ripple of fear tickled his conscience.

What if four were too many? What if that was enough to knock him out, to make him throw up again, and this time maybe after he was asleep. He could drown in his own vomit, couldn't he? They'd find him a few days from now, facedown in his own mess, and the report would read suicide—even if that wasn't the legacy he wanted to leave Brooke and the girls.

Already he could feel the tension in his arms and legs starting to ease. He wasn't going to pass out or die; no, he was simply going to feel normal again. Another swig of water and he returned the cap to the bottle of pills. But four was too many. Far too many. He set the bottle back on the table and squeezed his eyes shut. *Never again. Never take four pills again. Understand?*

He blinked his eyes open and rose to his feet, but somewhere in the distance he could barely make out the sound of someone laughing. A shrill, bone-chilling, evil laugh.

As he made his way to bed, he remembered that it was New Year's Eve, and somewhere—probably still in New York City— Brooke and the girls were celebrating it without him. The way they would celebrate all holidays from here out. The thought weighed like a cement blanket on his shoulders as he turned out the bedroom light and settled into his pillow.

Four pills made the difference, and sleep came easily. *Never again*, he told himself as he drifted off. *Never four pills again, no matter how bad it gets.*

※

Peter's promise was good until the next day at noon. He'd had a series of difficult patients, two old men with advanced cancer, both of whom needed hospice care. And a woman whose unborn baby showed signs of serious birth defects. He sent all three patients on to specialists, but the pills he popped between visits weren't doing the trick, weren't calming his nerves.

Worse, he'd seen Hayley's face everywhere. First he saw her in the terminally ill old man, then in the nurse who helped with his chart, and finally in the pregnant woman. Hayley was everywhere, looking to him, begging him to help her. After the third patient, Peter gripped the bag of pills in his pocket. No use fighting the inevitable.

He took four pills, and the relief was better than anything he could've imagined . . . for an hour, anyway.

※

As the days ran together, even four pills weren't enough and finally—three weeks into the new year—Peter realized the awful truth.

No amount of pills would ever be enough.

Only one answer remained, one that would forever take away the pain and anxiety and loneliness. One that would promise him an eternity without even once having to second-guess that Saturday with Hayley.

Just after three in the morning, he woke up in dire need of a fix. His toes and knees and ribs and elbows shook. Even his eyebrows trembled.

He took hold of the pill bottle near his bed and tore off the lid.

*This is it,* he told himself. *Figure out a way, West. It'll all be over in a few minutes.*

**Son, come to me!**

Peter froze and his eyes darted about the room. He hadn't heard that voice, the gentle warning voice since New Year's Eve, but now here it was again. He started to speak, started to answer that he couldn't come, had no way to come until he'd taken the pills. But before he could speak, another whispered voice, angry and hissing, pierced the silence.

*Take the pills, Peter. You want relief, right? This is the way . . . the only way out.*

Peter held his breath, too afraid to move. What had the voice said? Take the pills? The pills were the only way out?

He worked the muscles in his jaw and felt his body relax just enough so he could shake a pile of pills into the palm of his hand. Whoever had told him to come didn't understand. The second voice was right. He had no right to live, no reason anymore. The pills were the only way out.

His hand shook as he lifted the pills to his mouth, so hard that six or eight capsules fell to his lap. Peter lowered his hand and scooped the wayward pills back into his palm. *All of them,* he told himself. *Take all of them so there's no doubt about the outcome.*

**No, son. I will give you rest. Come to me.**

Peter wrapped his fingers around the pills and squeezed his fist to his midsection. "Go away!" He shouted the order into the vacant space before him. He was crazy; that had to be it. Already crazy. "Whoever you are, I don't want your kind of rest."

He waited, and the quiet, gentle voice was silent once more. The hissing voice was silent also, and Peter stared at his clenched fist. It was time—now, before any other voices filled the room.

Again his hand shook as he lifted it to his mouth, but this time he kept his fingers tight around the pills until the last possible second. Then he peeled his fingers away and thirty—maybe forty—

pills spilled into his mouth. He wanted to gag, but he wouldn't. Not this time. Instead he grabbed his water bottle, squeezed it over the pills and swallowed, swallowed hard enough to down the entire pile of pills.

There.

He blinked and set the water bottle back on the bedside table. It would all be over soon. Nausea grabbed at him, but he resisted. He wouldn't lose the dose again. Not when the only way out of the nightmare of his life was to end it. A strange warmth began making its way down his limbs and throughout his body.

The pills would be breaking up by now, releasing their potent chemicals into his bloodstream. A matter of minutes really—ten at best—and he would never again have to wonder what it would take to get his next fix, never have to guess if Brooke was going to call and invite him over for a movie, never have to look Maddie in the face knowing that he had robbed her of her little sister, never have to look at Hayley and . . .

A hissing, laughing sound started in the corner of the room. With every heartbeat it grew louder and louder. Louder than any other time. And then the laughter became words, words that spit at him and surrounded him and filled his soul all at once.

*That's right, Peter; I tricked you! Now you'll never say good-bye to Hayley or anyone else. The game's over, friend.*

*Game over?* Peter's mouth hung open and he gasped. Whoever . . . whatever was making that noise, the words only now made sense. He'd taken an overdose of pills and now he wouldn't get to say good-bye, wouldn't get to explain the torment he'd been in, the reason he'd had to take the pills. The reason he'd chosen to end his own life.

"Wait!" The word was a shout, a cry. But even as he spoke, he heard the way the letters ran together, the slur of his voice and his inability to say anything further. The pills were taking effect. They were making their way farther and farther into his system. This time there would be no turning back.

No second chance.

And suddenly he wanted to live. More than he'd wanted anything, more than he'd wanted even the pills and the wonderful feeling of peace, more than he wanted a permanent solution for his miserable existence, he wanted to live.

"Help me!" His eyes moved slowly about the room, his lids heavier than before. Where was the other voice, the kinder, gentler one? The one that had sounded like it was from God himself? "Help me, God!"

In that exact instant his eyes fell on the phone next to his bed. The room was already starting to spin—not the way it did when he needed a fix, but faster, more forcefully. In a way that signaled the end.

*Make the call, Peter.*

"God . . . help me!"

And with a strength that wasn't his own, with a steadiness that belied the medication coursing through his veins, he reached for the telephone. Then with unexplainably steady fingers, he dialed the only three numbers that mattered.

9-1-1.

He held the phone to his ear and waited, the receiver growing heavier with each half second. *Answer . . . please answer.*

"9-1-1. What's your emergency?"

"I'm . . ." The words didn't want to come, and he had to fight the urge to fall over, to give in to the unbearable pull toward sleep, toward death. *No . . . help me, God!* He held his breath and gave a single shake of his head. "I'm . . . dying."

The woman was saying something, asking what had happened and whether someone was in the house. But it was too late. Peter couldn't say another word, couldn't remember even why he had the phone in his hand in the first place.

Sleep.

That's what he needed. A good night's sleep. The receiver fell from his hand, and distantly he heard a tinny voice. Not the hissing voice or the gentle voice, but someone talking from the phone, saying something about his condition or the house or something he couldn't quite make out.

Not that it mattered.

Peace had finally found him and now—after so many nights of restlessness and dark evil voices, he was finally falling asleep. Sleep was a good thing, the one bit of respite he hadn't been able to find, right? It had to be good. But still, as he closed his eyes and gave in to the almost violent pull toward oblivion, he had one thought. One that didn't seem to make sense in light of the relief he was feeling. Or maybe it wasn't so much a thought as a knowing, a knowing that filled his waning consciousness.

*God.*

That was all. God was real after all. He was real—yesterday, today, and tomorrow. God would always be real. Real in the person of Jesus Christ. And somehow, Peter needed that same God now more than ever before.

But sleep was closing in fast and he was out of time, out of chances. He had one more thing to say, something he wanted to tell God, since God was real and he'd missed that fact while he was alive. But he couldn't remember, couldn't make the words come. Couldn't formulate even a thought.

And with that, Peter's eyes closed—still, silent, dark.

Forever dark.

# CHAPTER TWENTY-EIGHT

IT WAS MONDAY NIGHT, well into January, and Ryan Taylor was watching a late-night college basketball wrap-up, when the phone rang. Kari had a modeling job the next day and was already asleep upstairs. Ryan had no idea who'd be calling so late.

He grabbed the receiver and clicked the On button. "Hello?"

"Ryan Taylor?"

"Yes?" Ryan sat back down in his recliner and looked at the TV screen again.

"I'm Dr. Williams from the Bloomington Mental Health Hospital. We admitted Peter West on Friday, and this evening we finished our most intensive session."

The man paused and Ryan leaned forward. Peter West? In a mental hospital? A rush of realities flooded his senses. How long had it been since he'd talked with Peter? Before Christmas, at least. He'd called him twice since New Year's, but both times he'd left a message and heard nothing in response.

Now Ryan understood why. Things were worse than he'd thought. He waited for the man to continue.

"Mr. Taylor, I'm sorry about the late hour, but Dr. West is asking for you. We thought . . . if you were willing to come now . . . Dr. West might be close to a breakthrough."

A breakthrough? Peter West was one of the most respected doctors in Bloomington. How had he plummeted so far without someone stepping in and helping? Ryan realized the man at the other end was waiting. "Definitely." He used the remote control to flick off the television and headed into the kitchen for his keys. "I can be there in ten minutes."

Ryan wrote a note for Kari in case she woke up, and then he drove to the facility. It was a shaded two-story building, discreet and set back from the road, not far from the medical center. The place where people could hide and find help when their world was caving in on them.

People like Peter.

Ryan used an intercom to gain entrance and then filled out a form and passed a simple interview with a security guard. Finally, he was allowed in, where he met up with Dr. Williams in the hallway.

Dr. Williams clutched a clipboard to his side. "Mr. Taylor, your brother-in-law wanted me to tell you why he's here."

Ryan pictured Hayley, drooling from her wheelchair. "Okay."

"Some time ago he became addicted to painkillers. The addiction got out of hand, and last Friday he tried to kill himself. He tells us it wasn't the first time."

The information slammed across Ryan's soul like a tidal wave. Peter had tried to kill himself? Why hadn't he called . . . Ryan or John Baxter or Kari? even Brooke? Someone would've been willing to meet him, talk him down off a ledge before it was too late. Ryan raked his fingers through his hair. "How'd he get here?"

"Apparently he overdosed and then had second thoughts. He called 9-1-1, and they found him passed out in his bedroom. Doctors pumped his stomach and stabilized him. The next day he was brought here." The doctor pursed his lips. "He's in our most secure detox lockdown area."

"Detox lockdown?" The entire scene was surreal, happening to someone off the street or to a man with nothing to live for. But not to Peter West—definitely not. "Okay . . ." Ryan squeezed his eyes shut for a moment. When he opened them, he studied Dr. Williams's face. "Could you explain detox lockdown?"

"Yes." The man nodded. "We admit people to that unit when they come from the hospital. It means we take away belts, blow-dryers, electric shavers. Anything with a cord. Also anything that can be used as a weapon."

Ryan shook his head. "Peter isn't dangerous, Doctor. You've got the wrong man."

"He's dangerous to himself."

The idea shot through Ryan's gut and knocked him back against the wall. It was one thing for Peter to take too many pills. But to be considered a danger with a belt or a blow-dryer cord? "You said he's been here since Saturday. How . . . how's he doing now?"

"He was very addicted." Dr. Williams stuck one hand in his pocket. "We're past the hardest part, but his body is still scream-ing for relief. Obviously we've helped him through the process as much as possible, but at this point he can't leave without per-mission from the admitting doctor."

Ryan stared at a spot on the floor near his feet. What would Brooke think when she heard the news? And how was she sup-posed to deal with Hayley *and* Peter? He remembered the offer he and Kari had made to Peter and Brooke back when Hayley first had her accident. *Lord, we've asked you for opportunities like this. Use me, use us to bring healing to Peter's family. Please, God.*

*I am with you even now.*

The jumbled thoughts in Ryan's head cleared and he gave a slight nod. *Thank you, God . . . I feel you.* He lifted his head and looked at Dr. Williams again. "What can I do?"

"Well, as I said, we had an intensive session, and he talked about God. We're not a religious facility, Mr. Taylor, but when one of our patients expresses a faith, we try to involve the person that patient trusts the most with spiritual matters. In this case, that person is you. It took hours to reach a place with Dr. West where he wanted to see you, Mr. Taylor. We didn't want to lose ground by waiting until tomorrow to call."

"Is he—" Ryan pointed down the hall—"can I see him now?"

"Yes." The doctor motioned for Ryan to follow. "This way."

The hallway was quiet, most of the patients in the lockdown unit asleep. Dr. Williams led Ryan to the last room on the right. He used a key to enter and the two of them walked in.

Ryan stopped short the moment he saw Peter. The man was a shrunken replica of his former self. Ryan tried not to stare. He must have lost thirty, forty pounds since the last time Ryan had seen him. His skin was a lifeless gray, his eyes hard and empty. The hollows of his cheeks sank way in, accentuating his cheekbones and the fact that he'd lost weight.

"Peter . . ."

Their eyes met, but Peter said nothing. He was sitting in one of two chairs, part of the sparse furnishings that included only a bed and a small nightstand. His hair—which had always been short and neatly cut—hung unkempt an inch past his ears. He clutched the armrests, his knuckles white. He wore blue sweatpants and a white T-shirt, and his entire body vibrated with what looked like a constant tremor.

Dr. Williams took a few steps closer to Peter and cleared his throat. "Mr. Taylor has agreed to meet tonight."

Peter let his eyes fall to his lap and worked his mouth open and shut several times before finally saying, "Thanks, Ryan."

The shock was beginning to wear off, but Ryan was still too surprised to say anything. How had this happened? The last time he'd seen Peter, the man was still pretending to be fine, acting as if Hayley's drowning and his decision to move out were mere speed bumps on the road of life.

"Let's go ahead and begin." Dr. Williams pointed to the other empty chair a few feet from Peter. "Mr. Taylor, if you could sit there. I'll sit on the edge of the bed and monitor, in case the discussion needs direction."

Direction? Ryan stared at the doctor. "I think we're okay alone, Doctor."

"I'm sorry." The man took his place leaning against the end of Peter's bed, his feet planted on the floor. "At this stage of detox, conversations need to be monitored."

Ryan looked at Peter. He was staring out the darkened window, as if he hadn't heard the discussion. Ryan nodded at the doctor and took the chair near Peter. "Hey . . ."

In a slow, discouraged way, Peter turned toward Ryan and met his eyes. "They won't let me die."

A chill passed over Ryan's spine at the words of his brother-in-law. Dr. Williams was right; the situation was worse than anyone in the Baxter family had ever imagined. Ryan tightened his hands into fists. *God, give me the words.* "You don't want to die, Peter. Otherwise you wouldn't have called for help."

Peter's eyes went vacant.

When it was clear Peter wasn't going to say anything, Ryan continued. "Come on, Peter. Tell me what happened."

Peter's eyes grew more distant, glazed even. "Everything hurt." He shrugged and his bony shoulders poked up through his T-shirt. His expression changed. "I couldn't stand the pain."

"So you took the pills."

Peter hung his head and did a barely noticeable nod.

"And on Friday . . ." Ryan slid his chair closer and glanced at Dr. Williams. The man nodded, giving him silent permission to continue. Ryan looked at Peter again. "What happened Friday?"

"They stopped working." Peter kept his head down but lifted his eyes. "No matter how many I took, it still hurt."

Ryan was quiet, letting God give him the words to continue. "What, Peter? What hurts?"

Slowly, one feature at a time, Peter twisted his expression until his face mirrored all the pain in his heart. He covered his eyes with his fingers. "Hayley." He uttered a single moan, a cry that was without tears or sobs or anything other than raw, unbridled pain. "I miss Hayley." He peered through the spaces between his fingers at the ceiling. "God! I miss my little girl."

The lump in Ryan's throat made it impossible for him to speak. Instead he leaned over and hugged Peter, hugged him hard and tight.

Peter stayed that way for a while, pressing his forearm into Ryan's back as if he might not survive if Ryan let go. Finally he drew back and hung his head again. "I didn't watch her."

Of course it would come to this. The reason for his pain was Hayley, and Ryan couldn't imagine any kind of pill that would take away the ache. The picture of Hayley at the bottom of the pool. The memory of pulling her limp body from the water, and the knowledge that she would probably never be the same again, never look at him with a sharp-eyed alert smile, never be like the other kids in school or on the playground.

The pain was deeper than all the oceans combined. Ryan leaned back but kept his hand on Peter's knee. "No pain pill could take away that kind of hurt."

"But it did." Peter sniffed. "For a while it did. And when it stopped working . . ."

Dr. Williams uttered a small cough, and the sound surprised Ryan. Things had gotten so intense he'd almost forgotten the doctor was in the room. Ryan focused on Peter again. "It stopped because it never really worked in the first place, Peter. It masked the pain, but it didn't take it away. Only God can do that."

"Not this." Peter shook his head. "God can't take away this pain."

Ryan's heart sank. "You're wrong, Peter." He pictured himself at college, getting the news that his father had died of a heart attack, imagined himself lying paralyzed on a football field, his playing days over, and later getting the news that Kari was engaged to someone else. "Pain like you're feeling is part of living. The solution for it will never be found in a bottle of pills."

Peter twisted his face again and gave a single shake of his

head. "I want her back, Ryan. I see her . . . dropping rose petals at your wedding, and that's all I want. Hayley . . . Hayley whole and well again." His features relaxed some. "I can't live without her."

"You don't have to." Ryan's answer was quick and filled with a peace that surprised him. "Hayley's alive, Peter. She's getting a little bit better every day. No, she's not the same, but she's still Hayley." Ryan felt his eyes grow wet. "When's the last time you saw her?"

Dr. Williams shifted, and the movement caught Peter's attention. He looked from the doctor back to Ryan, his mouth half open, eyes wide. "I can't."

"You can." Ryan wasn't sure how hard to push, but Dr. Williams would let him know if he stepped out of line. "You can because God will walk beside you. Remember, Peter? The Twenty-third Psalm says he'll walk with us through the valley of the shadow of death." Ryan's words were slow, and something in Peter's expression changed.

"I don't know how to do it, Ryan. I've never hurt like this."

"You're not supposed to know how. God says he'll lead the way; he'll walk beside you through the valley." Ryan squeezed Peter's knee. "It doesn't say he'll take us on a detour around the valley of the shadow of death. It says he'll stay beside us while we walk through it."

"What if I can't?" Peter's voice was broken, racked with unresolved pain.

"That's the problem, Peter." Ryan slid closer to the edge of his chair. "For you, the valley is this pain you're feeling. You have to walk through it to get past it, to the next place along the road of life. You can't mask it or run from it. Or even die to escape it, Peter. You have to walk through it, and the only way to do that is with God."

Peter squeezed his eyes shut. "My little Hayley!" He moaned again, agonizing, louder than before. "I'm so sorry. I should've been watching you, baby. I didn't mean it; really I didn't."

Ryan swallowed. *Stay strong. For Peter, stay strong.* "God

knows that. He's here. Right now, ready to walk the valley with you. But you have to be willing . . ."

"Willing?" Confusion joined the other emotions ripping at Peter's expression.

"Yes." Ryan felt the corners of his mouth lift. "Willing to take the first step."

❧

Brooke took the phone call at work the next day.

She was between patients when the receptionist found her. "Your father's on line three."

Brooke nodded and took the call in her office. Her father didn't normally call her at work, and she had to fight her initial reaction that something was wrong. Something else. She pushed the blinking button on the phone. "Dad?"

"Listen, honey. I know you're busy but you need to know about Peter."

"Peter?" Brooke felt her heart skip a beat. She settled into her office chair and shaded her eyes with her free hand. He hadn't contacted her or the girls since before Christmas. Twice she'd called his office to make sure he was still seeing patients. He was last time she checked, but that had been two weeks ago. Kari had told her maybe she should give him space, time to realize how lonely life would be without her and the girls.

"Honey, Ryan called. Peter's at the mental-health facility in town. In the detox lockdown unit."

The words came across the phone line, but somewhere in Brooke's consciousness they hit a brick wall. Detox lockdown? That unit was for drug addicts, people so desperately addicted their very lives were at stake. Why in the world would Peter be there? "Dad, I . . . I'm not sure I understand."

"He's been taking painkillers. He overdid it on Friday and called for help."

298

"Help?" The walls of the office began closing in, and Brooke struggled to grab a breath.

"Paramedics responded. The hospital stabilized him, and they sent him to the mental-health facility the next day."

"He's been there since Saturday?" Brooke was buying time, getting the facts straight in her head so she could accept the truth of what he was saying. The suspicions of her family had been right after all. Peter had been writing prescriptions for himself, taking painkillers until he couldn't function without them.

And not once had he called her for help.

Brooke wasn't sure which truth hurt worse. She pinched the bridge of her nose and concentrated on her father's words. "Does . . . does he want to see me?"

"Not yet." Her father hesitated. "Ryan visited him last night."

"Why Ryan?" Brooke dropped her hand and leaned back in her chair.

"Because the pain pills aren't working anymore. Peter told his doctor Ryan was the person he trusted most, spiritually. I guess they talked about walking through the pain with God and coming out whole at the other end."

A single ray of light shone its way through the murky fog of desperation. Brooke held her breath. "And . . ."

"And Peter agreed that was the only way—his only hope."

Brooke released a small cry. "Are you serious?"

"Yes." Her father's voice was thick. "He's got a long way to go, Brooke. But he wants to find his way back."

The conversation wound down, but for several minutes after Brooke hung up, she sat there, her head bowed as she considered the situation. In the months since Hayley's accident, Peter—the confident, brilliant doctor she'd married—had become an empty, broken man. A man whose pain over what had happened to their daughter had almost cost him his life.

As difficult as the news was, Brooke didn't feel discouraged or desperate or any of the things she would've expected to feel. Instead she felt a river of joy—deep and vibrant and full of life—running through the barren places of her heart. God was working in the situation. Hayley was making progress, and for the first time in his life, Peter was a broken man.

Brooke wouldn't have wished anything else for her husband. Because only once he realized he was broken could God fix him. Knit them all back together again.

Whole and healthy and once more walking toward a future soaked in sunlight.

The visit came four days later, one week after Peter's admittance to the mental-health facility.

Peter's counselor agreed that he was far enough into his rehabilitation, far enough removed from the suicide attempt, that he could meet with Brooke. Besides, he'd been asking for the chance since seeing Ryan earlier that week.

That evening, Brooke had dropped Maddie and Hayley off at her parents' house and reminded herself to be calm. Believing rehabilitation was the best thing for Peter and visiting him in a detox lockdown unit were two different things. By the time she entered the facility and found the front desk, Brooke's fingers were freezing cold and she couldn't draw a full breath.

So much of what she'd prayed about had led them to this moment, this time together. And though Peter had asked to see her, Brooke had no idea what he wanted to talk about. Had his time at the rehab center made him reconsider his place in their family? Did he want to save their marriage after all? Brooke didn't know, and the counselor hadn't shed a single ray of light on the issues.

The woman at the front desk checked her in and nodded. "Mr. West is expecting you."

"Will his counselor be there?" Brooke sounded official, the way she always did when she was in a medical facility. But she was weak with fear, suddenly unprepared for whatever lay ahead.

"Yes." The woman pointed down a long hallway. "They'll be in 235, at the end of the corridor."

Brooke thanked the woman, and seconds later she made a cautious entry into the room. Peter looked thin, his face pale, but he had a look of hope in his eyes, something Brooke hadn't seen there in more than a year.

"Hi." He stood and nodded at her.

The counselor cleared his throat. "Hi, I'm Richard Camp, chief psychiatrist at the center." He paused and gestured to the space around him. "Don't mind me; I'll keep to myself over here." He adjusted his notepad. "Try to let your conversation be normal."

"Okay." Brooke ran her tongue over her lip. She needed water.

Tension hung in the air, and Brooke glanced at the counselor. She wasn't sure if she should cross the room and hug her husband or ask Dr. Camp for permission. In the end she did neither, opting instead to drop slowly onto the chair nearest the door. The moment was even more awkward than she'd expected. She met Peter's eyes. "Hi. I . . . you look good."

Peter shrugged. "Not really, but thanks." He took a long breath. "How're the girls?" She smiled, and the counselor jotted something down on his notepad.

"Good." A layer of sweat beaded up on Peter's upper lip.

Brooke tried to think of something to say, but nothing came to mind. She fiddled with her wedding ring. Had they run out of things to talk about? She sucked in a quick breath and thought about Hayley, how far she'd come and how much of her recovery Peter had missed. "You should see Hayley." She offered a stiff smile. "She's rolling across the floor now, making her way to me whenever I call her."

"Really?" Peter's eyes stayed flat. "What does her doctor say?"

"Nothing." The words were coming easier now, the counselor

less of a distraction. "She shouldn't be alive, let alone rolling across the floor."

A loud beeping sound came from the counselor's pager. He unclipped it from his belt and frowned at the Caller ID window. "Hmm." His eyes lifted to Brooke's and then to Peter's. "I have to take this." He hesitated. "Why don't I give you twenty minutes alone; will that work?"

Brooke felt the sting of fear. The question brought a mix of feelings. Alone would be good, but without the counselor she and Peter would have to face the obvious: They were sitting in a room at a rehab unit in the wake of his suicide attempt, with an unexplored ocean of tragedy lying between them.

The counselor was waiting, and Peter gave the nod. "Go ahead."

"Okay." The man looked from Peter to Brooke and back again. "Twenty minutes."

The counselor left the room and shut the door behind him. Brooke looked at her husband, and suddenly the atmosphere between them changed. Peter's forced smile faded. His shoulders slumped and his head fell forward until he was staring at the floor between his feet. A minute passed, and he said nothing. But then his upper body began to shake and he brought his hands to his face.

"Peter . . ." She slid to the edge of her seat and angled her face.

"I haven't . . . I haven't told you what happened." He raised only his eyes. "With Hayley."

Brooke's stomach tightened, and a wave of nausea hit her. She'd expected the counselor to be present, expected them to talk about his addiction or their marriage or his fragile recovery.

But Hayley?

"You don't have to, Peter." Adrenaline shot through her veins and she closed her eyes. "It doesn't matter now."

"It does." His voice sounded tight, pinched by the struggle. "I have to tell you. So you don't wonder forever."

She blinked and opened her mouth, ready to beg him not to

tell her, not to paint the picture she'd avoided since Hayley's accident. Better to never know, to not find herself falling asleep fighting images of Hayley underwater, Hayley at the bottom of the pool, Peter diving into the water. . . .

But before she could tell him no, before she could ask him to forever keep the details to himself, a glint of understanding dawned in her heart. What if this was part of his counseling? What if telling the story was Peter's first attempt at building a bridge between them?

"Why, Peter?" Her throat ached from the sudden tension in her neck. "Tell me."

He sat a bit straighter. "I can't feel . . . I can't feel close to you until you know." He dug his elbows into his thighs. "We need to talk about it. We should've talked about it a long time ago."

Brooke's teeth began to chatter, and she gave a shake of her head. *No, God . . . I don't want to hear.*

*Daughter, do not be anxious. . . .*

The verse that had struck her time and again these past months practically shouted at her: "Do not be anxious." The words played in her mind again and she gritted her teeth. Fine. She would hear the details. Maybe Peter was right. Maybe then they would get past that awful day and find a way to move ahead. Maybe even move ahead together. A long breath eased between her teeth. "Okay." She relaxed her jaw. "Tell me."

Peter fit his hands together and wrung them. The lines on his forehead relaxed and resignation filled his eyes. "It's all right. You don't have to hear."

"I changed my mind; I do want to hear." Brooke slid her chair across the tile linoleum until she was a few feet from Peter. With every passing second her statement was becoming truer. Hadn't she wondered about that day? Of course she had, and she'd wonder until the day she died unless Peter told her every bit of what had happened that Saturday. Her heart pounded as she spoke again. "Go ahead, Peter. I'm ready."

For a long moment, he didn't look like he would do it. He

raked his fingers through his short dark hair, and Brooke saw he had more gray than before. He looked weary and remorseful and terrified and nervous all at the same time. For another few seconds he massaged his temples, and then the story began to spill out. "After you left, I was watching the game with DeWayne and—" he shook his head and rubbed the back of his neck—"I don't know, maybe ten minutes later the girls came in, dripping wet."

Brooke lifted her fingers to her throat and massaged away the tightness there. The scene Peter was describing was a last time—the sort her mother had talked about recently. The last time Hayley had ever run into the house after a swim in the pool. The last time she'd started a conversation with Peter. At that point, her minutes as a normal, healthy child had been counting down fast even though no one knew it.

"Tell me." She nodded, giving Peter permission to continue.

He let his hands fall to his lap. "They asked me to take their life jackets off so they could have cake, and—"

Brooke fell back against her chair. There it was: the admission she'd known was coming, the explanation she'd imagined even that very same day after Hayley was taken to the hospital. Peter himself had taken off the girls' life jackets. He'd taken them off and never thought once about putting them back on until . . . until . . .

"Wait." She held up her hand. But even as she did, she caught herself. This was the reason he was telling her in the first place, so she'd never have to wonder what happened next.

"Brooke." Peter looked at her, his eyes narrow, intense. "I know what you're thinking. You told me to keep their life jackets on, but I thought . . . with them sitting at the table they should . . ."

"Don't, Peter." Brooke spread her fingers out in front of her. *Steady,* she told herself. *Stay steady.* She gave a sad huff. "Don't say it. Just go on."

He hesitated and she watched him, the way he worked his

fingernails into the palms of his hands. After half a minute he gave a slight defeated nod and continued. "Well, so a little while later Maddie came running into the TV room and . . ."

This time, the story spilled out in its entirety, the whole thing. The part about Maddie crying out to Peter, afraid, unable to find Hayley, and the way he'd noticed Hayley's life jacket swinging on Maddie's arm. His mad run toward the pool and Hayley's small body lying at the bottom of the deep end. The dive into the pool and the awful time it took him to swim her to the surface.

Peter's voice was a gritty monotone as he let the story come, every horrifying detail of it, and finally, when he was finished, he searched Brooke's face. "That's what happened. I took her life jacket off, Brooke." As he said her name, his voice cracked and he sank lower in his chair, still buried beneath the guilt. "It was my fault."

She watched him and for the first time she saw past Hayley's damaged condition to the reality of that Saturday afternoon. The girls had been dripping wet, wanting to eat cake. Wouldn't she have done the same thing? Wouldn't she have taken off their life jackets so they wouldn't drip water all over the kitchen? Clearly Peter had assumed the other adults would watch the children, keep them in the kitchen area. Wouldn't she have figured the same thing?

"No, Peter." She dropped to her knees in front of Peter, easing her hands up under his arms and around his back. Her voice was a mix of anguish and release. "I would've done the same thing. I promise you, I wouldn't have wanted them dripping wet, either. I . . . I should've been there."

Peter eased back some and studied her face. His cheeks were flushed, and surprise shone in his damp eyes. "You don't blame me?"

"How can I?" She sniffed and let her forehead fall against his shoulder. "You didn't want her to drown, Peter. Any more than I did." The side of her face nuzzled against his, and she felt him respond, felt him press his cheek next to hers the way he hadn't done in years. "It happened, that's all. It just happened."

"I'm still sorry, Brooke." A moan came from his chest and filled the room, the sort of moan that might come from a wounded bear. "I want her back whole. . . . I'd do anything to have her back."

❧

Peter couldn't let go.

Though they made no declarations of love that night, no apologies for their distance or his drug addiction, the embrace between him and Brooke held—desperate almost—and despite occasional interruptions from the counselor, they stayed that way much of the time until Brooke had to leave.

Now there was just one more difficult task Peter had to tackle: seeing Hayley as she was now, back at home in a wheelchair, drooling and rolling across the places where she once ran and played and laughed about tea parties with her dolly.

His first visit happened on a cold, slushy Saturday morning. Brooke met him at the door, hugged him, and led him into the living room. Maddie was upstairs reading, so they were alone, for which Brooke was grateful. The moment would be hard enough without Maddie jumping about and squealing that, at least for an hour, Daddy was back home.

Peter saw Hayley, dressed in a pink knit sweater and leggings, her blonde hair combed straight and shiny, and he felt a stinging in his eyes. "Hayley," the word was a whisper.

He went to her and knelt down in front of her wheelchair. He and Brooke had spent much of their time imagining how this meeting might go, talking about it, trying to diffuse the sadness of it, and not once had Peter broken down and cried.

But here, as Hayley's eyes found him, as the corners of her mouth turned up in a smile that said she remembered him, tears fell from Peter's face like so much gentle rain. "Hayley, baby, Daddy's here. Daddy's never going away again."

And as Brooke watched them from a few feet away, he could feel a quiet celebration beginning somewhere in his heart. A rejoicing because he was here and Hayley was smiling, and for too many dark days he hadn't been sure either would ever be true again. But most of all because he meant every word he'd just told his little daughter.

No matter what struggles they still had to work through, after this, he was never going away again.

# CHAPTER TWENTY-NINE

T HE RESIDENTS at Sunset Hills Adult Care Home were still asleep when Ashley arrived at work this morning.

Since New Year's, the early shift was working well for her. Twice a week she'd take Cole to her parents' house at seven, and her mother would give him breakfast and drop him off at preschool. That way she could do paperwork, visit with the residents after they woke up, and finish her work before noon. The rest of the day she'd spend with Cole.

The days when she didn't go in early, she spent the mornings painting. Anything to stay busy and keep herself from thinking of Landon.

Ashley opened a file containing the expenses for January. One of her goals was to trim 10 percent from the supply cost for the month of February, and now that February was nearly half over, Ashley wanted to make sure they were on target.

She worked her pencil over a column of numbers, but after a few minutes the figures blurred and her mind drifted. Hayley was doing so much better these days. Ashley and Cole had gone by to visit Brooke and the girls yesterday, and the improvements were shocking.

No, more than that. They were miraculous.

Hayley was rolling up onto her hands and knees, swaying her body and trying to crawl. No question she recognized people now, and her doctors had no idea how far her recovery might go. She still wore the facial expression of a brain-injured child, but every time Ashley stopped by, Hayley seemed a little more like herself.

"I've asked her doctors not to give me a prognosis." Brooke had been sitting on the floor, Hayley cuddled in her lap, while Maddie and Cole played with Matchbox cars on the wood floor nearby. "Only God knows how much of Hayley we'll get back."

Brooke seemed happier than she'd ever been. Peter was out of rehab, and the two of them were seeing a counselor several times a week. Peter was still living in his apartment, and so far he'd stayed away from painkillers. Brooke didn't want to rush things with him, because he needed to connect with God and get past his addiction before they could work intensively on their marriage.

And Brooke had finally convinced Ashley to make an appointment with an autoimmune specialist. She had had her first appointment with the man this past Thursday.

Ashley doodled a row of daisies along the bottom of the work sheet. Brooke had been right about the doctor's initial response. He wanted to start with blood work to see if anything had changed since Ashley's first test.

The numbers on the sheet in front of her came into focus again, and Ashley concentrated on the task at hand. Thirty minutes later she'd finished her assessment. Compared with January's supply costs, they were on track to save not 10 percent, but 12 percent.

She was about to open a stack of business mail, when she heard Maria's singsong voice in the background. "Good morning, Helen. How are you today?"

Helen's response was muffled, but it sounded dark and surly. Ashley smiled to herself and pushed the stack of mail aside.

Breakfast with her old friends was something she rarely missed. It gave her a chance to connect with them, make sure the Past-Present theory they lived under was still working, and get an overall feel for how each of the residents was doing.

She left the office and headed down the hall.

Irvel, Helen, and Edith were seated at the table when Ashley entered the room. In honor of Valentine's Day—coming up that Saturday—Maria had decorated the dining room with red crepe paper and hearts. Holiday decorations were a wild card around Sunset Hills. Sometimes it helped the residents feel more at ease, happier about their environment. Other times it left them troubled and confused.

The residents hadn't noticed her yet, so Ashley studied them from the entrance of the room. Helen gripped the arms of her chair and stared at the streamers overhead, suspicion written across her face. "I knew it," she said.

Edith keyed off Helen's concern and also looked up. Her mouth formed a perfect *O,* as she studied the decorations.

Only Irvel looked relaxed. Her delicate hands were folded neatly on the table in front of her, clutching something Ashley couldn't make out. Irvel smiled at Helen. "Excuse me. I don't believe we've met."

"I don't want to meet anyone!" Helen barked at Irvel. "I'm always meeting people."

"Very well." Irvel raised her brow and sat a bit straighter in her seat. "I shall call you Gertrude." Irvel glanced up, the way Helen and Edith were doing. "Are you looking for God?"

"No." Helen glared at Irvel and slammed her hand on the table. "Prison bars, that's what they are. Red prison bars. Spies brought us here and now we're in prison." She shot a look at Maria, who was putting together a serving dish of scrambled eggs in the kitchen. "What's it cost for a cup of coffee around this joint? A quarter?"

Edith picked up her fork and studied it, first one side, then the other. "Prison . . . prison bars . . . prison."

Ashley caught Maria's eye and nodded. She strode into the room as if she'd just arrived and smiled at each of the women. "Hello, Irvel . . . Helen . . . Edith. How is everyone this morning?"

All three stopped looking up at the red streamers and stared at her.

Irvel made a polite pointing gesture at Edith and Helen. "I think they're looking for God."

"Not God, you old bird." Helen slammed herself back in her chair. "The prison guy, the one with the key. I've gotta get out of here, I tell you. Today. Before it's too late and the spies . . ."

Helen kept talking, but Ashley tuned her out. She was too busy watching Irvel. The old woman looked pale—too pale. And her eyes weren't as clear as they'd been the day before. Ashley moved closer to Irvel's chair.

"Hi, Irvel. How're you feeling?" Ashley tried to make out whatever it was Irvel held in her hands, but the woman had it covered with her bony fingers.

Irvel lifted her face and squinted at Ashley. "God isn't up there, dear." In spite of the cataracts and white film, the woman looked more lucid than she had in months. "You know that, right?"

Ashley set her hand on Irvel's shoulder and ran her thumb lightly over the old woman's brittle bones. "Where is he, Irvel?"

Irvel smiled and pressed her hand against her heart. "He's right here." Then she shifted her gaze to an empty spot beside Ashley. Her words were slower than usual. "Well . . . hello . . . Hank!" She paused and then chuckled as a bit of color came to her cheeks. "Of course not. The girls wouldn't mind if you joined us for tea."

She turned to Helen, who had only just then come up for air. "Gertrude, do you mind if Hank joins us for tea?"

"Look," Helen released a hard sigh. "We have to get out of prison before we can have tea. Besides, it costs a quarter and it only comes from the warden."

Ashley released Irvel's shoulder and made her way around the table to Helen. "You're not in prison, Helen. Those are decorations. For Valentine's Day."

"No!" Helen gave several hard shakes of her head. "I'm in prison. Help me!"

Edith studied her plate. "Help me . . . help me."

Ashley figured she'd give the residents until after breakfast to get in the spirit of Valentine's Day, and if that didn't happen the decorations would go.

"Excuse me, Gertrude." Irvel tapped Helen on the arm and smiled at her. "Hank's waiting."

"Who's Gertrude?" Helen threw her hands up and looked hard at Ashley. "Will someone put that old bird out of her misery?" She pointed up at the streamers. "And what kind of food do you serve in this joint, anyway?"

"Eggs, coming up!" Maria entered the dining room with the scrambled eggs and a plate of buttered toast. Ashley helped serve, and when she came to Irvel, she noticed the old woman staring at the thing in her hands.

"Irvel . . ." Ashley set the bowl of eggs down and took hold of the back of Irvel's chair. "What do you have?"

She looked up at Ashley, confusion clouding her eyes. "Well, hello, dear. I don't believe we've met." She covered the item with one hand and held the other out to Ashley. "My name's Irvel." A smile lifted the corners of her mouth, and she nodded her head to the empty place beside her. "This is Hank."

Ashley smiled at the empty spot. "Hello, Hank." She looked at Irvel. "I'm Ashley. I'll be with you all morning, okay?"

"Ashley." Irvel narrowed her eyes and looked to the center of Ashley's being. "You seem so familiar, dear." Her gaze lifted some. "But look at that beautiful hair, will you? I've never seen such beautiful hair, dear. Does anyone ever tell you that?"

"Not today, Irvel." Ashley eased her arm around the woman's shrunken shoulders. "Is Hank having breakfast with you today?"

"No." She looked around as if she'd misplaced something. "Neither of us is hungry."

"Oh." Ashley looked once more at the object in Irvel's hand and again tried to make it out. But Irvel's hand still covered it.

"Hank's always wanted me to go fishing with him, and to-day—" Irvel gave Ashley a partial wink—"today I'm going with him. Just me and him and God."

Helen was midbite, but she stopped at that part and snapped at Irvel. "God doesn't fish."

Irvel patted Helen's hand, her smile more confident than before. "Oh, yes he does, Gertrude." She looked at Ashley. "That woman doesn't know much about God, I'm afraid."

Ashley contained a smile. Irvel was right about Helen, but this wasn't the place to say so. She pointed to the item in Irvel's hands and tried again. "What do you have there?"

Irvel looked down at the object and surprise filled her eyes, as if she had no idea what was in her hands or how it had gotten there. She turned it over, and as she did, Ashley felt her eyes water.

It was a framed picture of Hank, one of the smaller photos Ashley had placed on Irvel's wall several months back. She must've taken it from the wall and carried it with her to break-fast.

Irvel held the frame up so she could see it better and grinned at the picture. "Well, hello, Hank." She waited a moment, then lifted her eyes to Ashley. "Hank says we don't have time for tea today. The fish are biting early."

Edith raised her hand. "Can . . . can I have eggs instead of fish?"

Maria was at her side in an instant. "Yes, Edith, right here." She took Edith's fork and poked it at the small scoop of scrambled eggs on her plate. "Right here, Edith. These are your eggs."

Helen was intent on her breakfast for a moment, the red crepe-paper prison bars temporarily forgotten.

Ashley looked at Irvel again. "Sounds like a wonderful day, fishing with Hank."

"Yes." Irvel's eyes sparkled in a way that was almost otherworldly. "The good Lord told me it would be a nice morning, indeed." She looked at the picture of Hank again. "Do you know something, hair girl? I'm the luckiest woman in the world, because you know why?"

"Why?" Ashley's heart was full. She treasured this time with Irvel. Often their conversations were poignant, even humorous, but they were rarely this tender.

Irvel lowered her head a few inches and pointed to the Valentine's decorations. "Because I know what it means." She dropped her voice a notch. "It's not a prison."

Ashley followed Irvel's gaze. "The decorations, you mean?"

"No." Irvel's eyes shone. "Love. Love isn't a prison."

Just when Ashley thought she couldn't learn another thing from Irvel, the two of them would share a moment like this. Landon's face came to mind immediately, and she savored it for a moment. "No, Irvel. With a man like Hank to love, it isn't a prison, is it?"

"No." Irvel looked at the photograph again. "It's heaven."

Bert's distant voice sounded from his room. "Food! Time for food."

Ashley looked at Maria. "You get Edith into the bath, and I'll take a plate to Bert."

Maria nodded and went to Edith, helping her from the chair. Ashley leaned close and kissed Irvel's cheek. "You think about your fishing trip with Hank. I'll be right back."

She made up a plate of eggs and toast, took them down the hall to Bert. He was already sitting at the small table in his room. The saddle, anchored on the old sawhorse at the end of his bed, shone from the early morning shine Bert had already given it.

"Here you go, Bert. Eggs and toast, just the way you like it."

Bert watched her set the plate down and smiled at her. "Saddle's shining good today."

"Yes." Ashley gazed at the saddle again. "Nice work, Bert."

With the compliment, the man worked himself a bit straighter in his chair. The transformation never ceased to amaze Ashley, the way a man who had made his living, found his purpose in his work, could be brought to a place of cognitive understanding and self-worth because he had a job again, because he had a saddle to shine.

She was heading back down the hall when she heard Maria cry out.

Ashley picked up her pace and returned to the dining room to see Irvel motionless, facedown on the table. Ashley could barely find words as she tore across the room toward her old friend. "What happened?"

"I don't know!" Maria's voice was high-pitched, panicky. "I came back and she was like that."

Helen stared at Irvel and pounded both fists on her knees. "Don't just stand there." She waved her hands in the air. "Help the old bird, would you?"

Ashley's heart was racing, but she forced herself to stay calm. "Maria, help Helen into the other room, okay?"

Maria's eyes were wide, fearful, but she nodded and made her way to Helen. "Come on, dear. It's time for our TV shows."

Helen left with only one glance over her shoulder. The moment they were alone, Ashley took Irvel's wrist. It was warm but limp, completely nonresponsive. "Irvel, wake up!" With a forced calm, she checked the woman's pulse, but found none. Next she passed her hand in front of Irvel's nose and mouth, and felt no breathing sensation whatsoever.

"Irvel." Ashley bent close to the woman's feathery soft face and gave her shoulder a gentle shake. "Irvel, wake up. Come on. . . . You're going fishing with Hank today, remember?"

No response.

"Irvel!" Ashley's voice was urgent, more persistent. She eased Irvel's head back and only then was she sure about what had happened. Irvel's eyes were open, blue and translucent, forever still. Her hands were together, still gripping the picture of Hank, and on her face was the slightest trace of a smile.

"Oh, Irvel . . ." Tears stung at Ashley's eyes as she put her arms around the woman and hugged her.

Maria rushed back into the room, her task with Helen complete. "Ashley, what is it? What happened?"

She still had Irvel in her arms, but she looked up and met Maria's frantic look. Then, with a sadness she couldn't express, she shook her head. "Get her file, please, Maria."

Protocol at Sunset Hills was that they call for emergency help if one of the residents was suffering a heart attack or a stroke. But if the person had already died, the call would go to the funeral home—a detail each of the residents had on file.

Ashley had no doubt that Irvel was dead, and the loss was greater than she'd ever imagined. Irvel was her friend, the one who had convinced her to work at Sunset Hills in the first place. Ashley and Irvel had shared a hundred hours of conversation about Hank and God and the merits of tea. But now she was gone, and Ashley was sure her heart would never be the same again.

Alone with Irvel again, Ashley studied the woman's face and ran her fingertips over her wrinkled cheeks. "Thank you, Irvel . . . you taught me so much."

Ashley thought of all that would come now. She'd have to tell Cole that Irvel had died, and contact Irvel's family about a service. No matter that Irvel was safe in the arms of Jesus, the next few days would be some of the saddest Ashley had known.

She hugged her old friend once more. "Good-bye, Irvel . . . I'll miss you."

Working carefully, slowly, Ashley closed Irvel's eyes. She reached down to remove the photograph from Irvel's fingers, but then she stopped short. Let the caretaker remove the picture of Hank. Ashley couldn't bring herself to separate Irvel's fingers from the photograph any more than she could will the old woman back from the dead.

"God . . . be with her." Ashley whispered the words against Irvel's cheek.

Irvel's words from this morning came back to her, and a strange feeling made its way through her heart. Had she known? Had God given her some idea that this morning would be her last, that come this afternoon she and Hank would finally see each other again the way they hadn't seen each other for so many years?

Then suddenly Ashley was certain. Her old friend must've had an idea, because for the first time she hadn't planned to spend the day waiting for Hank to return from a day of fishing with the boys.

And now, at long last, the waiting was over.

Irvel was no longer an Alzheimer's patient living out her days at Sunset Hills Adult Care Home. She would never again get confused about Helen's name or wonder why some people were violent when all they had to do was love God to find joy.

No, Irvel was finally free from the binds of earth. And today, even at this moment, Irvel was a citizen of heaven, sitting on the banks of a lake in paradise, doing the very thing she'd planned on doing that day.

Fishing with her beloved Hank.

# CHAPTER THIRTY

T HE WAREHOUSE WAS fully involved in flames long before Landon and his engine company arrived at the scene. His position as captain had been delayed for two months because of a personnel switch, so he was still with his original station, the station Jalen had worked at, and this afternoon he'd been on duty five hours when the call came in.

A rush of adrenaline coursed through Landon's veins as his truck pulled up and waited for instructions. Huge balls of fire leapt from one side of the building, and for a fraction of a moment Landon stared at it, mesmerized. Jalen had told him about fires like this, but never—until now—had he seen one for himself.

Sure, the fires he and his men responded to were often major. Many had involved the rescue of civilians and other firefighters. But nothing Landon had seen had been as massive as the fire playing out before them now.

"Blake!" Captain Dillon's expression was tight with tension. "You and the others get a ladder up the south side of the building stat. Command says four men are trapped near the center of the roof."

"Roger that, sir." Landon led the way with Barry, John-John, and three other men behind him. Normally the ladder companies handled roof assignments, but they were the only available men, and there was no time to think about other options.

The group worked their ladder to the far side of the building, the place where the flames hadn't quite come through the roof. Landon and John-John grabbed hoses and scrambled up the ladder first. The moment they reached their position, the other four men climbed past them in search of the trapped men.

*Be careful, guys. . . .* Landon directed a spray of water at the most threatening flames, the ones that shot through the roof between them and the center of the structure. *Come on, God . . . let the water hit it right, take down the flames so we can see the men.*

It took three seconds for four of the men to disappear through the smoke and flames in search of the victims. Landon tightened his grip on the hose and gave it everything he had, but still the pressure wasn't enough. Another wall of flames shot through the roof, blocking off one of the few escape routes from the center of the building.

Landon could barely make out a host of sirens in the distance. More units were coming, but it didn't matter. The building was shaking, the roof shuddering beneath the ladder where he and John-John were anchored. Thick smoke billowed past them, cutting visibility to almost nothing.

*Steady, Landon . . . breathe steady.* He checked the fitting of his face mask and sucked in a slow mouthful of oxygen. His position on the ladder was steady, but the ladder rested on the roof. If the roof gave way . . .

Then suddenly a piercing crack filled the air, rising above even the roar of the fire. In slow motion, a rumbling began to build and grow until it was deafening, the sound of a freight train bearing down on them.

Or the sound of a collapsing structure.

Landon tightened his grip on the ladder.

"Hold on, Blake." John-John's voice sounded over the radio

monitor in his helmet. The man was hanging from the other side of the ladder, looking like he might fall at any minute.

Just then another crash sounded and shook the flaming building, and the ladder jolted a few feet to the side as a cloud of debris rose out of the thick smoke.

Landon used all of his strength to keep his grip. The smoke and debris were so thick, he couldn't tell what had happened, couldn't see if the roof was still intact. Loud static sounded in his helmet, and he could barely make out a handful of words.

"Evacuate the roof . . . evacuate the roof."

The command was muffled, and Landon wasn't sure he heard it. Why would they want him to evacuate? He continued spraying the hose, staring through the relentless smoke, desperate for a sign of life among the flaming beams.

Beside him John-John began making his way back down the ladder. He motioned at Landon once and then continued toward the ground.

"Wait!" Landon shouted the word into his face mask and felt his grip on the ladder loosen. He was suddenly so tired he wasn't sure he could hang on another minute. Landon felt the ladder shake again, and he closed his eyes.

*I can't leave those men, God . . . not if I can help them.*

*Son . . . obey. I'll take care of the men.*

The thought came to him so directly Landon wondered if maybe he'd heard it over the radio. But when he opened his eyes, he was completely alone. John-John was gone, descended through the cloud of black smoke. And still he had no way of knowing whether the roof was even intact, let alone whether anyone was trapped there.

He hesitated for another moment, and then once more his ladder sank several feet closer to the roaring inferno below.

*Go, son . . .*

Landon gritted his teeth and with the hose still spraying, he began his descent. Inside his sweltering uniform he was drenched with sweat, barely able to breathe, blistering from the flames beneath him. One step, another. *Breathe, Landon . . . keep going.* Another step, two more.

Finally, after five minutes, he reached the ground.

Immediately he was whisked away from the building, and only then did he realize he was in trouble. His feet wouldn't work, and he felt sick to his stomach. Heatstroke, the condition that lulled a number of firefighters to their death each year. Landon allowed the men on either side of him to drag him to a staging area, where they ripped off his helmet and held a cup of water to his lips.

Landon wasn't sure what was happening. Everything seemed to move in slow motion, and more than anything he wanted to sleep. He uttered a weak cough and felt his knees buckle.

"Drink." It was Captain Dillon, and when Landon didn't reach for the cup, the captain splashed half of it onto his face. "Come on, Blake; drink the water."

The cold wetness against his face snapped Landon to attention, and he gave a hard shake of his head. "Wait . . . what . . . what happened?"

"Drink." The captain had more water.

This time Landon smacked his lips. They were parched and swollen. He opened them as wide as he could and let the cool water run into his throat. Medics joined them now and gave the captain a full bottle of water, which he held to Landon's lips.

"Keep drinking."

"Let's get him to the truck." One of the medics led them toward the bumper of the closest fire truck, and Landon worked his legs in front of him, then stumbled. His feet wouldn't work and his legs were shaking. Not just his legs but his arms, hands, even his mouth. Almost as if he were shivering. The medics peeled away his uniform until his turnouts were off.

"Heatstroke." One of the medics covered Landon's mouth with an oxygen mask. "Breathe deep. You'll be okay."

Five minutes passed while Captain Dillon and two medics alternated giving him water and oxygen. Finally, seven minutes later, Landon's head cleared some, and he started to remember. He'd been at the top of a ladder, spraying water onto the flames coming through the roof, and . . .

"What happened?" he asked.

Captain Dillon ignored the question. "You okay, Blake?"

"Fine." Landon straightened, searching the firefighters milling about for the faces of his friends. "Where's Barry and John-John?"

The captain clenched his jaw and gave a shake of his head. "The roof collapsed."

"What?" Landon's heart thudded hard. "Where're the men?"

"On their way to the hospital." It could've been the smoke, but the captain's eyes were red and damp. "Eight of them were trapped in the collapse."

Eight men? The four who were trapped initially, and four from . . . "Four from our engine company, sir?"

"Yes." The captain narrowed his eyes, wrinkles bunching up at the corners. "You're a praying man, right, Blake?"

"Yes, sir." Landon wanted to run, chase after the ambulance and make sure his men were okay. Make sure all the men were okay. "Are they hurt bad, sir?"

The captain paused, and for a moment his gaze fell to the ground. "Pray, Blake. Pray hard."

By seven o'clock that evening, everyone in the department had the news.

The collapsed roof had claimed the lives of six men, one of them Barry, Landon's colleague and friend. Combined, fourteen children were fatherless that night because of one New York City fire.

One lousy fire.

Landon arrived at his apartment just before eight o'clock and fell onto the sofa. His clothes still reeked from smoke. He'd spent two hours getting intravenous fluids at the hospital, orders of Captain Dillon, and his body was no longer in trouble. But his heart was devastated.

How had it happened?

Four men were trapped, so how had they lost six? Six men who had gone to work today the same as any other FDNY man, only tonight they lay dead, their families devastated. Because of what?

A warehouse fire.

The fire would've burned out eventually, so who had sent them skittering to the roof to spray water at it? Landon crossed his arms and willed himself to stay calm; he could do nothing about the losses now. And the department had been following protocol. When a warehouse was involved, they could often stop the fire by attacking it from the top.

And that meant putting men on the roof.

He stayed there for a while, anchored to the sofa, his legs stretched out. *God, I asked you to help.*

*Men are like the grass, son. . . . What is your life but a mist?*

The Scriptures were ones he was familiar with, verses that had struck him on several occasions before. Verses that reminded him that life was too short to hesitate, words that had pushed him to come to Manhattan in the first place.

He closed his eyes and he could hear Jalen again.

*"Fighting fires in Bloomington is a pastime, man. But in New York City it's a passion."*

Hadn't Landon thought about that when he made the decision to come? Life was short, little more than a mist. Why wait around Bloomington for Ashley when his job could become a passion in New York City?

But now, in light of the day's losses, the Bible verses made him wonder why—if life was so short—he'd want to spend it putting out warehouse fires a thousand miles from home.

The thought buzzed around in his head until he was thirsty

again. The doctor at the hospital had told him he'd be thirsty through the night and the next day. Night had fallen outside, and Landon flipped on a light as he headed for the kitchen and a glass of water.

As he walked by the phone he noticed the message light blinking on his answering machine, and he paused long enough to press the button.

The voice that sounded through the speaker was John Baxter's. Landon reached down and turned up the volume.

"Hey, Landon, wanted you to know that Irvel died this morning." Mr. Baxter's voice was mixed with sorrow and compassion. "Ashley was with her, and . . . well, she's taking it pretty hard. The service will be Sunday at one o'clock." He paused. "Just thought you'd want to know."

Landon hunched over the machine and hit the Off button. *Not Irvel, too, God.*

There was no response this time, and Landon gripped the countertop. What was he doing, so far away from everything that mattered to him? Hadn't he come to this truth before, after finding Jalen's body in the rubble of the collapsed World Trade Center? and again before Kari and Ryan's wedding?

And what about his week with Ashley after Christmas?

Hadn't he known he could never live without her? Sure he could convince himself that Ashley had made up her mind, and that the captain position was God's way of showing him a different plan, one that didn't involve Ashley Baxter.

But what was God telling him now?

Life was short, a mist that appeared for a little while and then vanished. He could stay in New York and devote his life to putting out flaming warehouses. Sure, once in a while he'd help with a rescue and maybe save a life. But there was one person who needed him more than any fire victim ever could. Because there would always be a firefighter to take his place at the department.

But no one else would ever love Cole Baxter the way he did.

And even if he never convinced Ashley to let him love her, there was still Cole. And without a dad in his life, without a man who could take up where John Baxter would leave off one day, Cole could very easily slip through the cracks.

Suddenly the smoke in his life cleared, and everything about his future came into focus. It was only a matter of time before the body that slipped through the roof of a flaming building was his. And where would that leave Cole? He wasn't afraid to die, not hardly. Rather he was afraid to miss out on living, on embracing the kind of life that would be filled with meaning and joy.

Landon stared at the phone and thought about the calls he needed to make in the morning. He would call Captain Dillon and put in his two weeks' notice. Then he'd contact his old captain back at the Bloomington station and see if he could get his job back. He'd thank Jalen's parents for the use of the apartment this past year, and he'd pack up his things.

But first, he had a memorial service to attend, and that meant one phone call he could make tonight.

A phone call to the airlines.

# CHAPTER THIRTY-ONE

VERY FEW PEOPLE remembered Irvel at her service on Sunday.

The memorial was held at a small downtown church, a place Irvel had never attended, since she hadn't lived in Bloomington except for her time at Sunset Hills.

Ashley had given the pastor a brief sketch of Irvel's life, the fact that she'd loved Jesus and Hank, not always in that order. And the truth that even after Alzheimer's had taken her mind, she remembered to be kind and compassionate, a Christian woman with grace and manners.

Three of Irvel's grandchildren and two nieces made the service and sat in the front row. Her grandson would take over her affairs, since he lived the closest.

Ashley's parents and Cole sat with her also, near the front of the church. Maria and a few other workers from Sunset Hills sat in the row behind them. Ashley had thought about coming by herself, without Cole, but she wanted her son to see this, the closed casket and the parting words for someone who no longer lived on earth, but had crossed over to heaven.

Beside her, Cole tucked his hand in hers as the organist began to play. Ashley had picked the music, too, and she felt her heart lurch as the first refrains of "Great Is Thy Faithfulness" filled the small church.

Ashley could see her still, Irvel, sipping her tea and humming the words to the old hymn: "Great is thy faithfulness, O God my father. . . . "

The song played on and Ashley stared at the coffin. It was simple, inexpensive, a plan Irvel's family had paid for long ago. A spray of red roses covered the top, and at the center stood a picture of Irvel and Hank. Already the caretaker had placed the other photograph—the one Irvel had died holding—inside the coffin.

Next the organist played "How Great Thou Art," another of Irvel's favorites. Ashley remembered watching the old woman and marveling at the brain's ability to remember. Irvel hadn't been sure of her whereabouts or the people at her breakfast table each day, but she could remember every word and note of her special hymns.

Amazing.

Ashley caught her father looking at her. She smiled in his direction, and he mouthed the words, "I love you."

She returned the feeling, holding up the thumb, pointer finger, and baby finger on one hand—"I love you" in sign language. Her mother leaned forward and gave her a sad smile, which Ashley also returned.

The pastor was talking now, saying something about how Irvel had lived a good life, a long life. "But most of all, she lived a life of love." The pastor glanced at the few faces in the crowd. "At the end of our days on earth, it should be the goal of each of us here to say we did as Jesus asked. We loved and were loved. The message is the crux of First John, that we might love because he first loved us."

The man smiled at them. "Irvel understood that, and so today we celebrate her life."

Minutes before the memorial ended, Cole slid his little body closer to Ashley and pointed to the casket. "Mommy." He whispered her name near her ear. "Is Ms. Irvel in the box?"

Ashley started to answer him, but her throat closed in and made it impossible. How many times had she sat at the Sunset Hills dining-room table, enchanted by Irvel's genteel demeanor, amused by her steadfast determination that Helen mind her manners, by her insistence that their time together was simply a wonderful afternoon of tea with the girls?

Now she was gone, and Ashley felt buried beneath the sadness. She thought about Cole's question and the answer was obvious. She made a quiet clearing of her throat. "No, Cole . . . Ms. Irvel's not there." Ashley closed her eyes for a moment and hesitated. In her mind she could see Irvel, large as life, smiling at her from across the table, holding a cup of tea to her lips. *"Why, dear, what beautiful hair you have? Has anyone ever told you that?"*

"But Mommy . . ." Cole's whisper was louder than before. "If she's not there, where is she?"

Ashley placed her hand on the far side of his small face and drew him closer. "She's fishing with Jesus, buddy. Sitting near the prettiest lake in all of heaven."

The graveside service was held right after the memorial. Ashley's parents took Cole home, since it was Sunday afternoon, and he always took a nap on Sundays. Ashley's way of helping him get ready for the busy week ahead.

Only two rows of chairs were set up on the grass near the place where the casket stood, ready to be lowered into the ground. Again the service was short, and when it was over, Irvel's family invited Ashley to a small lunch at her grandson's house.

Ashley declined. "I think I'll sit here for a while." Her eyes stung, ready to tear up at any moment, though so far she hadn't cried. "Irvel was very special to me."

They took turns hugging Ashley, and Irvel's grandson was last to say good-bye. "My grandma lived her last few years a happy woman." His eyes glistened. "That's because of you." His chin quivered and he pursed his lips, trying to maintain his composure. "You allowed her to live with Grandpa this past year, every day as if he were right there, just down at the lake or around the corner cleaning fish with the boys." He shrugged and a sound that was part laugh, part cry came from him. "She talked about him all the time, and—" he looked at the other family members gathered behind him—"all of us saw it. She was at peace, happy with God and Grandpa and herself."

He dragged his fist across his cheek and held Ashley's eyes for a moment longer. "Thank you. We . . ." His gaze fell to the ground for a moment and he shook his head. Then he handed Ashley the photograph of Irvel and Hank, the one that had been on top of the casket back at the church. "This is for you."

Each of them repeated the same sentiment, thanking Ashley and letting her know how wonderful Irvel's last year had been. Then, very quietly, they left, and Ashley was alone with Irvel's casket. As often as Ashley told herself that Irvel wasn't there, that she was fishing in heaven with Hank and Jesus, the moment at hand was still the saddest of all.

Because it was Ashley's last chance to say good-bye.

She eased herself from the chair and went to the casket, still covered in red roses. Ashley had taken care of the floral arrangements, and she'd chosen red on purpose. The color Hank would've given her for such a grand occasion, the passing from life to life ever after.

Ashley placed her hand on the polished wood and closed her eyes. "Irvel . . . I miss you. I miss you so much." Her voice was quiet, and the sound of it mixed with the crisp February air and faded through the still-barren tree branches across the cemetery.

How much had she learned since coming to Sunset Hills?

She tried to remember how she'd felt that first day, the morning when that awful Belinda woman had mocked her and told her she'd never make a difference, never find a way to reach the likes of Irvel and Helen and Edith.

Hot tears flooded Ashley's eyes and ran down her cheeks, and this time she did nothing to stop them. Belinda had been wrong then, and she was still wrong now. God's love and Ashley's desire to show that love to the people at Sunset Hills had indeed made a difference. Wasn't that what Irvel's family had just told her?

But it hadn't made a difference for Irvel and her friends only. Ashley had been changed, too. Changed dramatically and permanently. Before Irvel, Ashley hadn't understood what love really meant. Not God's love or any other kind of love. She'd assumed that her parents merely tolerated her, and that no one would care about her after what she'd done in Paris.

Irvel convinced her otherwise.

The love that woman had for Hank convinced Ashley that life had to be memorable, that one day all she would have left were her memories, and if she didn't take a chance and let herself love Landon, she would have nothing to remember.

No, she couldn't sentence him to a lifetime of risk. But the times she'd shared with Landon this past year would stay with her the rest of her life. She loved him; she still did. Loved him with all her heart, even if it was better for them to be apart.

Of course, Irvel's legacy went even beyond Ashley's love for Landon. She had also learned to love her precious son, the child she had never known quite what to do with. And hadn't it gone beyond that? Weren't things better in her relationship with her parents and her sisters, even her relationship with God?

Ashley pictured the wall of Hank photographs in Irvel's room, the glow on her face as she studied them each morning and night. Irvel had loved in a way that was not defined by worth or perfection or even life itself.

For Irvel, love went way beyond even the grave.

It was still true, because here and now, in the chill of a February afternoon, Ashley could feel Irvel's love as surely as if the casket weren't standing before her, but rather Irvel herself.

Very simply, before meeting Irvel, Ashley hadn't known how to love. And now everything was different—everything. And all because God had allowed one special woman to show her the importance of love.

Ashley let herself lean against the casket. "Irvel . . . I hope you know how God used you."

It was time to go, but Ashley couldn't pull herself away. She gazed toward the heavens and thought about the mercy of God, letting her find her way to Sunset Hills, using a woman as dear as Irvel to change her entire view about love.

"God, give her a good spot at the lake. Right near Hank, okay?" Again her words faded on the breeze, and for the longest time Ashley only stood there, her hand on the casket, eyes intent on the fading afternoon sun.

After a while she heard something behind her. She knew. It would be the caretaker, of course, patiently waiting for her to leave so he could lower Irvel's casket into the ground and bury it.

She let her gaze fall to the casket once more, to the spray of red roses shouting one last time about the love of a woman who would be sorely missed. "Good-bye, Irvel . . . thank you."

The moment had come, and she was about to turn around when she felt a hand on her shoulder. Then, inches from her face, in a gentle voice laced with sorrow and passion, she heard him.

"You have the most beautiful hair. Has anyone ever told you that?"

"Landon . . . " Her voice was more of a quiet gasp, the sound of shock because, of course, he couldn't be here, couldn't have known about Irvel, couldn't have found a way from New York City to the small graveside service in Bloomington.

But as she turned she saw she was wrong. There, as real as life itself, stood Landon Blake, his eyes damp and locked on hers, and before she had time to figure out how he had come she was in his arms, lost in his love and the realness of his presence, there amidst a sea of death.

He held her for a long time, rocking her and letting her cry for the friend she'd lost in Irvel. After a while he eased back and searched her eyes. "I'm sorry, Ash. She was a special lady."

"Yes." Ashley blinked. "Yes, she was."

He studied her face then, using his fingertips to brush her bangs back from her eyes. "Have you said good-bye?"

"Yes." Ashley nodded and for a moment she let her head fall against his chest. She'd told him the truth; she'd said good-bye and now it was time to go, time to begin the celebration of Irvel's life, and the gifts Ashley would always have because of their time together. She lifted her head and gave Landon a sad smile. "I've said good-bye."

"Okay, then." He stared down a pathway that led from the cemetery to an adjacent park. "Wanna take a walk?"

"Sure." She set the framed photo down on the nearest chair and slipped her hand in his, amazed that he had come, that he'd cared enough to be by her side at a time like this.

She realized something as they headed along the path. She'd needed him these past few days, yet she'd never admitted that even to herself, but now—now with him by her side, matching her step for step, their bodies brushing against each other as they walked away from Irvel's casket—now the colors in her grateful heart were more vivid than any she'd ever painted.

Landon waited until they crossed from the cemetery into the park. He led her to a quiet bench ten yards from a small play area. "Sit here?"

"Okay." She sniffed, her heart still aching at the loss of her friend. "You always do this."

"What?" He leaned back on the bench, weaving his fingers between hers and clutching her hand to his chest.

"You always come." She turned to him, and the light from the waning sun stung her swollen eyes. "Whenever I need you,

you're here. I don't have to ask; you just—" her eyes drifted to the trees, the path in front of them—"you just show up." She worked the corners of her mouth into a smile. "All the way from Manhattan."

He angled his head, studying her. "That's what I want to talk to you about."

Ashley felt her emotions shifting. No. He hadn't come here today to talk to her about their future again. Her heart skittered into a strange rhythm. Her soul was still too hurt, too raw to have that discussion now.

She shifted her position, placing a few inches between them so she could see him better. "Meaning?"

"Meaning I don't want to talk about us anymore." He gave her a sad, lingering smile. "I'm tired of talking."

Ashley held her breath. She wasn't sure where the conversation was going or how she'd feel when it got there. "Okay . . ."

His eyes were deep, and they looked into a part of her heart no one else ever saw. "So this time, instead of talking, I did something about it."

"What?" She searched his eyes, his expression, looking for signs. When she saw none, she reminded herself to exhale. "Landon, you're talking in circles."

"I'm sorry." Sorrow filled his face. His free hand came up, and he framed her jawline with his fingertips. "Three days ago I took a call and an hour later six men were dead. One of them was my buddy Barry, remember him?"

"Landon, no . . ." Ashley was on her feet, staring at him, terrified, reminding herself that whatever horrible thing had happened, the man talking with her wasn't a ghost. Six men might have died, but Landon was here, alive. Her mouth hung open, and she waited for him to finish.

"It was a warehouse fire, fully involved. We were told to rescue four men from the roof, and—" he looked a foot to the side of her, his eyes distant as he remembered—"and everything fell apart." His eyes found hers again. "The roof caved in, Ash. Eight guys fell into an inferno. It's a miracle two came out alive."

"You were . . . you were up there? on the roof?" She was breathless picturing it. How would she have survived if she'd lost him? Even though she'd planned to never see him again, she couldn't have gone on if something happened to him on the job.

"I was on the ladder." Landon stood and faced her, taking hold of both her hands. "I held on, but Ash . . . I came close. Very close."

"Landon . . ." She pulled him close, hugged him, grateful in so many ways that he was here, alive and strong, his body next to hers. Things could've been so different.

He eased back and searched her eyes. "When I got home that night, I found out about Irvel, and I made a decision." His voice was tender, a caress against her face. "I called the captain the next day and quit, Ash. I told him I couldn't give the rest of my life to the FDNY, not when I would spend every day wanting to be here in Bloomington with you."

Her head began to spin and the sidewalk buckled beneath her feet. "You . . . you quit your job?"

"Yes." His eyes shone again. "I gave them two weeks, but after what happened at the warehouse, they told me I could collect my things and be done. They understood."

Ashley was glad Landon was holding both her hands. Otherwise she was sure her knees would have given out and she'd fall in a heap on the ground.

"I'm tired of talking about it, Ash. You're all I want. Sick, healthy, broken, whole. I don't care. For six months I've let you talk me into staying away from you." He drew her slowly to himself and spoke with his lips barely touching hers. "Not anymore, Ash. You can't make me go now."

He kissed her then. Not the kind of kiss they'd shared on New Year's Eve, when every desperate moment felt like their last. But the kiss of hello and possibility and forever, all mixed into one.

After a while, when she had her bearings and she was sure she

wasn't somehow dreaming or imagining the past fifteen minutes, she leaned away and studied him. "You really quit your
job?"

"In New York, yes." He gave her a mischievous smile, one that
tugged hard at her heart. "But I start work in Bloomington a
week from Monday."

"What?" The story grew more unbelievable with each passing
second. "Landon, are you serious?"

He kissed her, longer this time, and drew back only long
enough to tell her yes, he was serious. Then he led her back to
the park bench, and he pulled a familiar velvet box from the
pocket of his denim jacket. "Ashley . . . I asked you before and
you turned me away. But this time you must know one thing."

Ashley wasn't sure whether to laugh or cry. She pressed her
fingertips to her lips and waited, alternating her gaze from his
eyes to the velvet box and back again.

Landon allowed himself a lopsided smile at her reaction. Then
he held her eyes once more and continued. "This time I'm hanging around, Ash. I'll be at your house every Saturday morning so
Cole and I can watch baseball games, and when you show up at
your parents' for dinner, I'll already be at the table."

"How can you love me so much? After all I've done . . ." Fresh
tears nipped at her eyes, and she hung her head for a minute. She
had tried everything she could to grant freedom to the man sitting beside her, freedom and a life without worry, without risk.
Not because she didn't want him.

She did. With every part of her being she wanted him.

She'd sent him away time and again because she'd wanted to
do the right thing. Only now . . . now he was telling her he didn't
want the chance to be away from her. He wanted her. Whatever
tomorrow might bring, he wanted her and Cole and however
long God gave them together.

"I'm not finished, Ash." He lifted her chin and found her eyes
again. "This time I'm giving you the ring." He opened the velvet
box, took the ring from inside, and held it out to her. "Marry me,

Ashley. Whether we have a moment or a lifetime, please . . . marry me."

Her answer filled her to overflowing, spilling from her heart and soul and eyes until she couldn't help but share it with him. "Yes, Landon. Yes, I'll marry you." She held her hand out to him and saw that her fingers were trembling.

"Good." He eased the ring over her finger and grinned at her. "You were getting the ring either way."

Ashley stared at it, white gold with a glistening round solitaire in the center. For the briefest instant, she doubted herself again, and she winced as she looked at Landon. "Are you sure? There are no—" she searched for the right word—"no guarantees."

"I don't want guarantees, Ashley Baxter." He kissed first her lips, then her hand, and finally the place where his ring shone from her finger. "I want you. As long as God gives us each other, I want you."

They kissed again, and after a while, Landon whispered against her cheek, "Here's something strange. It wasn't the men at the fire that got my attention. Really, it was Irvel's death. Knowing that her entire life was all about loving Hank." His lips moved briefly against hers. "The way my life is all about loving you."

Ashley admired her ring, the way it caught what was left of the sunlight and splashed it across her hand. Nothing about the day was real, but Ashley didn't care. She'd never felt so much in a single day. "I thanked God for Irvel earlier, because she taught me how unforgettable love could be. How it can consume a person and change a person and bring light to a waning life, even until the last breath is drawn. Irvel showed me that."

"She did, didn't she?" He took her hand and rubbed his thumb in light circles over the ring.

"The way Irvel loved Hank, the way he loved her—that kind of love kept her warm inside years after life grew cold." Ashley met Landon's eyes again. "Theirs was a love worth remembering, a love worth celebrating."

"And one day, my precious Ashley . . ." Landon eased her to

her feet. For a few brief seconds, they came together and swayed to the music of all that tomorrow suddenly held.

"You were saying?" She breathed the words against his neck, intoxicated by the nearness of him.

"Yes. A love worth celebrating." He nuzzled his face against hers. "One day that's exactly what people will say about us."

# CHAPTER THIRTY-TWO

BROOKE PARKED HER CAR in a lot adjacent to the hiking trail and peered out the front window.

Other than her sedan, the parking lot was empty, and suddenly she wasn't sure if she'd read the card right. It had come on a bouquet of yellow roses and white carnations delivered to her house the day before.

"Happy anniversary, Brooke. Meet me at the rock at noon tomorrow."

Brooke was touched. Obviously the card was from Peter, and it could only mean he wanted to talk with her again, maybe even find a way to love her the way he had before everything had gone so bad. They were in counseling still, twice a week now, and the counselor had hinted that it might be time for her and Peter to have a trial run at living together again.

"That's the goal," the counselor had said at their last meeting. "I think we're getting close."

Brooke had mixed feelings. Part of her couldn't wait to have Peter home. He'd been drug-free since the hospital had checked him into rehab, and these days he was wonderful with

Hayley. He stopped in several times a week and worked with her, massaging her muscles and stretching her so she stayed limber while her brain tried to remember what to do with her arms and legs.

Still . . .

She wanted to love him the way God wanted her to love him. Honoring him, putting him first, building him up as a doctor. But that would only come as she trusted him, and she wasn't sure he was ready for that kind of love again. Mostly because he hadn't said he was ready.

But in the message at the bottom of the card, he'd written something that took her breath away. Something the old Peter would've said to her: "Meet me at the rock at noon tomorrow."

The rock was a midpoint in a hike they'd taken a hundred times when they were in med school. The path veered off from the campus and wound its way into the hills that surrounded the university. Two miles along the path stood a boulder-sized rock, a place they'd come back to on every one of their first four anniversaries. In order to reach the top of the rock, they would climb up one side, using ledges and grooves in the stone.

It took several minutes, but the view from the summit was well worth it.

The summit—a plateau really—was just large enough for two people, and it was Brooke's and Peter's favorite place. The view covered miles of sprawling, rural Bloomington, and the two had spent hours there, talking and watching dozens of sunsets. But after they had the girls, life became too busy for hikes or rocks or breathtaking views from little-known summits.

So much time had passed since they'd visited the rock, Brooke wasn't even sure he'd meant this one, the one on the hiking trail near campus. Maybe he meant for them to meet at a rock near the rehab center. Or one that stood as part of their landscaping at the home where Brooke and the girls were living.

But just in case, in case maybe he'd started back on campus and hiked the whole thing, Brooke made her way onto the path and walked the short distance from the parking lot to the rock. And there it was, tagged with simple graffiti: "Jaime loves Jake" and "IU girls rock" and the like.

Brooke studied it, the slope of it and the height of the summit. It was smaller than she remembered. But still it remained. Brooke leaned against it, savoring the feel of it and all it represented. She stood waiting, looking around and remembering every good memory she and Peter had ever shared here.

For a moment she listened, hoping to hear Peter's voice or footsteps. Maybe this wasn't the place he'd referred to on the card. She checked her cell phone. Five after twelve. Peter must've meant a different rock, and why not? It had been years since they'd been here. He probably didn't remember this old rock at all. She was about to turn away when she heard someone call her name from down the path.

"Brooke . . ."

Peter's voice. It was his voice, and her heart soared the way it hadn't in far too long. He was coming for her, and that meant yes, he'd walked the entire two-mile trail. But more than that— far more than that—he'd remembered.

He rounded the corner then, and the moment he saw her he stopped. "Brooke . . ."

"You . . ." She took a few steps toward him. "You remembered our rock."

The path was empty except for the two of them. Peter searched her eyes, and in his she saw a depth that hadn't been there in years. He came to her slowly, his eyes never leaving hers. "You're so beautiful, Brooke." He took her hands in his. "How come I stopped seeing it?"

She'd never answered that question in counseling. But here, now, being honest with him seemed the most right thing to do. Because the problems they'd suffered were not only his fault.

They were her fault, too.

"Brooke . . ." He studied her, and she liked the image he made. He'd gained back some of his weight, and he looked almost as good as ever. As if the nightmare of the past five months had never even happened. "I'm not sure I understand."

"It was my fault, too, Peter." Her stomach felt suddenly nervous. "Because I stopped needing you."

There. She'd said it.

And as she did, she winced. How wise was it to have this conversation with Peter now, on their anniversary, and without the assistance of a counselor? This was the first time they'd been alone since Peter had been admitted to rehab. What if something went wrong and they lost ground? She closed her eyes for the briefest moment and thought of the Bible verse she'd clung to these past months.

The words ran over in her head: *"Rejoice in the Lord always. I will say it again: Rejoice! . . . Do not be anxious about anything." Thank you, God. . . . Help me rejoice even now.* She opened her eyes and looked at him.

"You stopped needing me?" He cupped her elbows with his palms, looking at her eyes, wanting more information.

Brooke let loose a sad sigh. "I think so. I've thought about it, and yes—" she squinted at him—"I think that's what happened."

He was quiet, waiting. Finally he lowered his brow and his voice at the same time. "And now? Do you need me now, Brooke?"

"Yes." Her answer came so quickly it took even her by surprise. She pictured him working with Hayley on the floor of their living room, pictured him reading to Maddie. And mostly the way her heart hurt when he said good-bye at the end of a visit. "Yes, I need you, Peter. I need our family back together, the way it was."

He lifted his hands and eased them alongside her face. "I need you, too, Brooke. That's why I had to come here."

He led her to the side of the rock and helped her start the climb. They weren't as smooth as they'd been last time they were here, but in a few minutes they were both on the summit, sitting side by side looking out over Bloomington.

"You see all that." Peter stretched out his hand and fanned it across the width of the horizon. "Between Ryan and you and the counselor, God's let me see how that's our future. Wide-open, full of beauty, and spread out before us."

He turned to her and took her hand again. "I'm so sorry, Brooke. You're a wonderful doctor, an amazing mother, and if I'd give you half a chance, a beautiful wife. I need you, Brooke. I want to come back home and try again. Please."

Brooke's heart thudded hard against her chest. This was the moment she'd waited for, the one she'd dreamed about long before Hayley's accident. "Are you sure?"

"Yes." He kissed her then, the first time he'd kissed her in a year. "The months away from you have shown me that I never want to leave again. I love you and the girls so much, and after Hayley . . ."

She tightened her grip on his hand. "Don't do that to yourself, Peter. It wasn't your fault. It could've happened to anyone."

"The blame is mine, but that's okay." He held up his hand. "Ryan's teaching me that it's okay to feel that kind of pain, to see Hayley and know she may never walk normally. That's the valley of the shadow of death, and God doesn't promise to take us around it." Peter's voice fell some. "He promises he'll walk us through it."

They kissed again, and the feel of his lips on hers, the breeze against their faces as they sat on the rock's summit, was more than Brooke could believe. "Happy anniversary, Peter." She raised an eyebrow. "So, how soon are you thinking about coming back?"

The answer she wanted was something she didn't dare hope for, so she waited instead, watching him process the sensation of their being together.

Peter smiled at her and looked at his watch. "Well, the funny thing is, I have this truck back in the university parking lot, and inside . . . well—" he shrugged and gave her an easy grin—"inside the truck is everything I own."

Again her heart took wing, because at that moment she understood. "Everything?" She smiled, playing with him.

"Yes, indeed." He looked at his watch. "So actually, I was thinking about moving back home today. You know . . . in a few hours. You know . . . in time for that anniversary dinner."

"Anniversary dinner?"

"Yes. The one I'm taking you to this evening."

Brooke giggled. "Okay." He'd had the whole thing planned; that was the only explanation. "I think we could use a little celebrating."

"Mmm-hmm." Peter held her hand, his eyes locked on hers. "But this time, I promise you, Brooke, the celebration will never end."

MORE ABOUT THE BAXTER FAMILY!

*Please turn this page for a bonus excerpt from*

# R E U N I O N

*the fifth book in the*

## R E D E M P T I O N   S E R I E S

*by Karen Kingsbury with Gary Smalley*

# CHAPTER ONE

THE IDEA OF MEETING with the birth mother gave Erin a bad feeling from the beginning.

Their adoption attorney had warned them against it, but with four weeks before their baby daughter's birth, Erin couldn't tell the woman no. Sam agreed. Whatever the outcome, they would meet the birth mother, hear what she had to say, and pray that nothing—absolutely nothing—damaged the dream of bringing home their daughter.

The meeting was set to take place in thirty minutes at a small park not far from Erin and Sam's Texas home, where they would spend an hour with their baby's birth mother—Candy Santana—and her two children.

On the way out the door Erin's stomach hurt. "Sam?" She stopped near the nursery door and gazed inside.

He pulled up next to her and followed her gaze. For a moment neither of them said anything. Then he sighed. "You're worried."

"Yes." The nursery had pink walls, a white crib with pink bedding, and a dresser topped with pink teddy bears. Erin folded her arms tight against her stomach. "Everything's worked out." Her eyes found Sam's. "Why now?"

"I don't know." He kissed the top of her head. "Maybe she wants to see how excited we are."

The possibility seemed like a stretch. Despite the warm, late-March afternoon, Erin shivered and turned toward the front door. "Let's get it over with."

Half an hour later they were at the designated picnic area when a young woman and two small girls came toward them from the parking lot. Next to her was a thin man with long hair and a mean stare.

"Who's he?" Erin whispered near Sam's ear. They both sat on top of the table, their feet on the bench, as they waited.

Sam gripped his knees. "Trouble."

The approaching couple held hands, and as they drew closer Erin felt the knot in her stomach grow. Candy was very pregnant, dressed in worn, dirty clothes and broken flip-flops. The man's arms were dark with tattoos, one of a rooster with a full plume of feathers and the word *cock* in cursive beneath it. The other arm had the full naked figure of a woman framed on top by the name *Bonnie*.

Erin swallowed to keep from shuddering. She lowered her gaze to the little girls, running a few feet in front of the adults. Candy's youngest daughter was maybe two years old and wore only a droopy diaper. The other girl, not much older, had a runny nose and matted hair. Both children had lifeless eyes and a vacant stare, the look of neglect and emotional disconnect.

The same way Candy's unborn child would grow up if something happened in the adoption process, or if Candy changed her—

*No, God, don't let me think like that. Please . . . get us through this meeting.*

The couple was a few feet away now. Erin could feel the color draining from her face.

"Hi." Candy gave them a look that fell short of a smile. The right side of her upper lip twitched, and she rubbed her thumb against it. "This is Dave. The baby's dad."

*The baby's dad?* A thin wire of terror wrapped itself around Erin's neck. "Uh . . ." She forced up the corners of her mouth. "Hello. I'm Erin."

Sam held out his hand to the tattooed man. "Hi."

Not once did the man look at Erin or Sam. Instead he shifted his stare from Candy to the girls, to the ground, and back to Candy again. He grunted something that might've been a greeting. Erin wasn't sure.

For a moment no one said anything. Then Candy cleared her throat and glanced at her daughters. The younger one had picked a dandelion and was chewing on the stem. "Hey!" Candy pointed at the girl and let loose a string of inappropriate words. "I told you a hundred times don't be stupid, Clarisse, and I mean it. You ain't a dog, okay?"

The girl lifted her eyes in Candy's direction. "No!" She put the flower stem back in her mouth.

Candy mumbled something as she stomped over to the child and grabbed her arm. "Let it go!"

This time fear filled the girl's eyes. She threw the flower a few feet away and made a face at Candy. The woman released her daughter's arm and returned to the table, where Erin and Sam sat watching. Candy looked suddenly nervous, as if she hadn't realized she was being watched. She managed a frustrated, forced smile. "Stupid kids."

Erin didn't know what to say. She looked at her hands, at her wedding ring. *What's this about, God?*

The tattooed man cleared his throat and seemed to give Candy some sort of signal.

Candy nodded and turned to Erin. "We . . . uh . . . we have something to talk to ya about."

The knot in Erin's stomach doubled. She felt Sam take her hand and give it a firm squeeze. "We thought so." Erin reached for Sam's hand and squeezed it, her way of telling him how frightened she was. "We're . . . we're very excited about the adoption. Nothing's changed."

"Has something changed for you, Candy?" Sam's voice was even, but his words made Erin's heart miss a beat.

Candy and Dave exchanged a look. Candy's lip began to twitch again. "No, it's just . . ." She looked at the ground for a moment. "We kinda ran into some money troubles, you know? Tough to get a job and all when you're, you know, pregnant and everything."

The instant Erin heard the word *money*, she relaxed. Was that all this was about? Candy was short on rent and needed a few hundred dollars? Their attorney had warned against giving Candy additional money. Her financial needs during the pregnancy had already been taken care of, and Candy had signed a paper agreeing not to ask for anything more.

Erin's heart rate slowed some. But if Candy needed something extra, then so be it. A few hundred dollars and they could all move on like before. She pictured her baby's face, the smooth skin and fine features, the way she'd always pictured her. Everything would be okay after all. Everything.

"That happens." Sam was nodding, looking at Candy. A fine line of moisture had gathered along his upper lip. "Money gets tight sometimes."

Dave looked up and shifted his weight to the opposite foot. He gripped the tattoo on his left arm. "What she's saying—" he cocked his head—"is we need more money."

There it was. Erin swallowed. In case they had any doubts, now the request—a request all of them knew was against the rules—was out in the open. She caught Sam's look and gave him a silent go-ahead.

Sam stared at Candy. "Have you talked to the lawyer? We agreed on what you needed."

"It wasn't enough." Candy glared at Sam. "You try raising kids and being pregnant on that kind of money."

*Raising kids?* Erin gritted her teeth. Candy wasn't raising the girls; their pastor had confirmed that on several occasions.

"Here's the deal." Dave pressed the toe of his worn work boot into the ground and dug his hands in his pockets. He grinned, and for the first time, Erin could see a gold stud in the center of his tongue. "We need more."

For a while no one said anything. The girls were quiet, still playing a distance away. Finally Erin found her voice and directed her attention to Candy. "How much?"

Above them, a cool wind played in the trees that lined the lake. Candy's lip twitched worse than before. "Fifteen thousand."

*Fifteen thousand?* Erin had to grip Sam's arm to keep from falling off the table. The adoption had already cost them their entire savings; they would never get hold of that much additional money, not at this late date. Candy was saying something, trying to explain, but Erin couldn't concentrate, couldn't hear anything but the number. *Fifteen thousand dollars.* Every word tore at the picture, the picture Erin had created in her mind of a baby girl cradled in her arms. She gasped for breath and turned toward her husband. "Sam . . ."

The figure was still crashing about in Erin's mind when Dave delivered the final blow.

"Fifteen thousand in twenty-four hours." He flashed an evil smile. "Or the deal's off."

The blood test was the doctor's idea.

Not because he doubted whether Ashley was HIV-positive but because he wanted a complete panel on her, a breakdown that would determine what method of treatment to take.

Ashley expected the results to come by phone, the way they had the last time. But this afternoon, stuck in the middle of a stack of mail, was a thick envelope from the lab. She stared at it as she made her way back into the house. Cole was inside, writing the alphabet on a piece of paper, and he grinned at her from the dining-room table as she walked in.

"Hi, Mom." His feet didn't quite reach the floor, and he swung them under his seat. "I'm on *T* already."

"Really?" Ashley's eyes were back on the envelope. "That's great, buddy. Tell me when you're done so I can check it."

She went into the kitchen and set the rest of the mail on a desk by the telephone. Then she stared at the envelope, slipped her thumb beneath the flap, and pulled out the stapled document.

Next to her name, the top sheet read "Lab Results."

Ashley had no reason to feel nervous or strange about the results. She already knew she was HIV-positive. It was only a matter of how her blood was holding up under the compromise of HIV and whether any progression could be seen toward full-blown AIDS.

Her eyes darted over the page, anxious for the summary lines, the places where any untrained person could make sense of the numbers and calculations. Then, at the bottom of the first sheet, she saw it. A simple few lines with only a few words that made Ashley's heart skitter into a strange and unrecognizable beat.

She sucked in a quick breath and blinked hard.

It was impossible; she couldn't believe it, wouldn't believe it. Someone had to have made a mistake.

Her head began to spin, and she gripped the counter to keep from falling to the floor. She had to call Landon, had to tell him.

"Mommy . . . I'm all done!" Cole's singsong voice called out to her from the adjacent room. "Come check for me."

"Okay." Ashley's face was hot and tingling, the way she felt when she got too close to a campfire. "Just a minute." She pressed her hands against her cheeks and jerked back at how cold her fingers were. Then once more she let her eyes read the results line at the bottom of the first page. They couldn't be right, could they?

A chill made its way from the back of her head, down her

spine, and into her feet. *Is it true, God? Is it really true?* Then one last time she looked at the lab results and began to imagine that maybe—just maybe—they were right. It wasn't possible, but still . . . what if? What if she'd come this far, given up so much, only to find this out? She wasn't sure whether to scream or shout or fall down on the floor and cry. But she was sure of one thing.

If the results were accurate, from this moment on, her life would never be the same.

※

Elizabeth Baxter found the lump on March 7.

She was in the shower, and at first she brushed past it, figured it to be nothing more than a bit of fatty tissue or a knotted muscle or maybe even a figment of her imagination. But then she went over it with her fingertips again and again. And once more, until she knew.

No question: it was a lump.

And a lump of any kind meant getting an immediate checkup. This was a road she'd traveled before, and as a breast-cancer survivor she knew the importance of self-checks. She stopped the water, dried off, and called her doctor while still wrapped in a towel.

Two days later she met with the man and had a mammogram. A biopsy was performed soon after, and now, on a brilliantly sunny day in mid-March, in the private office of Dr. Marc Steinman, Elizabeth sat stiff and straight next to John as they waited for the results.

"It's bad; I know it is." Elizabeth leaned a few inches to the side and whispered so that only John could hear her. "He wouldn't have called us in if it wasn't bad."

"You don't know that. It's probably nothing." His words were strong, meant to assure her. But his tone lacked the usual confidence, and something wild and frightened flashed in his eyes. He tightened his grip on her hand. "It's nothing."

Elizabeth stared straight ahead. The wall held an oversized, framed and matted print of a pair of mallard ducks cutting a path across a glassy lake. *No, God, please . . . not more cancer. Please.* She closed her eyes and the ducks disappeared.

Suddenly a parade of recent memories marched across her heart: Ashley and Luke sitting side by side at Luke and Reagan's wedding reception, reconnected after so long apart; Kari and Ryan exchanging vows at a ceremony in the Baxter backyard; little Jessie taking her first steps, and Maddie and Hayley holding hands for the first time after Hayley's drowning.

*They need me, God . . . they still need me. I still need them. Please, God, no more cancer.*

Footsteps sounded in the hall outside, and Elizabeth's eyes flew open. "Help me, John." Her voice was high, almost panicked.

"It'll be okay." John pushed closer, letting her lean on him.

The doctor entered the room, a file clutched beneath his arm. He stopped, nodded, and sat at the desk opposite them. Then he opened the folder and pulled out the top sheet of paper. "Thanks for coming." He looked up and his eyes met first John's, then Elizabeth's. "I have the results of your biopsy."

"She's fine, right?" John's tone sounded forced.

The doctor opened his mouth, but Elizabeth already knew. She knew the news would be bad. And in that instant, she couldn't think about surgery or radiation or how sick she was bound to get; she couldn't think of how she'd break the news to the kids or how John would handle another go-around with cancer. Instead only one question consumed her.

How in the world would her family live without her?

# A WORD FROM KAREN KINGSBURY

 OFTENTIMES WHEN I write a novel, God presents me the opportunity to live through things he wants me to tell you about. During the writing of countless novels, I marveled at the strange similarities taking place in my life. But the situation that came along as I wrote this novel was almost more than I could believe.

Four months after I'd written the first chapter of *Rejoice,* the chapter that sets up Hayley's drowning, I got a call from a close friend in Arizona. Her sister—another friend—needed prayer because her nineteen-month-old son, Devin, had fallen into an irrigation canal in central Arizona and drowned.

Little Devin traveled the canal for nearly a mile—eighteen minutes—before a neighbor saw his body and pulled him from the water. Eighteen minutes. Devin's body was blue and lifeless; he was not breathing, and he had no pulse.

Nevertheless, the neighbor administered CPR while a helicopter was called to the site. Devin was life-flighted to Children's Hospital in Phoenix, where he was put on life support. The lead doctor pulled aside Devin's mother and told her that the next two days were bound to bring about brain swelling, a condition that would push Devin even further from the possibility of ever waking up. To make matters worse, the family was asked to consider organ donation since Devin was basically brain-dead, being sustained by machines and pumps.

On the phone with me that day, my friend's request was simple. Pray. Pray for a miracle for Devin.

I'd like to tell you that when I hung up the phone, I rejoiced in God's healing power and prayed exactly as my friend had asked. But I didn't do anything of the sort. Instead, I begged God to let Devin go home. Let him run and skip and jump and catch frogs along a lake in heaven, where he would be free from the prison of his brain and his body.

You see, Devin looks very much like my little Austin. White blond hair, tanned skin, blue eyes. A boy with more testosterone than blood coursing through his body, one who had found his greatest joy running and jumping and living life to the absolute edge.

The same way Austin does every day.

I closed my eyes and tried to imagine Devin confined to a hospital bed, barely cognizant of the people around him, unable to run or jump or ever play again. And the picture was more than I could bear. I added up the facts and told myself that eighteen minutes underwater would never result in a miracle. Never. And if Devin couldn't smile or get out of bed again, then what was the point? *Take him, God,* I prayed. *Set him free in the fields of heaven.*

Two weeks passed, and against all medical odds, Devin was still alive. My friend would call on occasion and give me updates. Good news was always tempered with the reality of his situation. He could cry, but he couldn't recognize his mother so he couldn't be consoled. He could open his eyes, but the drowning had left him blind forever. He could turn his head, but he had no control of his arms and legs.

That month, I was asked to speak at an event in Phoenix. The way the flight schedule worked out, my plane arrived five hours before the event, so after checking into my hotel, I took a cab and met my friend and her sister at the hospital, at Devin's bedside.

He was awake, looking even more like my Austin than I remembered. Nurses had him propped up in bed with blankets. Padding was wrapped around his arms so he wouldn't hurt himself when his body seized, as it did several times each minute. Nestled beside him was a red Elmo doll, his favorite. In a slow, brain-damaged way, he moved his head from side to side and made a deep, throaty sound. He blinked, but also in slow motion.

His mother went to the opposite side of the bed. "Devin." Her voice held a hope and love that showed she had gotten past the initial shock of seeing her changed son. "Laugh for Mama, Devin."

And that's when it happened.

Devin followed the sound of her voice and looked at his mother with vacant eyes. His lips lifted into a little-boy smile and he laughed. It wasn't a normal-sounding laugh, but it was a laugh anyway. A response. Proof that somewhere beyond the obvious brain injury, Devin still lived.

The tears came then.

They streamed down my face, and though I was able to carry on a conversation through much of the next two hours, the tears never stopped. Not once. Not while Devin's mother talked to him, not while his legs seized straight up in the air, and not while I massaged his calf muscles in an effort to ease the tension there.

Through it all, I wept. Very simply, I was caught up in one of the saddest moments I'd ever been a part of. But it wasn't only because lying before me was a little boy who, until a few weeks earlier, was wonderfully vibrant and whole. It was that, for sure. But it was something else.

Watching Devin, seeing him interact with his mother, told me that I'd prayed for the wrong thing. Never mind the statistics and medical understanding of a child who had been underwater eighteen minutes. My God is bigger than all of medicine combined, bigger than brain damage and drownings, bigger than any limitation our bodies might put on us.

There and then I was convinced beyond any doubt that God could heal Devin. I held that little boy against my chest and let my quiet tears fall on his cheeks. Then I rocked him and leaned my face close to his ear the way I would with my own children.

And I begged God for a miracle for Devin.

I saw in that hospital room a family who was choosing to rejoice rather than give up. Rejoice rather than medicate their pain. Rejoice rather than believing the dismal reports from doctors.

When I left that afternoon, I could only do the same.

I went home and told my family about Devin. My parents assured me they would pray. Don and our kids looked at pictures of Devin and prayed along with me. My friend had a specific prayer, which I lifted to God every day: that come August, Devin would be off feeding tubes. That when he turned two years old, he might be able to eat his own birthday cake.

The first significant good news came two weeks later. My friend called with an update, and I went to my parents' house to tell them the news.

"I've been wondering how he is." My father hugged me. "I've been praying every day for God to give Devin back his eyesight. For some reason that's been on my mind morning and night."

"Dad . . ." My heart skipped a beat. "That's the news. The doctors have done a series of tests and they're sure. Devin can see again!"

I'll never forget the way my father's mouth hung open, the way he brought his hand to his face and let his head fall forward. My father had believed God was able, and now his tears were those of joy.

Since then, Devin has continued to improve. On his Web page, www.devinsmiracle.org, click the word *prognosis* and you'll see a brief testimony to the truth. It says, "Devin's family rejoices in God's goodness." They refuse to give a prognosis, since only God knows the plans he has for Devin.

Obviously much of what you've read in *Rejoice* was taken from my time with this precious little boy, my heart for him, and his recovery time. Please pray for him. If you have children, tonight before you hit the pillow, take a moment and thank God.

I'm glad you journeyed with me through the pages of *Rejoice*. My family is doing well. God has brought us two more kids—this time a nineteen-year-old who lived with us for six months, and a twenty-one-year-old—two young men who in our home seemed better able to follow the Lord and make good choices. Depending on the day or the month, the total number of kids in our house is often eight, sometimes more: three biological, three we adopted, and a handful who have adopted us.

Life is full, with constant reason to rejoice.

Oh, and I just received another bit of news from my friend in Arizona.

Devin turned two last week, and at a party attended by friends, family, and the neighbor who pulled him from the irrigation canal, he ate a piece of his birthday cake.

God is good!

Until next time, in his love,

*Karen Kingsbury*

P.S. Oh, one more thing. The poem Elizabeth wrote for Luke before his wedding was something I'd first written for my own children. The idea that we miss out on our children's last moments in a given stage is something I've thought about for years. After discussion with my husband and kids, I turned Elizabeth Baxter's *Let Me Hold You Longer* into a children's picture book, a special story you can share with your children—whatever age.

Tyndale will publish *Let Me Hold You Longer* in fall 2004. Though my primary focus will always be life-changing, emotionally gripping adult fiction, I'm thrilled to bring you this special children's book. The illustrations are light-hearted and whimsical, so that your kids will be laughing, even as you are holding back tears.

As always, I'd love to hear from you.

e-mail address:  **rtnbykk@aol.com**

Web site address:  **www.KarenKingsbury.com**

Please come visit and check out the reader forum and the guestbook links so you can see what other readers are saying and meet new friends.

# A WORD FROM GARY SMALLEY

B Y N O W Y O U ' V E figured out that the title *Rejoice* didn't mean this book was full of only good times and celebration. Rather, the calling of every member of the Baxter family was to find joy in the midst of great trials and pain. Jesus tells us to be joyful always, to consider it pure joy when we face trials of many kinds, to rejoice in the Lord always.

Rejoice. It is the command of Christ that his people keep a positive outlook, that we find a reason to smile even through our tears. And the reason?

Because we are what we think.

In my years working with relationships, I've seen two of the principles in this book played out time and again. First, the idea that couples struggle when tragedy befalls them. And second, the truth that couples always do better when they choose to be joyful, regardless of life's circumstances.

The following are five life seasons in which you will better serve your relationships by choosing to rejoice.

## REJOICE IN THE MUNDANE

Though we will all go through hard times, most of us are not in the midst of a situation as difficult as the one faced by the Baxters after Hayley's drowning. The key, then, is to find joy in the ordinary times. Many marriages are dying slow deaths because people walk through life half awake, passing each other in the halls and barely remembering to say hello. A woman once told me that she attended a barbecue with friends, and partway through the meal the host had her laughing hysterically over a funny story.

"I remember that it felt strange to smile, and then it hit me," she said. "I couldn't remember the last time I had smiled at home with either my husband or my kids."

Sometime this week, when you're doing nothing more than hanging around the house, catch your reflection in the mirror. If you haven't smiled in the past hour, smile. Rejoicing in the mundane makes dull times become happy. Remember, act with your head. Your heart will follow.

REJOICE IN THE DETAILS
Life is full of countless hours spent sorting mail, paying bills, balancing checkbooks, and managing debt. These details are necessary, but they don't need to rob us of our gladness. Next time you're in the middle of such a task, put on uplifting music—worship songs or something that makes your heart sing. If music isn't available, allow yourself to converse with the King of the Universe as you pay bills or sort mail. This type of determination will cause you to feel a kind of deeper joy, the joy God commands we have if we are to walk as a Christian.

I know a woman who does all such mundane tasks seated with her family watching a warm or fun-loving movie.

"I've never been much into movies," she told me. "But that way I'm surrounded by those I love, and they think I'm watching a program with them. The tedious nature of paying bills or balancing a checkbook simply disappears in that setting. It's my way of choosing to be filled with joy even while I'm doing something so simple."

REJOICE IN FRUSTRATION
Recently a friend of mine told me about a bad day her twenty-year-old son had experienced. He had just spent a couple thousand dollars fixing his transmission, and that afternoon he had to be at the fire station for a professional picture with the rest of the firefighters. When he went out to his car, less than twenty-four hours after getting it back from the shop, the engine wouldn't even turn over. He took his mother's car and went to

get his hair trimmed, but his hairdresser yelled at him for coming in before his hair had fully grown out. Flustered, he set out for the photo shoot and took the wrong exit off the freeway. By the time he found the right location, the picture had been taken.

He went home that day and gave his mom a hug. "The devil wants me to be mad, Mom. He's been poking at me all day." The young man grinned. "But not this time. It's a great day, and you know what? I'll figure out the car, things will be fine with the hairdresser, and next season I'll make the photo shoot." He shrugged. "No point wasting today over it."

Therein lies the lesson. Don't waste today by letting life's little frustrations rob you of your joy. Determine to be joyful anyway. Practice makes perfect in this area. Pretty soon when someone asks how you are, you'll answer, "Good!" And guess what? You'll mean it!

## REJOICE IN RESTORATION

Sin is one of the great thieves of joy. Our happiness can be robbed quickly when we get sucked into a familiar sin or any sin that causes us to be lost in shame, guilt, and the dark shadows of wrongdoing. One client of mine was having an affair for a year before the people at his medical office caught on.

"We were a group of Christian doctors, and we'd made our reputation that way," the man explained. "They told me they wanted me to seek a period of time away from the office, a time for restoration."

Initially, the requirements this man's friends demanded of him seemed overwhelming. "I was more depressed than ever," he said.

But then one of his closest friends reminded him of James 1, and the command of God to be joyful in trials. The man realized that God was pruning him, developing his perseverance, and that by choosing to embrace the discipline joyfully, he would grow from it.

As soon as his attitude changed, as soon as he began rejoicing about his restoration, the process began to unfold miraculously. He met with counselors, kept an open book of his life before his peers at the medical office, and six months later he and his wife were happier than they'd ever been.

"I'm sure it wouldn't have happened," he told me, "if I hadn't determined to rejoice in the restoration process."

## REJOICE IN SORROW AND TRAGEDY

God understands grief. Jesus wept when he saw the crowd's response to Lazarus in the tomb. Death, illness, and painful trials were never God's intention for his people. Since the fall of man, it has been the way of the world. But even so, God gives us a way out of the misery.

Be joyful! Rejoice always!

This doesn't mean you'll never cry. To the contrary, if your heart is soft for God, you'll cry often. You'll weep when it's your turn to stand vigil at a hospital bed, or when you stand there on behalf of someone else. But if you make a decision to rejoice, then deep inside you will always have a reason to go on, a reason to get up in the morning. Your grief won't be that of a person without hope; rather you will grieve because pain and death and tragedy are sad. Very sad. But you will have hope because you will believe the truths that go along with faith in Christ. God is in control. . . . He has a plan for everyone who loves him. . . . Death is merely a door for those who believe in him. . . . And he will make good out of every situation.

See?

What other response could we have to that kind of God but joy?

For more information about how the concepts in the Redemption series can save or improve your relationships, contact us at:

The Smalley Relationship Center
1482 Lakeshore Drive
Branson, MO 65616

*kingsbury* • *smalley*

Phone: 800-84TODAY (848-6329)
Fax: 417-336-3515
E-mail: family@smalleyonline.com
Web site: www.smalleyonline.com

# DISCUSSION QUESTIONS

Use these questions for individual reflection or for discussion with a group of reader friends, a circle of people at church, or your family members. Maybe, like the Baxters, God is calling you to a more joyful place. Even if the season you're in now is one of your most painful.

1. Statistically, the tragic loss or accidental injury of a child is one of the most difficult situations for married people. Discuss situations you are familiar with where such a tragedy led to a troubled marriage.

2. Why do you think so many marriages end in divorce after such a time?

3. Doubt has a way of creeping into any dark time. We saw that with Luke after September 11, and now with stalwart John Baxter in light of Hayley's accident. Why do doubts plague us who have faith? Where does it have its roots?

4. What does it look like to rejoice during a trial? Talk about a time when you or someone you know chose to rejoice during a hard time. Compare that to a time when you or someone you know chose to respond differently.

5. Why do you think God asks us to respond to hard times by being joyful?

6. Use as many adjectives as possible to describe *joy*.

7. Is it possible for doubt to exist in a joyful setting? Why or why not?

8. Is God asking us to hide or bury our true feelings about pain? Is he asking us to be happy about bad situations?

9. God has given us free will. As such, we have a number of ways we can respond to a tragedy. Think back on some of the Baxter family members and how they responded to Hayley's drowning: Elizabeth . . . John . . . Brooke . . . Peter . . . Ashley . . . Maddie . . . Cole.

10. Peter's response to such a horrific trial was to numb his pain. Explain why that didn't work for Peter. Discuss what other issues came about as a result. Share a time when numbing pain didn't work for you or for someone you know.

11. What price did Peter's family pay for his response to their tragedy?

12. How would things have been different for Peter and his family if he had chosen to rejoice in the midst of such a terrible ordeal?

13. God promises to give us a way out of any situation we find ourselves in. That was true for the Baxter family in this season as well. Explain Brooke's reaction and decision in light of Hayley's accident.

14. Read James 1:1-4. How did this passage play out for Brooke, and later for Peter?

15. Read Philippians 4:4-6. Explain how these verses apply to Ashley's reaction to these painful events. What biblical connection exists between rejoicing and finding peace?

16. Explain how you've seen that connection play out in your own life or in the life of someone you know.

17. More than one issue was presented in *Rejoice*. Another was letting go of a child, the way Elizabeth had to let go of Luke. Discuss a time when you had to let go of a child or someone you loved.

18. Elizabeth had two choices: She could begrudge Luke for choosing to marry young and move to New York with Reagan, or she could rejoice at his happiness, even as tears made their way down her face. Which did Elizabeth do? How did her choice relate to God's command that we rejoice in all situations? What could have happened if she had responded differently?

19. Kind, old Irvel had an amazing impact on Ashley's life.

Explain how joy played out in Irvel's life even after she developed Alzheimer's disease.

20. What did Ashley take away from her time with Irvel?

# The
# REDEMPTION
# SERIES
## by Karen Kingsbury and Gary Smalley

Novelist Karen Kingsbury and relationship expert Gary Smalley team up to bring you the **Redemption series**, which explores the relationship principles Gary has been teaching for more than thirty years and applies them to one family in particular, the Baxters. In the crucible of their tragedies and triumphs, the Baxter family learns about commitment, forgiveness, faith, and the redeeming hand of God.

## REDEMPTION
a story of love at all costs

## REMEMBER
a journey from tragedy to healing

## RETURN
a story of tenacious love
and longing for a lost son

## REJOICE
a story of unspeakable loss and
the overwhelming miracle of new life

## REUNION
a story of God's grace and redemption,
his victory even in the most difficult times

Other Life-Changing Fiction by
# KAREN KINGSBURY